Mark Lemon

Wait for the End

A Story

Mark Lemon

Wait for the End
A Story

ISBN/EAN: 9783744749619

Printed in Europe, USA, Canada, Australia, Japan

Cover: Foto ©Andreas Hilbeck / pixelio.de

More available books at **www.hansebooks.com**

WAIT FOR THE END.

A Story.

BY MARK LEMON.

"He came to some hard substance, which he judged rightly was the long-buried box."

[Page 376.

LONDON:

BRADBURY, EVANS, AND CO., 11, BOUVERIE STREET.

1866.

"I haven't got so much for my own sake as for the child's." Page 173.

TO

MRS. FRANCIS KEARSEY,

OF BURSTOW HALL,

THIS VOLUME IS

𝔍𝔫𝔰𝔠𝔯𝔦𝔟𝔢𝔡

WITH MUCH ESTEEM, BY

MARK LEMON.

VINE COTTAGE, CRAWLEY.

CONTENTS.

WAIT FOR THE END.

CHAPTER I.

OCTOBER the 10th, 18—, was a great day for —— College. It had scored 169 against 140 on the return match with M——, and as Gerard Norwold had bowled or caught out nine wickets in the first innings, and seven in the second, his "side" had invited him to supper at Charlie Craven's, who was the fortunate possessor of the largest rooms in the College.

Gerard Norwold was what is usually called a good sort of fellow. He attended chapel and lectures pretty regularly, gave no great promise of future distinction, was a first-rate cricketer, a good runner, an accomplished horseman, and had been known to drive a tandem. He was a general favourite, and those who knew him intimately had for him the warmest regard. His half-brother Gilbert was strikingly opposed to him in appearance and pursuits. He was an extravagant dresser, much given to purchasing showy jewellery, addicted to betting, billiards, and card-playing. Indeed, he carried his passion for the latter vice so far, that it had been rumoured more than once, that he and another man of the same College had made a bank for *rouge-et-noir*. He was known to have lost and won large sums, and his brother Gerard had often remonstrated with him on a course which had compelled

B

frequent application to home for money, and led to more than
one unpleasant interview with the College authorities.   It
had been hinted, also, that upon one occasion when a New-
market favourite had died on the evening preceding the race,
Gilbert Norwold, having had private information of the
dangerous condition of the horse, had improved the occasion
to his own advantage.   The brothers were in fact so widely
separated by their tastes and dispositions, that they were
rarely seen together, and Gilbert had not been asked to the
supper-party at Charlie Craven's, although many men of
other Colleges had received invitations.

At eight o'clock Charlie Craven's rooms were thrown open
to receive company.   His neat little camp bedstead was soon
covered with the caps and hats of the guests, who scrambled
for places, and gave assurance by their loud laughter and
noisy ejaculations that a merry evening was to succeed to a
day of triumph.   Charlie Craven was called to the chair by
acclamation, and as a matter of course the guest of the evening, Gerard Norwold, occupied the place of honour beside
him.   The attractiveness of the viands produced a momentary
lull in the vociferous storm which broke forth again with
redoubled force during the distribution of the good things
upon the table, and it was not until the entire party had
settled down to their work of destruction that moderate
weather prevailed.   One generous fellow, however, who had
come up the same year as Gerard, and who had for his
prowess and social qualities the highest admiration, was not
to be quieted.   He had knelt down in the Cricket-tent on the
declaration of the score, and vowed "to pour a libation"
whenever the name of Gerard Norwold should be mentioned
that day.   The necessity for fulfilling his vow had occurred
so frequently, that a naturally strong head had yielded to the
potency of the offerings, and continued to emit unlimited
melody prematurely and vexatiously.   At the persuasion of
two judicious friends, Pylades consented to retire into the
bed-room, and was subsequently reported to be as well as

could be expected among the hats and caps on Charlie Craven's camp bedstead.

The tables having been cleared and glasses of divers fashions placed thereon, bowls of steaming Bishop and frothing milk-punch succeeded, and the revel began in earnest. When an assembly of orators insist on the right to be heard at the same time, it is difficult for the most practised ear to note accurately the gist of any individual speaker's obser-vations, and as no conglomeration of words would convey a notion of the universal conversation of Charlie Craven's guests, the reader must be content to remain as uninstructed as he would have been had he been present. At last some-thing like unanimity prevailed, and the cry for a song rose above the general hubbub. The suggestion was favourably received, and the request so earnestly enforced that it seemed for some time that the demand was considered equal to the supply. By much hammering on the part of the Chairman and his adherents, and the loudest vociferations for silence on the part of the most persistent disturbers, vocal harmony prevailed.

The song had been heard a hundred times before within these old college walls, but its charm seemed undiminished by age, and could only have been indebted for its universal and university popularity to its unintelligibility. *Ex. gr.*

> " I'll sing you a one O ?
> Green grow the rushes O !
> What is your one O ?
> When your one is all alone
> It ever more shall be so.
>
> " I'll sing you a two O !
> Green grow the rushes O !
> What is your two O ?
> Two, two lily-white boys
> Clothèd all in green O !
> When your one is all alone
> It ever more shall be so."

And so on until it promised to monopolise the remainder of

the evening.   When the welcome cry of "Chori-us" was
heard, every man gave tongue according to his fancy, producing a discord that would have driven the dummiest Mus:
Doc: crazy.   The applause which followed can only be fitly
described as the concentrated essence of sound, and it was
exciting to behold the glasses and candlesticks and other
moveables upon the table dance to the drumming of the en-
raptured assembly.

The chairman rose.   His position was instantly acknowledged by many kind inquiries after his health, and the expression of anxious doubts, whether he felt himself equal
to the situation.   Having repeatedly and most good-humouredly satisfied his questioners upon both points, he
made nine attempts to propose the toast of the evening,
seldom getting further than "Gentlemen, I rise."   Concluding at length that eloquence would be unappreciated at that
moment, he contented himself with filling a goblet to the
brim (*loud cheers*), and shouting as only an under-graduate
can shout in a confined space and oppressive atmosphere,
"Gerard Norwold's health and wickets!"

Then up rose every man in answer to the pledge, and as

> "The war-horse at the trumpet's sound,
> Erects his mane and neighs and paws the ground,"

so each loud hurrah! excited those convivial spirits to mount
the chairs, and ultimately to set foot upon the tables, until
the oppressed mahogany, staggering beneath the weight, upset
one of the sconces into the Bishop bowl, and rendered un-
stable the positions of "slip" and "longstop," who, clinging
to each other for support, fell together to the floor.   Song
followed song, and cheer succeeded cheer; but amid all this
merry riot not one unseemly word was spoken, nor was one
ungentle act committed; none "drunk, but nobly mad," and
all resulting from the unrestrained enjoyment of generous
natures, as yet uncorrupted and unsaddened by contact with
the world. ·

It was now eleven o'clock, and the house rose. It became necessary to rouse Pylades from his slumber before Craven could "speed his parting guest." Pity, earnest pity, for the loss of such an evening saved Pylades from making atonement for smashed beavers and broken trenchers, and more than one generous hand proffered beakers of hock and soda or some more powerful stimulant.

Pylades—his name was Leyton, now perfectly recovered from his temporary obfuscation—and Gerard walked leisurely towards their respective rooms in the quadrangle. The night was sultry, and many of the windows were opened, though lights shone only from two or three.

"My brother has a visitor to-night," said Gerard, as they approached a room on the ground-floor, and whose window was open and lighted from within. Gerard drew aside the curtain with the intention of wishing his brother and his guest good night. Before he could speak, however, something he saw in his brother's room alarmed or distressed him so greatly, that he seized Leyton's arm as though to save himself from falling. Leyton naturally inquired the cause of this sudden change; but Gerard remained silent, still grasping the arm of his friend and hurrying from the window.

When they reached Leyton's rooms, Gerard asked for drink of any kind, and it was not until he had emptied a large water-goblet filled with wine, that he appeared capable of speech.

"Leyton," he said, "if what I have seen to-night in my brother's room be true, I and he and all of us who bear his name are most unhappy. Ask me nothing more to-night, but I promise you, that if I require aid or counsel, I will come to you. Do not go to bed for half an hour—I may return."

Gerard hastened to his brother's room. The light still shone within, but the outer door was closed and fastened. Gerard knocked violently, and called for admission at the same time. When Gilbert opened the door, he was evidently

startled at the expression of his brother's face, and could not
forbear asking what had happened? 'Gerard did not reply,
but seated himself at the table where a freshman, named
Mariott, was sitting, half stupefied by the strong wine he
had drunk and the excitement of the play in which he had
been engaged, evidently, as there were cards upon the table.

"Well, Mariott," said Gerard, as soon as he could speak,
"you will not listen to advice; you will not be warned,
but are here again losing your money, and muddling your
brains."

"Is that all you have come to say?" remarked Gilbert.
"The morning would have been time enough, surely, for
lectures."

Gerard did not reply to his brother, but spoke on. "You
have lost again to-night, Mariott; you have lost largely."

"I can pay what I have lost, Mr. Norwold," said Mariott,
rising, and taking a roll of notes from a silken note-case, he
counted about thirty pounds and threw them upon the table.

"Take that money again, Mariott," said Gerard—"at
least until to-morrow—until my brother asks you for it."

"I always pay my debts of honour immediately," answered
the half tipsy loser, "and I allow no one to dictate to me on
such a matter. Good night, Norwold, it is getting late, and
as your brother seems disposed for a family row, I am in the
way—Good night."

Gilbert did not seek to stay Mariott, but when he had gone
he closed the door, and turning abruptly to his brother,
said :

"Gerard Norwold, attend to what I am about to say. If
we are to continue on terms of friendship, you must leave off
these impertinent meddlings and intrusions. I admit no right
of yours to choose my friends or to regulate my amusements.
You have your pursuits, I have mine, and if I am again
annoyed as I have been to-night, I shall cut with you
altogether."

"Have you done?" asked Gerard, after a pause.

"For the present," was the reply.

"Then hear me, Gilbert Norwold, and perhaps for the last time. Did you not bear my father's name, you should not hear me at all, and I would cut with *you* altogether; but as anything which affects your honour affects him—affects me— I have come here to-night with the determination to check you in your disgraceful practices, and compel you to make reparation to those whom you have injured."

Gilbert's face became livid, and his lips trembled either with rage or with the dread of the revelation his brother was about to make. He was not left long in suspense.

"Gilbert Norwold, you are a cheat, a mean despicable cheat. Don't speak! Don't move. I am the stronger man, and I will hold you in your chair and tell you of your villany. You have won large sums of the poor idiot who has just left us, not only by your greater skill in such miserable acquirements, but by stooping to play unfairly. You would deny it —I see it in your face—but I have had the evidence of my own eyes to prove this horrible accusation. Passing your window to-night, I drew aside the curtain to wish you a brotherly good night—I saw you deliberately place at your back one card and substitute for it another which you had previously placed behind you. I heard you exclaim, 'Game again!' and what I saw—what I heard, I dare no more keep secret, nor would I, than I would the knowledge of a murder."

Gilbert was taken completely by surprise. He did not dare even to deny his brother's accusation, and could only stammer out—"So, Mr. Gerard Norwold descends to play the spy upon me."

"Tush!" exclaimed Gerard. "I have told you how I came by my knowledge of your dishonour, and you believe me. Now, no evasion. You had better be truthful for the future. How much have you won of Mariott?"

Gilbert made no reply, but stood gazing sulkily upon the ground.

"Gilbert, this matter shall not rest until restitution has been made. If you have not the means of doing so, let me assist you. If you refuse, I have only one other course. I shall communicate with our father. You know him—you know that if he found you capable of this crime, he would turn you on the world, even if it broke his own proud heart to do so."

Gilbert still remained silent.

"What is your determination?" asked Gerard, after a pause of some moments.

"One question," said Gilbert. "Would you, supposing I deny this charge—would you, regardless of my mother—I do not say of me—would you tell this to my father?"

It was now Gerard's turn to be silent for some moments. He then said, taking his brother's hand, "Gilbert, your question, I am sure, does not require an answer. You will not make such an alternative possible. You will trust your brother, and tell me the worst. I will help you to the uttermost. Come! do not hesitate. Speak the truth."

Gilbert went to his writing-desk, and from a secret drawer within it, brought forth a small note-book in which he had put down his late card winnings and his earlier losses.

The latter had been large, and not until the name of Mariott appeared on the page had his gains been great. Gerard, after a time, his distress rendering calculation difficult, reckoned up the sums Gilbert had obtained from his victim, and the total reached to nearly two hundred pounds.

"The amount is large," said Gerard, "larger than I had expected, but it must be paid. We must write home for money."

"That will be useless," replied Gilbert, "at least so far as I am concerned. Sir John has refused to send me more. I have had money unknown to you, for I have lost considerably by betting, and the trustees of one of my tradesmen have been pressing me. I can get no more."

"You must ask your mother, then, for help," said Gerard.

Gilbert shook his head. "Useless! useless!" he replied. "Her pin-money is not great, and I have already had a hundred pounds from her."

Gerard was puzzled. "I dare not ask for more than fifty pounds, as I promised not to exceed my allowance. What is to be done?"

"There is one chance," said Gilbert, after a pause. "Jasper Jellifer has lent me money at times, and which my mother has repaid him.—He may have the means to help *us*."

Gerard looked up suddenly.

"I mean help me, although he told me that my mother's security was of no value. I think he would assist if he had your promise to see him repaid. In fact he said as much."

Gerard held out his hand to Gilbert, and instantly proffered to do all that was required provided the money could be obtained.

"Very well, then," said Gilbert. "I will write to him to-morrow, and go down to Morden on the following day, and if I find Sir John away from home, I will see my mother."

The course of action having been determined, Gerard proceeded at once to draw up the required security. He was unskilled in such compositions, and it was not until he had made more than one attempt that he succeeded in completing the important document.

It was comprised in three short lines, with Gerard's signature attached, and yet it changed the current of more lives than one.

Leyton remained at his open window waiting the return of Gerard, his well-beloved friend. "All right, old boy," said Gerard, very cheerfully. "I cannot tell you what I have been saying to Gilbert: but it's all right. Good night."

Often and often, in after years, Gerard Norwold remembered this parting from his true Pylades, and regretted bitterly his silence upon what had passed in his brother's rooms.

Gilbert put out his lamp, and threw himself upon his bed dressed as he was. He could not sleep, but again and again he went over the exciting scene just enacted, and strange unthankfulness! he always ended by repeating Gerard's words: "I have only one other course, I shall communicate with our father."

That thought was the last in his mind when he fell asleep.

CHAPTER II.

No one entering Morden at its north end could fail to
observe a large old-fashioned house, built, it was said, as
early as the time of James the First. On one side was a large
pond, whereon floated plump geese and ducks, like argosies,
to be freighted hereafter with savoury stuffing, whilst overhead blue-rocks and runts, jacobines, nuns, and tumblers
were gyrating and traversing to and from a spacious dovecote,
surmounted by a gilt vane. Its sloping roof, covered with
grey stone healing, dotted here and there with tufts of stone-
crop and houseleek, harmonised well with its white front,
relieved by oak framework, painted black, and filled with
latticed windows. A large porch of carved oak, with seats
on either side, and partly concealed by creeping rose-trees
and jasmine, marked the principal entrance, which was
approached from the road by a broad gravel path, bordered by
flower-beds and well-kept lawns, studded about with clumps of
evergreens and flowering shrubs. Two giant elms, which
overshadowed the garden gate, gave their name to the place,
which had been occupied for several generations by the family
of the Spraggatts, but the freehold itself belonged to Sir John
Norwold. The homestead of the farm was near the house,
partly hidden by a grove of elms, whereon a colony of rooks
had been long established. We shall have much to do presently with the inmates of this old house, now occupied by
John Spraggatt—Jack Spraggatt he was called usually—his
widowed mother, and two fair sisters.

The Elms was about half a mile from the High Street of

the neighbouring town, which extended nearly to its boundary
meadow. Morden was an improving place, and had taken
a fancy to march southwards, so that the High Street, which
had formerly been the principal place of trade, had fallen
into poverty, being separated from the thriving market-place
and New Street by the bridge, which crossed the shallow
river flowing through the town. The Town Hall, however,
still gave an importance to High Street; and at election
times, or on corporation festivals and ceremonials, the old
street held up its head again, and claimed its place in Morden.
The houses in the market-place had grown up at various
dates, and had been built without any attempt at uniformity,
so that the old church, which stood in one corner, and had
been frequently repaired and beautified, according to the
taste of the churchwardens for the time being, did not appear
such a mass of incongruity as it would have done had its
neighbours been more regular in their construction. The
shaft of the old cross had been kept in tolerable repair since
its conversion to Protestantism, and looked picturesque enough
on market days when surrounded by the butter sellers, generally farmers' daughters, and who always appeared, if not in
their Sunday clothes, at least in their second best. We miss
those rustic beauties sadly now-a-days from English market-
places : they passed away when Capital bought up the small
farmers, and turned out their little households to seek for
other occupations, or new homes in the New World. The old
farm-houses and their small homesteads still remain here and
there, but changed, how changed! from what they were.
The parlour-kitchen, with its clean brick floor, the cosy
ingle, where the bright iron dogs glistened in the sun in
summer time, giving place in winter to those of ruder make,
when the crackling log blazed upon the hearth, the well-
stored bacon-rack above your head, that told of savoury
broils adorned with eggs like marigolds, the corner cupboard,
which hid away the choicest crockery (heir-looms reserved
for high days and holidays), the well-polished oaken dresser,

on whose shelves were ranged pewter and blue delft plates, kept for the same high occasions;—(the wooden platter was thought good enough for working days;)—the square rush-bottomed chairs, broad enough to seat a Falstaff at his ease; the eight-day clock, whose tick—the voice of time—could, in the stillness of the night, be heard in distant chambers—are only memories. The carter and the ploughman, hard worked and ill paid, are now the men in possession, and manage someway to labour and live. No doubt the change is for the better; all changes are so now-a-days; but those were not evil times, when the rustic toiler was certain of a coarse breakfast and supper of bull-broth and brown bread, a liberal dinner of fat bacon and strong cabbage in the farmer's outer kitchen, and a hard, warm bed in the farmer's garret. God helps those toilers some way in our money-loving times, as they bear their lot so patiently.

In one corner of the market-place was the shop of Jasper Jellifer. He was not particular as to the commodities he sold, and they ranged from peppermint drops to mill-stones. There were few wants of the farmer or the farmer's woman-kind that Jasper could not satisfy out of his *omnium gatherum* of a shop, and being a smooth-spoken fellow, he rarely lost a customer that had once given him a trial. He was a shrewd man, no doubt, and never took his eye off the main chance, as it is called, and when his neighbours had small difficulties which baffled their own ingenuity to overcome, Jasper was the man they consulted. When asked, he always gave advice, generally of a practical character, and the knowledge he thus obtained concerning many of his neighbours' affairs, invested him with an influence which he failed not to turn to his own profit. Always in a fair way, however, for though Jasper was known to drive a hard bargain, he gave good weight and just measure in all things. Still he was not a popular man with his fellow town's folk, with whom he rarely sought a close intimacy, and many who had profited by his shrewdness and caution, spoke of Jasper as a screw or a close shaver, or a money-grubber, and in truth he deserved those appellations, for no man ate at his board or drank of his cup. Philanthropic ladies and gentlemen in those days had not learned the art of being charitable at the expense of other people's pockets, or they would have called in vain on Jasper Jellifer. When a fire destroyed the tools of seven poor carpenters, and the market-place made a subscription, Jasper avoided giving a shilling on the pretence that he had no change, and declined to put his name to the subscription list in case he should forget it. Being much pressed, at last he contributed in kind, and] presented a few second-hand tools for the benefit of the sufferers. He did love money, no doubt of it, and the passion became stronger and stronger as he grew older and richer.

We said that no man ever shared his hospitality. We retract. We should have said that Raymond Ray, the miller, was Jasper's crony, and of late had been a frequent visitor and guest. And this intimacy was somewhat strange, as Ray was not a native of the place, but had come from the neighbourhood of London to work the water-mill outside the town. Nobody knew anything about him, but he was a pushing fellow, and having money at his command, he soon made his way with the good people of Morden. He was rather a loose liver, it was said, and, being a bachelor, and seemingly inclined to keep so, the scandal-mongers over their gossip-water did not spare him. His mill was turned by the stream which flowed through Norwold Park, and formed a pretty object as seen from the library window of the Hall. Looking also from the footbridge which crossed the water near the entrance to the park, it would have made a good subject for a painter. Some limes planted upon the margin of the stream had grown aslant until their lowermost boughs dipped into the water, and through these sylvan arches the old wheel could be discerned splashing, splashing and scattering the water-drops about like some prodigal distributing fairy diamonds. The house attached to the mill was overgrown with ivy, and had a gable end, with latticed windows, which almost overhung the mill-stream. The holly hedge by which it was surrounded was neatly clipped, and like most millers' gardens, Ray's was a mass of flowers and shrubs.

It had been a rare sight at one time to have seen Jasper Jelliffer away from his shop, except on business, but since his intimacy with Ray he might be found once, and even twice a-week in the dusk of the evening walking in the miller's garden, although he was known to care nothing for flowers, or indeed for little else in which he did not traffic.

> " A primrose by the river's brim
> A yellow primrose was to him,
> And it was nothing more."

He was there one evening earnestly reading a book—it was bound in rough calf with a brass clasp—as he walked up and down, when a farmer rode up to the mill.

"Hallo!" cried the new-comer, looking over the garden hedge. "Jasper Jellifer, as I live! What are you studying man—the Ready Reckoner, or the Art of Short Mensuration?"

"Neither, Master Spraggatt," replied Jasper, smiling, and putting the volume into his pocket. "I'm studying a leaf out of your book, sir, and learning the art of being idle."

"You're too old and too knowing to go to my school," said Jack Spraggatt, dismounting and fastening his horse's bridle to a ring in the gate-post. Before he could open the wicket, however, Jasper was at the entrance.

"Ray is at home, I suppose?" remarked Jack.

"Yes—I believe so — that is, he was here just now," answered Jasper, with some hesitation of manner, which, however, was not noticed by his questioner.

As Jack's business was with the miller and not with Jasper, for whom he entertained no great respect, the young man made his way at once for the house. As he did so he observed there was a light in the miller's parlour, or counting house, but on Jasper calling out, "Mr. Ray!" it was extinguished instantly. Jack thought nothing of this until he reached the door, when he heard the lid of an iron chest, which he knew stood in one corner of the miller's room, close with a noise, as though it had been shut down hastily.

"What's in the wind, I wonder?" thought Jack. "Jasper wouldn't be idling away his time here for nothing, and Ray evidently did not want to make me as wise as himself."

Whatever the mystery, there was no reading it in the miller's face, for when he opened the door he looked as beaming and spoke as cheerily as any man could, who was fresh from the accomplishment of some good action.

"I hardly expected you here to-night, Mr. Spraggatt," said Ray; "but come in and try our last brewing. Unless," added the miller, opening the parlour door and leading the way, "you prefer a glass of French brandy or Dutch Hollands; I have both at hand."

Jack preferred the ale, and the miller's handmaiden soon brought in a foaming jug of nut-brown stingo which would have astonished the degenerate topers of bitter beer.

Jack had come to make a bargain for the sale of some wheat, for which the miller had offered a price some shillings below its value. Buyers, however, were scarce, and Jack wanted money. So did Ray, at least that was his excuse for the badness of his offer, and he could only buy by borrowing at interest, and therefore the wheat must pay the loss.

Jack's need was urgent, for unless he paid some money at next day's market his credit would be damaged, if not lost altogether. Ray knew this also, and professed to become a purchaser more to oblige Mr. Spraggatt than from any hope of gain by the transaction. There was nothing for it but to take the miller's price, and the little sample bag of wheat was drawn forth from Jack's pocket with a sigh that told a tale which few suspected who knew the light-hearted farmer on his daily walk, for Jack Spraggatt had a cheerful smile and pleasant word for all, even when night had brought no sleep, and the light but small comfort.

Ray had left the room to get so much of the money as was needed for the morrow, and Jasper Jellifer's presence at the mill was accounted for by the young farmer, when he heard the miller call his name.

Ray was absent a short time, and when he returned he brought with him a lighted candle, for the evening had closed in. The usual formalities gone through, and two hundred pounds safely deposited in the breast pocket of Jack's coat, he rose to take his departure.

As he did so, something sparkling on the ground caught his eye, and to his surprise he picked up a diamond ring—a lady's diamond ring.

"Ha! how careless of me," cried the miller, almost snatching the waif from Jack's fingers. "I would not have lost that ring for a hundred pounds. It was my—my mother's. Thank you, Mr. Spraggatt."

Jack knew the ring did not belong to him, and therefore believed the miller's story without further question, but Ray scarcely spoke another word until they reached the garden gate and bade each other good night.

Jack Spraggatt rode on with a full pocket and a heavy heart, for he knew that many bargains similar to the one he had made that evening would complete his ruin.

Jack had many friends, some of them true friends, as the world goes—and was always sure of a welcome. He had great natural spirits and a happy-looking face, two things which pass current for much more than they are worth too often. Many who had returned his cheery greeting or valediction had envied the happy Jack, and wondered how he managed to put aside Care, or to avoid the old carker altogether. Had they peeped under his hat as he rode or walked along, solitarily, they would have seen a bent brow and a sad face that told of sorrow hidden from all, perhaps, and known to himself alone. Whatever it was that was gnawing at his peace, like the Spartan boy, he hid his destroyer bravely.

To see Jack at his own table was to see him in his glory.

His aged mother seated in the place of honour, and on either side a blooming sister, kindly careful of their frequent guests, whilst Jack filled a chair which death had made vacant some three years before our story, by taking away the kind grey-headed man who had loved that household dearly—aye, too dearly.

No shade of sadness then! No word, no look to pain that widowed mother and those trusting sisters, nothing to mar the bright hopes that mingled ever with the talk of Letty's coming nuptials—she was the elder of the two—or that sought to check the prodigal love which was so lavish in devising adornments for the happy bride. Ray's purchase would empty the bays of the great barn, and when that sorrow was passed, they should be covered over with green boughs and flowers, and all should

"Go merry as the marriage bells."

Yet Jack had a great skeleton in his cupboard—larger than that of the Irish giant—or the mastodon even, and it would come out in the still night and terrify him into wakefulness. It would greet him in early morning as soon as his eyes were open, it would often and often look at him from behind his mother's and sisters' chairs, and scare him for a moment; but Jack, by a cheerful look and a merry word, would drive it away, to meet it perhaps again when he smoked his pipe walking among the flowers in the garden, or sitting in the rose-covered porch, and at other times when he ought to have been most happy.

This grim attendant was none of Jack's own seeking. It was bequeathed to him by his father, who told him the day before he died never to let his mother see the unsightly thing, but to hide it from her, if possible, until the time came when she should lie down to rest in the green church-yard. Jack obeyed his father, although it made his young life at times a blank, and closed his heart against a love which knocked at it loudly for two long years, and which turned away at last to find another home. Now and then, when the malign influence became almost intolerable, he had thought of asking Lucy—his favourite sister Lucy, to share with him in part this terrible knowledge; but fearing that it might become as fatal to her and to her peace, as it had long been to him and to his happiness, he elected to bear it alone, and until the end, if that were needful.

Jack found two neighbours awaiting his return from the mill, and a merry supper was the result. The young ladies and Jack were excellent singers of homely songs and glees and catches, and one of the guests prided himself on the profundity of his bass. So they sang some old part-songs, such as years and years ago the early tenants of that ancient dwelling had sung under the same oak roof-tree, and whose delighted ghosts perhaps still hovered around, and wagged their spectral jaws to an inaudible chorus.

Mrs. Spraggatt had retired to rest somewhat before the party broke up, although the clock struck ten only as the two guests departed. Jack went to his little sitting-room, adjoining the one they had just left, with the intention of depositing his money in an oak box where he kept his account books, but found that his mother had the key. As she was now asleep, possibly, he took his treasure to bed with him. The mirthfulness of the last hour or two had scared Jack's skeleton into its cupboard, and the young farmer soon fell into a sound but short slumber. When he awoke, the moonlight was shining on his face, and had helped to rouse him, he thought. Rasper, the house-dog, was barking at intervals down at the homestead, but that was his custom, whenever Jack forgot to unloosen him, and he had done so that night. The weathercock on the pigeon-house was creaking sadly. That was strange! because Jack had seen it oiled not a week ago. Yet it did creak, and that continuously. There was a fox or a strange dog about the place, no doubt, for Rasper was very noisy, and Jack had half a mind to get out of bed and silence him, but sleep was stealing over him, the creaking of the weather-cock had ceased, and so what evil was at work that night remained unseen by Jack Spraggatt.

He found it out in the morning, however, and fearing to alarm his mother and his sisters, never talked of it until years and years afterwards, when he and one other were alone in a far-off land—alone in a great wilderness, sitting at night by a bright wood fire.

Jack discovered in the morning that two men (there were the foot-prints of two men) had filed the catch of the window of his little room (he thought it was the creaking of the weather-cock), and having entered, had forced open the lid of his oak box, and thrown all his books and papers upon the ground. Nothing else was disturbed. Nothing stolen.

Jack replaced his books and papers, took off the catch of the window, and thought how good a thing it was to have friendly neighbours look in to compel one to make merry sometimes in spite of oneself. Had Mrs. Spraggatt not taken the key of the oak box to bed with her, Jack would have lost the bank-notes he had obtained at such a sacrifice.

CHAPTER III.

NORWOLD HALL, the residence of Sir John Norwold, was a
fine old building, of somewhat later date than Elizabeth's
time, but partaking of some of the architectural characteristics
of that period, when fortified houses were growing into dis·
use, although the great mansions still preserved traces of
caution, and appearance of strength. Its large bay windows
were partly filled with stained glass, depicting the armorial
bearings of the house of Norwold, and of those families who
had been united to it by marriage in the time of its greater
prosperity—its fortunes were more humble at the time of our
story. In its great hall, cavaliers had mustered to do battle
for King Charles, and many keen sportsmen had gathered,
often "to boot, and to saddle," and to "burn powder" in
sylvan warfare. The grounds about the Hall had been exten-
sive at one time, and there was still much that told of their
past glories. Thick yew hedges, broad enough to allow the
construction of bowers in their midst, proclaimed themselves
to be the growth of more than one century, and there were
terraces of green turf, whereon, so tradition said, Henrietta
had once walked in queenly pride and beauty, and many
other stately dames, also, in after time, when Norwold Hall
had been the scene of a large hospitality. The approach to
the house was by a gentle rise, and through an avenue of
noble trees, once all but condemned to become timber, by the
needy politician who had lately held possession, but family
pride cancelled the sentence.

The park was only separated from the town of Morden by a stream which flowed through it, turning Ray's mill in its course to the adjoining river.

Many of the smaller houses in Morden were the property of Sir John Norwold. They had been bought by the present Sir John's father for election purposes, and were invariably occupied by " free men," who, when tractable, were desirable tenants before the Reform Bill deprived them of much of their birth-rights. The management of those political serfs had been long intrusted to one David Locke, a small corn-dealer, but a shrewd fellow, and a first-rate pot-house politician. He was in his way a diminutive " man in the moon," and managed matters so cleverly, that his votes defied scrutiny. The borough had been frequently and hotly con-tested, but David Locke's man was always at the head of the poll, and the means by which his victories were obtained were never doubted. He brought up his men in shoals whenever occasion required them, and he ticked them off as they polled with most annoying effrontery. His mode of bargaining was unique and open. The Rock Club, held at a small public-house in Morden, was composed of certain free and indepen-dents who were banded together for their own interests and security, contriving by their combination to keep up the price of votes, and prevent any underselling of each other. On the eve of an election the Club met, and invited Mr. David Locke to attend, and state the political opinions of his candidate. When pipes and beer, those necessary adjuncts to deliberation, had been supplied, Mr. David Locke rose, stick in hand, and proceeded to business.

" Gentlemen of the Rock Club," he would say, " I am here to solicit your votes and interest for Mr. Blank. As time is of consequence to all of us, I will at once state the opinions of my principal. He is a man of his word, and his political opinions extend to —." Here he would give two blows with his stick upon the table.

This declaration would be always highly unsatisfactory to

the meeting, and loud cries of "Oh! no! that won't do!" compelled the orator to proceed.

"Mr. Blank, gentlemen, is not an obstinate man, unwilling to be guided in some way by the opinions of his constituents, and therefore, I do not hesitate to say for him "—three blows with the stick, followed by more dissatisfaction.

"There is reason in roasting eggs," Mr. Locke would continue, " and, gentlemen, I can assure, you, that Mr. Blank will retire from the contest—and will do so with my concurrence, and by my advice, unless you are satisfied with "—five blows of the stick.

The fathers of the club would then put their wicked old heads together, and whisper mysteriously for a few minutes. During their deliberation, Mr. David Locke resumed his hat, buttoned up his coat, every button, and placing his divining rod under his arm, awaited calmly the result of the conference. If the chairman of the club then struck five times upon the table, Mr. David Locke again removed his hat, and repeated the mystic number of blows. If on the other hand the chairman exceeded that number by only one tap, Mr. David Locke looked his contempt of the assembly, and retired without a word. Need we say, that the blows upon the table indicated the number of guineas at which Mr. Locke was willing to have those political brutes knocked down to him?

The late Baronet, Sir Robert Norwold, had been a great House of Commons man, and had contested three elections for Morden, paying so dearly for his whistle, that when he died, his estate was found to be greatly encumbered. Sir John, his son and successor, set to work to get back as much of his father's outlay in bribery as he could by pinching his tenants to the uttermost. Those free and independent persons had been so long used to pay their rent in kind, that it was no easy matter to make them recognise the new order of things, and pay in money; and Mr. David Locke found his political influence diminishing daily by the intrusion of the broker and his myrmidons into the dwellings of the recusant tenants. But being one of those practical philosophers who decide that half a loaf is better than none, Mr. Locke determined to take care of himself, and arranged with Sir John Norwold to allow him a good commission for collecting his rents in specie and promises; so after awhile matters went on pretty smoothly.

We have said thus much of Mr. David Locke, as a sudden illness threatened to close his rather equivocal career, and leave his collectorship open to a successor. The precarious condition of Mr. Locke was known to very few persons only, and Jasper Jellifer was one. The collectorship had been long desired by the persevering Jasper, and had Mr. Locke's illness not been so sudden and dangerous, he had intended to have devised some plan to have obtained, at some future day, the reversion.

Jasper Jellifer had always been a lucky man, and fortune had not tired of serving him. Sir John Norwold was well known to be a proud, selfish, overbearing man, and most of his deeds of good or evil were referable to the state of his temper for the time being. Jasper was afraid of Sir John.

Lady Norwold was a second wife, and had been promoted to that position from a respectable but rather humble condition, and her recognition by Sir John was more that of a superior housekeeper than of one whom he had promised to endow with all his worldly goods, and to cherish and comfort to the end of their mutual lives. It seemed, therefore, hardly possible to induce a lady so circumstanced to interfere on behalf of a person who was only known to her as a small tradesman that occasionally received the honour of her custom.

But Jasper Jellifer was a lucky man, and a letter of introduction was put into his hand by the postman. It bore the Cambridge post-mark, and the handwriting appeared familiar to him. He retired into his back parlour before breaking the seal, and was gratified to find that the letter was from Gilbert Norwold. It was earnestly worded, and urgently requested the immediate loan of 200*l*. The largeness of the amount made Jasper start. The letter went on to say, "So great is the necessity for this money that I am sure my mother, Lady Norwold, will guarantee the repayment when I can explain circumstances to her. My brother Gerard is also so concerned in this matter that he will give his written undertaking to see the money repaid. I shall follow this letter to-morrow and be with you at night, when I trust to find you prepared to help me." Jasper read and reread the letter, and then thought over the course he should pursue. To lend so large a sum, even if he had the money, on such security, would be absurd. Nevertheless the letter empowered him to see Lady Norwold; and out of an interview and the knowledge of her son's necessities, something might arise to obtain her inter-cession with Sir John for the desired collectorship. He dressed himself in his best, and started at once for the Hall. He walked briskly, and as he passed under the grand old trees which formed the avenue leading to the house, visions of future advancement and larger gains presented themselves. The collectorship once obtained, other trusts might follow, and some day Jasper Jellifer might aspire to be steward of the Norwold properties. Two hundred pounds was a large sum to invest on such a dream. A spendthrift's promise was soon forgotten, and Lady Norwold was slenderly dowered. A quarter of that sum would show his willingness to help, and give him a hold upon the lady's gratitude. Well, there was time enough to decide, after he had seen her ladyship. He went to the servants' entrance, but as it was forbidden to have strangers in the offices, he was shown into the great hall, there to wait until Sir John and Lady Norwold had finished breakfast. As he sat there, patiently, he fancied he heard Sir John speaking loud and angrily, and when the door of the breakfast room was opened by the footman who had been in attendance, his conjecture was confirmed. The foot-man shrugged his shoulders, and made a grimace at Jasper, whom he knew, saying:

"The old game! Sir John's in a towering rage—his temper gets worse and worse. You haven't come to see him, I hope?"

"No," replied Jasper; "but I want to see her ladyship very particular."

"I don't expect she'll see you or anybody this morning—she never does after these rows. I don't envy 'her ladyship,' I can tell you," said the footman.

"What's the matter?" asked Jasper.

"Oh, the old story—money. Master Gerard has writ home for 50l., and Sir John has gone into fits about it. He says it's all Master Gilbert's fault a-setting him a bad example, and that Lady Norwold encourages 'em in extravagance. Hark! he's a-coming out," and the prudent footman retreated with an alacrity that was surprising, considering his full condition.

The door of the breakfast-room was thrown open by Sir John, who paused to say :

"Now write and tell them so, Madam. Tell them both that I'll not give them a pound more than their allowance. If I do——" here followed a coarse expletive which at that time was not so uncommon as to be thought brutal, even by those to whom it was addressed.

Jasper wished himself back in the market-place, but retreat was impossible.

"Well, who are you?" cried Sir John. "Oh, I see! the chandler's shop-keeper—Well, what do you want?"

Jasper was nearly bewildered, but as the collectorship was uppermost in his head, he stammered out—"Mr. Locke, Sir John, is dangerously ill—dying, I believe, Sir John——"

"So much the better!" interrupted the fiery old gentleman. "If he had died forty years ago it would have been all the better for me. An old bribery-monger. How do you know he's dying?"

"Please, Sir John, the doctor was with him three times yesterday——"

"That's enough—sent any message to me?"

"No, Sir John, but——"

"Then why the devil do you stop me here talking——"
Luckily for Jasper, at this moment the gardener's boy was
discerned by the passionate Baronet wheeling a barrow across
the lawn, and as this was a proceeding strictly against orders;
Sir John rushed out, his angry voice and the howling of the
boy giving assurance that the prohibition was being forcibly
impressed on the memory of the delinquent. Jasper sank
down upon the hall-settle, almost resolved to abandon the
coveted interview, but the fear of meeting Sir John on his
way through the park kept him sitting. At last, to Jasper's
great relief, he saw the dreaded old gentleman ride down the
avenue, and if the truth be told, he cared not whither.

When Lady Norwold passed into the hall, Jasper noticed
that she had been weeping, but his self-interest was too much
concerned to admit of any display of delicacy on his part. He,
therefore, advanced towards her, almost calling, "My lady!"
Lady Norwold stopped, and Jasper instantly opened his
business.

"I beg pardon, my lady, but I want to speak to your
ladyship for a few minutes."

"I am rather indisposed, Mr. Jellifer, just now, and must
trouble you to call again——"

"But my business is very pressing, my lady," said Jasper.
"I have a letter from your son, Mr. Gilbert."

"From my son?" said Lady Norwold. "My son written
to you? Pray follow me," and she led the way into a small
room which she usually occupied when alone.

"Did I understand you rightly, that you had a letter from
my son, Mr. Gilbert?" asked her ladyship, seating herself as
though her anxiety already oppressed her.

"Yes, my lady," replied Jasper. "A letter which has
perplexed me a great deal, I can assure your ladyship; and I
thought it my duty to come on to you at once, my lady.
Here is the letter, which will speak for itself."

Lady Norwold drew a deep sigh before she ventured to read a communication which, she feared, would bring her more sorrow. As she read on, large tears fell upon the paper, and when she had finished she hid her face in her handkerchief, and sobbed aloud. Jasper was very sorry to witness her distress, for he thought he could not very well touch upon the collectorship at present, and he dreaded the return of Sir John.

"This is a very sad, sad letter," said Lady Norwold, after a pause of some moments, "and will go nigh to break my heart, unless Gilbert has some satisfactory explanation to give. What do you propose to do, Mr. Jellifer? Is it in your power to help my unhappy boy?"

"Why really, your ladyship," said Jasper, hardly expecting such a point-blank question so early in the interview, "I assure your ladyship that it is quite out of my power to do what Mr. Gilbert requires."

"Then why did you come to me? Why did you come to give me pain, if you have not the power to help my poor son?"

Jasper saw all his new-blown hopes fading away if he hesitated.

"Your ladyship would not hear me to an end," said Jasper. "I was about to say that I would see Mr. Gilbert, and hear if he really wants so much as 200*l.* If fifty would help him, and I have your ladyship's promise of repayment, I would try—yes, I would try to advance that sum."

"Thanks, Mr. Jellifer. Mr. Gilbert must make that sum sufficient, for I do not hesitate to tell you that Sir John is tired of supplying his sons'—both his sons'—extravagances, and that I am myself subjected to much annoyance on their account. Sir John is very unreasonable at times, and is not particular upon whom he vents his ill temper. I knew when you gave me that letter that it was about money. As I read how dear Gilbert's imprudence was distressing him, poor boy, and saw how large was the amount required to release

him from his difficulties, I was perfectly overcome, knowing
that I am almost penniless at present. Mr. Jellifer, you will
do your best in this unhappy business, and I promise you
shall be repaid. Of course I depend upon your honourable
secrecy, and——have you anything else to say?"

Yes, Jasper had, and he intimated as much by his
manner, when he saw her ladyship about to leave the room.

"I beg your ladyship's pardon for detaining you," said
Jasper; "but Mr. David Locke, Sir John's collector of rents
in Morden, is dying."

"Poor old Mr. Locke dying, indeed! Well!"

"I am most anxious to have the appointment at his death,
and if your ladyship would intercede for me with Sir John,
I should be deeply grateful."

"Mr. Jellifer, I will say what I can for you. You know—
all the world in fact knows—what a strange temper Sir John
is, but he has his lucid intervals, and I will avail myself of
one of them to prefer your suit. Good morning—though,
Mr. Jellifer, I must make one condition."

"Pray name it, your ladyship," said Jasper, thoroughly
satisfied and delighted.

"You must let Mr. Gilbert have a hundred pounds. Tell
him, from me, that he must do with that. Good morning"
——and her ladyship glided from the room.

She had always been a cold, selfish woman, and married
Sir John, her senior by many years, for position, relentlessly
breaking whole quires of written vows of constancy and love
to one who had believed them. Her married life would have
been an unhappy one had she coveted a husband's love, or a
wife's place in her husband's home; but, asking neither,
finding neither, she had concentrated all the woman's nature
she possessed on her only child, ever seeking his advantage
at the expense of his brother Gerard, using mean trickery and
double dealing to secure her ends, and too frequently employ-
ing the agency of her own child, until she had made him as
selfish, deceitful, and dishonourable as herself.

The last condition of Lady Norwold was not over acceptable to Jasper, but as he walked down the grand old avenue
his former dreams of greatness and profit returned, and he
resolved to consult his friend the miller.

Ray, he knew, had been to London, but would return by
the mid-day coach, and he might as well call upon him at
once, and not wait until the evening for the settlement of
some matter of business between them. So Jasper sat down
on a bench in the garden to await his friend's return.

We have hitherto said nothing of Jasper's wife, and
although she will have little to do with our story for some
time to come, she is a person not to be altogether overlooked.
Jasper had smuggled her, almost, into Morden, for none knew
of his wooing or of his marriage, and the lady herself was a
stranger to every one. She was rather a showy person to be
Jasper Jellifer's wife, but she proved to be an industrious
woman, and drove as hard a bargain, and loved money as
dearly as did her husband. Her maiden name she told to
many, had been Harrison; and it was by her introduction, it
was said, that Ray and Jasper had become friends. Some
persons, indeed, fancied they could trace a family resemblance
between Ray and Mrs. Jellifer, but people in country towns
will have strange fancies.

Ray returned punctually by the mid-day coach, and he
and Jasper were soon closely closeted together. Ray's jovial
laugh came now and then pealing through the open window,
overpowering poor Jasper's feeble chuckle, which rarely had
an independent innings. An hour or so had passed when
Gregory, the miller's man, was summoned to the house, and
desired to witness the signatures of the two friends to a paper
which had been prepared in London. The man was rather
frightened, as persons of his class frequently are, when asked
"to put their names to paper;" but Ray for some reason,
and despite his *bonhomie*, was not a person any one would
willingly disoblige when he required a service of them.

"Now have a glass of wine, Gregory, if only to impress

this matter upon your memory," said Ray; " and I hope it may be a long day before you are required to give your evidence."

Both friends laughed in concert, and Gregory grinned and drank off the wine, and never forgot to his dying day the signing of that paper.

" Your mind is at ease now, I hope," said Ray, when Gregory had left the room ; " by to-morrow's post the other deed will arrive, and when that is signed, sealed, and delivered, all will be straight between us."

The next day Gregory was again summoned, but no wine was forthcoming, and for that reason among others, he remembered when his head was grey the signing of the second paper also, when Mr. Ray was the miller at Norwold Mill.

CHAPTER IV.

MR. JELLIFER PROVIDES AN OFFERING, AND RAY, THE MILLER,
OFFICIATES AS A PRIEST OF MAMMON.

THOSE who remember the old coaching days—forgetting,
perhaps, many of their discomforts, delays, and dangers—are
wont to contrast them favourably with the hurry, noise, and
monotony of a journey by rail. It was certainly a pleasant
change for the daily worker, whether student, trader, or
craftsman, to find himself seated on a well-appointed four-
horse coach, whirling along through pleasant country scenes,
such as England presents, whichever way we travel, silently
enjoying the ever-changing landscape, now of broad cultivated
plains, rich with their promised or accomplished harvests;
now of great moorlands, golden with the blossoms of the
furze, or purple with the flowers of the heather; the distance
studded with farmers' homesteads or lordly mansions, and
changing then to the glorious woodlands, watered by noble
rivers or placid streams, until the wearied mind forgot its
toils and cares, and felt that the beauteous earth might indeed
have been a Paradise. The fresh breeze came like the breath
of health, and made the pulse beat quicker, whilst the brisk
clatter of the dashing team became a cadence that was almost
music. The entrance of the coach into the country town or
little village was an event to be regarded. The busiest
and the idle, the old and the young, had eyes for nothing
else, and every passenger, on the outside at least, felt "a
lion" for the moment. What delicious ale you drank at the
Change! What luscious ham and delicate fowls you ate at
the dinner, and what a princely price you paid for the enjoy-

ment! You pay as nobly now, but *minus* the pleasure. Then the after weed! When did a cigar ever seem so fragrant, so etherial, as when smoked upon a coach-box, with no better companion at your side than the chatty coachman, whose skill you admired, and whose universal popularity you almost envied. Mr. Babbage, that sorely tormented gentleman (may his tormentors eat dirt!—by the bye, they do that), would have forgiven the strong-lunged guard for the melody produced by his straight horn or key bugle, and paid his tip at the end of the journey with the readiness of gratitude. Soho! our ride by coach is ended, and what is written may seem rhapsodies, but many shared them on the day when Gilbert Norwold obtained his "exeat," and left Cambridge for Morden.

The ride was a dreary one for him, and when he arrived in London he almost determined to retrace his road, and dare Gerard to his worst rather than proceed on his humiliating mission. He thought, however, that Gerard would not be diverted from the resolution he had expressed to see restitution made; and he knew that his father would feel the family honour compromised, and against that conviction his parental affection would weigh as a grain of sand. So, he must on to Morden, and purchase his redemption from Jasper Jellifer at whatever price he might be pleased to require for the service to be rendered.

The coach would arrive about nine o'clock, and to avoid recognition, Gilbert had requested Jasper to meet him with his covered cart about a mile from the Elms, and his request had been obeyed.

As Gilbert had made frequently secret runs home, the guard and coachman (to whom he was well known), were not surprised at this arrangement, and both knew their business too well to allude to the circumstance when they made the next change at Morden.

"Well, Jellifer," said Gilbert, as soon as they were seated in the cart, "are you ready with the money?"

D

The inquiry was somewhat abrupt, but Jasper was undisturbed by it, and the more especially as he was not about to ask any favour from Gilbert.

"The sum you require is far above my means," he replied —"very far, and you ought to have known that, sir."

"I don't believe you, Jasper; that's flat!" said Gilbert. "I am sure you must have the money; but I suppose now that you know the infernal strait I am in, you want to play the Shylock. You need not hesitate to ask your price—I am prepared to pay liberally; that is, to promise to pay, and my brother Gerard will do the same."

"I tell you once again, sir, that I have not the power to help you to so much as 200*l*. I saw her ladyship this morning."

"Ah! What did she say?"

"She was very much cut up, sir, when I told her what you had written about. Very much cut up:" said Jasper, with emotion.

"She always cries before she puts her hand in her pocket, I know," replied Gilbert. "But she gave you her security?"

"Not so; she has given me no security, because I told her as I tell you, I have not the money."

"Then you must borrow it," cried Gilbert, much excited by Jasper's coolness and protestations. "My honour, my future welfare, is concerned, and you must find me the money, you cold-blooded fellow."

"I am not what you call me, Mr. Gilbert, and I will prove it to you at once. I offered to give you all the money I have —some fifty pounds or so—and your lady mother said that you must make that sufficient, as——"

"How can she know what is sufficient?" cried Gilbert. "She ought to be able to manage better, and make Sir John more liberal with his money. I tell you once for all fifty pounds is of no use to me."

"'You *may* make it a hundred,' said her ladyship, 'and I will see you paid;' and being anxious to serve you, sir, and her ladyship, I have been to my friend, **Mr. Ray**—the miller, sir—and he hopes to be able to make up another fifty pounds to mine. We will go down this lane, and then cross the river in a boat. My cart would be known in the market-place, and people would wonder what business I had at the mill so late at night."

Gilbert sat silent for some minutes, and then said :

"A hundred pounds, eh? Hm!—Gerard will get fifty from Sir John, and that might be made sufficient."

"You must not calculate upon that, sir," said Jasper. "As I was sitting in the Hall this morning, I could not help hearing Sir John desire her ladyship to write to you both, and refuse your brother the money."

Gilbert swore a strong oath for so young a man, but he had been accustomed to hear such phrases from his father's mouth.

"Please, don't swear in such a fearful way, sir," said Jasper. "I am not a religious man, but we are about to cross the river in a boat, and I don't like the water even by day-light."

By this time they had reached an old boat-house on the banks of the river, and Jasper had made all needful prepara-tions, as a boy was waiting to ferry them across to Norwold Park, after the horse had been put up at a neighbouring stable.

The night was star-light, and the fine old Hall looked grand amid its surrounding of stately trees as Gilbert and Jasper walked under the shadow of 'the park palings to Norwold Mill. They found Ray waiting for them at the garden gate, and the miller raising his hat to Gilbert, led the way to the house in silence.

The room they entered was the one in which Jack Spraggatt had found the ring, but now the shutters were closed, and thick red curtains drawn before them. Supper was laid upon the table, and as the evening had been somewhat chilly, a bright wood fire was burning, and both were heartily wel-

comed by the two wayfarers. The miller's pleasant manner
and cheerful face were not lost upon Gilbert, and he soon
went heartily to work at the excellent supper provided for
the party. No word was spoken on the matter which had
called them together until, the table being cleared and the
materials for grog brought in, the domestic was dismissed for
the night.

Ray broke ground.

"Mr. Jellifer has told me, sir, of your wants, and of his
own inability to meet them, and has come to me, who am
quite as poor as himself, to help in the matter."

Gilbert bowed slightly, and said, "Just so. I understand
that Mr. Jellifer has explained my present position to you,
and that you have kindly undertaken to help me, if you can."

"That 'if,'" said the miller, "is the difficulty."

The clock in the passage struck eleven.

Jasper rose hastily, and said that as his wife, who knew
nothing of this business, would be alarmed at his absence,
and possibly be making inquiries for him, he begged to be
allowed to go.

Ray knew all the particulars, and Mr. Gilbert had arranged
to remain at the mill until the early morning, when Jasper
was to call for him with the covered cart. As there was no
reason why he should remain, Ray saw him to the garden
gate, and after a few minutes returned to his guest.

"To tell the truth," said he, "I am glad Jellifer has left
us. He is a good fellow enough, but he has seen nothing of
the world, and has all the narrow prejudices of a provincial
shopkeeper. Your grog is not to your liking, I'm afraid,
sir?"

Gilbert assured him that it was capital, and the miller went
on, having first produced some cigars of excellent quality.

"I do not wish to force myself upon your confidence, or to
take advantage of what I already know, but being a burnt
child myself, I am very anxious to help you, if I can." He
paused for a few moments, and then continued. "If I had

had an adviser when young, I should not be a huckstering miller, nor the intimate of such a man as Jasper Jellifer; but I made one mistake, and was unforgiven—turned out into the world to fight the battle of life—to sink or swim as best I could. I know what I have suffered, and seen what others have suffered also."

There was silence, and both sat looking at the bright fire.

" I have no right to say more," continued the miller—"no right to ask you to tell me anything; but the sum you—a young man—require is so large, and the need of it so urgent, that—" he paused.

" That, what?" asked Gilbert.

"That I would make a great effort to help you, if I believed it would save you from the evil consequences of a boyish folly."

Gilbert was touched by Ray's tone, and kindly manner almost more than by his words, and he said, " Thank you, thank you, Mr. Ray. The money would indeed save me from a very painful difficulty."

"Yet you will not trust me, because I am not your equal. Is it not so?"

" That is not my reason," replied Gilbert; "on my honour, no! and I will hesitate no longer. I only desire that what I say be not communicated to Jellifer, or indeed to any other person."

Ray gave the required assurance, and Gilbert continued :

"I have a brother, as you know, a half-brother only, and older than myself. He is up at Cambridge with me. Our pursuits, our habits, are widely different; and whilst he, I believe, is considered a thoroughly good fellow, I am regarded by his set as a rather loose fish. I accept the distinction, because I know I deserve it. Gerard rarely touches a card, and I am fond of play, and latterly I have——, I have——"

" Lost your money," remarked Ray, as Gilbert made a pause.

" No; I have won somewhat largely, and principally of a
freshman."

" Well, no harm in that," said Ray, as Gilbert again ceased
speaking.

" You are mistaken ; all the harm I fear is from that cause.
' Easy got, easy go,' is an old adage, and so it has been with
my winnings. Pressing debts and some fresh extravagancies,
have disposed of all my gains. That had been all very well; but
this is my difficulty : my good and worthy brother has come
to know of the matter—how does not signify—and because
my opponent chances to be a rich young fool, Gerard desires
me to restore the fellow his losings, and that forthwith ; pre-
tending that our family honour, or some such nonsense, is
concerned."

" And what, if you refuse to comply with such an unreasonable request ? " asked Ray, with a smile.

" The blackguard threatens to tell my father, knowing his
ungovernable temper, and that he would turn me out of doors
as likely as not; for I have never been a favourite with him,
and he has forbidden us, again and again I own, to play for
money."

" Would your brother do this, think you ? "

" Yes—remorselessly. He has said he would, even when
I pleaded for my mother. He is sneak enough to keep his
word," answered Gilbert.

" Your position is indeed desperate ! " said Ray, with a
sigh; " for I know of what evil things your *good* young man
is capable. It was a ' good young man ' that made my
father close his door on me, and changed the whole purpose
of my life. You want 200*l.* ? "

" Yes.   Jellifer will advance fifty pounds, and Gerard
wrote home for fifty more, and has been refused."

" That I know, as Jasper saw your mother this morning,
after a stormy breakfast with Sir John," said Ray. " I wish
I were rich enough to help you ; from my soul I do ; but I
have a hard fight to keep my place, poor as it is. However,

I have not asked this confidence without a reason. Had you needed this money for any ordinary purpose, I should have added a little to Jasper's loan, and so have ended. But your case is too desperate to hesitate, from false delicacy, perhaps, to tell you what can be done. Your brother has everything to gain by your exposure; but from some sense of decency he has made this home request for money, knowing it would be refused, and proposed to give his security to Jasper, knowing it to be worthless, has he not? I guessed at something of this, and therefore have not been idle in your behalf, although only partially successful. Fill your glass again, Mr. Gilbert, and then I will tell you all that can be done."

Ray made up the fire, and threw on another log or two, muttering audibly as he did so, "Poor young fellow!" He then seated himself, and said:

"I have been to London on this matter, Mr. Gilbert, unknown to Jellifer. I have brought back the money, and here it is in this pocket-book. It is at your service conditionally, and pray bear in mind that the terms I am about to propose are not mine, but of the man from whom the money comes. Were it mine, there should be none. I have obtained one hundred and fifty pounds from a money-lender—one of the most cautious of his class. He has known me long, too long for my advantage, but as I never deceived him, he will at all times take my word, and not my security. He knows my real circumstances too well. Yet, as I say, he will trust to my word and to my honour. He will lend you this money on one condition only. Mind, it is he who speaks. He will have some tangible security, such as, he says, Lady Norwold can easily give if she be so minded. She must have jewels, diamonds, and those he will have, or I am bound to return him this money."

Gilbert started from his seat, exclaiming, "Impossible! She will not risk my father's anger."

"She will," said Ray, calmly; "she will, when she knows it will save her son from the ruin which is before

him. Sit down, sir, and let us talk quietly. Reflect—has
Lady Norwold no jewels which she seldom wears. Your
family will not go to town until Christmas, and before that
time your mother can easily obtain—for women have great
tact—the money from your father to redeem any pledge she
may now give. Reflect—has she nothing that you can ask
her to lend you at this terrible emergency?"

"Yes—she has one ornament which she rarely wears—a
diamond bracelet given her by Sir John, I have heard her
say, shortly after they were married," replied Gilbert.

"Ask her to lend you that," said Ray, coolly.

"But how to see her, even if I wait until to-morrow?
I dare not go to the Hall, and she is not always at liberty
to leave home."

"Go to her to-night," said Ray. "She and Sir John occupy
separate chambers—do they not?—whenever there has been a
domestic breeze, and one blew pretty stiffly this morning, I
hear. It has been whispered, Mr. Gilbert, that you could
find your way into Norwold Hall without troubling the
porter." And the miller smiled.

"I thought that secret was known only to myself,"
answered Gilbert, smiling also, and colouring deeply. "There
is an entrance, but then one door will be locked to-night, and
I have not the key."

"Where there's a will there's a way," said the miller,
laughing, and going to one corner of the room where a
portrait hung. "Secret for secret, Mr. Gilbert. Here is my
Hassarac's cavern. Open Sesame!" As he spoke he pressed
upon the moulding of the picture frame, the canvas flew up,
and disclosed a very shallow recess behind it. "A present
this, from my old friend the money-lender, and I use it for
odds and ends that else would get astray. Here are some
keys of various sizes. One of them, perhaps, may remove
your difficulty."

Gilbert looked at the bunch; there were some dozen or so,
and at last selected three which appeared to be available.

The ring to which they were attached was rusted, however, and would not open.

"Take them as they are," said the miller, "and remember what you have at stake. Home and fortune, or a life of struggle, not ending perhaps—in a mill."

The moon shone very brightly, and the stars glistened like the eyes of angels, when Gilbert Norwold entered the grand old avenue to steal into his father's house like a thief in the night. Again and again his heart failed him, but all that Ray had spoken came back to him, hissing in his ears, and roused him to proceed.

The door through which he had often passed secretly at night, was in the wall of a small yard, which had been formerly used for poultry by the first Lady Norwold; but had been long neglected. From the roof of a small building within it, Gilbert could reach a staircase window which was without a fastening, and through this he had passed often and often. The lock of the door was of the commonest construction, and one of the keys he had readily opened it.

He soon reached the roof of the neglected aviary, and walked along it towards the window which had frequently given him access to the house when he had been absent without the knowledge of, or against the wish of his father. As he drew nearer to the house, his shadow rose up before him on the wall, as though to warn him of impending danger, or to drive him back from the commission of a crime. It startled him for a moment, but again the miller's words— "Home and fortune—a life of struggle,"—came back to him, and he opened the window.

When Gilbert Norwold stood in his father's house his heart beat violently, and he felt how mean an act he was committing. How many a wretched hour had he spared himself and others, had he listened to the still small voice within that called to him to go back.

Noiselessly, as one stealing to do murder, did he approach

his mother's dressing-room. The thick curtains shut out the moonlight, and he was afraid to proceed until he had carefully withdrawn the hangings and let it in. Silently he reached the door of the bed-chamber, and found it locked. He tapped once, only once, upon the panel, and no one spoke, and he feared to knock again, thinking his mother could not be in that room.

What was to become of him? If all that Ray had suggested should come to pass! If Gerard should be the false-hearted treacherous brother that he had made him appear to be! If he could have seen his mother alone but for a few minutes, he knew her love for him was so strong, herself so weak, that she would have yielded to his prayers for assistance. What now was to be done?

The moonlight streaming through the half-opened curtains fell full upon the small cabinet wherein his mother kept her trinkets. The thought which passed through his mind when he saw this, almost deprived him of the power to move. There was deliverance behind those painted doors. Again the words of Ray came back to him—Homeless! Portionless! and all by the word of a false brother. His hand almost instinctively sought the keys in his pocket; he drew them forth—one, two, three, were tried without effect. Again he paused in his guilty work, and again Ray's words were in his ears. His mother would save him, did she know all. He would tell her all to-morrow or the next day, when he would write to her. A key was found at last, one painted door was opened, and there, on the little shelf where he had seen it lie so often, was the bracelet case. He opened it, took out the bracelet, and returned the case. His brain was numbed now, and his heart almost still, but the click of the closing lock set both at work again. How he reached the park he could not remember, but he must have returned the way he had entered, as he found the keys in his hand. Uttering a sharp cry, he hurled them away, and running down the avenue, would have fallen to the ground, had not Ray suddenly advanced to him from the shadow of some trees which stood near the pathway leading from the park to the mill.

It was some minutes before Gilbert could proceed, even with the assistance of Ray, who kept silent, fearing to provoke a return of his young friend's faintness, by any inopportune question.

When they had entered the miller's parlour, where the fire still burned brightly, Gilbert burst into tears and laid his head upon the table; and Ray did not speak for some time, not until the sobbing ceased.

" Has the interview been so painful ? " he asked.

" Oh, most painful! most painful! never to be forgotten from this hour by me. Say no more, sir. It is over! There is the bracelet." He almost threw it upon the table, and Ray, who did not care to increase Gilbert's distress, took it up and examined it carefully. It was of diamond work surrounding a portrait of Sir John Norwold. Ray held it in his hand for some time, and a smile of satisfaction passed over his pleasant features.

Gilbert sat with his face covered by his hands, and so Ray proceeded to count out 200*l*., and to write some memoranda on a sheet of paper.

" Now, sir," he said at length, " Jasper's cart will be here directly, and we may as well conclude our painful business. There are notes for 200*l*., and I must trouble you to give me your brother's undertaking for Jellifer, and to sign these memoranda for the other money. They are receipts for these two sums, and here is another signed by me acknowledging the possession of this bracelet, and the amount, 200*l*., for which it is pledged. Mr. Jellifer will arrange his own charge for interest."

Gilbert did not observe the cold vicious tone in which Ray now addressed him, but signed the papers, and gave Ray Gerard's letter acknowledging his responsibility. He had scarcely finished when Jasper's covered cart drove up to the mill, and Gilbert shaking the miller warmly by the hand, joined the clever agent, who had helped him to such a generous friend as Miller Ray.

When the miller returned to the house, he saw that Gilbert had left the paper acknowledging Ray's possession of the bracelet behind him. Ray shook his head, and placing the paper in his cash-box, opened his Hassarac's cavern and deposited them within it. The bracelet, and the receipt signed by Gilbert, he put into his pocket, no doubt intending to give them to the money-lender, who had such remarkable reliance on his word and honour.

On the evening of the next day, Gilbert Norwold entered his brother's rooms at Cambridge his whole appearance so changed, that to any one slightly acquainted with him, he would have been hardly recognisable. His face so haggard that the deepened lines added years to its expression, whilst his curved shoulders seemed bent down by the weight of the heavy heart within. He did not offer to sit down, and hardly accepted the hand his brother Gerard extended to him. Gerard was surprised and pained at the change, and more so when Gilbert said in a low, hollow voice :—

"I have brought back the money. Jellifer lent me £50 on your security. For the rest I am indebted to my mother. I leave to you the restitution."

"My dear Gilbert, you are ill," said his brother. "Is it fatigue, or have you had words at home?"

"I am fatigued," replied Gilbert. "I have not closed my eyes since I left Cambridge. Our father's honour—your honour—is preserved."

"And yours also, dear brother," said Gerard, taking Gilbert's hand. As he did so he felt that a shudder passed through his brother's frame, and saw that on his forehead large drops of sweat came suddenly and fast.

"Lie down on my bed. You are ill; I am sure you are," said Gerard. "Let me send for the doctor."

Gilbert instantly appeared to rouse himself, and replied : "No necessity for that, Gerard. My interview with—with

Jellifer and his friend, who advanced the money, was long and humiliating. It lasted throughout the night, and I have travelled here since I saw them—I will go to my own rooms. You will see Mariott. I suppose I need not ask you to spare me as much as possible. You will do that, however, for your own sake. There are two hundred pounds in notes."

" I suppose," said Gerard, unwilling to reply to his brother's taunt—" I suppose the terms exacted by the lenders are somewhat hard."

" Yes," answered Gilbert : a shuddering shook him this time unnoticed by his brother. " You may know some day what it is to be in desperate need and wanting a helping friend. When that time comes, Gerard, remember how sharp the ordeal has been to which you condemned me."

" I condemned you ?"

" Yes, you—my brother. Your wicked threats of exposure here and at home, have well nigh driven me mad; and now that I have done what you required of me, let me alone. Do not come near me so long as we are 'up' here. When we go home I will try to behave to you as I have always done. I will spare no effort to do so, but until the vacation I desire to be let alone." And then, without another parting word, Gilbert left the room, whilst Gerard, surprised and silent, had not power to question him as to the meaning of his words.

" The poor fellow's ill—excited," he thought. " Perhaps annoyed at the wretched discovery I have made, and afraid that Mariott should guess the truth. That he shall never know from me." Gerard went to bed, and laid an hour or more awake devising the construction of the note to be sent to Mariott in the morning.

On the next day, Julius Mariott, of —— College, Cambridge, when seated at breakfast, was greatly surprised by the following note :—

" DEAR MARIOTT,—You are such a good fellow, that I am sure you will feel no offence at what I write, and will heartily

coincide in the course which my brother and myself have
considered it our duty to adopt with reference to Gilbert's
winnings at various times of you and others.

"My father is a man of very violent temper and prejudices, and did he know that either of us had disobeyed
any particular injunction of his, I am afraid—nay, I am sure
—that the consequences would be most serious to our future
welfare. One of the promises which he exacted from us both
on coming up here was, that we should never play at cards
for money. I am ashamed to say that we have forgotten
that promise. A strong sense of the impropriety of this
conduct, and of the danger attending it, has made us resolved
to throw ourselves upon your generosity, and ask you to
enable us, as far as it can be done, to undo the past by not
hesitating to receive the enclosure.

"Mariott, you will not refuse us—you must not. We
know how repugnant such acceptance of lost money must
be to you; but like a noble, good fellow, waive your right to
be angry and offended, and place us in a position to tell our
father, should he question us, that we have not altogether
disobeyed his injunction or broken our promise. This is,
I grant you, a mean equivocation at the best, but it is the
nearest approach to truth and right which we can make.
You will not refuse us, will you?—I am faithfully,

"GERARD NORWOLD."

"What the devil am I to do?" thought Mariott, when he
had finished reading. "This isn't fair to a man. Nobody
ought to ask you to do such a thing under any circumstances."
He glanced at the letter again, and did not feel quite so
certain of his conclusions. "They have put it in such a way
that it seems beastly to refuse them. And yet I really can't
accept—I can't. I should cut with myself if I did—if that
were possible." Another hurried perusal of the letter left
the young gentleman more undecided. "Well, it's not fair,
that's all I can say, to ask a man such a thing, and in his

first term too. Suppose I send it to some charity. Well, perhaps that gets over the difficulty," and Mr. Mariott walked out into the High Street so obfuscated that he nearly came to grief by passing no less than three Dons without capping them.

How a single act of good or evil oftentime changes the colour of all our future lives?

Gilbert Norwold, so late the thoughtless, pleasure-seeking youth, was now a moody miserable creature, made so by one guilty deed, which he must hide for years to come within the secret chamber of his own bosom. No, not from every one. His mother must know the dreadful thing he had done, and he would write to her at once. He began to narrate the disgraceful story; but the words he wrote blinded him, and he tore up the paper. To-morrow the confession should be made. Another terrible night passed over, and the theft he had committed appeared more mean, more criminal, and he could not write down the record of his own degradation. He would wait until he returned home, and then he would tell her of his evil doing. The vacation was close at hand, and then he would confess to her his sin, and be forgiven.

Two days only of the term remained, and his resolution had not strengthened; so, when Mariott pressed him to spend a week with him before he returned to Norwold Hall, the unhappy criminal felt it as a reprieve, and thankfully accepted the invitation.

The ailing man who suffers day by day from some torturing malady, will often hesitate to seek the aid of the physician, because he fears to learn the worst or bear the pain of cure, until those dreadful words, "Too late," are his sentence to the grave. Gilbert Norwold was like the ailing man, and his moral sore grew and grew, until it killed his peace.

CHAPTER V.

SACRILEGE AND MATRIMONY AT MORDEN.

The long vacation had commenced, and Gerard had come home to Norwold Hall. He had undergone more than one wigging from Sir John on his presumed extravagance, and borne them patiently, convinced that his college bills would bear scrutiny, and that he should deserve, if he did not obtain, the parental blessing. Lady Norwold, though dying, as she said, to embrace her boy, was nevertheless glad at his temporary absence, as Gerard had to sustain the first outburst of his father's ill-humours, and Sir John was soon forgetful of most of his resentments.

Shortly after Gerard's return from Cambridge, Sir John was much occupied with his magisterial duties, as Morden church had been entered and robbed of its valuable communion plate, almost under the nose of the beadle. On all similar occasions, it was Sir John's practice to issue warrants against every person suspected of poaching; and although the accused were generally acquitted, the justice of the peace was gratified in thinking that he had caused annoyance to some of the vagabonds who preferred night-walking after his game, with the occasional chance of gaol allowance, to hard labour for eighteen-pence a day, and the certainty of the short commons such earnings could procure.

The scandal of this sacrilege made the local authorities more than usually fussy; for, strange to say, in no instance of burglary had the county constabulary been successful in discovering a trace of the perpetrators, or of the lost property. The only man in Morden who seemed to have any particular suggestions to make on the matter was Miller Ray, and he earnestly advised that communication should be established with the London police, as there was no doubt but the thieves came from the metropolis, and would undoubtedly dispose of their evil gains in the same locality. The suggestion was accepted by the whole Bench as a very good one (although Sir John insisted upon having a few poachers bagged for his own satisfaction); and the clerk of the court considered the facility with which Mr. Ray drew up the particulars of the robbery as something remarkable in a miller.

Mr. Ray laughed, and assured the functionary that it must be a natural gift, as he had never cultivated it, and its development was only attributable to the honest indignation he felt, in common with the other inhabitants of Morden, at the loss which the church had sustained, not to mention his detestation of the perpetrators of such an act.

Sir John being thus occupied, Gerard was left to his own resources for amusement, and it was therefore no wonder that he was daily with Jack Spraggatt, who was an especial favourite with every one at the Hall.

The Elms were more than usually attractive at this time, as great preparations were in progress for the marriage of Letty, Jack's elder sister, and Gerard displayed such taste in assisting Lucy to decorate the barn wherein the wedding breakfast was to take place, that he might have been born the son of an upholsterer, rather than the heir to an ancient baronetcy. A looker-on might have thought that he occupied more time than was really necessary in peering into Lucy's pretty face, asking her questions as to the effect of his arrangements, or requesting assistance in carrying them out, than became such an adept. Lucy's face was very pretty, certainly, and when she smiled, and her bright blue eyes sparkled also, it was not an easy matter to look away from it. Her rich auburn curls were fitting adornments for such features, and almost wooed the fingers to play with the silken tresses. Her voice, too, was a pleasant sound to hear, making the commonest words seem like notes of music.

E

Her figure would have been injured by any less simple dress than that which she generally wore, and flounces, and braids, and fringes would have been as much out of keeping as they would be upon Canova's masterpiece. Yet she appeared unconscious of her beauty, although, no doubt, she and her looking-glass were no strangers to each other. She was well educated as middle-class girls were taught then, and could sing and play such simple songs and melodies as make the music festivals of home. She had paid long visits to London, and could talk of other things beside farm-stock and poultry, and had not lost her love for the duties of her country life, as the dairy and store-room could testify. She was the light of Jack Spraggatt's home, and he rejoiced in his heart of hearts that it was Letty who was about to leave them, and not Lucy.

The wedding-day was close at hand, and a great day it was to be! Jack Spraggatt was not so lively as he ought to have been, Gerard said, but Lucy thought she could divine the reason. The bridegroom elect was a Frenchman, whom Letty had met in London. He was a young man of a good Protestant family, but the Spraggatts had their national prejudices, and would rather have had their new connection one of the family of John Bull. The fates had willed it otherwise, for Letty, who was a pretty, weak-minded girl, and consequently very obstinate, had, despite many domestic engagements with the family, compelled them at last to lay down their arms and surrender at her discretion. It was Jack's dislike to the Frenchman (or something else, perhaps), that made him very moody at times, and a little cross when new expenses were proposed, or the list of invitations was extended.

It is surprising what interest all women take in weddings. Marriage is certainly a great event in a young girl's life, and should be productive of happy anticipations, even when her nurture has been gentle and her home a loving one. Still, there is change before her, a future which may differ widely from the past, a newer love to be trusted than the one that has watched over her from the hour of her birth, and been prodigal of all which has constituted the happiness of her life. Alas! no past, however free from cares, can ensure a future equally happy, and the old must die and leave the young to trust in one another.

It is wonderful, 'we repeat, the interest women take in weddings, even in those where they themselves are not the principals. Mothers, sisters, aunts, cousins, friends and servants, when a wedding is in prospect, display a consequence and an excitement entirely unusual with them. The family conversation (and we doubt not that of the collateral relations we have enumerated) lapses occasionally into other subjects, but the grand staple is of the bride and bridemaids, wreaths, dresses, presents, and wedding-cake. Money, labour, time, are all accounted subservient to the one grand object, as though a great sacrificial ceremony was about to take place, and every one was bound to be prepared with an offering.

The Elms was no exception to other households, and the number of volunteer needlewoman was immense. Willing pens were busy day and evening inditing invitations to friends distant and near, until poor Jack thought that the Big Barn would be fuller than it was before Miller Ray emptied it. He ventured once or twice to hint at a limitation of numbers, but such excellent and unanswerable reasons were given why the list should be increased rather than curtailed, that he always retired discomfited.

Gerard invariably sided with the ladies, unless, indeed, Lucy voted with Jack, and then he thought no more of giving a plumper in opposition to the opinion he had previously expressed than would a free and independent voter who had listened to the eloquence of the late Mr. David Locke during a contested election.

The wedding-day arrived at last, and the Big Barn looked like a sylvan bower, so well had Gerard and Lucy devised, and willing labourers had worked. The tables were covered

with home-made delicacies, whilst the plate-baskets of relatives and dear friends had been laid under contribution, and
their contents glittered as brightly as the glasses.   Lucy ran
to take a peep just before going to church, although arrayed
in her bridemaid's dress of simple white, dotted over with
lilies gathered from her own garden, and was surprised to
find Gerard there, giving the rustic servants the benefit of his
more refined experience.   With gentlemanly delicacy he had
not called at the house, as Jack had not presumed to ask him
to the church, although he had invited him to the breakfast,
and therefore Gerard came to Lucy and apologised for the
liberty he was taking, in directing the arrangements of the
wedding-feast.

Oh, that blushing cheek ; that radiant smile which thanked
him as much as the sweet voice for such kindly consideration,
and Gerard saw and heard them long after Lucy had gone to
the distant church, long after, when he had seen no other
face he knew for many weary months, and when he sighed to
think he should never meet Lucy more.

None must believe them to be lovers.

Had Gerard Norwold suspected that he had in his heart a
spark of love for Lucy, he would have crushed it out by his
will remorselessly.   He was the heir to an old ancestry,
and would have died any death rather than have disgraced it
by a marriage with any one beneath him in station.   He knew
her only as dear old Jack Spraggatt's pretty, graceful, happy,
honest-hearted sister, and so he esteemed her.   Had Lucy
believed that the pleasure she derived from her association
with Gerard Norwold was other than the gratification of a
respectful friendship, she would have despised herself, for she
never forgot the difference of station which existed between
them.   No! none must believe them to be lovers.

The bridal feast was a merry one, and

> " Laughter holding both his sides,"   •

seemed to have taken the chair for the occasion.

The oratory was rather discursive, and the metaphors somewhat mixed, but the hearts of the speakers were in their words; and when that is the case, any one, to our thinking, is a Demosthenes.

Thresher's flails had made noisy clattering on the floor of the Big Barn times and often, and the drowsy bats, nestling in the roof, had slept on in peace, but the hearty response to the health of the bride and bridegroom, roused them from their slumber, and scared them into the daylight.

Jack Spraggatt's face beamed with the sunshine in his heart, which did not leave it when his French brother-in-law, M. Fichard, broke down in his English, and finished his "return thanks" in his own language, as though he had been the personification of a French and English vocabulary.

The bridal feast had lasted long enough—to judge by the hubbub which succeeded, and the general desire on the part of the gentlemen to shake hands with each other; whilst their happy, healthy faces, showed in the richer brown which stained them, that the good wine had reached their hearts as well as their heads; therefore, a final glass was drank, and a parting cheer was given so heartily that it overpowered the church bells which had been ding-donging for the last quarter of an hour as a summons to the lingering bride and bridegroom.

The lawn at the Elms might have challenged the county for a display of beauty and rustic elegance. Matrimony is considered by the highest authorities to be epidemical; and such whisperings and smilings, such daring attempts at pressing of fingers, and, in one or two instances, of waist encirclings, that any one might have surmised that more than a dozen couples, strolling about Jack's garden, had taken the infection that happy morning.

When the time arrived for the departure of the happy pair, the poor pale face of the bride was made rosy with kisses, as she passed up the garden walk to the gate, and some agitated young gentlemen became sufficiently confused and excited to salute the bridemaids, whose screaming was delightful to hear. Be merry, happy youth! Lose no innocent pleasure, nor indulge in a sinful one! Gather every flower that your hand can reach. Listen to every pleasant song that charms your ear. Dance! Dance! whilst your heart is light, and be thankful for your beauty, before wrinkles steal into your face, or a silver thread shines in your soft hair! God gave you youth for enjoyment, that the remembrance of its delights may come back to you in age, and solace you with its happy memories—but happy only when pure and innocent.

The bride and bridegroom departed with all the time-honoured ceremonies, the old slipper reposing in the bosom of M. Fichard's full-frilled shirt. There were willing hands enough to clear the tables, and prepare the barn for dancing, and nimble feet to keep the town band constantly employed in playing country dances, reels and jigs, for as yet the solemn quadrille had not been introduced generally to the Morden Terpsichoreans. Those were the dancing days of Old England, putting to shame our shambling, hopping, sliddering times, and hands across, down the middle, up again, and pousset had been performed twenty times at least before Sir Roger de Coverley wound up the ball by exhausting the most persistent dancer after a bout of three-quarters of an hour, and so a happy morning ended with a happy night. At least all said as much the next day, excepting Gerard, who having missed Jack from the ball-room for some time, went in search of him.

Jack was not in the house, and one of the servants said she had seen him walking in the garden. Gerard sought his friend in the direction indicated, and found him at last standing in the shadow of a yew hedge, his face covered by his hands and his broad bosom heaving painfully.

"My dear old fellow!" said Gerard. "What is the matter with you?"

Jack recovered himself instantly, and answered: "Nothing,

Gerard; nothing, really. The heat of the barn—the excitement of the day rather overpowered me."

"Forgive me, Jack," said Gerard, "but you are not telling me the truth. Surely you do not regret this marriage? I know it was not a matter you would have desired, but——."

"I am glad, very glad, that Letty has found so good a husband. Do not ask me to tell you—at least, not now—what has disturbed and unmanned me. It is something to be thankful for to know that you, my kind warm-hearted friend, can never be unhappy from the same cause, unless you create it by your own free will, and that I believe to be impossible. No more now. Let us go to my friends, and ——. No, I will not ask you to be silent as to what you have seen, for you are a gentleman."

Jack returned with Gerard to the dancers in the barn, and for the next hour was the merriest of them all. It was not very long after that he and Gerard made strange revelations to each other.

As there was a bright moon that night—bright as the coming honeymoon, which was to shine on a whole month of wedded happiness—Gerard had arranged to walk home, having engaged a bed at the inn in the market place, as Sir John objected, when he was not the cause, to the servants at the Hall sitting up. He had entered the High Street, and was walking leisurely on, when a man passed him, bidding him "good night." Gerard returned the salutation, and at the sound of his voice the man turned, and accosted him by name.

"Yes, I am Mr. Gerard Norwold," he replied.

"You are a friend, I believe, of Mr. John Spraggatt, sir," said the man.

"I am. What then?"

"You have just left his house, I conclude?"

"Yes. What then?"

"Do you know, sir, whether any of his men servants sleep in the house to-night?" asked the stranger.

"That is a question I decline to answer," replied Gerard. "As you are unknown to me, I beg you to leave me."

"You would not, if you knew the motive I have in making the inquiry," said the man.

"Perhaps so; but as I do not, I will thank you to keep the way you were going, and allow me to follow mine alone."

"Very well, sir," said the man. "It is of no great consequence, perhaps. Good night, sir," and to Gerard's surprise, he saw his unknown questioner take the way to the river. In a few moments he heard the plash of oars, and soon after a boat struck against the opposite bank.

"Quite an adventure," he thought to himself. "If he has any intention of paying Jack an unseasonable visit, I should not advise him to select to-night for doing so." Thus musing, Gerard reached his inn without further interruption.

Jack went to bed soon after midnight, having secured safely in the great oak chest the borrowed plate, which had added so much to the splendour of the breakfast; but sleep came not. No, the skeleton in the cupboard was waiting in his bed-chamber to recall to him the past, and to remind him of the present and the future. As he lay thus occupied he heard the same creaking noise as had attracted his attention when the window hasp had been filed, and the old chest ransacked. He rose at once, and opening his window noiselessly, looked out, and saw two men at work beneath him. Before he could think upon his course of action, a low whistle from the road startled the burglars, and with the swiftness of guilty men they fled up the garden, and joined the confederate who had given the signal. That man's figure appeared to be familiar to him. Who was that man?

Jack crept softly down-stairs, and was rejoiced to find the great oak box safe as he had left it. He laid himself upon it and fell asleep.

CHAPTER VI.

THREE days after the wedding and its glories had passed
away, Gerard came to the Elms for a day's fishing with his
friend Jack. He found Lucy alone in the breakfast parlour,
as Mrs. Spraggatt was indisposed, and Jack was busy arrang-
ing the tackle in his own room.

Gerard was completely at home at the Elms, therefore he
had entered without ceremony, and was surprised to find
Lucy so occupied with her thoughts, that she was not conscious of his presence for some moments. Her thoughts were
sad ones, as Gerard read them, and it was not until he had
wished her good morning, that her habitual smile returned,
and bade him welcome. As it was the first time that Gerard
had ever seen a shade of sadness upon those sunny features,
he had during the few moments it had remained there thought
of Jack in the yew walk, and connected the two meetings
with each other.

The shadow had gone, however, like the one passing cloud
on a summer sky, and all was sunshine again in that sweet
face, and placing her hand in Gerard's with the freedom of
her honest friendship, she wished her guest good morning in
such a cheery voice, that he almost mistrusted the evidence
of his eyes.

Jack answered to her summons with a cheery voice also,
and instantly joined his friend at the breakfast table. A
capital breakfast it was, and the two young men, with a long
day's sport before them, did complete justice to it. Jack

managed to monopolise the talk, and seemed so elated at his prospective holiday, that any one might have supposed he had never had a day's fishing since his school days.

"We will try Drayton Water first, Gerard," he said; "there used to be the best trout in the county from the mill up to the stone bridge, unless the rascally poachers have taken them. If that fails us, we will drive over to Basston, and have a try for a jack or two. I have sent on to the Drayton Arms, and ordered some live bait to be ready. And Lucy has packed up a hamper for dinner, so that we may make a long day of it, as the evening often makes amends for the bad sport of the morning. Our luncheons we can take in our pockets. Dinner we will have at the Drayton Arms, and old Mrs. Morgan will think herself well paid by half-a-crown, and what the men will have to drink. You've brought a couple of rods, I see. You need not have burthened yourself with a landing net, as I have a couple. Another cup of tea, Lucy, and tell Joe, when he comes home to dinner, to take the black horse to be shod. He ought to have seen that his fore shoes are worn as thin as a sixpence. I've not had a day's fishing, Mr. Gerard, since we went out together last autumn. Don't hurry your breakfast, I have a short note to write, and the chaise-cart will be at the door by the time I have done—say half-an-hour from this; and Lucy you will see to the rest, dear, I know; I shall not be more than half-an-hour—no, not more than twenty minutes," and Jack left the room.

There was nothing in this common-place talk to call up again the sad look in Lucy's face, yet it was there, and Gerard saw it with some anxiety.

"Jack seems in high spirits this morning, Miss Spraggatt," said Gerard; "but they are natural to him, I believe?"

"Yes, Mr. Gerard," replied Lucy; "that is, they used to be, and indeed when either my mother or myself are present he is always cheerful. But——"

The hesitating manner with which she said this, and then

her sudden pause, assured Gerard that Jack was not such a clever actor as to deceive the sister who loved him.

"You were about to add something more," said Gerard.

The tears came into Lucy's eyes, and she rose and closed the door leading into Jack's room, having first satisfied herself that her brother was not there. She returned and took her seat again quietly at the table, and looking at Gerard as she had never looked at him before, for her eyes were full of sorrow, she said, almost in a whisper—

"Mr. Gerard, I know you are my brother's friend—one that he values more than any other in the world—and I have longed for some days past to speak to you concerning him. For many weeks before my sister's marriage, I observed a great change in him. Whenever our conversation turned on that subject—and it did so necessarily very often—I have seen his expression alter, as though our, perhaps, silly talk of dresses and arrangements pained him. Sometimes he would leave the room; but if he remained, he seemed by an effort to recover his usual cheerfulness, although his banter would now and then sound very like remonstrance."

"I fancy," said Gerard, as Lucy again paused, "that Jack was not over pleased with your sister's selection. That was, perhaps, the cause of what you observed."

"I thought so, too," continued Lucy, "until the wedding-day had passed, but the hearty manner in which he received Mons. Fichard convinced me he had overcome his objections, for Jack is no hypocrite, unless he is now practising an hypocrisy, which God forbid."

For a moment her tears choked her utterance, and then would have way.

"May I venture to ask," said Gerard, "what you now think?—that is, if you believe that I can be of any service."

"Yes, Mr. Gerard, and it is because I think you may be of service to my dear brother, that I have been so bold, as to speak to you now. I am sure he has some secret sorrow—some grief which he will not let me share. It is nothing shameful, of that I am certain, but he fears to give me, perhaps our dear mother, pain by the revelation. What it is I do not guess even, but I cannot let him suffer alone and be silent, when so true a friend as you are to him is at hand."

"You make me proud to think I am so considered by you, Lucy. Tell me, do you think he is in love?" and Gerard smiled.

Lucy strove to smile also as she replied, "No. Jack is too hard to please to be in love, I fancy. There was a most dear and beautiful friend of mine that we once thought he admired, and oh! how happy I should have been had he done so! I am sure he would not have been an unsuccessful wooer; but shortly after my father's death, Jack was so occupied with business matters that he avoided all opportunities of meeting her, and of late their intercourse has ceased altogether. No—Jack is not in love."

"What, then, do you desire? That I should endeavour to ask his confidence?"

"Yes! Yes! Mr. Gerard, do not let him suffer alone. Tell him, if you will, that I entreat him to confide in you, or if he dare, in me—his sister. If his grief, whatever it may be, can be shared by me, implore him not to keep it from me, for there is nothing my love could not endure or strive to do for the dearest, kindest brother that ever a sister had."

Gerard did not speak until Lucy's tears had ceased, and she again looked at him for a reply.

"I will make the attempt, Miss Spraggatt, and I think I may not be unsuccessful"—the meeting in the yew walk coming back to him. "If I succeed and find that I can be of help to him, there is nothing I will not do. My power to be of service is very limited."

"Oh, no!" said Lucy, the shadows all gone once more— "oh, no! for you can be his friend, his confidant; perhaps his adviser. And you will?"

Gerard took the hand she offered now, and pressing it

between his own, vowed in his heart to be a faithful knight and do the lady's bidding.

Before the growling old clock in the passage had struck the half-hour, the chaise-cart was at the door, and rods, creels, and hampers safely stowed away, with Jack ready to mount beside his friend, and only waiting to give Lucy a parting kiss, as ever was his wont. When her lovely face was turned upwards to receive her brother's salutation, Jack started and paused for a second; but Lucy threw her arms around his neck, and kissing him a score of times ran into the house, and waved them good-bye from the window.

Jack gave a short cough as they drove away, as though something had displeased or surprised him. He was almost sure that Lucy had been crying. Why? Gerard could not have been saying anything to annoy her, or——. No, he was too true a gentleman to cause her pain in any way, and to excite false hopes would be to do a cruel thing. So Jack soon recovered his good spirits, and on they went to Drayton Waters, where a man was waiting to take the chaise-cart and horse to the Drayton Arms.

The anglers soon went to work, and a gentle breeze, ruffling the surface of the water, gave promise of sport. We are unskilful in the practice of the gentle craft, and have preferred to take our trout and goodly perch in the pleasant pages of honest Isaak Walton (as it is the phrase to name that torturer of worms and live bait), and are free to own that in our own piscatorial essays, we have found our pleasure in the contemplation of the bright stream and clustered water plants, and flickering insects that haunt the drooping boughs, or when stretched at length beneath the umbrageous shadow of some stately tree, our rod and line neglected in the stream —we have watched the pale blue smoke our lips had breathed, curl upwards to the clouds, and called our dreaming peace.

Nevertheless, we can imagine the ecstatic pleasure others have professed to have known at the success of their skill and cunning in hooking a two-pound trout, or a formidable jack,

the tyrant of fresh waters, or, braver still, the noble salmon.
How the prey was fairly hooked, and played, and landed,
makes better after-dinner talk than much of the prosing of
sages, philosophers, and politicians.

As Gerard Norwold and Jack Spraggatt were enthusiasts at
the sport, both deeply learned in the entomology of the craft,
and clever manipulators of silk and feathers to lure the wiliest
fish; and knowing exceedingly in all baits, whether ground,
live, or dead; it was no wonder, therefore, that Gerard on
turning a bend of the stream, saw with great pain his friend
leaning on his rod, and busied with other thoughts than how
to fill his creel.

So occupied was Jack Spraggatt that he did not hear
Gerard's approach until his friend's hand was upon his
shoulder. The poor dreamer tried to wake without a struggle,
but the sorrow at his heart made it impossible to conceal his
agitation.

"My dear old friend," said Gerard, "again in the yew
walk, for this good stream and this favouring breeze are
nothing to you this day. Come, let us sit down and have a
chat, Jack; for I am commissioned to drag this sorrow—
whatever it may be—out into the light."

"By whom?" asked Jack, with a frown.

"One whom you love the most in the world, except your
mother. Your sister Lucy! I have given her my promise
to speak to you—and no better time than now. Let us sit
down."

Jack obeyed, and clasping his knees with his hands,
looked gloomily towards the stream that flowed past so
merrily.

Gerard then recalled word by word as nearly as he could
remember, the conversation with Lucy, and as he did so, the
face of his auditor now flushing red, now overspread with a
deadly pallor, revealed how closely the recital touched him.
When Gerard had repeated all that had passed between Lucy
and himself, he added:

"I have now told you all, and you will believe, my dear Jack, that I would not have attempted to obtain the confidence I ask, if your sister had not urged me to do so."

"I know it," answered Jack. "I know it. I saw that she had been crying, and was puzzled to guess the reason. Your question is soon answered. One little word tells all the story."

"Love?" said Gerard.

"No?" exclaimed the other—"Debt!"

"Debt! is that all!" said Gerard, smiling. But the expression and earnestness of his friend almost frightened him.

"Is that all, Gerard Norwold? I told you on my sister's wedding night that you could not understand the nature of my sorrow. That all! There is not a good gift that God has given me—loving relatives, earnest friends, health, cheerfulness, a pleasant home, and welcome labour, which is not changed into bitterness by that accursed debt. It comes to me in the dead of night and breaks my sleep. It stands by my bedside when I lie down or rise up. It walks with me wherever I go, and sits at my table, only scared away by the effort of a strong will and a sense of duty to those I love."

"My dear Jack," said Gerard, when his friend ceased speaking, "try and calm yourself. Let us look this devil in the face, and see how we can lay him. The mouse once saved the lion, and I may nibble a hole in the net which enmeshes you. How stand matters?"

"You must have patience, and hear my story. Until two days before my father's death, I believed, whenever I thought of the matter—that we were wealthy—wealthy for our station, I mean. We all thought the same—my mother and sisters. My father sent for me two days before his death, and when we were alone, said to me: 'My poor boy, I leave you a sad inheritance, I fear; but you must not flinch from doing your duty to those who will soon have no friend but you to provide for them.' I will not dwell upon particulars—

enough that he told me during the three preceding years he had met with great losses, and that every endeavour to retrieve them had only made bad matters worse, until he should leave me many difficulties to overcome as best I could, and which he believed, had his life been spared, he could have mastered. He died, dear, kind, ever loving father, and I took up the load he had laid down only beside his grave. Young and hopeful, I went to work with a will, but I found matters much worse than I had believed them to be. I, too, tried by bold ventures to redeem our fortunes, but all that I touched turned out a loss. Wool, hops, corn, all went against me, and now I see no help for it but to sell off all that we have, and pay our debts."

"This is bad news, indeed, my old boy," said Gerard. "You have friends—."

"Yes, and they have stood by me to the uttermost, and must not be losers by me. To go on is to be completely ruined ourselves, and to ruin others."

"Suppose the worst you have described inevitable, you are still young enough, and there is a new world opening, we hear, to all who are not afraid of work," said Gerard.

"Do you think that it is for my own future—nay, my own present, that I care? No, Gerard, but when I see my mother's grey hairs, and remember how many years of peace and honour she has passed beneath our roof—when I see my dear, dear sister, whose life has hitherto been clouded by only one sorrow—my father's death, and know that there will be no longer a home for her—that she must fight the battle of life by my side, and share my fortunes, be they what they may, my heart grows sick, and I dare not—truly dare not, disturb their present peace, although I know their dreams must soon be roughly broken."

For some time the two friends sat silent, Jack being exhausted by the pain his confession had occasioned him, and Gerard, bewildered by the difficulties which presented themselves, necessarily, to one unused to business complications.

" I have been thinking," said Gerard, after awhile, " what you ought to do with regard to your sister. You do her a wrong in not confiding your position to her. She will not be so unhappy in knowing all you have told me as she is now, doubting the cause of your distress. She ought, also, to be prepared for this change, if it be unavoidable; or, who knows? her cleverness may devise some mode of extrication for you."

Jack shook his head at this last improbable contingency, and did not reply at once; but springing to his feet, he took his rod and began whipping the stream in, as Gerard thought, a most inartistic manner. His success was commensurate with his unskilfulness, and he returned in a quarter of an hour with his creel no better stocked than when he started. He held out his hand to Gerard, and said, " My dear friend, I have decided what to do; I will take counsel with Lucy— and you, if you will be of the party. I will look matters boldly in the face, and if it must come to an end in England, why, be it so. I have a friend there who is doing well. He has been some three years in the colony, and sends home very cheering accounts of his success; and what he has done, I may do. So no more at present, but as you have been cheated of your lunch, let us go at once to the Drayton Arms and have dinner."

They soon reached Mrs. Morgan's little roadside inn, and put the worthy hostess into a fluster by arriving an hour before the time appointed; the more so, as it was hay-making time, and the labourers at the adjoining farm were waiting for their " 'lowance o' beer." The two friends, therefore, expressed their willingness to wait Mrs. Morgan's leisure, and strolled into the garden.

A rough country lane ran at the bottom of this garden, and as Jack Spraggatt stood looking over the hedge two men in a higgler's cart drove up. The driver was a powerful flashy-looking fellow, his broad-brimmed hat cocked knowingly on one side, and his sharp fresh-coloured face peering out of a

F

series of bandanna handkerchiefs tied loosely round his neck.
He wore a fustian shooting coat with large metal buttons,
relieved by a faded livery waistcoat. Altogether, he was not
a very presentable person. His companion was less objectionable in appearance, at least as much as could be seen of
him, as he was nearly buried in a hat much too large for
his head, whilst his neck and chin were lost in the folds of a
worsted comforter, despite the heat of the weather. A vel-
veteen jacket, as much too small for him as his hat was too
large, was kept together by a piece of string, and he held
between his knees a narrow square box carefully covered with
green baize, and which he embraced with both arms, as though
he owned a treasure that he was prepared to defend with his
life.

"Hallo, mister," said the driver, addressing Mr. John
Spraggatt; "is this the way to the Drayton Arms?"

"Yes; the next turning brings you into the main road,"
replied Jack.

"Much obliged," said the man. "My friend here in the
hat undertook to pilot me; but, as he always travels a-foot,
he brought me down this infernal rutty road, which has
been nigh breaking my springs and sending my fowls into
fits.—Much obliged," and then he drove on.

"Who was that, Jack?" asked Gerard.

"I don't know. A queer-looking fellow, whoever he may
be, and one I shouldn't like to meet on a dark night, without
a thick stick for my companion."

"I know his voice," said Gerard. "I seem to have heard
it very lately, and under unfavourable circumstances. Ah!
I remember now; it was on the night of the wedding. He
spoke to me in High Street." Gerard then narrated, for the
first time, the conversation he had had with the strange man
who was so inquisitive about Jack's household.

"That was a strange meeting," said Jack, "and connects
itself with an unpleasant circumstance which occurred on that
very night. I have never spoken of the matter at home, as

my mother is a very nervous woman, and I did not wish to alarm her." Jack then acquainted Gerard with the attempt which had been made to force the window, and also the result of the first visit of the burglars.

"And who was the man you thought you recognised?" asked Gerard.

"No, that would not be fair to the man I suspect," replied Jack. "It is more than probable that I was mistaken. We will have another look at my friend the higgler when we have had dinner."

Mrs. Morgan soon announced that Lucy's good things were on the table, and the two friends, both relieved in mind by the morning's revelations, enjoyed their meal as though there was not a care in store for either of them. Who that has lived out half his life would seek to raise the veil which shrouds the future; for though the present has its sorrows and its trials, there is hope to sweeten the bitterness of the cup.

The gentle breeze which had rippled the water in the morning had gathered strength as the day advanced, and brought up a thunder-storm, which soon drove the hay-makers from the field, and some of them sought shelter in the Drayton Arms. The rain continued after the thunder had ceased, and then from the tap-room came sounds of a jingling melody, which defied the knowledge of the two friends to determine by what instrument they were produced. Their curiosity became so excited that they resolved to seek out the minstrel in the tap-room, and found, on proceeding there, that it was the higgler's companion, and that the mysterious case which he had carried between his legs was a box strung with wires upon which he performed, by beating upon them with two sticks, and producing the jangle which they had heard. The minstrel was uncovered, and showed to his delighted auditors a round smiling face, in which were inserted a pair of bright piggy eyes, peeping about from beneath two shaggy brows, attached apparently to his straight coarse hair, which

had been cropped by some artist who was insensible to
the advantages of what a scientific operator would call
" pointing."

On the settle which occupied the now fireless ingle, sat the
higgler, smoking his pipe and carefully scrutinising the
assembled rustics. He only gave a momentary glance at
Gerard and Spraggatt when they entered the room, as though
he considered he had made a sufficient acknowledgment for
the civility of the morning.

"And what do you call that instrument?" said Jack,
when the player had ended his tune.

"Dulcimer!" answered the minstrel; "thirty years old;
belonged to my feather. He played it, too. Like a song,
gentlemen? I sings as well."

The proposal was accepted without a dissentient voice,
and the musician proceeded to administer a course of verses
which left the two friends in a state of mental prostration
from their endeavour to extract the meaning of the muddle
of sounds he uttered. As Gerard, with Jack's assistance,
contrived at a later period of the afternoon, when they had
secured the services of the minstrel to themselves, to take
down his utterances, we venture to transcribe them, regretting
that we cannot convey the tune, and the manner of the
minstrel as he gravely delivered himself of the following copy
of verses :—

1.

" I'll spread these green bushes although I am young,
So well do I like my love, so sweetly she sung—
Was there ever a mortal in so happy a state,
As I'd be with Floro, fair Floro so swate ?

2.

" I'll go to my Floro, and to her I'll say,
' We both will be marrièd, it wants but one day.'
' One day !' says the fair one, ' that day is to come ;
To be married so early, my age is too young.

3.

" ' I'll first go to sarvice, and when I return,
We both will be married in the next town.'
' Will first go to sarvice ? and leave me to cry ! '
' O yes, love ! fine shepherd ! I've toud you for why.'

4.

" As it happen'd, to sarvice, to sarvice she went,
To wait on a lady it was her intent ;
To wait on a lady, a lady so gay,
Who clothed fair Floro in constant array !

5.

" A twelvemonth, or better, a letter he sent,
He wrote a few lines to know her intent ;
She wrote ' that she lived so contented a life,
That she never, no, never ! 'ud be a poor shepherd's wife.'

6.

" These words by experience appear'd like a dart,
' I'll pluck up my speerit, and cheer up my heart !
In hoping she never might write so no more,
Her answer consumed me as ofttimes before.

7.

" ' My yows and my lambs too I'll bid them adieu !
My ship-crook and black-dog, I'll give them to you !
My bagpipe and budget, I leave you behind,
Since Floro, fair Floro, has chang'd her mind ! ' "

The rain having ceased at last, the higgler and his bard prepared to take their departure, and were on the point of doing so, when two of the county constabulary drove up, and somewhat peremptorily ordered the higgler's cart to be taken back into the yard.

" What's up now, gentlemen?" said the higgler; "you seem to know my business better than I do myself. I don't want to stay here now the rain is over."

The county constables were not accustomed to be addressed

so familiarly, especially when on duty, and by a person of the higgler's questionable character.

"Don't you make a noise," said one of them. "Just step this way, whilst we have a word of a sort with you."

"No objection in the world," said the higgler, "so that neither on you is a member of Parliament, and wants to talk by the yard. After you's manners—Oh! if you wish it, certainly," and the burly fellow swaggered into the little parlour where Jack and Gerard were seated.

"Ask your pardon, gentlemen," said the higgler, not allowing either of the officials to speak. "Ask your pardon for intruding, but I do so at the request of these intelligent gentlemen, who will now, perhaps, explain what is their little game in detaining me."

The young friends were both known to the county constables, who briefly apologised, and then explained the purport of their visit.

It seemed, according to their statement, that for some time past many burglaries had been committed in the county, and evidently by London thieves. It had been ascertained that wherever a robbery had been effected, the higgler and his companion had been seen immediately afterwards, as some said, and often before, as asserted by others. The magistrates had, therefore, issued a warrant for the two men, and they had been followed to the Drayton Arms, and intercepted as we have narrated.

"Very well, gentlemen," said the higgler, "you have got hold of some valuable information, and I wouldn't mind laying glasses round that some day you'll see a hole through a mill-stone. Now, just hear what I've got to say. You and your masters do this at their peril; I am an honest man, following an honest calling, and so is my musical friend in the hat. I am engaged in finding a particular breed of five-toed hens for a noble lord in London, and that takes me about to many places in and out of your county. However, duty is duty, and I know you must do as you're ordered. I make no resistance, nor does little Dulcimer. Only I wish to say this, that I'll bet you more glasses round that I'll meet you here, or at any house in Morden to-morrow evening, provided I have my hearing in the morning."

"Why, you impudent fellow," said Gerard, unable longer to keep silence. "Do you fancy I do not recognise you as the man who spoke to me, some four nights ago, in High Street?"

"Mr. Gerard Norwold has good ears," replied the man, making a bow, "and I never contradict a gentleman. Now, my men," addressing the constables, "we are with you—I've only one more thing to say; be careful, very careful of little Cobby's dulcimer, for at the price he sets upon it he'll ruin you in damages, if you injure a wire."

The officers and their captives soon drove off, Jack and Gerard watching them from the inn window, little dreaming then, how much the after life of both of them was to be influenced by the burly higgler.

CHAPTER VII.

In the morning Jack Spraggatt acquainted his sister Lucy
with all his troubles, and Gerard, who had arranged to assist
at the family council, was delighted when he arrived to find
them sitting in the summer-house, and talking cheerfully of
the future. "We both owe you a thousand thanks, Mr.
Gerard," said Lucy, "for compelling this naughty boy to
admit me into partnership in his tribulations. They are sad
ones, truly, but if I understand them rightly, as I think I
do, I see no cause for despair."

"No, no!" cried Jack. "Nor do I now."

"Jack has one sad fault, Mr. Gerard; he is deficient in
self-reliance. He will not look at the future as a field wherein
he may win victories, but strews it over with the dead hopes
of the past, and is ready to surrender to the first difficulty
that approaches. Is it not so?"

"Yes, I own it," answered Jack. "I do fear the future
when I see how many interests beside my own are in peril
from failure upon my part. Lucy, dear, you should have
been the man and I the woman of this family."

"If I had been, I would not have allowed my poor little
sister to have imagined all kinds of dreadful things, when
half an hour's quiet chat could have made her as happy as I
am now, you naughty boy." And she gave Jack's broad
cheek such a loving kiss, that Gerard almost wished that he
had been born a twin-brother of his yeoman friend.

"We have been reading over this terrible list of debts,"

said Lucy, referring to a sheet of foolscap paper which she held in her hand, "and I see nothing to fear so very much. Our creditors are chiefly friends who have helped Jack through many difficulties, and I am sure would not withdraw from him now. We must all be more careful of our means, and learn to speak that difficult word—No!—and so I doubt not in a few brief years to be emancipated from the slavery of debt."

"Spoken like a brave, true-hearted sister, Miss Lucy," said Gerard, "and Jack will be unworthy of you, if he ever shows the white feather again."

"White feather!" replied Jack. "I hardly think I have been a coward. I never feared for myself; it was for those I loved—for those who had trusted me. My dear Gerard, may you never have like cause for such endurance. You have no reason to fear it, as riches, honour, station, are all before you! May they bring you the peace they should do when rightly used."

"Ah! Jack, never was there a wiser proverb than 'It is not all gold that glitters.' There are sad hearts often enough at Norwold Hall," replied Gerard. "That is the reason you are plagued so frequently with my company. My father's temper gets more violent, and now that he has a personal call from the gout, there is little cause for any one to envy my lady mother-in-law. Our College bills arrived to-day, and such a storm was raging in the breakfast-room that I doubled back, and came on here to invoke your hospitality."

Lucy rose instantly, saying, "I am so glad you have named it;" and then, pausing, she placed her arm around her brother's neck, and looked into his face so lovingly, that Gerard thought there was nothing in Norwold Hall, either of art or luxury, that he would not have exchanged willingly for such deep sympathy as that look conveyed. "My dear old Jack," she said, "we two may soon be all that is left of our little household. Our father awaits us in the happy land, and our dear mother is hastening fast to join him. Our sister Letty has a home apart from us, and we shall regard her by-and-by as one whom we have loved, but may see no more. We then shall be alone. From this hour, then, promise me, in the presence of your dearest friend, that no sorrow, no anxiety shall come to you without giving me my sister's share. As I have partaken in the fruits of your labour and your care, I claim a right to have my portion of the ill. I cannot work with my hands, but I can with my heart, and a few words of honest love—perhaps of woman's wisdom—will make your burthens lighter. You promise to do what I now ask of you?"

Jack clasped her in his arms, and the big, stalwart man—we must chronicle truths as they arise—blubbered like "a great lubberly boy."

A brighter face, however, never shone through tears in the course of a few moments than Jack's; and the whole party, as happy as though all debts had been really paid, and had not to be worked for, hardly worked for, both with brain and hand, passed through the porch into Jack's parlour.

There was nothing uncommon in the components of Gerard's luncheon, yet never were viands so grateful to the taste, or nut-brown ale such incomparable tipple! It was the last pleasant meal Gerard was destined to have beneath that roof.

The last day's fishing which had passed so strangely was to be compensated for by another holiday in the ensuing week, and Lucy was to be caterer again. Why should not Lucy and her favourite gossips be of the party also? There were many pretty nooks by Drayton Waters, where they could dine and make merry, much better than in Mrs. Morgan's tobacco-smelling parlour. Why not ask some other pleasant friends? And Jack should take down his fiddle from the peg, where it had hung for twenty months or more, and recover his fingering, and be prepared to make music to which the rocks and trees might dance if they pleased, like their classical ancestors. What a merry day was in store for them!

Time, the old scene-shifter, obeys no human prompter's
whistle. The Fates have written out his scene-plot, and as
the changes are set down upon that scroll, so will they come
and go, and we, the actors, strut and fret our little lives
away. The curtain will soon rise upon our story, and show
a change indeed!

The saucy higgler had been as good as his word. When
taken before the magistrates—Sir John Norwold, despite his
gout and ill temper, being in the chair—the higgler bowed
respectfully to the Bench, and appeared to be a very different
man to the noisy blusterer of the preceding evening. The
county constables gave their evidence with the usual circum-
locution, and promised to bring forward witnesses to substan-
tiate their statements, if the prisoners were remanded for a
few days.

Gout and ill temper concentrated in the person of a justice
of the peace, are not usually favourable to the interests of a
prisoner, especially when appearances are against him, and
the higgler had taken some pains to place himself at a disadvantage, so far as his wardrobe was concerned; and Cobby,
the bard, though looking simplicity or stupidity itself, was not
sufficient to counterbalance the unfavourable impression created
by his friend, innocently employed, as he said, in searching
for five-toed hens.

"Well, man," said Sir John, "what have you to say for
yourself? This cock-and-bull story of yours is not credited by
the Bench. If you've nothing better to say for yourself, and
that other fellow who stands blinking like an owl, we shall
commit you on remand, as the constables require."

"Will your worship be kind enough to look at this letter,"
said the higgler, coolly.

"No written characters here, sir," replied Sir John. "We
know how such things are concocted, eh, gentlemen?"

"I hope you will not decline looking at that paper, Sir
John," said the higgler, very mildly. "It will save your
worships a great deal of trouble."

"Here! pass it to me—make haste, sir!" cried Sir John, to a slow-moving usher. "You officers ought to have been prepared with your witnesses, and not have given the Bench so much trouble."

The letter had reached Sir John's hands by the time he had done speaking, and he read it with evident surprise.

"Dear me, very odd! Gentlemen, we had better adjourn to our private room," said Sir John, rising, the gout giving him an ugly twinge at the moment, and producing an expletive not quite in accordance with the judicial character.

As the J. P.'s retired from the bench, the sensation in the small court-house was immense! The only unmoved persons were the prisoners at the bar, until the higgler whispered something in the ear of the minstrel, which set that stupid person into limited hysterics. The magistrates' bell rang, and the spectators in court buzzed. Now for the explanation! No—the two prisoners were ordered into the magistrates' room, and in a few minutes after, an officer came out to announce sulkily that business was over for the day.

In the afternoon, the mysterious higgler and his faithful minstrel were seen smoking their pipes in front of the inn in the market-place, when the three-o'clock coach from London drove up to change horses.

Mr. Gilbert Norwold had arrived by it, as well as a small parcel addressed to Mr. John Jones, and for which the higgler had made previous inquiry. He dropped it carelessly into the pocket of his shooting jacket, and continued smoking his pipe until the coach and its attendant porters, ostlers, and idlers had departed. The parcel contained a letter, which appeared to dictate to the higgler a course of immediate action, as he instantly walked rapidly to the court-house, and sought an interview with the town-clerk. We shall learn more of his business presently.

Gilbert Norwold's reception by his father was anything but affectionate or satisfactory. His College bills were large— very large—and contrasted unfavourably with the more moderate expenditure of his brother Gerard; and as this condition of things made Sir John's reproaches more acute, Gilbert felt the anger he had nourished in his heart for many weeks past against Gerard turn almost into hatred. Humiliated and wrathful, he sought his own room; and recalling all he had lately suffered by the inspiration of Gerard, the moral poison worked within him until it destroyed at once, and for ever, all brotherly union between them.

As Gilbert's return had been unexpected, Gerard had gone with Spraggatt to a neighbouring market, and was, consequently, not at the Hall to receive him. Gilbert was glad of this; the more so, as he had resolved, when he could see his mother alone, to make to her the terrible disclosure of his turpitude. Lady Norwold, however, had been so distressed by her husband's violence in the morning, that she had retired to her own room, and given emphatic orders that she was not to be disturbed by any one that day. Poor lady!

Gilbert bore with this patiently, for he dreaded the ordeal, and gladly accepted the compulsory respite until the morrow. He was not destined to be the arbiter of his own fate.

The Miller Ray had just sat down to tea in his little parlour when the two county constables, who had been so at fault in the morning, entered the room without ceremony, looking like men who were sure of their game this cast. The miller started, naturally enough, at the advent of the two officers, who, without waiting to be questioned, declared him to be their prisoner.

"Prisoner! Your prisoner!" said Ray, with a loud laugh. "Why, you are mad!"

No, they were dull fellows enough, but they were not mad. They had their wits—such as they were—about them; for one placed his back against the door, and the other took his stand at the open window looking into the miller's garden.

"We've a warrant to take you into custody, Mr. Ray, for the charge of being directly and indirectly concerned in several burglaries in this county and in London. The warrant's signed by a Bow Street magistrate, and I produce my authority," said one of the officers.

Ray glanced at the strip of paper, and did not laugh again, but attempted to pour out a cup of tea. His hand shook so violently that he abandoned the attempt.

"We are sorry our duty obliges us to trouble you with these," said the officer who had spoken, producing a pair of handcuffs; "but we've no choice in the matter, and must do our duty."

The miller's powerful frame shook from head to heel as the glittering manacles were extended towards him.

"Stay, my good friends. I will not attempt an escape; but you have taken me so by surprise—made such an unfounded charge against me—that I am quite unmanned. I'll take a glass of brandy, and——"

"No," said the officer, interposing, "how do we know it is brandy you are going to take. I hope you won't be rusty, but let me put on the handcuffs like a man."

"You are right to be careful. I know it is your duty, and submit. You will not object to send one of my men with a note to Mr. Jellifer in the market-place?" said Ray.

The officer did not object, and Ray wrote a few lines requesting Jasper's instant attendance. The man was called, he who had witnessed so unwillingly the signing of the papers a short time ago, and dispatched with the letter. Ray then sullenly submitted his wrists to the fetters, and the three men sat in silence until Jasper came in.

"What is the meaning of this?" said Jellifer. "What has happened?"

"I am in custody," replied Ray, deliberately measuring his words as he spoke. "I am in custody on the charge of being concerned, directly or indirectly, in certain burglaries committed in this county and in London. That is the charge, I believe, is it not?"

"Yes, sir; them's the words of our warrant," replied the officer appealed to.

"As the warrant is signed by a Bow Street magistrate, I shall be taken, I conclude, to London to-night."

Jasper sank into a chair, and appeared to be overpowered by the perilous situation of his friend.

"I don't want a woman's nonsense, now," said Ray. "I want a man to act for me. You must follow me to-morrow, if you cannot come with me to-night. You understand, and I shall expect you. You will take possession of the mill, and see that some one is put in charge whom you can thoroughly trust."

"Oh, we shall take care of your property, Mr. Ray, depend upon that," said one of the officers, with a smile.

Ray smiled also as he replied: "You are clever, careful fellows, I don't doubt; but as I am certain to be acquitted of this charge, I would rather make my own arrangements."

Jasper promised to do all that was required of him, and when he shook hands with Ray, as the officers were taking him away, he found left in his own a piece of paper, which he carefully concealed until the final departure of the prisoner and his escort.

On opening the crumpled slip he read thus: "Secure all the papers in the H. C." Having read the line twice over, Jasper tore the paper into very small pieces, and then scattered them to the winds. If he understood the meaning of what he had read, he was too prudent or too good a man to aid a suspected felon in defeating the course of justice, and it was well for him that he acted as he did, for standing near the window, and looking into the room, was Mr. Higgler, in a very different costume to that he was pleased to wear in the morning, as was Cobby, the minstrel, also. They now had blue coats, with metal buttons, and very bright red waistcoats, which they were entitled to wear as Bow Street runners. Cobby could not change his stupid face, but he had removed the straight-haired wig and bushy eyebrows, and displayed his own short crop of bright red stubble, and no eyebrows at all.

" Well, Mr. Jellifer," said Higgler, that being his proper
name, and in no way connected with his ornithological
calling, " my friend Mr. Cobby and I have come to relieve
you from your responsibilities, and take possession of the
mill for a short time."

" Very glad to hear it," said Jasper; " but I suppose I had
better send some one here for the present."

" Well, perhaps, you had," replied Higgler. " Cobby,
call the other constable."

Mr. Cobby proved his possession of other musical qualifications than those with which we are already acquainted, and
by putting his two fingers into his mouth, and distending his
rubicund cheeks, he produced a whistle with variations that
might have been heard, and possibly was, in the market-
place of Morden. A feeble squeal responded, followed by
the appearance of another rural thief-taker, and who had
more the appearance of a gamekeeper than of any other
profession.

" Now, Master Johnny," said Higgler, addressing the new
comer, who stared at the name presented to him, " Now,
Master Johnny, help my friend Mr. Cobby and myself to
remove this iron chest."

There was not much difficulty in effecting this operation,
and when it was done a small trap-door was discernible on
the spot the chest had occupied.

" Locked, I fancy, Cobby?"

" Yes," was the reply, " but you have the plan in your
pocket."

Higgler drew forth a piece of paper, on which were traced
certain lines and references, and having consulted it, he went
directly to the portrait, or Hassarac's Cave, and pressing
the secret spring, obtained an insight into that ingenious
receptacle.

Producing from it two keys tied together, he soon unlocked the trap-door, and discovered a Hassarac's Cave indeed;
for there lay, in admired confusion, much plate and many

jewels. Amongst the former, the communion plate of Morden Church, battered and defaced, was conspicuous. Higgler expressed no surprise, nor did Cobby, neither did Jasper, strange to say; but possibly he was prepared to learn the worst of Ray, having once had his suspicions aroused. A careful inventory was made of the various articles discovered, and then the iron chest was opened. It contained only Ray's account books, but one of them was kept in cipher. This Higgler secured, but upon Jasper objecting to its removal, on the plea that it might be wanted in the business, Higgler returned it to the chest with a knowing smile at Mr. Jellifer.

"Let us see what more is inside this respectable old party," said Higgler, standing on a chair and looking behind the portrait; "some more keys, a cigar box—extravagant rascal —a bundle of papers, and a cash box. I wonder what that contains? Nothing valuable, I expect, as it is unlocked." Mr. Higgler glanced carelessly over the contents of the box until he came to two pieces of paper enclosed in the cover of a letter. He read them very attentively, and then placed them in his waistcoat pocket. It was surprising how unconcerned Jasper had been throughout this discovery of his friend's delinquencies, but there was a look of wonder in his face when Higgler pocketed the papers.

"Now, Master Johnny, ask for a sack, and you shall take these precious matters to the court-house in the cart you brought with you." The constable obeyed.

"You'll have to stay here, Mr. Cobby, for a time, I fancy; but no doubt Mr. Jellifer will see the miller's maid—of course there is one?—and take care that you are made very comfortable. Eh, Mr. Jellifer?"

Jasper undertook to give instructions to have Mr. Cobby duly installed as master of the situation, although the miller's arrest had thrown his terrified household into considerable confusion.

The cart having received its precious freight, in addition to the portly persons of Mr. Higgler and the county constable,

G

was about to be driven off, when Mr. Higgler beckoned
Jasper to him, and said in a whisper, "Meet me at Norwold
Hall to-night, at nine."

"At the Hall!" said Jasper, turning very pale at so simple
a request.

"Yes, at nine o'clock, not a minute later, if you please,
Mr. Jellifer," answered Mr. Higgler, like a man not to be
questioned, and then gave the word to proceed.

Mr. Ray's case was very soon disposed of by Sir John and
his fellow magistrates, who had been specially summoned;
and the miller, escorted by another Bow Street runner, who
had come down in the morning specially to take charge of
him, left Morden for ever by the afternoon's coach.

Sir John had arranged to take an early dinner with one of
his brother magistrates, and though suffering slightly from
gout, remained until nearly nine o'clock, not having been
able to resist the temptation of some excellent old port selected
by the late Bishop of the Diocese. He rode home unattended,
and had nearly reached the house end of the avenue when he
was surprised by Mr. Higgler stepping from the shadow of a
tree and politely requesting permission to speak a few words
with him in private.

"Why not have told me your business this afternoon, Mr.
Higgler—I have had enough of justice for one day. Won't
to-morrow do?"

"No, Sir John, as I must return to London by the earliest
coach I can get, and my communication concerns you and
your family so nearly, that I am sure you'll excuse me making
so bold as to ask you to listen to me now."

"What, out here in this night air. No, —— if I do."

"As you please, Sir John, only it must be where we-are
alone," replied Higgler.

"What's in the wind new?" cried Sir John. "Come
along after me, Higgler—We'll stop at the keeper's cottage."

The cottage was close at hand, and the keeper out on his
evening round, so the wife was sent on to the Hall with

the quiet old cob, and Sir John and the officer were left
alone.

"Now then, Higgler, make haste and tell me your
business. My gout promises to be troublesome to-night, and
I want to get to bed early. What is it?"

Higgler had opened the door leading into the back kitchen,
to satisfy himself that there were no listeners,—an act of professional caution,—and then standing by the table, at which
Sir John was seated, he said:—

"When searching the hiding places in the house of the
man Ray, this afternoon, I lighted in one of them, on two bits
of writing, which as they have nothing to do with the
charges under investigation, I took the liberty of putting into
my pocket."

"Well, what are they about? Let me see them," said Sir
John, testily, as his foot was getting rather painful.

"One moment, if you please, sir; I fancy they will
surprise you even more than they did me, and I wish you to
consider them as coolly as you can," observed Higgler.

"I'm always cool, sir! Always when business is before
me. Give me the papers."

Higgler presented one of them, but as the light was
failing, the Baronet requested him to read it, as he already
knew its contents, and Higgler did so. It was Gerard's
engagement to repay any money advanced to his brother,
and was worded as follows:—

"I undertake to repay you any sum you may advance,
provided the money is forthcoming immediately.

                                "GERARD NORWOLD."

The date was within a month of the time of this conversation.

"What's that?" cried Sir John, springing up and snatching the paper from Higgler's hand. He hurried with it to
the window. When he had read it, he exclaimed, "The

                                                    G 2

young scoundrel, I remember about that time he applied to me for 50*l.*, and I refused him. And then he had recourse to a common thief,"—but our page must not be sullied by the fearful words that came from the lips of the infuriated man. It was some time before he could speak calmly, at last he said: "Well, Higgler, that money must be paid, thief though the fellow be who lent it. You must see to that for me. Well, now for the other paper! What's that about?"

"I really fear to give it to you, Sir John, seeing how you are affected by your son's indiscretion."

"Indiscretion, why—but never mind, I have had my burst out, and I won't give way again," said Sir John, holding out his hand for the paper. He paused, however, and then asked Higgler to read it to him.

It was a sad record.

"'I hereby acknowledge to hold as security for the sum of two hundred and fifty pounds, advanced by me to Mr. Norwold,'" Higgler paused.

"Go, on! sir, go, on! There can't be anything worse than that."

"Don't be so sure, sir," said Higgler, who then continued to read. "'A miniature portrait of Sir John Norwold, set with diamonds. The same to be returned, when the said sum of 250*l.* is repaid to me.

"RAYMOND RAY."

The date a day after the other.

Sir John did not move when Higgler ceased reading, neither did he say one word until a little stream of blood trickled from one of his nostrils. The relief thus afforded soon restored him to himself again, and he spoke much more quietly than he had done before during the interview.

"My good fellow, you have rendered me a great service in bringing these papers to me. I don't understand them at present, but I will before I sleep. My honour, the honour of all my family, dead and living, is concerned in this matter, perhaps. You shall not go unrewarded for your consideration. You see I am not quite myself just now. I shall be in the morning. Don't you leave Morden without seeing me again, and I will hold you harmless with your superiors. Good night, Mr. Higgler."

As he said this, he folded the papers carefully one within the other, and placed them in his pocket, and, having repeated his valediction two or three times, strode at a rapid pace to the Hall, as though the gout had never been known to him. As the hall door was unfastened until the family retired to rest, Sir John entered freely, and passed at once to the drawing-room, in which were seated Lady Norwold and Gilbert, she having left her room on hearing of her son's arrival. They both were reading. When she looked up, hearing the door open, she was alarmed and terrified at her husband's appearance, as the blood had stained the large frill of his shirt, and his face was deadly pale.

"O my dear Sir John, what has happened? Are you hurt?"

"Yes," he replied; "but not as you suppose. Come with me; I want you!"

Gilbert sat panic-stricken as his mother left the room. No other word had been spoken than those we have recorded; but he knew—he felt certain that his guilty secret had been discovered, and he was lost! utterly lost! He could not have moved! he could not have spoken one word, even to have saved himself from ruin, for his limbs were powerless, and his tongue dried up within his mouth. No chance of escape! None. All the evil he had done and thought, to hide this miserable theft, had been wickedness in vain.

Unless—he went on? Ah! there was another pact to be made with the fiend that had so tempted him! Would he listen to it?

When Sir John had reached the drawing-room containing Lady Norwold's cabinet, he paused, and looking his wife in the face, said slowly: "Emily, on your honour as a wife—as a noble lady, answer me truly. Have you ever—for any purpose—at any time—lent valuables to *my* son, or to *our* son?"

"My dear husband, never!" replied the wife.

"Then open that cabinet."

It was done.

"Take out your jewels. No; not those. Ah! that case."

As she removed the object to which he had pointed, he took it from her saying, "What should this contain?"

"Your miniature; the one you gave me on your birthday the first year of our marriage."

He opened it, and showed her that it was empty.

Lady Norwold gave a shrill scream—it reached Gilbert sitting in the drawing-room—and then she swooned in her husband's arms.

Her cry brought some of the servants to her assistance, and when she recovered, and before Sir John could say more, she proclaimed her loss, but not knowing whom to accuse. When she became calmer, Sir John conducted her to the drawing-room just as Gerard had returned from his pleasant holiday with Jack Spraggatt.

"You have returned in good time, sir," said Sir John to Gerard, before he could greet his brother. "Stand where you are until I have done with you. You know a man, a dishonest thief, named Raymond Ray."

"No, sir, I do not!"

"You are a liar, sir! a liar to your father. Is not that your writing?"—and Sir John showed him one of the papers.

"Yes, Sir John, I own that to be my writing; but——" Gerard paused, it was his brother's secret, not his, that was asked of him.

"This morning that paper was in Ray's possession, and yet you dare lie to me, and say the man was unknown to you."

"I do not lie, Sir John, nor shall you say so uncontradicted," replied Gerard, his blood rising at the accusation. "I own the paper to be my writing—the obligation to be mine, and for no unworthy purpose."

"There was more money had from that man—a much larger sum."

"Yes, there was a larger sum required and obtained." It was Gilbert's secret still that was demanded from him.

"On what security?"

Gerard raised his shoulders merely in reply.

"Again, I demand to know on what security? If you do not at once reply, and reply truly, though you are my son—my heir," (no! the oath must not be recorded), "I will turn you out into the world a beggar."

Gerard knew his father's violent temper, and guarded his reply.

"I cannot tell you the security that was given."

"You dare not, you degenerate cub. You dare not confess that you have so far forgotten your father's name, your dead ancestors, your own honour, as to own that you have stooped to be a thief, and the companion of thieves."

"This is past endurance, Sir John Norwold. You forget that you are my father, and compel me to lose a son's reverence. I tell you that you speak words you would not dare utter to any other man living that claims to be a gentleman."

"A gentleman! You have lost the title to be called even an honest man. Read that paper, if the words do not blind you—there is evidence of your shameful theft!"

Gerard took the paper, and as he read it, a faintness overcame him, for he divined the truth! Whilst he stood thus overpowered, Sir John, whose rage had risen to its height, turned to Gilbert, who almost crouched at his mother's side, and said with violent action and terrible words: "You know of this? You must have known of this! and you were silent? Speak, fellow!"

"He is my brother, sir.   He is my brother!"

Those words which the Evil One spoke by the mouth of Gilbert sealed Gerard's fate.

With fearful oaths the maddened father drove his generous son forth from his home that night never never again to stand beneath its roof.   The father's curses clung about the walls long after they were uttered, and not even the purifying fire could destroy the memory of them!

CHAPTER VIII.

THE moon in the heavens was as bright as Gerard's young life had been an hour before, but at intervals it was obscured by clouds, black and impenetrable as the change which had come upon him. He remembered walking from the lighted drawing-room through the crowd of domestics assembled round the opened doors, and passing down the stairs and through the hall, out unto the park. He remembered passing down the old avenue, dark as a great vault, and seeing the glittering of the lights in the town of Morden, hearing all the while the loud voice of his excited father repeating the awful words which cursed him and sent him forth a wanderer. His walk through Norwold Park, from the Hall to the little bridge which crossed the mill-stream, never left his memory— never. He believed that he must have crossed the river without going through the market-place, but why he did so he could not conceive, as he remembered nothing more than this—that when he had crossed the mill-stream he entered the church porch—his dead mother was at rest within the church —and there he vowed never again to set foot in Norwold Hall! Never to see his father's face again! That when the night should have passed, he would be "as one that was dead." And once he tried to pray to be forgiven his trespasses, as he should forgive them who had trespassed against him; but he felt the words he uttered were only words. His thoughts were all entangled one with another! The bright drawing-room, the dark avenue, the passionate father, the

listening servants passed and repassed before his eyes, whilst
the awful words which cursed him, and made him an outcast,
were roaring in his ears.

Jack Spraggatt had put on his slippers preparatory to going
to bed, and Lucy had risen also, when they heard a violent
thud at the front door, as though some heavy body had fallen
against it, and then followed a rapid knocking. Jack had
the heart of a lion, so he hastened to answer the summons;
and Lucy, who was as brave as a loving woman always is,
followed, carrying a light. Jack asked who knocked?

" Gerard Norwold."

Absurd, that was not Gerard's voice, those hollow, husky
sounds. The door was opened at once, and there, with
haggard face, great staring eyes, red as fire, and disordered
hair,—no hat had been cared for—stood the dearest friend of
the household, Gerard Norwold.

Before either Jack or Lucy could speak a word, he stalked
into the parlour, and sat himself down in the chair which
death had made vacant, looking not unlike the phantom of
himself. Jack's bold heart beat so fast, that he could not
question his friend; whilst Lucy, with ready coolness, mixed
some brandy with water, and then held the glass to Gerard's
lips, who drank the draught readily. It revived him, and he
seemed to recognise the place—the friends—and then covering his face with both his hands, he gently sank down on his
knees, and crouched, as it were, upon the ground.

Lucy and Jack knelt down on either side of him, and implored him to speak. Speak! when great sobs were bursting
from his heaving breast, and hot tears flowing from his
burning eyes.

He suffered himself to be raised up after a time, and when
he was calm enough to articulate words—the words were
nothing, but his passionate utterance kept the listeners silent
—he said:

" My friends—my only friends now in the world, I have
come to you in the excess of my misery—I know not why—I

know not for what—but I have come here without reasoning —by the mere instinct of our long friendship, Jack—and of yours, Lucy Spraggatt—knowing I should find some human thing that would not look at me like a fiend, curse me like a fiend, and drive me out into the world as though I were the wickedest creature living."

He paused, but before either of his auditors could speak, he went on as though unwilling to be interrupted, until he had "unpacked his heart."

"To-night—to-night my father—before his wife, before his servants, has called me a thief, and with horrible, most horrible curses, turned me out of his house. Do either of you believe me a thief?"

He started up, and looked at his two listeners.

"I see you do not. If I had seen the shadow of doubt in your face, Lucy, or in yours, Jack, I should have gone mad! —stark mad!"

Again the sobs and tears!

"Gerard Norwold a ——. No! I will not repeat the word," cried Jack. "Nor can I guess why such an epithet could be applied to you—and by your father?"

"Yes, by my father! my own father! No inquiry! No consideration of circumstances! But a conclusion formed in passion, in madness! and he has dared to stigmatise me—his heir—his own flesh and blood, as a thief! a mean, dishonourable thief! And those who listened believed it; for not one of my kindred, not one of the servants, who had known me from my cradle, dared to deny the possibility of such a name being deserved by me."

He walked rapidly up and down the room, and no one spoke for some time.

"I confess, Gerard," said Jack, "that I am at a loss to understand what has happened. If it will not distress you, tell me; or perhaps you would rather go to rest, and in the morning——"

"In the morning, Jack, I hope to be many miles away

from here. Don't interrupt me, if you please. I wish, when I can master myself, to tell you what has occurred."

" Perhaps, Mr. Gerard, I had better leave the room," said Lucy.

" No, Lucy—no—I wish you to hear from my own lips a story that will be repeated, I doubt not, often enough when I am gone. I could not endure to think that you should ever have occasion to blush that you have owned me for a friend."

He then as calmly as though nothing particular had occurred, revealed the events of the evening, from the time he had parted from Jack, dwelling upon the minutest details, naming the people he had seen, the objects which had attracted his notice, as though he were anxious to delay reaching that point in his narrative when his father made the cruel accusation against him.

" From that time," he said, " I remember nothing distinctly, except my father's awful curses, and his damnable accusation. If anything else was said, I heard it not—I saw nothing but that incensed and cruel man, until I turned away to quit his house, and then I met the glaring faces of the servants ! I know that they stood on either side to let me pass through them—that the hall-door was open to hasten my departure. That the avenue looked like a monstrous vault, which the glittering lights beyond made darker and more dismal. I turned to look back once upon the old Hall. It was discernible only by the lights seen through the windows. A momentary burst of moonlight fell upon it, and then the dark thick clouds hid it again. I stood in the church-porch, as it were, by my mother's grave, and vowed to renounce home, name, and kindred for ever ; and I will keep my oath. How I came here I know not. I know that you two were every now and then in my mind, and so I wandered on, I suppose. You have heard my story—Lucy—Jack—and when it is told by others, I know you will deny—as I do now from the depths of my heart—that I ever did knowingly,

a dishonourable act in my short life. Now, good-bye, my
dear old friends. Give me some covering for my head, and I
will be off again."

" Not to-night, Mr. Gerard."

" Yes, Lucy, to-night. In the pauses of our conversation
I have resolved upon the course I mean to take. If that
proud, passionate old man has one spark of a father's love in
his heart, I will blow it into a flame which shall torment him
to repentance."

" Surely," said Jack, " you will make an effort to disprove
the charge made against you."

" I might have done so had I had a father to deal with,
and not a madman. To free myself, I must condemn others
to the same fate as that my father has decreed to me. The
vow I made to-night—rash, wicked, as it may be—I will
keep. My dear friends, good-bye. I am obeying my father,
my wicked unjust father, and parting from you is not the
least of the miseries to which he has condemned me."

" Oh, Mr. Gerard," cried Lucy, clasping his hand in hers.
" Do not! do not go away to-night with such a troubled
spirit as now possesses you. Stay here until the morning ;—
stay here until you have prayed to God to guide you aright,
and go not away with only your great wrong and your bitter
grief to direct you. You have always been good, noble and
generous, and be sure that your father will remember this to-
morrow, and know that he has been deceived, and you will
be dearer to him than you have ever been, and he to you."

"Lucy, he has cursed with the words of a fiend—he has
believed me capable of dishonour. Neither love, nor the
recollection of what my past life has been, weighed as one
feather in my favour. He has driven me forth, and the
punishment shall be shared between us! I can endure, and
I will revenge my wrongs."

" It is right to endure, it is wrong to revenge," said Lucy,
as though a reproving angel spoke. " Do not, Mr. Gerard,
leave us to-night. Stay here for a few days, at least, until

you have recovered from the first shock of this unaccountable injury. You cannot find more truthful, loving friends than you have here, and you have seen in our own case so recently that it is not good to bear our grief alone. Think me your sister, Mr. Gerard, and believe what I would do to comfort you in this distress. The neglected scratch, so slight in itself, grows dangerous and painful; the ghastly wound, deep almost to death, is rendered often an aid to future health when carefully tended, even by unskilful hands. Let us be your surgeons, Mr. Gerard. Do not leave us with this great wound in your heart, which may become so dangerous as to destroy your peace of mind for ever."

"You will stay, Gerard, I am sure you will," said Jack, trying to take his friend's hand; but he drew it away, closing his fingers firmly together.

"I dare not stay near that accursed house yonder, remembering what has been said, and knowing who are within its walls. Chance might make me a parricide. No, I will fly beyond that danger. I dare not pray, or I would say, God bless you both."

"Stop one moment, Gerard!" He was moving towards the door. "Since you are determined to go, you must not go alone; I shall go with you. Lucy, my boots, dear." His sister was not surprised at Jack's resolution. She knew that he would not desert his friend in the strait in which he was, and left the room, returning in a few moments, bringing a fur travelling cap belonging to herself, as all her brother's head-gear was much too large for Gerard.

"What is this?" he said. "I remember! your travelling cap, Lucy. Thanks; I am glad to carry something of you with me. It will help to keep down evil thoughts, perhaps, and to remind me that one spot on earth contains two friends true as steel." As though it were a thing of course, he took her head between his hands, and kissed her forehead. "I will go into the porch whilst you get ready, good, true, honest, old Jack," and then he left the room.

Jack soon pulled on his boots, and stowed away the flask which Lucy had filled, and hastened to join Gerard; but when he looked into the porch no one was there. He called "Gerard! Gerard!" but no answer came. Jack hastened to the road, but the night was too dark, and the light wind rustled in the trees, so that he could neither see nor hear anything of the runaway. With a heavy heart, Jack returned into the house, and then he and Lucy sat long into the early morning talking of poor Gerard and his changed fortunes, and sowing seeds that bore abundant fruit hereafter.

It was eight o'clock when the tidiest of old ladies was surprised at her breakfast by the appearance of Gerard Norwold. Her little handmaiden was surprised also to hear her mistress cry with delight, and hug that road-stained, haggard-looking man to her capacious bosom. He had often lain there when a helpless babe, and drawn from its living fountains the life he now valued no longer. Yes, Mrs. Bland had been Gerard's nurse, as after he was born his mother was long an invalid, and Gerard owed much of his iron constitution to the then buxom widow Bland, whose only child had died the same day as her young husband. Baby Gerard therefore succeeded to all the poor widow's love, and as her mother's fancy saw in the heir of Norwold's face the lineaments of her own dead child, he became to her a son indeed, making her love almost idolatry. Gerard never passed a vacation without visiting Nurse Bland frequently, though she lived some ten miles from the town of Morden. No wonder, then, that he brought his bruised heart to her for cure.

It was strange, he thought, that she had not been the earliest remembered when the blow came,—even before Jack and Lucy,—and so thought she when he had told her the story of the past day and night.

"My darling boy, my dear darling boy," said the old nurse—all the motherly feelings of other days returning, "I never thought this hour would come, although your beloved mother often foreboded some such evil times. Sir John was always a vile tempered man; brutal ever, when his angry fits were on him; and they were so frequent that they wore away your mother's life long before her time. When she felt that she was dying, she said to me—oh! so calmly—so sweetly. 'Nurse, I shall soon leave you, and my dear child will have no mother then but you. Care for him as you have done; and for his sake, and for my sake, bear with my husband's fearful temper, and do not be driven from our darling boy. You promise me this?' I did, of course; and kept it through many and many a day of sore trial, Gerard. Your mother went on to say: 'Nearly all my small fortune I have given at various times to help my husband in the payment of his debts. There is, however, enough in this pocket-book to keep you from want, and find you a humble home. Earn it, dear Nurse, by what you will have to bear for the love of my darling—for the love of his dying mother.'

"I did bear what few could have borne; but you had been sent to me by Heaven when my own sweet babe and his honest loving father had been taken from me: and I loved you dearer than my life. Thank God that you have come here in your trouble. It is your mother's home that shelters you. It is your mother's bounty that I now ask you to share."

Poor Gerard! The voice of the old nurse retained the same music as had soothed his earliest sorrows, and he did not resist when she laid his head upon her bosom. He soon recovered his composure, and then having eaten and drunk, though sparingly, he retired to her bedroom—the nursery he called it, with the first smile his face had worn for many hours, and obtained the repose he so much needed.

He slept soundly through the night, and when he awoke he found Nurse Bland sitting by the side of his bed, as he had done hundreds of times before, when he was hardly more helpless than at present. He was feverish and prostrate, but his old nurse was skilful in the healing arts required for his restoration, and by the end of the third day, he had talked over and over again the cruel past, but without finding any relief for the agony it occasioned him.

It was late in the evening when he bade his kind old nurse farewell, and though her tears fell fast, yet there was no hopeless sorrow in her honest face, and so with her we bid adieu to Gerard Norwold.

The river which flowed past Morden, a sluggish stream, widened on its passage to the sea, and receiving two important tributaries a few miles below the town, became a rapid river. On the banks, near the confluence of the lower stream, a coat and waistcoat were found on the morning following, and on the lining of both was written " Gerard Norwold." Such a fact proved nothing, whatever surmise it occasioned, and when Sir John was told of the discovery, he laughed scornfully, and denounced it as, "A trick—a very stale trick, which could deceive no one but a fool."

The time was approaching when he would have given all his wealth to have known the truth.

Jack Spraggatt was not so easily satisfied. As soon as the story reached him, he set off at once, and for three days continued his inquiries and search, on both sides of the river, and it was not until the third day that he bethought him of Mrs. Bland, and that possibly her foster-son might have gone to her in the hour of his greatest need. Jack met with a cordial welcome from the old nurse, by whom he was well known and esteemed, and after an hour's serious talk with her, he sought for Gerard Norwold no more, and ever after studiously avoided speaking of his friend's disappearance, although for some time both he and Lucy wore a slight mourning in memory of their friend.

We must return to the Hall, soon to be deserted for other scenes and unexpected changes. Sir John's rage had not exhausted itself on the hapless Gerard, and when he left his ancestors' house at his father's bidding, it raged for a time against the guilty and terrified Gilbert. With the same vehemence as he had used in discarding one son, did he threaten to visit with a similar consequence any further disobedience on the part of the other, and almost included his trembling wife in this denunciation. A momentary compunction which Gilbert had felt at his brother's undeserved fate, and which might have impelled him to have confessed the truth had a gentler course been pursued, died away under his father's continued violence, and when he left the room, almost fainting with terror, he went forth like another Cain, fearing that his brother's wrong would cry out from the very walls. He walked into the garden, and the cool night air revived him slightly. It was well for him, he thought, that Ray had been taken to London before the discovery had been made, which was now only known to his father and the family. Yes, there was Jasper Jellifer! He might lead suspicion towards him, if he thought it would serve his ends. No, his mother was engaged to interest herself with Sir John, and Jasper would not make her his enemy by uttering any conjecture that would injure her son. So he strove to lull his guilty conscience into a little peace.

Higgler had brought Jasper to the Hall to prove Ray's writing on the memorandum relating to the bracelet, which, strange to say, could not be found or traced anywhere.

Jasper's testimony was not required, as he was, of course, entirely ignorant of Ray's proceedings. He had believed him a clever, pushing fellow, and as such they had had dealings together; but of his nefarious pursuits Jasper had never entertained a suspicion, and he feared that he should be a loser by the confidence he had reposed in him.

Mr. Higgler smiled as Mr. Jellifer made this statement.

Jasper was evidently a true friend either to Ray or to himself, for he had sacrificed the comfort of his home to secure the property at the mill, and had placed Mrs. Jellifer in possession. This lady gave little Cobby infinite trouble, as she was as restless as a ghost, and glided about from one place to another, so, that the wary Bow Street runner, from professional habit, felt compelled to follow her, and neglect his beloved dulcimer, which was at once his solace and delight. There was no doubt Mrs. Jellifer had a reason for this inquisitiveness. Sir John had offered £100 for the recovery of the bracelet, and, as this liberal reward was, she thought, a secret between herself and Jasper, she set earnestly to work to deserve it; but the cleverest of us are but fools, and whilst Mrs. Jellifer was searching the mill diligently, Cobby was on the watch continuously, knowing her purpose, and would have pounced upon her and the treasure trove, and claimed half the reward. Mr. Higgler took a more direct course to discover the missing jewels.

Ray had been brought up several times before the Bow Street magistrates, and numerous charges of receiving stolen goods, both in London and the provinces, having been proved against him, he was committed to Newgate for trial. Newgate prison was a terrible contrast to the pretty home which Ray had just quitted. It would have been terrible even now-a-days when so much has been done to mitigate the olden cruelties, when the prisoners within its gloomy walls were packed away like slaves in the hold of a slave ship, and lived like human devils, in the midst of profanity and drunken riot. The untried and the condemned were herded together, at the mercy of venal warders, who made a profit of their vices when they had money, or left them almost to starve if they had not the means to bribe their gaolers, or procure the necessaries of life. The grim, smoke-blackened walls of the great London prison, were a sad exchange for the neatly-clipped hedges of the miller's garden, and the brutal songs of the half-drunken prisoners, for the twittering and melodious notes of the happy birds, and the fierce besotted faces which met him at every turn, for the pleasant flowers then blossoming in all their beauty. The murky cell and hard pallet, haunted by the memories of hundreds of criminals, some of whom had hung upon Tyburn tree, or had suffered out the remnants of their evil lives in Van

Diemen's Land, or the worse *Inferno* of Norfolk Island.
Murderers, forgers, burglars, highwaymen, and even such as
he, Raymond Ray, the tempter to crimes, he had not the
courage to commit, had preceded him as occupants of the
narrow dungeon wherein he must abide until he also should
go forth to endure for years and years the bitter lot of a
transported convict. He could not sleep at first with such
horrible thoughts always at work in his once clever-scheming
brain, but exhausted nature yielded at last, and the gaol-
bird ceased to flutter in his gloomy cage.

Jasper came to see him as often as the prison rules
allowed him to do so, but then they spoke to each other
with iron gratings between them, and the visitor left no
hope behind when he departed. Jasper never spoke of the
diamond bracelet, prudent man that he was, fearing to
invoke suspicion of complicity in Ray's criminality in the
mind of any chance listener. Not so, Mr. Higgler, who had
requested an interview with the prisoner the day after his
committal to Newgate.

"Good day, Mr. Ray," said the officer, "I suppose you
bear no ill-will to a man who has only done his duty, and
will not object to a few minutes' conversation with me?"

"None in the least," replied Ray; "I have not too
much pleasant society in this infernal place. What have
you to say, sir?"

"I suppose, Mr. Ray, that you have calculated the
chances of the game you have been playing so many years,
and are not afraid to pay your losings manfully. You have
had a long run of luck, but I fancy you see that you are
beat at last."

"I don't know that," answered Ray. "A jury may
think me as innocent as I am."

"No doubt of it," replied Higgler, knowingly; "and if
they do, your position will be a bad one. It is no use
fencing the question with me, Mr. Ray. I could not, if I
wished, make your case worse than it is, and you know it.

I have not come to try to do so, but to see if I cannot square a certain matter between us, and make things easier for you."

Ray's heart beat quickly, for he thought there was a hope of escape in the officer's words.

"I don't understand you at present," he said. "You must speak more plainly, if you please."

"I will. When I was searching the mill, I found two pieces of paper behind the portrait in the corner of the parlour. They had reference to certain money transactions between you and young Norwold. They had nothing to do with my charge against you, and so I have not produced them at present." Higgler paused, and then said abruptly, "What have you done with the diamond bracelet you had in pawn?"

Ray was too cool a rogue to be caught so easily.

"That is my affair, Mr. Higgler," he replied. "Why do you want to know, and what am I to gain by telling you?"

"I want to know," said Higgler, "because Sir John wishes it back again, and if you will put me in the way of restoring it, I will make him use his influence in high quarters to ease your sentence. That's plain enough, I hope."

"Sir John can do this, you think; but will he?" asked Ray.

"Yes. He will pay the money lent to any one you please to name. His family honour is concerned, you see; and though he has turned his son Gerard out of doors, he don't wish the matter to go further."

"His son Gerard, did you say?" asked Ray, earnestly.

"Yes. He's a rough customer, is Sir John, and the most violent old fellow I ever met. They say Gerard was his favourite son, and that he'll fret himself to death at his loss. Nevertheless, he cursed him both hot and strong, so that if, as the saying goes, 'Curses come home to roost,' I don't envy the old gentleman his lodgers."

Ray did not appear to hear what Higgler was saying, but sat lost in deep thought. His cool, scheming head was at work again in its old way, and he saw a chance of escape, unperceived by even the wily Bow Street runner.

"Well, Mr. Ray," said that officer, after waiting a minute or so, "what do you say?"

"The bracelet," replied Ray, "is with the man who lent the money. He has been a good friend to me, and I should not like to involve him in any trouble——"

"Jasper Jollifer?" asked Higgler, quickly.

"No. Not Jasper Jollifer, nor any such chicken-hearted fellow like him. I will think the matter over, Mr. Higgler. I conclude Sir John is to pay you for this business, and I will try not to spoil your bargain, if it don't injure myself. Can nothing be done *before* my trial?" said Ray, with emphasis.

"Nothing. The other business is too clear against you, and you know it. Had there been only one case, *that* might have broke down; but there are four—and you must see that what you hint at is impossible."

"I fear so," replied Ray, sadly. "Well, Mr. Higgler, I shall know the worst on Tuesday; so come to me the day after, and we will talk over the subject again."

Mr. Higgler shook hands in the most friendly manner with the man he had tracked down so cleverly and perseveringly, and parted from him as pleasantly as he could have done had Ray been a pot companion at a tavern door.

Ray slept soundly that night, and the next also, although the morning which followed was to declare his future fate.

As Higgler had prophesied, the cases against Ray were proved too clearly to admit the least doubt of his guilt, and the twelve intelligent men in the jury-box retired, merely as a matter of form, to consider their verdicts, returning in a few minutes after each case to pronounce the word "Guilty," their faces beaming with self-satisfaction at their own acumen.

Then, police officer after police officer stepped into the

witness-box, and told how they had known the prisoner at the
bar under many *aliases*. That he had been convicted of swind-
ling, card-sharping, and other mean vices. That he had been
long known as a trainer of thieves and a receiver of stolen
goods, but by great cunning and address had eluded detection,
until London becoming too dangerous for him, he had disappeared. That Mr. Higgler, from information which he had
received, had found out his whereabouts, and brought him to
trial that day. He was thought to have come of a good
family, though no one, except a woman he called his sister,
and Mr. Jellifer, a neighbour, had cared to own him for many
years past.

The sentence was transportation for life.

The persons in court who had heard the trials, and the long
catalogue of previous iniquities, stared with wonder at the
pleasant face and manly bearing of the convicted felon, who
bowed respectfully to the Bench, and walked firmly, but
without bravado, from the bar.

Ray did not sleep that night. The reminiscences of his
bad life, recounted by so many witnesses during the past day,
kept sleep from his eyes, and the wickedness he had done now
began to be his punishment. With the daylight his hardihood
returned, and when Higgler came according to promise, Ray
had adjusted his mask again, and seemed an unmoved man.

" I have thought over what is to be done," said Ray.
" You may tell Sir John that you have brought me to a state
of penitence and confession, and so have earned your wages.
When you have done that to your satisfaction, bring the old
gentleman here, and I will make my own terms with him.
I have more to restore to him than his wife's bracelet; and,
valuable as that is, he would give a hundred times what it is
worth for the other affair."

Mr. Higgler was rather astounded, and would have fished
out Ray's secret if he could have done so, but abandoned the
hope of success when the felon said:

" You have nothing more to gain by me, nor I by you

Make what bargain you can with Sir John: my words will
be worth the money, be it what it may. As I shall leave
here for the hulks in a few days, you had better make an
early appointment. You will always find me at home, as I
shall quit London without the formality of bidding adieu to
my friends. I am not beat yet, Higgler; at least, I hope
not."

Mr. Higgler, again shaking hands with his friend Raymond, as he now called him, took his departure, and calling
a hackney coach, ordered the driver to proceed to an hotel at
the West-end, where the Norwolds were expected to arrive
that day.

CHAPTER IX.

MRS. JELLIFER had gone to London the day before Ray's trial, leaving Mr. Cobby, the man in possession, after thanking him for the constant attention he had paid her during the time they had been together. Mr. Cobby was not surprised at her departure, as the certainty of the miller's fate was known in Morden, and Mr. Cobby had more than once, explained to Mrs. Jellifer the state of the law as affecting the miller's property in the event of his being found guilty of the offences with which he was charged. The Crown would then become possessed of all the felon's goods and chattels, and therefore there seemed to be no necessity for Mrs. Jellifer's supervision of the proceedings at the mill. On the second day after the trial, however, when Cobby was relieving the monotony of his existence by performing on his beloved dulcimer, and by no means discoursing most eloquent music himself, he was surprised by the arrival of Mrs. Jellifer, accompanied by a well-dressed gentleman, and two men of humbler appearance.

Cobby went to the door to receive them, but Mrs. Jellifer wishing him a curt good afternoon, brushed past him into the house, and requested her friends to follow her. Mr. Cobby was a brave man, but he was also a small one, and with a discretion which was to be expected from one of so much worldly experience, he offered no opposition to their ingress.

"What's up now, ma'am?" said Mr. Cobby, seeing the lady quietly seat herself in the easy chair he had just vacated, and motion the respectable gentleman to take a place beside her.

"What's up, sir?" replied the lady, with a slight sneer. "If you mean by that to inquire why we are here, I beg to inform you that we have come to take possession of the mill and its contents, and to dispense with your further attendance, Mr. Cobby."

"Dear me," said the officer, "I shall be sorry to have any difference of opinion with a lady for whom I have so much esteem; but you can't take possession, and you can't dispense with me."

"Indeed, sir, we shall see," replied Mrs. Jellifer.

"Yes, ma'am," said Cobby; "that gratification shall not be denied you;" and diving into a side-pocket of his coat, he produced a little brass staff and an official-looking paper. After carefully opening the latter, he proceeded: "this, ma'am and gentlemen, is a document which I have received this day from London, empowering me to hold, on behalf of the Crown, all the goods and chattels of Raymond Ray, a convicted felon, now lying in His Majesty's gaol of Newgate."

"Indeed," said Mrs. Jellifer, "then I am afraid the Crown will be disappointed for once, as this"—almost snatching a paper from the hands of the respectable gentleman—"as this is a bond or a bill of sale, or whatever it's called, making over to my husband, Jasper Jellifer, as security for money lent, all that Mr. Raymond Ray was possessed of some time ago; and now I leave you and our lawyer, Mr. Williams, of Lincoln's-inn-fields, London, to fight the matter out between you."

Mrs. Jellifer then rose and left the room.

The legal battle was not of long duration, Mr. Williams being well-known as a highly respectable person to Cobby, and he did not therefore hesitate to accept the assurance of that gentleman, that the document which gave Jasper Jellifer's claim the preference over that of the Crown, was perfectly valid, the more especially as Mrs. Jellifer returned, bringing with her from the mill the affrighted man who had attested the signatures of the parties to the legal instrument. Cobby was by no means cast down at this defeat, but, requesting Mr. Williams to give him a written declaration of the authority under which Mr. Jellifer claimed possession, he pocketed his sceptre and declared his willingness to abdicate.

"I thought we should make short work with you," said Mrs. Jellifer; "no reflection on your size, sir. And now if you will kindly remove yourself, and your box of music, as you're pleased to call it, to some other place, I shall be extremely obliged to you."

Cobby inquired whether it was absolutely necessary that he should retire so precipitately, and whether he might not remain until the morning, as his business in Morden would then be at an end, and he proposed to return by an early coach to London.

"Well, yes!" said Mrs. Jellifer; "you may remain conditionally."

Cobby inquired the terms on which his evacuation of the mill could be delayed.

"These," said Mrs. Jellifer, with savage emphasis. "As I intend remaining here to-night, to lock-up and make an inventory of certain things, I require that you tie up in its green bag that horrible instrument of torture upon which you are continually thumping; and that, if you want to sing, you go into the mill and remain there until you have exhausted the contents of that 'Little Warbler,' which you seem to have swallowed at some time or the other."

Cobby was hurt, painfully hurt, at the mention of these conditions, and from that hour to the end of his existence, hated Mrs. Jellifer.

It was six o'clock in the evening when Higgler reached the hotel where Sir John Norwold was staying. The old baronet was in an execrable temper, two or three circumstances having occurred to make him more than usually unamiable. One was that he had been engaged with his lawyer for an hour or two in making a new will. He never

paused halfway in any course which he had resolved to
pursue; and in order to disinherit Gerard as completely as
possible, he had willed to his son Gilbert all that he could
devise to him. The entailed property was small, as during
his father's lifetime Sir John had imprudently allowed much
of it to be sold to pay the heavy election expenses incurred in
contesting Morden. Another item was a list of the improvements required in Lady Norwold's wardrobe, and which she
declared to be requisite for her proper appearance in public.
The slightest reference to such a subject always brought on a
violent fit of swearing, and certain allusions to the domestic
economy of the ancient Britons strongly adverse to the
progress of civilisation. If he had lived in these days of
crinoline, Lady Norwold would have gone into society a
perfect fright had she conformed to Sir John's notions of
amplitude as applied to a lady's skirt. Another circumstance which tended to his irritability was this, he wanted
his dinner; and like other savage animals, he growled loudest
when he was hungry. Mr. Higgler's mission was made,
therefore, under a most unfavourable condition of things;
and that worthy officer had to submit to numerous interruptions during the narration of his interview with Ray, all of
which would have been distressing to a less regulated mind
than that of the Bow Street runner.

It would be worse than useless to give the conversation in
detail, as Sir John declared that he would have hung Ray
without the formality of a trial, and expressed his regret that
such a catastrophe was not awaiting that criminal person
with such ornate flourishes of language as prevent repetition.
The excommunication of the Jackdaw of Rheims might have
been read (had that remarkable objuratory poem been written) as a blessing beside Sir John's maledictions. Mr. Higgler
knew his man, however, and having heard a great deal of
bad language in his time, was patient and enduring. He
succeeded at last in obtaining Sir John's promise to meet him
at Newgate on the following day, and to amply reward him

should Ray's communication prove of the consequence he professed it to be.

Through the long weary night which succeeded Ray's last interview with Higgler, the wretched felon slept but little. The prison clock striking the hours and the quarters roused him from his feverish slumber, and he remembered that the passing minutes brought him nearer to the interview which might produce some mitigation of his dreadful doom, or destroy his best hope of any future peace this side the grave. And then he recalled his past evil deeds, and their bitter consequences to others, and wondered that he had thought so lightly of the usual ending of such a life as his had been, or why he had put those thoughts, when they did come, so readily aside. He remembered also the few evanescent, unsatisfying pleasures which his evil gains had brought him. He had had, it is true, an unwedded mother and a libertine father, who was no father in his love or in the discharge of his duties towards his unhappy boy and girl, and who had allowed them to be reared in short-lived luxury, to be cast upon the world when death transferred his abused wealth to his high-born heirs, who would acknowledge no kindred with those whom the law refused to recognise. He thought of all this wrong, and sought to find some palliation for his own misdeeds in the selfish cruelty of the dead. But conscience would not admit the plea, and cried out " Guilty " almost as loudly as he had heard that fatal word pronounced in court not very many hours before.

Time, that stays not either for the just or for the unjust, brought the hour appointed for Ray's meeting with Sir John Norwold.

Mr. Higgler was waiting to receive the baronet, and to usher him into the governor of Newgate's little office. Sir John had passed a sleepless night also, and looked haggard and nervously excited. He glanced with an angry look at the grim ornaments of the little room. Manacles of notorious malefactors, labelled with their names, as though they were

relics too precious to pass into oblivion. Above them, on
shelves, were casts of hideous heads, their features distorted
by the violent deaths they had died—hideous also, from the
crimes with which they were associated, and which had given
them their Newgate value. There were two or three more
precious relics of the gallows still than those memorials
made by the hands of man : there were the skulls, the
once living bones of departed scoundrels, not hidden out of
man's sight in the earth, but kept as lures to the warder's
show-box.

"The place smells of death," Sir John said, and he desired
to be taken to Ray, or to have Ray brought to him as soon as
possible.

The latter civility might have been accorded him had he
been more regardful of the turnkey's feelings, and not spoken
disparagingly of his criminal museum ; but having offended the
man's professional prejudices, Sir John was led through the
gloomy passages of the old prison, along which many had
passed on to "dusky death," until he came to the cell wherein
Ray was confined, and where he now remained pleading illness, thus avoiding the necessity of taking his place in the
felon's yard. As Ray rose up on the entrance of Sir John,
his fetters clanked, and sent a cold chill through the frame
of his visitor, although, as a magistrate, he was not entirely a
stranger to the inside of a prison.

The warder stood waiting at the door until Ray expressed
a wish to speak with Sir John alone, and as Higgler had
supplied a liberal garnish, the turnkey expressed his willingness to retire, provided Sir John was not afraid.

"Afraid ! What do you mean by being afraid, fellow ? I
never feared any man yet, and don't care for this manacled
scoundrel."

. The door of the cell, therefore, was closed, and Sir John
and the convict were alone together.

"Now then, Ray, what is it you wish to say to me ? I
should not have come, but I have had so many surprises of

late, that perhaps you may have something to astonish me, also."

"I have, Sir John, or I would not have requested your attendance here," said Ray. "You can well believe, sir, that a man with such a dreadful future before him as I have, may strive to get one ray of hope by a boldness which he would not have dared to exhibit under other circumstances; and as two matters which I have to communicate are of the gravest importance, I believe, to you, I must make conditions before I speak."

Sir John was disposed to use harsh words, and to call bad names, but at last deigned to ask to have the conditions named.

"I propose to reveal to you the most important secret first, and I require your promise that, if my revelation be of the value I profess it to be, you shall exert your influence in my behalf, and obtain some mitigation of my terrible sentence. I mean, sir, to obtain for me, when I reach my destination, some less severe task-work than falls to the lot of the common convict. It can be done—it is often done—and you can obtain this favour for me by asking for it in a quarter I can mention."

Sir John did not reply immediately, not until he recalled much that had happened of late, and in some way connected it in his mind with what Ray had to tell.

"I promise to do what I can, provided your communication is of the importance you pretend it to be," said Sir John.

"My second communication shall be made before I leave England, provided my first produces the result I hope for. Don't be angry, Sir John. I do not doubt your word, but you may not estimate what I am about to say as I do. I trust to your honour."

Ray then proceeded to narrate all that had occurred at the mill. How that Gilbert came at night to borrow the large sum of 200*l.*, bringing with him no other security than Gerard's promise to repay the loan. He did not mention

Jasper's name, and he had good reasons for his silence. He then described how, sympathising with Gilbert's distress at not being able to comply with his brother's requirement that the money won should be repaid at once, he had told Gilbert of the money-lender's conditions, and pointed out the possibility of help being obtained from Lady Norwold. How Gilbert went away taking the keys with him to open the outer gate, the time he was absent, and how Ray had met him on his return—exhausted, as he then thought, by his interview with his mother; how he threw the bracelet down, and the words he used when questioned. Ray then assured Sir John that he knew not until the day after his trial that the diamonds had been stolen (he did not say that Jasper had told him this), and that Gerard and not Gilbert had been suspected as the thief—Gerard, the noblest, most self-sacrificing gentleman that ever lived, and who had borne his father's anger rather than breathe a suspicion of his brother's dishonour.

As Ray dwelt on all the incidents of the narrative we have indicated briefly, the violent emotion of Sir John was painfully apparent, but Ray had his own point to gain, and did not pause to consider the effect he was producing on a listener of such a violent and excitable character as the man who sat before him.

As Gilbert's guilt became evident—as Gerard's innocence came to light, the struggle of the father completely overpowered him.

He started up, clutching at his cravat, and shaking his head to and fro exclaimed, "Let me out! Let me out of this infernal hole, or I shall be suffocated."

The warder heard him instantly, and on opening the cell-door Sir John rushed past him, and as it were by instinct, made his way along the passages until he reached the intervening gates, which he shook in his desire to escape into the air, and then with Higgler passed into the street, where a carriage was awaiting him.

"Come to-morrow—tell them to drive home!" was all he said.

Higgler watched the carriage out of Newgate-street, wondering what could have been the communication which had evidently had such powerful effect upon Sir John. He re-entered the prison, and went to Ray's cell, but the prisoner would tell him nothing, not one word of what had passed. Ray saw the effect he had produced, and did not wish to have it weakened by any interference of Mr. Higgler.

Ray did not deceive himself into the hope that his sentence would be revoked—he knew that was impossible, but he tried to recall all the stories which he had heard of criminals who had obtained concessions from the authorities in Van Diemen's Land, and who had by skill and honest-dealing risen to be men of wealth and position in the colony. He thought that the worst he should endure would be the miseries of the passage out in the transport-ship, trusting that the influence he had secured by the revelation he had made and had to make, would free him from the convict's chain and harassing labours. Why should he not thrive as others had done? He would apply the cleverness he had hitherto used for dishonest pursuits to make himself a reputable position, and so end his days peacefully. If he could obtain the limited freedom accorded to many other convicts he could do this, for he had not been deprived of all his illgotten gains — no! thanks to his forethought—and there would be friends left in England who were bound to befriend him whenever the time arrived for the exercise of their assistance. So he comforted himself with this Alnascar's dream, although he had already unwittingly destroyed the fragile means which were to realise his pleasant anticipations.

When Sir John Norwold's carriage stopped at the West-end hotel, and the footman opened the door to let out his master, he was horror-stricken to see him lying back on the seat, apparently in a deadly stupor. His face was dark red, and one hand still clutched the white cravat, bound, as was then

I

the fashion, tightly round the neck. Sir John was instantly removed into the house, and medical aid procured only in sufficient time to save him from instant death.

Lady Norwold had ventured during her husband's absence to send for her dress-maker, and was busy with silks and laces and other vanities when the carriage drove up to the door. She saw it arrive from the window, and terrified at the explosion of angry words which she believed would be sure to succeed Sir John's discovery of her pardonable delin-quency, hurried her milliner and her goods from the room, herself condescending to carry a basket of no mean di-mensions.

Poor lady! She was never to hear that angry voice again! Passion had done its work, aided by remorse, and the living man brought into her chamber was already as powerless for good or evil as the dead. Throughout the night he laid motionless almost, his deep stertorous breathing painful to hear, and it was well for one watcher by his bedside that he did not know whose act it was that had quenched the life of his father, and made him almost a parricide. That knowledge was mercifully spared him, but never throughout his after-life was that death-bed scene forgotten. Before it quite closes we must return for a short time to the Elms.

Jack Spraggatt had evidently found another little skeleton, but he only concealed it for a day or so after his visit to Nurse Bland, and in conformity with his promise to Lucy, he made her a partner in his new possession. Nurse Bland had told him more of the circumstances connected with the expulsion of Gerard than he himself had done during their short excited interview; and Jack strongly suspected that his poor friend was bearing the consequences of some disgraceful act which his brother had committed. He had mentioned the conclusion at which he had arrived to the old nurse, and with which she appeared to coincide; but when Jack proposed to make some effort to vindicate Gerard, she peremptorily for-bade him taking any action for that purpose, in compliance with the most earnest injunction of his lost friend. Jack was not satisfied with this state of things, nor was Lucy either, and they determined to set off at once to Nurse Bland and discuss the matter over again.

Had Jack known half as much as Jasper Jellifer, he would have gone at once to Sir John, and had justice done to Gerard; but the self-seeking, prudent Jasper could discover no particular gain to himself, but, on the contrary, the prospect of considerable loss by revealing all he knew of Gilbert's transactions with Ray, and therefore he preserved a selfish silence.

It was otherwise with Jack Spraggatt; Gerard's honour was as dear to him as his own, and he believed his friend to be utterly incapable of an unworthy thought. There were many circumstances not amounting to evidence, perhaps, which led Jack to conceive the possibility of Gilbert having been betrayed into the commission of this wrong; he had always been treacherous and cowardly, and Jack could not bring himself to believe that he was doing his duty by his friend without communicating his own suspicions to Sir John Norwold.

A short drive through pleasant country lanes soon brought Jack and his sister to Mrs. Bland's cottage. Its small garden was crowded with bright blooming flowers and rose-bushes, among whose bells and leaves the honey-bees were busy from morn till night. The greenest of ivy grew mid-way up the cottage front, leaving its red tiles in no unpleasant contrast, as they were pierced with latticed windows, draped within by the whitest of dimity. As no cottage is perfect without a porch, this had one; and there Nurse Bland would sit on sunny days to knit or sew, and exchange gossip with a passing neighbour. The settle was unoccupied when Jack and Lucy stopped at the gate. The parlour and upper blinds were down, and no one came for some minutes in answer to Jack's lusty summons, although more than one of the inmates of the neighbouring cottages ran out to learn the cause of the knocking and shouting. At last the door was slowly opened by a purblind old man as deaf as he was blind, and from him Jack contrived to learn that Mrs. Bland was away from home, and he was left to take care of the house. He could tell no more, but he rather thought "that Master Piggott, at the shop, knowed more about 'um." And so to Master Piggott they went.

He did know a great deal that surprised Jack, for he had never thought for a moment that Mrs. Bland at her time of life, and after having lived some fourteen years in her little cottage, could have invested Master Piggott, or any one else, with authority to let the house and sell by auction all her goods and chattels, save and except certain articles which she had distinguished by a chalk cross, and which were to be removed before the day of sale.

"They were matters of small value," Mr. Piggott said; "being two or three portraits of children, and such like, together with an old clock, which he believed had come from the nursery at Norwold Hall."

This news was a great disappointment to Jack and his sister, and set them wondering more and more, whether it was not their duty to see Sir John without loss of time; for it was evident that Gerard was either dead or had resolved to carry out his determination to return home no more. In the first case Mrs. Bland had evidently left a neighbourhood which had, now, such painful associations; in the next, she might have resolved to share Gerard's fortunes, for all knew that she had the love of a mother for her foster-child.

They had just reached the Elms, when the sound of the horn announcing the approach of the "London up," decided Jack; so buttoning his great coat and giving the reins to Lucy, he exchanged his seat in his gig for one on the outside of the coach, and in due time arrived safely in London, as the clock of the inn-yard struck nine.

A hasty toilet and a substantial breakfast having been accomplished, Jack set out for the West-end hotel where Sir

John Norwold was lying unconscious of all around him. Whilst his name was being taken up-stairs, Jack heard with much concern the dangerous condition of the sufferer, and would have left at once had not Lady Norwold expressed a desire to see him. She had some vague idea that he had come from Gerard, and had thought it right that the outcast should know the state to which his father had been reduced. Gilbert, also, connected the coming of Jack Spraggatt with his injured brother, and walked to the window when the young farmer entered the room.

The usual civilities were hardly exchanged when the nurse came from the adjoining chamber to announce that her patient had suddenly rallied, and, as she thought, had muttered the name of Lady Norwold. Her ladyship immediately followed the nurse into the bedchamber, leaving Jack and Gilbert together. Gilbert felt he was bound to say something, and therefore remarked—

"This is a sad state in which you find Sir John, Mr. Spraggatt."

"Yes, sir," replied Jack; "and by me quite unexpected. He looked so hale and hearty that one might have taken a lease of his life for years. I wished to have seen him very much—very much indeed!"

Gilbert made two or three efforts to speak before he could even say—"On business, I presume?"

"Oh, yes, sir—on *his* business principally," answered Jack. "He was always a just man when—not in a passion; and he——" but recollecting to whom he was speaking, he paused; and then added—"But it is too late, I fear, to—too late!"

The silence which ensued was broken by the entrance of the nurse.

"Sir John has certainly rallied wonderfully," she said. "He evidently recognises her ladyship, and tries to tell her so. You can see him, if you stand here."

Jack accepted the invitation of the nurse, and looking

through the half-opened door, he saw the father of his injured friend, propped up with pillows; his lips twitching slightly now and then, whilst his glazed eyes were fixed on those of Lady Norwold, who sat by the bedside holding his hand. He was dying, no doubt of that, and the last feeble rays of life just lighted up his face.

The nurse was called into the room, and instantly returned to request Mr. Gilbert to go to his father, as her ladyship fancied Sir John had asked for him.

The eyes of the dying man had wandered to and fro whilst these communications had been made, and when Gilbert went to his father's bedside they became fixed upon him. As soon as the confused mind of Sir John could comprehend the presence of his son, a redder flush suffused his face, his eyes dilated, and his breast heaved slowly, slowly, and then with a deep sighing the spirit passed away.

Two men who looked upon that bed of death and saw the dart strike home, remembered it in after years, one to find only remorse in the retrospect, the other to add another comort to a happy life.

As Mr. Higgler had nothing now to gain through the agency of Ray, he paid no more visits to the convict, and that person, therefore, being dead in the eye of the law, might have been actually defunct for what any one not interested in his safe keeping seemed to care for him, and he left England unconscious of Sir John's death, attributing the neglect which he experienced to the want of honour on the part of the baronet, and to the callous selfishness of Higgler, who, having been paid for his share of the business, cared nothing for the poor tool with which he had worked. So, using a bad man's logic, he reasoned himself into the belief that he was an ill-used person, and resolved, if fortune gave him the chance, to revenge himself in the new world to which he was going. We shall meet with him again in after years, and learn how he prospered, and how he did a good turn when it was least expected.

Jasper Jellifer came into possession of all the late miller's property, Jack Spraggatt's wheat amongst other valuables, and it was calculated by those who took the trouble to mind other people's business as well as their own, that Jasper had made a very good bargain, although the money he had received might have been a little cleaner. Jasper always had been a lucky man, everybody said, and by adding and adding honest earnings to the gold he had picked out of the dirt, his gains became so mixed, and grew so bright by being jingled together in the same bag, that there was no one in Morden who could tell one coin from the other, and therefore they came to respect lucky Jasper for a great deal more than he was worth.

CHAPTER X.

TWELVE months had passed since the death of Sir John Norwold, and it was well for Jack Spraggatt that his tangled affairs had given him constant employment to get them straight, or he might have thought more of the loss of his dear friend Gerard, and of the injustice he had suffered, than would have been good for his peace of mind ; but he and Lucy had to exert themselves to the uttermost to surmount the difficulties which surrounded them. Jack needed all his sister's hopefulness and bravery to keep him now and then from desponding, as he would sometimes talk of giving in ; but she always discovered some earnest way of going to work, and Jack only wanted such a prompter to play out the part which had fallen to his lot. Their mother had died in ignorance of her children's struggles, and many retrenchments which could not have been made in her lifetime without exciting her inquiries became possible, and were made cheerfully. The accounts of the continued success of Jack's friend in New South Wales were every now and then arriving, and would set him thinking of a new home in that distant land ; but then, his household gods had been set up so many years at the Elms that it seemed like sacrilege to abandon them for other lares, however advantageous the change might seem. His father's fathers had tilled the land around him, and their graves, and those of others whom he had loved, were in the neighbouring churchyard ; and, foolish as it may seem, he thought that he could not put the seas between him and them. They were only mounds of earth to the passers-by, but to him they were green shrines where he had often stood and prayed that he might not bring dishonour on their honest names. A foolish fancy, perhaps, but all his life he had seen the seed which he had buried in the earth spring up into flowers and golden grain, and so he could gather loving thoughts from the graves of his departed kindred. Lucy, too, had to be considered, and where could she be as happy as in the old house at home? She would marry some day, no doubt selecting a farmer for her husband, and then the Elms could be managed between them, for without Lucy the place would be home to Jack no longer. The gossip of the neighbourhood had already found her a match in the son of Mr. Hayes, whose farm adjoined their own. The old man was reputed to be rich, and his eldest son Robert would doubtless possess all, as the younger was, although not eighteen, a sot and an idle fellow. True Robert was not exactly the man Lucy was likely to fancy, as he was given to low sports, and had been known to have visited more than one prizefight. Such amusements were, however, countenanced by the highest in the land, and might be abandoned if he became amenable to a better influence. Indeed, Robert Hayes had said to more than one confidential friend, that for Lucy Spraggatt's sake he would do anything in the wide world. He had never made any advances to Lucy, for, like most men of low pleasures, he was abashed in the presence of a modest girl, and it was long after his admiration for Miss Spraggatt was known to most of his intimates that he plucked up courage to speak to her brother on the subject.

Jack told him very frankly the objections he saw to the chance of Lucy accepting him for a lover, but Robert Hayes was ready to make oath there and then, that all which was objectionable should be amended, for the happiness of his life depended on her decision in his favour. Jack thought over the matter for a day or two, and generously put forward all the good qualities of the would-be suitor. He was industrious, steady, moderately good looking, and very well to do in the

world. His faults were only those of a not over educated
young man. There appeared, therefore, no reason why he
should not make the venture, and it would rest with Lucy to
refuse or accept his proposal. Accordingly Jack brought
Robert Hayes home to dinner, and acting as a good brother
ought to do, tried to display his sister to the best advantage
by exhibiting her household qualifications, and then to
present her admirer at his best by directing the conversation
into channels adapted to the flow of his ideas. Mr. Hayes
floundered about considerably at first, and made a very indifferent dinner, appearing to have much difficulty in swallow-
ing, even when taking a custard. The home-brewed of the
Elms had a local reputation for excellence, and Mr. Hayes
seemed inclined to draw his inspirations from the contents of
a brown jug, with a silver rim.

Jack at last hit upon a subject on which he knew Mr.
Hayes could talk, and his inquiry as to the pedigree of Ponto,
Robert's favourite pointer, unloosed the young gentleman's
tongue, and set his eloquence flowing.

"He's of the best strain in the country, Miss Spraggatt,
if not in all England," said Mr. Hayes. "His great-great-
grandsire came direct from Spain, and he has as good blood
in his veins as the King of England."

"Not a very loyal comparison, Mr. Hayes," remarked
Lucy, not knowing what else to say.

"I beg pardon, Miss, but I think it is. That dog never
makes a fault. If the ground's as dry as a biscuit he never
once runs over his game; and I'd be bound if he made a
point, and the game didn't rise or run, he'd stand for a week
—ay, until he was starved to death. Why last season "—
and Mr. Hayes shot over again days upon days wherein
Ponto had distinguished himself so greatly, that, according
to his admiring master's appreciation of his merits, he deserved to be chiselled in stone and set up in the market-place.

Jack mounted him next upon a favourite mare, and the
excited orator rode his hobby for nearly half an hour, leaving

Lucy much opportunity to reflect upon the acquirements and other recommendations of the speaker, although she did not anticipate to what end all this display was directed.

Lucy was country bred, and had an interest—a modified interest—in good dogs and horses, and in all, indeed, that pertained to the true sports of the field; but a young man whose knowledge and tastes appeared to have no further range than the stable and the dog kennel, did not excite in her gentle bosom the amount of admiration necessary to make a proposal of marriage acceptable. Jack Spraggatt perceived the ill success of the aspiring wooer, and after a short absence from the room was, therefore, not surprised to find Mr. Hayes looking the picture of despair at having had his hand and heart respectfully declined by Miss Spraggatt, who had very considerately retired to her own chamber after inflicting this necessary pain on her brother's visitor.

' Jack having good-naturedly walked home with the unhappy Strephon, received a sisterly wigging on his return, for having been a party to such an absurd and embarrassing proceeding.

"And now, my dear Jack," said Lucy, "a word or two as to the future. Should any other young gentleman make such a proposal to you again—it is not very likely, I own, but still it is within the range of possibility—I beg you to say that I have neither the wish nor the intention to marry. My course—our course of duty—is clearly defined. We have to get out of debt, in the first place, and in the next we have to provide for the future. This will be my home so long as I can be useful in it, dear Jack, to you, and when you find another mistress to your liking, I will trust to your generosity to provide for me, for I shall never marry. There, that is what I want you to remember; and that you may not forget it there is a beautiful kiss, one for each cheek, and I wish you a very good night, you bungling, dear old matchmaker."

Jack was very glad that Lucy had rejected Robert Hayes.

When he saw them sitting in the same room—when he heard him talking so rapturously about dogs and horses and nothing else, he felt that even Letty's French husband was a very desirable connection by comparison.

And yet he did not admire Lucy's parting words—" I shall never marry." Why not? No young girl of twenty makes such a declaration as that and means it, unless her young love has been stolen or given away unworthily. Jack puzzled over this riddle for more than four years, and then never guessed it. He only knew it when the solution was told to him.

The knowledge of Lucy Spraggatt's refusal of Robert Hayes soon became public property by the liberal confidence of the rejected suitor, and nearly everybody blamed the young lady for her folly in not accepting such an eligible offer; the more especially as old Hayes died shortly afterwards, and left Robert his son several thousands of pounds. Morden had its scandalisers, and some said the Spraggatts had always been thought a little too proud owing to their London connections, and Jack's intimacy with Gerard Norwold, who had turned out such a bad fellow; and though no one could remember any exhibition of this objectionable quality, so far as themselves were concerned, yet they all had heard somebody else say so, and therefore it must be true. Where there was smoke there was sure to be flame. Stupid old adage.

However, the nine days' wonder soon passed away, and there was another subject of popular discussion which retained its interest for a much longer period of time. It was another windfall for lucky Jasper Jellifer. Old Hayes had appointed him the guardian of his younger son William, with an allowance of 150l. a-year until the lad should be of age, when he would come into possession of 2000l., left to him by his maternal grandfather. What perplexed every one was the reason that Mr. Hayes had selected Jasper for such a trust; but the old man had been a frequent visitor to the shop in the market-place, and as his son's " goings on " had been usually uppermost in his mind, Jellifer had been favoured with a knowledge of the case, and gave such excellent advice as to what he would do with so rebellious a subject, that old Mr. Hayes walked one day direct to his lawyer's, and added a codicil to his will, appointing Jasper guardian to his son. Young William objected strongly at first to this disposition of his person; but as he was a great trouble at home, his brother and his father's executors insisted on submission, and he was therefore domiciled with the lucky Jasper. Not that that there was much to be made out of the 150*l.* a year, but there were possible contingencies to arise hereafter, quite unseen and unthought of by every one except by clever Jasper Jellifer.

We must be of those, kind reader, with whom " time gallops withal," and pass over another year until the time when Gerard Norwold would (if living) have been twenty-three years old, and, in accordance with the custom of the Norwold family, have attained his majority. That day had been often spoken of by the dwellers in Morden and at Norwold Hall as one when there were to be great merrymakings, as there had been in other days, and from time out of mind. But there was a cloud over the great House, and those who remembered the day as an anniversary of the birth of its heir, shrugged their shoulders, or spoke sadly or disparagingly of the departed Gerard. In one household, however, he was remembered as his kindly, generous nature entitled him to be regarded, and with a strange combination of joy and sorrow. Jack Spraggatt would not believe that he was dead, although the closest inquiries had failed to discover the slightest trace of him after he had quitted the cottage of his old nurse, who had also gone none knew whither. That circumstance gave the Spraggatts and other of Gerard's friends hope that the evidence found on the bank of the river was a device to deceive those who might be interested in his fate, and Jack declared a determination, for his own part, to keep Gerard's birthday as though he were with them in the flesh. He would have the church bells

rung, and give a bullock to be roasted, and have a meeting of
all the Norwold tenants at the principal inn in the market-
place, and defy the family anger. Lucy, however, dissuaded
him from all this. She, too, could not bring herself to believe
that their dear friend had played such a cowardly part as to
free himself from the sorrows of the present by breaking God's
canon against self-murder. Nevertheless, there was no proof
that he was living, and such rejoicings would have been a
mockery of the dead, provided he was dead. Again, she
urged, such a display of friendly rejoicing could not be desired
by Gerard, or he would have taken means to have communicated his present condition to some relative or friend. No—
he had vowed in the paroxysm of his grief never to claim
kindred with his father's house, and though those words were
uttered rashly, Lucy believed that they would bind Gerard to
their fulfilment unto his dying hour. Jack yielded to the
reasoning of his sister, and they resolved to observe the day
as they did the anniversaries of the deaths of their father and
mother, not sorrowfully, but resignedly and in the belief that
the grave was but the portal to a world where love would be
eternal. So Gerard was lovingly remembered on that day,
and as he was for many long years to come.

Again and once again we must turn over the hour-glass of
time, and end for some years our visits to the Elms, as that once
happy home-circle was destined to be broken, and by his hands
who had made it such a pleasant abiding-place for so long.
Jack Spraggatt, Jack Spraggatt! the bark you are about to
steer over thousands of miles of the great sea will be freighted
with the whole happiness of your loving sister's life, and woe
to your own if you make shipwreck of your venture.

The morrow would be Gilbert Norwold's birthday, when
he would be twenty-three, and the possessor of all the wealth
his mistaken father could bequeath to him. There was to be
some show of rejoicing at the Hall, but as neither Lady
Norwold nor the young heir had made themselves many new
friends since Sir John's death, and had kept but little inter-

course with their old ones, the day did not promise to have much hearty enjoyment in store for those who were to take part in the festivities.

We shall have to accompany Jasper Jellifer to the Hall in our next chapter, and therefore for the present we will linger at the Elms. The more especially as Lucy has to meet a new wooer, one who will press her earnestly for her love, although he has a place in her heart already. Will she refuse him as she did Robert Hayes? Perhaps not, as her suitor now is— her brother Jack.

The postman had brought a letter to the Elms—a full-bodied responsible-looking letter, and the post-mark was New South Wales. Jack had but one friend in that distant land he knew, and therefore he did not puzzle himself much to divine the sender, although the handwriting of the super-scription was unknown to him. When he opened it and read on, the caligraphy became quite familiar to him, and he was obliged to pause more than once or twice, indeed many times, before he could finish that long, long letter. There was much on those sheets of paper which told of great suffering and hard struggles, ending in successful mastery of difficulties, and a future of promising prosperity. For such revelations Jack was not unprepared when he knew who was the writer, but of that which came after he had never dreamed in all the times when he had thought of the after-fortunes of his sister Lucy, and he was fairly puzzled how to proceed.

Two years had passed since Mr. Hayes had received his credentials as suitor for the hand of Lucy, but the words she had then spoken had come back to her brother's mind again and again: "I shall never marry." How those words had perplexed him at the time they were uttered we have already chronicled, and he was not wiser now as to their meaning. There was nothing for it, therefore, but to take counsel with Lucy herself after he had read the greater part of his long letter again, and so when they were seated by a bright fire early in the evening, Jack produced his budget.

"I have received," he said, "a long letter from an old friend this morning from New South Wales."

"Oh, yes—our old playmate!" she answered. "I trust that he is well and prospering as usual."

"Yes, dear, our friend is prospering bravely, after many difficulties and many trials."

Jack then read from his letter much that we shall know if we wait for the end, and then he came to a part which concerned Lucy more nearly than any letter she had heard read in all her happy life. The writer said :—

"And now, my dear friend, my head fails me—my heart almost fails me when I need them both more than ever I have done since I could think or feel. I have told you all that I can remember of my sufferings and trials and of my present prosperity. I ought, I fear, to make an end, but I can see before me two futures; one a life of ungratifying toil, another of honest exertion rewarded by the peace of home, and the happiness of an assured love. Should I hesitate in an endeavour to secure the happiest because I may be subjected to more pain, more regrets than I have yet endured? Would it not be cowardly to do so? Believing that I hear you answer 'Yes,' I now make my venture, praying with the whole strength of my soul, that God's blessing will be with my imperfect words.

"There was one I left behind me in the land of my kindred that I believed to be possessed of all womanly virtues, and you believing that also, can understand how nearly my friendship had become love. It needed but what has passed to destroy the only impediment to the stronger development, and the change came. It came, and I despised myself for the miserable thoughts which had kept my love down, and would have stifled it, 'had I not known tribulation.'

"The more I dwelt upon the excellence I had had so long about my path, and yet had estimated only in part, my own demerits rose so strongly to my mind that I felt the poverty

of all that I could ever hope to offer in exchange for the treasure I coveted, and—I despaired.

"As time went on my love grew and grew, until it has
come to be too'great a burthen to be borne in silence, and I
now ask you, dear Jack, dear friend, to lend me help in this
great need. I dare not write down what I am, for my faults
would outnumber my few virtues. You must recall all your
old friendship thought me to be, and tell it to her as truth,
which coming from your lips she will believe.

"I dare not ask you to send away the light of your home,
dear Jack—to send to this distant land the dearest treasure of
your great brotherly heart, unless—what a momentous condition!—unless you find—how dare I write? I will be bold
in despair, and say, unless Lucy loves me—loves me well
enough to leave all—even you, her happy home, old friends,
old memories—and trust her future life to my care in this
distant land. To come to me and make my life as happy as
she has made yours."

The letter contained many more passionate words, which
were only intended to be known to Jack and Lucy, and would
be read as foolishness by those whose hearts were not concerned in the perusal. It was signed George Warner, and
the hand had trembled as it traced the letters which composed
the name.

When Jack had finished reading, Lucy knelt down at his
knees, and taking his hand in hers, pressed it to her lips. Her
touch was as cold as death. "Dear brother," she said, "what
you have read to-night must never be read to me again. I
have already told you—I told you what I had determined
upon as my course of duty, and that—and that I should never
marry."

"Ah! but that was Robert Hayes."

"Do not interrupt me, please, dear Jack, until I have ended.
You must not read that letter to me any more, nor must you
ever speak to me again about it. I am but a weak woman—
with a woman's nature, and such words and thoughts as you

K

have read may affect my peace and make my life a sorrow.
Two have passed away out of this house, and whose love
watched over us to increase our joys and lessen our sorrows.
We two are left alone, dear Jack, and thank God we are not
divided by distance or death. If it be decreed that we should
part it must be by the hand which directs all things, my dear,
dear, brother."

"I think I understand you Lucy," said Jack, "my heart
would be a stone did I not understand you, and refuse the
sacrifice you are making for my sake. I never until to-day
suspected even that—that he loved you, nor did you I am
certain. I never knew until this night that you loved
him."

"No! no!" cried Lucy, "I have said nothing to make
you infer that."

"Nothing plainly, I grant," said Jack, "but do you think
that I am blind, Lucy. That I cannot see all the love in your
heart. As I look in your face, now pale as snow, now red as
fire. If you have hidden this love, you have acted womanly
—wisely, because it might have been unprized and unasked
for. But now you know how it is sought and valued, it is
your brother's duty to see that you do not wrong yourself."

"I never loved him, Jack; never had a warmer feeling
than——"

"Was proper and right. I know that," interrupted Jack.
"Dear Lucy, do not trifle with your love, do not believe that
you can ever stifle it in your heart, or that time or anything
else can entirely conquer it. No, darling, no. You think it
overcome, you think it dead, you fancy it will be forgotten;
but some trifling thing, a flower, a song, a word, a well-known
place, and back it comes again as strong as ever."

"You only say what you have read or fancied," said Lucy,
coldly. "You must have felt love to know what it really
is, I have heard say."

"And I have felt it, Lucy—feel it now," replied Jack.
"Would that it were not so. No man loved more truly, more

fondly than I loved one ;—you remember,—I think she would not have rejected me, and, if I had spoken, I might have found a loving answer. I did, I do love her, though it is almost guilt to do so now. I do not blame her. She must have thought me vacillating, cold, insensible, to have avoided her as I did, and I was glad, yes, I was glad for a time when she married, because I fancied no thought of me, nothing which I had said or done, had touched her heart and could ever make her unhappy."

"Why did you neglect her? Why did you, knowing your own feelings, lead her to believe that she was indifferent to you?" asked Lucy, with much excitement in her face and manner.

"Because my father died, and I saw the change, the struggle that was before me. I knew that I had debts to pay, difficulties to overcome, for the sake of those who had a prior claim upon my love and my exertions."

"And shall I not remember the lesson you have taught me, dear, dear brother," cried Lucy, throwing her arms around his neck. "Shall I forget for any selfish love that dear old Jack has bruised his honest heart to do his duty; that he has waking nights that might bring desponding days, if there were not one to see his sorrow and use her best skill to cure it. Leave you! No, not to be queen of the world!"

"That's —— nonsense!" (Yes, he did! It was very wrong, but knowing what Jack meant, "the recording angel as he wrote it down dropped a tear upon the word and blotted it out for ever.") "My difficulties are nothing now, my creditors are nearly paid, my prospects for the future are brighter, and my spirits and my self-reliance are now equal to anything."

"It is no use, my dear Jack, trying to dissolve our part-nership," said Lucy, smiling. "We have still *our* difficulties, *our* creditors, and *our* prospects. You may have a very high opinion of your clever friend abroad, and his log-house and his bush-farming, but I am quite contented with my stupid

K 2

scheming brother, the dear old Elms, and a tabby cat. So, go pull off your boots, put on your slippers, and get your pipe, whilst I brew you such a glass of gin-punch as will make you ashamed of this shabby attempt to get rid of your housekeeper."

Jack felt himself out-generaled, and therefore he obeyed the commands of his conqueror, glad that the terms of capitulation were so agreeable. He might have been required to have dried up Lucy's tears, or to have fumigated her out of hysterics. Lucy exerted herself to prevent the conversation turning into the forbidden channel, but Jack was evidently crest-fallen at his defeat, or scheming how he could resume the offensive. Lucy, perhaps, suspected as much, and when the old clock growled as it was wont, before striking ten (or any other hour), she gave Jack his good-night kiss and prepared to leave the room.

"Just one question," said Jack. "You are positively determined never to marry?"

"Positively, dear boy—I—will—never—marry. Good night."

"Good night," said Jack, as Lucy left the room. "You never—will—marry," imitating Lucy's manner. "Very well. Now hear me, ye old beams and rafters that for so many years have covered the heads of the Spraggatt's, by the last sip of punch remaining in this old tumbler, I will make her marry; and more, I'll make her marry the man of my choice."

The gin-punch had been more potent than usual, perhaps, but that tyrannical brother repeated his terrible threat as he put on his nightcap preparatory to getting into bed.

CHAPTER XI.

THE festivities at the Hall on the morrow were to be very
limited, merely extending to a dinner-party of some of the
neighbouring gentry, and a few additions to the servants'
table. The snow which began to fall promised from the
appearance of the clouds to continue throughout the night,
and would necessarily make travelling disagreeable and difficult, and the unconsidered inhabitants of Morden prognos-
ticated a limited attendance at the old Hall, wherein great
merrymakings had been held in olden times. Jasper Jellifer
had obtained from the executors of Sir John the much-coveted
collectorship, and now became nervously anxious as to his
possible retention of the office under the new reign about to
commence on the morrow, the more so as a smart London
gentleman, who had been located for some days at one of the
inns in the market-place, had paid two or three visits to the
Hall, besides making a great many impertinent inquiries concerning the tenements and various properties on the Norwold
estate. Jasper, we know, was a shrewd man, and he came
to believe that the smart London gentleman might possibly be
preparing himself to supplant him in the position he had occupied during the past three years. This notion had no sooner
possessed him than he set about devising measures for his own
security, and early in the morning Jasper Jellifer trudged
through the deep snow to Norwold Hall. The family had
been early astir, and therefore he found easy access to Mr.
Gilbert Norwold, who, having had breakfast, was sitting in

the library conversing with his mother through an open door
which led into the little room where Jasper had had his
former interview with her ladyship.   Gilbert Norwold had
not passed unscathed through the fiery furnace which he had
kindled with his own hands, for time had brought no repentance, and he had sought in a freer indulgence in his old vices,
forgetfulness of the past.   He succeeded often in hushing
the still small voice that will be heard at most unwelcome
seasons, and amid the most unlikely scenes for the intrusion
of such a monitor, and the consciousness that this appeal
might be heard when least expected, made him more reckless
in his pleasures, and impatient of restraint in his pursuit of
them.   He inherited somewhat of his father's irritability of
temper, and his own unquiet mind rendered him petulant,
dogged, or morose, as circumstances affected him, and therefore his society was as little courted in the world as it had
been when he was at college.   He was sensible of his un-
popularity, and at times the knowledge stung and mortified
him into such retaliation as his selfish and cunning nature
enabled him to inflict, and had he been as needy as he was
revengeful, he would have been a desperate man to his own
cost as well as to that of others.   All this was known to
Jasper, who nevertheless sought the present interview with
less trepidation or misgiving of success than he had experienced when he first asked for the appointment which he
was about to solicit again.

"Well, Mr. Jellifer," said Mr. Norwold, "what brings you
here so early?"

"In the first place, Mr. Norwold," replied Jasper, smiling
his best, "I will venture to offer you my heartiest congratu-
lations on this auspicious day, and to wish——"

"Thank you.   Some other business I conclude brought
you here?" asked Gilbert, curtly.

Jasper bowed, and smiled again as he said; "Certainly,
sir, or I should not have dared to have intruded upon you.
For nearly four years, sir, I have had the honour to collect

the rents of certain properties in Morden, and to the satisfaction, I believe, of your late excellent father's executors and your trustees."

" I have heard nothing to the contrary," said Gilbert.

" I therefore have ventured to hope that now that the property has passed into your own hands, I may be permitted to retain the collection of the rents."

" You are a sharp man of business, Mr. Jellifer, a very sharp man of business, as I have reason to remember ; but early as your application is made, another has been before you," replied Gilbert.

Jasper was not so much startled or disturbed by this announcement as might have been supposed.

" But though the application has been made," said Jasper, " I presume it has not been granted."

" Why do you presume so ? " replied Gilbert, sharply.

" Because," and Jasper spoke in a low tone, glancing at the open door as he did so; " because I cannot believe that you would have quite forgotten the small services I have rendered you when they were so much required."

Gilbert rose and closed the open door before he replied.

" For those services, Mr. Jellifer, you were liberally paid. To what they led you no doubt remember, and it is partly because you do so, and partly because I require assistance now, that I contemplate making my London agent the receiver also of my country properties."

" You only contemplate, then," said Jasper. " You have not decided. I am glad of that, because I think you will find me equally useful in all ways."

" You have profited by success, I see, Mr. Jellifer, and can be pertinacious instead of obsequious, as formerly."

" I can be of use to you, Mr. Gilbert," said Jasper, with a smile; "and will be, if you will allow me."

" As you are persistent I must be positive," replied Gilbert. " I decline to continue you as my agent. I am afraid of you."

"You need not be," said Jasper, with perfect coolness, "if you use me fairly."

"Fairly, sir!" replied Gilbert, reddening with anger. "Use you fairly! I have always done so, and shall hear no more." He again rose and went towards the bell.

"Stay, Mr. Norwold! a very few minutes, and I have finished. The Miller Ray——"

"The scoundrel! the villain!" cried Gilbert. "How dare you speak of him to me?"

"Because I desire to speak of him to *you*, and to no one else," answered Jasper. "If I leave this room deprived of the appointment I have now enjoyed for four years, I shall depart an injured man to my thinking."

"And what then, fellow?" asked Gilbert, loudly.

"Why, then, I will not answer for myself. Injured men brood over their wrongs; and I might do so over mine. I might be led to speak of what I would not utter even within this room."

"What can you say that I should care the world to hear?" asked Gilbert. "That to pay some youthful follies I was fool enough to apply to you; that you introduced me to your friend, the scoundrel Ray, and that I had to obtain from my mother the loan of a bracelet, which the villain sold, or pawned, or made away past recovery. You have been paid the sum I borrowed under that mysterious bond of yours. It was lucky for you, I fancy, that a closer inquiry was not made into that transaction——"

"Pardon me, Mr. Norwold, that would not be my story," answered Jasper, his lips livid with suppressed anger.

"No! what then, Mr. Jellifer?" asked Gilbert, speaking loudly as he had done during the latter part of this interview.

"I should say, sir, that wanting this money most pressingly you had come to me, who was too poor to help you, that you then sought the assistance of the stranger Ray, who mistrusting your ability to pay, demanded security. That by the aid of false keys you entered your father's house, that you returned with a bracelet, how obtained your dead father has declared, that one of a bunch of keys given you by Ray fitted your mother's cabinet, for the officer Higgler found the keys after a long search in your father's park, and at my suggestion. That you stood by and heard your brother accused of a theft which you could have disproved, and did not. This I might say, Mr. Norwold, under the remembrance of injuries, but which I will carry with me to the grave, if I am fairly used by you. Pray, sir, consider if I cannot serve you. Money if you need; secresy if you desire it."

During the culmination of this speech Gilbert's hand sought something in the drawer of the table at which he sat. At the conclusion when Jasper's voice and manner changed to their usual subserviency, Gilbert hurled behind him some heavy substance, and which the other did not affect to observe. Dreadful thoughts had passed through the mind of Gilbert Norwold; and many minutes were required to chase them away completely, as he walked to and fro without regarding Jasper Jellifer.

As soon as Gilbert could obtain sufficient command over himself to allow him to speak, he turned abruptly upon Jasper, and said—

"Who told you that disgraceful story? Was it Ray? It was that cold-blooded villain! Or were you a party to the whole scheme, Mr. Jellifer?"

Jasper protested that it was not until after Ray's conviction that he had been made acquainted with the circumstance, and when he had vainly urged the miller to disclose to whom the bracelet had been consigned.

Gilbert paused again for some moments, still pacing the room as though he were taking time to enable him to make his next inquiry.

"Did Ray—did Ray communicate this story—to my—to any one beside yourself, Mr. Jellifer?"

Jasper saw that the arrow which he had shot had struck over the barb, and was fixed for ever, and so he answered—

"You mean to Sir John? No, sir." That was a lie, and Jasper knew it to be so.

Gilbert paused in his walk, and beckoning Jasper to him, pointed to a small pistol lying upon the ground. "You see that instrument of death, Mr. Jellifer; you might have seen me cast it away some minutes ago. Can you guess why I took it from my drawer?"

Jasper fixed his eyes full upon Gilbert's, and said quite calmly, "Perhaps with the intention of destroying me, the sole depository of your secret."

"No," said Gilbert, "I am not so mad as that. I have thought again and again that a day might come when some voice, from the grave even, would proclaim the story of my shame and guilt as you have narrated it this day. I thought also, that should such a revelation ever be made I would not live, and that weapon was provided for my own death. I have heard my crime, my shameful crime, described with all its miserable details, and have cast away the instrument of death and dare to live. I have heard how terrible the story sounds from your lips, and will never hear it again if it be possible to buy your silence. You shall have all you ask, more if I have ever the power to grant it. Your interests shall be bound up with my own. I know I cannot touch you nearer, Jasper Jellifer. Let us meet as seldom as possible. Is this agreed between us?"

Jasper was a shrewd man, and saw at once that as his object was gained, he had better close the interview. "The confidence you place in me shall never be abused, Mr. Gilbert, and if I have spoken too plainly I hope you will pardon me. I am a self-seeking man I know, an unforgiving man I grieve to own, and had I left you with a sense of wrong, I know not into what I might have been betrayed. You have trusted me, Mr. Gilbert, and there is no power on earth, no temptation of advantage which can now make me unfaithful to your interests. Good day, sir."

Jasper bowed respectfully, and without waiting to speak to

any one, took his way homeward through the snow, which fell so fast that his footsteps were soon obliterated by the stainless flakes, and yet his track round about the house of Norwold could be traced for many years to come.

As Jasper left the room, Gilbert heard a low, rustling noise at the door which led into his mother's apartment, and on opening it he was startled to find her lying in a swoon close beside it.

"She has been listening," Gilbert thought. "What has she heard, I wonder? Enough I fancy to make her regret her meanness." He raised her up, and having placed her in a chair, rang the bell, which was answered by Lady Norwold's maid.

"Your mistress is not well, Jackson," said Gilbert, "I will send the housekeeper to you, and when her ladyship recovers let me know."

He made his way to the billiard-room, where some of the persons staying in the house were amusing themselves; wondering as he went why he had never divulged the truth to his mother, feeling how little he was disturbed now by the supposition that she had listened to the story told by Jasper. He had become less frightened at his sin now that he knew he had a sharer in the guilty secret.

More than an hour elapsed before he was summoned to his mother's apartment. He found her looking very pale, but exhibiting a constrained cheerfulness which he did not care to disturb by any inquiries, and neither of them referred to the event of the morning but in the most general terms.

The snow still fell fast and continuously, as some of the guests who lived near to the Hall arrived. It needs a warm-hearted friendship to take men and women from comfortable firesides on a rough snowy winter's night, miles away, to meet old familiar faces, and how much more to a formal dinner-party. The Norwolds were not surprised, therefore, that when dinner was announced as served, many of their invited friends were absent. Few trifles have a more depressing influence on an assembly than a dinner-table around which there are vacant chairs, and not even when the expected guests are despaired of, can the best Amphitryon rally the flagging spirits of his party. Lady Norwold seemed incapable of making an effort to overcome the effect produced by the absence of her friends, but looked more like the skeleton at an Egyptian feast than the proud mother of a son attaining his majority. She was still very pale, and every effort she made at conversation seemed painful to her. Her friends attributed her condition to disappointment at the absent, and kindly strove to cover her deficiency as hostess by chatter among themselves. Gilbert, also, was ill at ease, it was evident, but having his feelings more under control, he soon mastered his mortification at what his guilty conscience made him suppose, the intentional slight of his absent guests, rather than a necessity imposed upon them by the weather. And so passed the dinner until the family orator rose to propose the health of the youthful host, and as he was a man of many words, and set phrases, he repeated those fulsome panegyrics which we were wont to hear after dinner, and still read upon tomb-stones. The toast was drunk with enthusiasm by those assembled to do honour to the occasion. One only could not pledge the heir perhaps of Norwold, but there she sat with a fixed gaze and livid lips powerless to moisten them with the cool wine in the glass before her. Not even the shouts and clapping of hands which hailed her son a man broke her dreaming, and it was only when tears rushed from her heart into her eyes that she appeared conscious of her place in this, by her, long desired ceremony. None there doubted the cause of her tears and of the succeeding weakness. Was she not Gilbert's widowed mother? Had he not been the idol of her life, to whom she had offered up all the woman's love her heart contained? Was not this day one to be noted and remembered all her life long? Ah! yes, it was never forgotten until all else passed into oblivion with it. It was remembered daily, almost hourly, but in silence. No word recalled its morning or its evening in any after conversation with Gilbert; and when she had learned to pray, taught by her broken hopes and her chastened selfishness, she entreated pardon and blessings for her son.

There was mirth and to spare in the servants' hall, for those good men and women bear complacently enough the sorrows and mortifications of their masters and mistresses. Why should they do otherwise? They are not paid for their sympathies, and are soon taught "that service is no inheritance." There are exceptions to this teaching. Good servants, who reckon kindly words and actions as matters to be accounted for at the ending of each day, and just masters, who consider the services of an active and devoted youth as debts to be cancelled only by a generous care of a less profitable old age.

It was a Norwold custom to brew a hogshead of strong ale on the birth of a son to the house, and this brewage was not tapped until the infant arrived at his majority. This ceremony had been duly performed by the old butler, and the strong liquor produced in the servants' hall in a veritable black jack, which, it was said, had performed a similar duty when the first knight of Norwold won his spurs. The potency of the liquor was soon declared by the increased clamour which followed the circulation of the black jack, and at last it became necessary to conduct the head keeper (whose once curly poll had grown grey in the service of the house) to his cottage in the park. As he was led by his subordinates beneath the windows of the dining-room, he could not be restrained from giving vent to certain opinions which he entertained, but which, from prudential considerations, he usually kept to himself. The strong ale would be heard to-night, and Gilbert, who had returned alone to the dining-room, opened one of the windows to ascertain the cause of the riot, just as the keeper expressed himself to the following effect:—

"I say Mr. Gilbert bean't a Norwold. Not a bit on't. He don't care a brass farden for shooting, 'unting, or fishing, and he han't got a Norwold heart in 'um, I tell 'ee. Mr. Gerard was another guess sort of chap altogether! He'd a made the old pleace what it wor in his feather's time—that is, when his feather was young and I was a boy! I· tell 'ee what, Bill! Mister Gilbert is a bad 'un, and choused his brother as sure as my neam's Joe. I never emptied a horn to-night as I didn't say Mr. Gerard's good health until he cooms back again—and back he'll coom some day as sure as my neam's Joe——'' And then the tipsy mutterings of the old keeper were indistinguishable by the listening master, who felt a coldness about his heart that night—colder than the frosty air which had changed the breath of. the guests upon the windows into fairy forest trees—as he knew the tipsy man had spoken the truth, and that it would be repeated again and again, until it might be heard to his destruction. His first impulse was to dismiss from his service the ungrateful servant; but the question would be asked by his household, in Morden town, and at the market-table, why was old Joe the keeper sent away from Norwold Hall? and he dared not provoke the answer.

There had been merry-making also in the town of Morden, and the most noisy and the most intoxicated of the revellers was certainly Jasper Jellifer's ward, William Hayes. Jasper had done his duty honourably by the young satyr so long as he could control his conduct—all the neighbours said that. He carefully regulated his outgoings and incomings, and curbed his passion for drink, limiting his potations. Jasper managed this so adroitly that young Hayes vowed there was not a kinder, better fellow in the world than Mr. Jellifer. But when young Hayes came of age matters changed for the worst, and he was often seen in the mornings with bleared eyes and a flushed face. By-and-by his hands trembled, and rumours were abroad that the doctor had been called in to repair, if possible, the ravages of his debauchery. Young Hayes was seldom seen in the market-place, except on his way to one of the inns for his morning's draught, and which was frequently so deep that his steps were unsteady when he returned, although he rarely remained after mid-day.

At last the doctor was a very frequent visitor at Jasper's house, and then it was announced one day, to the surprise of no one in Morden, that young Hayes was dead—dead from drinking brandy continually.

Jasper's patience had been long worn out, and as he despaired of conquering the young drunkard's love of drink, he had retired from the contest, and yielded up to him the key of the cellar! Poor William Hayes, like mad Tom, "found ratsbane by his porridge;" for brandy was his poison, and he took it and died.

Jasper had not suspected, he said, the consequences likely to follow his own goodnatured imprudence, and would have taken this calamity greatly to heart, no doubt, had he not found an unexpected consolation. He was always a lucky fellow, and now he reaped the reward of the care and trouble he had bestowed on his late ward, William Hayes. The grateful drunkard had bequeathed to Jasper Jellifer all that he was worth, and which amounted, according to popular calculation, to nearly twelve hundred pounds. How all Jasper's windfalls fructified, blown down as they were at his feet, we shall see, if we have patience to wait for the end.

CHAPTER XII.

JACK SPRAGGATT, much to his credit, had been very unmindful of his sister's injunctions, and had frequently pleaded
the cause of his absent friend, without, however, appearing
to shake Lucy's determination in the least. He had not obtained the slightest admission that the proposal would have
been acceptable to her under any circumstances, but fraternal
love quickened the brother's perception, and he had satisfied
himself that the happiness of Lucy was absolutely dependent
upon a course of conduct opposed to that which she had
declared her determination to pursue. Jack was an obstinate
fellow when he believed himself to be in the right; particularly obstinate when he thought the best interests of others
were under his influence; and at last he determined to compel
Lucy to accept the only man he had ever thought her capable
of loving as a husband. Had he arrived at a correct estimate
of his sister's feelings? He was sure of that, as he had found
her frequently alone, and when her eyes gave evidence that
she had been weeping; and he knew that she had no cause
for any other sorrow than that which must have resulted
from the struggle which she had so nobly maintained between
her love for the absent and her sense of duty towards her
brother. Jack, therefore, resolved upon a course of action
which he knew would prove effectual in deciding this painful
question, and in order to avoid any controversy with his
sister he kept his plans to himself until it was quite beyond
her power to controvert them.

He then communicated them to Lucy by affixing to the wall of their breakfast-room a placard, headed

THE ELMS,

and whereon was set forth in varied types the startling announcement that Mr. Peter Mallett was instructed by the respected tenant of that very productive and eligible farm to sell by auction the remainder of the lease, together with all the stock, live and dead, farm implements, and household furniture pertaining thereto, without reserve, on the last day of the month following.

Lucy was not quite unprepared for this announcement, as Jack had latterly thrown out vague hints that he had a duty also to perform, and that he would not have the self-reproach of having sacrificed the happiness of his sister to a sentimentality which could be manfully overcome.

" You see, my darling," he said, smiling, " to what extremity you have driven me; and though no loving heart but yours will greet me in the distant land to which we are going together, I shall leave none behind me from whom a separation would be a continual sorrow. I confess that the first sight of that great bill sent a pang to my heart, but that has passed away; and the few regrets which will remain when I shall look upon this old house for the last time, will be compensated for a thousand fold, by the conviction that the beloved dead would approve an act which will pluck from my sister's life that ever rankling thorn—a love unsatisfied."

Lucy's head was resting on his bosom as he said this, and the look which filled her face when she turned it up towards his, told him that he had read truly the secret of her heart, and that she was as grateful as she was happy.

The little world of Morden was busy enough when the knowledge that the Spraggatts were to be sold up, became general, conjecturing, and inquiring as to the cause for such an unlooked-for event. The more the gossips discussed the subject the more perplexed they became, especially as Jack

always appeared to be in the highest spirits and the best of
humours.   More than one friend who had stood by the
Spraggatts in their recent troubles, were ready to help again
if that were needed; but Jack only thanked them from the
bottom of his full heart, and assured them that he should be
free from debt and have plenty to spare, when all at the
Elms had been knocked down to the highest bidders.   There
were, however, exceptional times when Jack was not so
cheerful, and when big sighs and grave looks betrayed the
latent pain which comes with a broken home.   There are
many living memories associated with household things which
make the insensate materials almost as dear as though they
had life and feeling, and one could sometimes resent their
rough handling, and indifferent estimate by the callous broker,
who sees in them only lots to be dispersed according to conditions of sale, leaving behind them a residuum of commission for selling to be paid by the purchaser.   Poor Jack
had more than one sharp struggle before he would consent
to surrender an old chair or table, or piece of ancient crockery
that had home legends tacked to it, and some few matters
were found to be too sacred to be permitted to pass into
strangers' hands, and were crowded away into Jack's little
counting-house, to be carried to the new home, wherever that
might be, giving infinite trouble, and costing ten times their
value in transport by sea and land.   They were held to be
more precious for their cost, and were worth the money
and anxiety, bringing back as they did for years and years,
pleasant remembrances of departed loved ones, and of the old
house at home.

Lucy shared in all these weaknesses, but knowing for whom
this great household sacrifice had been made, she hid her own
emotions from Jack, and went about her necessary work bravely,
not showing how hard it was to part with so many old familiar
things until the morning of the sale, when she prepared to
leave the Elms to stay with a neighbour; and then she lingered about the rooms which had echoed to now silent feet,

and to her own voice from childhood to that day, until she thought (but only for a moment), that the future should be indeed a bright one that could compensate for this severance, as it were, from a past so full of remembered happiness. She wept very sadly as she knelt down in the chamber wherein her parents had died, and repeated the simple prayers she had said at her mother's knee, as though she had hoped to hear that mother's voice blessing her again, as it used to do when she laid her down to rest.

Jack saw something of Lucy's sorrow, and avoided her—great, stupid, coward that he was—and went out busying himself in doing nothing particular, until Lucy was driven off in their neighbour's gig. He then went back alone into the house, and looked very red and flustered when he came out again.

The stock, both live and dead, had a good reputation, and the persons who came to purchase were numerous and respectable. There were plenty of idlers, also, for there are many people who flock to a sale, as others do to a funeral, and not always from the most charitable motives. If there were any present who came to rejoice over the dead fortunes of the Spraggatts, they must have been mystified to have seen how Jack bore himself. He cracked jokes with some, descanted to others all the prime qualities of his favourite breeds of sheep and oxen, and exhibited his samples of grain with as much cheeriness as he had ever done at the market-cross, and when prices were rising. He was selling himself off because it pleased him, and so thoroughly enjoyed the fun, that no doubt he could have mounted the auctioneer's rostrum, in the parlour, or its peripatetic substitute, the wheel-barrow, out of doors, and knocked down his own lots. It was customary, and perhaps, it may be so at present, to feed the competing buyers before the business of the day began, and Jack's guests were numerous and hungry enough. The slices of beef, roast and boiled, which disappeared were truly marvellous, and the home-brewed ale was neither weak nor sparingly supplied.

Many a timid man who had set a very moderate price on
some desired lot came forth a resolute buyer, and would not
be outbid by any one who dared to compete with him.   The
bold became more bold, and paid liberally for their entertainment by "springing a little," when good-humouredly taunted
by the auctioneer for "their want of speerit."

The small British farmer of other days was a dull fellow
enough when met at his plough-tail, or at dung-carting, or in
the harvests fields, as dull as the oxen he drove, or the beasts
he fattened.   He knew nothing of phosphates and sulphates,
and all the other great agents of agricultural chemistry, and
would as soon have thought of threshing by steam as going
up in a balloon to catch larks.   He was contented to farm as
his feyther had farmed afore him, and only knew that "plenty
of muck, plenty of crop."   He brightened up greatly on
market days, whether he was buyer or seller, and it was
difficult to dip your fingers into his leathern money bag more
deeply than was conducive to his own interests.   He worked
hard for his money, and generally knew how to keep it.   But
he was brightest at a sale, where he always made up his
mind to get a bargain if he could, and approached the object
he desired very charily, taking shy looks at it, and never
closely examining into its merits so long as a possible com-
petitor was at hand.   When he had satisfied himself of the
desirableness of the commodity, he showed no further interest
in it until it came under general notice, and then it was to
ascertain if others had as good an opinion of it as himself, and
an intention to purchase.   If he could say a word of dis-
paragement, he did so, and then mostly retired to the outer
circle, where he could catch the eye of the auctioneer without
attracting attention to himself.   His bids were always made
by winks, and when the offers of others had nearly reached
the limit of his estimate, he would thrust his hands into his
pockets and take a few turns to keep down his rising anxiety.
As the seller dwelt upon the last bid, he would return to his
station, and wait until the hammer appeared descending

finally before he winked again. He would then fix his eyes
on the competing adversary, until it was evident that he
would rather have pulled off his coat and fought out the
difference between them. When fortunate enough to have
been the purchaser, he usually gave his name with a blush, as
though he were ashamed of his bargain, or had been detected
in an act which reflected upon his prudence, and would
expose him to the small wit of the market-table. He had
bought a bargain, be certain of that, and was no more to be
blamed for his caution and cunning than the dowagers who
decry the cracked china which they have commissioned Mr.
Moses to buy at any sum.

The Spraggatt sale lasted three days, and the lots fetched
excellent prices, but no one, not even Mr. Mallett, the
auctioneer, could get at Jack's secret, for selling off; this, he
said, still remained "reserved" and was not to appear in the
catalogue.

The three or four days immediately succeeding the sale
were possibly the most painful Jack Spraggatt had ever
known! The cattle and other stock were driven away, and
the stalls and sheds left empty. Well, that had happpened
in part often enough before. The farm gear had been subject
to change and removal, so let that go! But those empty
rooms! Those terrible empty rooms which had been never
without some dear face, some old familiar object since he
could remember! There were dirty foot-prints and littered
straw then over the floor, and the bared walls were stained
here and there with the marks of picture, map, or weather-
glass! All gone to the homes of strangers, or to the broker's
shop in the market-place! Jack blinded his eyes with his two
closed hands, to shut out the desolation about him; but the
visions which he then saw, the phantasmagoria of what had
been in those old rooms, were more than he could bear, and
he walked out into the garden to the yew hedge, where he
had been wont to go when his dark hours were upon him.
And then he recalled his old struggles with the dreadful

skeleton which he had buried at last, and remembered who
had given him courage for the contest, and that he owed to
her all the happiness of his life.   Could he have remained
indebted to her for so much when, by the sacrifice of so little,
he could reverse their positions, and make her the debtor?
No! a thousand times no! and there was comfort in the
thought.

The last evening that Jack Spraggatt was to pass at the
Elms arrived, and closed in darkly and stormily.   Lucy had
gone to London to stay with some friends preparatory to
seeking her new home, and poor Jack might therefore be
excused feeling lonely and depressed, in spite of all his philo-
sophy.   His thoughts had been occupied with the past more
than with the future, and, at last, not being able to endure
his solitariness any longer, (it had been his own election that
he was alone,) he put on a rough coat, and walked towards
Morden.   The market-place was almost deserted, but the
lights shone brightly in the shop windows, more dimly perhaps in those of the thriving Jasper Jellifer than in any other,
as he had always been equally economical in oil and candles
as in most other things.   It was his shop, however, that Jack
entered, but he found only Mrs. Jellifer at home, and that
worthy lady's surprise was excusable when Jack asked for her
husband, as his visits to them had been of rare occurrence
at all times.   Jellifer, she said, was down at the mill, which
he had continued to tenant since Ray's forcible desertion of it,
although it was seldom that the old wheel made its pleasant
music.   It was principally used as a store-house for some of
the larger commodities in which Jasper dealt, and its once
pretty garden was now neglected, and its shrubs and evergreens allowed to grow wild.   Thither Jack Spraggatt took
his way, guided in some degree by the patches of unmelted
snow which lay in the fields and by the roadside, as the night
was dark.   When Jack reached the mill, there was a light
burning in the room where he and Ray had driven their hard
bargain some few years before, and he could see through the

uncurtained window that Jasper was engaged with some one within, whose figure, as he stood with his back to the window, was not altogether unknown to him. Without thinking of what he was doing, Jack continued a quiet spectator, and saw that Jasper was paying money, and for which he took no receipt. The man then turned to go, but as his face was partially concealed by the brim of his hat and a large necker-chief which he wore, Jack was no wiser than before as to his identity. The unconscious spy then became sensible of the impropriety he was committing, and being rather ashamed to be detected in such a position, walked to the door, as Jasper opened it to let out his visitor. The stranger threw a hurried glance as the light fell upon Jack, but contenting himself with observing, "A dark night, sir," walked away like one well acquainted with the road which led to the town. The voice, the figure, were both known to Spraggatt, but not sufficiently well to be recognised positively, and as Jasper made no reference to his departed friend, Jack, conscious that he already knew more than he ought to have done, was silent on the subject.

"You make your visits late to the mill, Mr. Spraggatt," said Jasper. "The last time I met you here, some years ago, I remember was at the same hour."

"You have a good memory, Mr. Jellifer," replied Jack; "and I remember also, you were in the garden when I came on business with that—man, Ray."

"And to-night, have you come on business with me?" inquired Jasper, without asking Jack to sit down, although they had entered the parlour.

"I have, Mr. Jellifer, though you may possibly consider what I am about to say a little impertinent, but as we may not meet again, for some time, I hope you will excuse me."

"Pray sit down, sir," said Jasper, evidently a little confused, and desirous, perhaps, to recover his habitual coolness, adding : "I am sure you will not willingly offend me."

"" Certainly not," replied Jack, " no honest man would be offended at what I am about to say ; and I am sure you are— you will not be."

Jack should have called Jasper an honest man, but somehow, he could not get the words to his lips.

"You remember, I am sure," continued Jack, " the painful circumstances which occurred at Norwold Hall, some four years ago." Jasper bowed. " You were fortunate to escape loss by what followed so soon after to the unfortunate man who then owned the mill." Jasper bowed again, but more slightly than before. "I have never been able to disconnect those two events with each other," said Jack, " although from the strictest inquiries which I have made, I have learned nothing to justify me in doing so." Jasper bowed again, but smiling as though he would imply, " he should think not ;" and Jack paused, before proceeding to say more, as doubting how to put the question, he was desirous to ask, inoffensively. He was not very successful when he did speak.

" It was evident to every one, Mr. Jellifer, that you and Ray had much business together, and trusted each other in many things."

" Mr. Spraggatt," said Jasper, " I must remind you that Ray proved to be a thief, and the associate of thieves—I only knew him as a neighbour, who bore a respectable name, and to whom I foolishly entrusted my hard earnings."

" All which you recovered, Mr. Jellifer," replied Jack, not caring to be hood-winked by Jasper's repudiation of Ray. " You came into possession of all the felon's property, and with that—as I hope—some of his secrets."

" I don't understand you, sir," said Jasper, in an offended tone.

" Pray don't *mis*understand me," replied Jack. " I mean that you saw him more than once after his conviction, and after Higgler—by the by, did he not leave you to-night when I arrived ?"

" No, sir," answered Jasper, flatly.

¦ "I am mistaken," continued Jack. "I was about to say, after Higgler had tried in vain to obtain the knowledge that I now seek. You know, or you may have heard, that Mr. Gerard Norwold honoured me with his friendship." Jack could not proceed for some moments. "I am ashamed of this weakness, but I loved him very dearly, and hold his memory very dearly also. I am about to leave England, perhaps for ever, and since I have taken my resolution to do so, I have thought again and again, that it would be a great satisfaction, to me and to my sister, if by any effort of mine his fair name could be restored to him."

"His family and friends have not been idle to discover the means of doing so. I am sorry to add, without effect," observed Jellifer.

"There is one person, possibly, who could do him justice?" said Jack, fixing his eyes steadfastly on Jellifer.

"What man?" asked Jasper, compressing his lips closely together, as though to restrain any exhibition of anxiety.

"Possibly yourself, Mr. Jellifer," answered Jack; "or if not you, the person who still has possession of the diamond bracelet, which, as there is a heaven, Gerard never had in his possession."

"How do you know that?" asked Jasper, earnestly.

"Because Gerard has said it, and he was too noble for falsehood. The man who holds that bracelet could prove it also, possibly. There might be some slight incident connected with his possession of it, which would cast a clearer light than has been yet thrown on that dark transaction. Are you the man?"

"I am not the man," replied Jasper, with pardonable warmth. "You do me great injury in supposing that I could be the man."

"Pray forgive me, Mr. Jellifer; I ought not to have encouraged such a thought; but as certain papers were found in this room that led to the terrible accusation of my dear friend, and as you became possessed of so much which had

been Ray's, I hoped that you might—— I mean that for
your own security—a pardonable fear of implication——"

"I might have been as bad a man as Raymond Ray. I
thank you, sir;" said Jasper, rising. "I have hitherto
borne an honest name, Mr. Spraggatt, and thought myself
secure from such an insult as you have offered me."

"I cannot recall what I have said, Mr. Jellifer. If I have
given you pain I am sorry for it. One question more, and I
have done. As you will one day have to answer for all evil
done in act or knowledge, I ask you if you know who does
possess that bracelet?"

Jack rose up as he spoke, and Jasper recoiled from him, as
though he feared some violence; but seeing that his questioner had no such intention, he answered firmly—and
truthfully—"I do not know. I cannot even guess who
had it."

"Then the mystery must continue unresolved, and a fair
name remain dishonoured," said Jack, with great emotion.
"It matters nothing to the dead, and little, I fancy, to the
living; and so good-by, Mr. Jellifer. Let us part friends.
Life is too short for evil thoughts or evil actions. Good-by,
sir."

They shook hands, and Jasper led the way to the door.
The night was intensely dark, and as they walked to the
garden-gate, a sudden light shone for a moment and disappeared.

"Was that lightning?" asked Jellifer.

Before Jack could reply it shone again, but now continuously, and when they turned to find the cause, they saw
that Norwold Hall was in flames. The first impulse of both
men was to run to the burning house, but Jack Spraggatt
went no further than the wicket which led into the park, and
from which he could see the flames through the avenue of old
trees, which now formed, as it were, a frame to the fiery
picture.

"What should I care if every trace of that house wherein

such wickedness has been done, should perish in the fire! Let it burn; and may the injuries inflicted within its walls be forgotten and forgiven! Strange! strange! that my last walk to my old home should be by the light of such a torch as Norwold Hall!"

Jack took the road to the Elms, occasionally pausing to look back at the fire, and listen to the clanging of the church bells, as they were rung backwards, the inharmonious noise awakening the early sleepers, and rousing the convivial sitters in the town of Morden. Very soon every man's face was towards the burning Hall, and women and children ran beside them to see the great house on fire; but Jack Spraggatt turned his back upon the blazing mass which lighted up the heavens, and cast his shadow before him on the pavement of the old High Street, and the pathway beyond it, almost to the porch of the Elms, on the last night he was to call that old house by the name of home!

CHAPTER XIII.

OLD FRIENDS IN A NEW WORLD.

"Tum to tea, untle Jack, tum directly, minute," cried a bright-eyed little girl, standing in the doorway of a log-house on the borders of the Bathurst country. An old English mastiff, the terror of the native dingoes, lying basking in the sun beneath the verandah which ran round the house, merely wagged his tail in recognition of the speaker, but half rose up when a full manly voice came pealing across the stock-yard in reply, as though the old dog was watching for the coming of his beloved master. None could doubt that the settlers were from England when they saw the neat garden filled with the prettiest flowers of the country, interspersed here and there with a few English exotics, which appeared to be cherished tenderly. The house and outbuildings were all of unsawn timber, and the great stock-yard was surrounded by palisades of a regular height, but only trimmed by the axe. Far away stretched Bathurst Plains, with here and there great growths of forest trees, then brown with their summer foliage. Beautiful birds!—but songless, alas!—flew about in the bright sunshine, whilst groups of parrots screamed at each other, hardly compensating by the brilliancy of their appearance for the horrible discord they created. The interior of the house was as cleanly and as orderly as any true Englishwoman's home is sure to be, and here and there were evidences of a better taste than is always to be found in the rude dwellings of the Bush. Four years ago the sole owner of this location had been George Warner; but he had taken to himself since then two partners, one for life, and the other a sharer in his toil and worldly gains, in the person of his brother-in-law, John Spraggatt. It was he who, in answer to his niece's summons, now came from tending cows, and horses, and bullocks, in the stock-yard, and toward whom the old mastiff bounded the moment he knew his attentions would be acceptable. No one meeting Jack Spraggatt now, in Morden market-place, would have recognised the smart young farmer of former days. His beard had been allowed to grow, and showed a productive harvest. His shirt was of blue flannel, and his breeches of strong drab cloth, fastened round his waist with a leathern strap. His boots were of horse-hide, with the hair preserved on the outer side, and the spurs attached to his heels were odd ones, and none of the brightest. Before entering the house he made his way to an outbuilding, and there completed a satisfactory toilet by the aid of a tub of water and a clean jack-towel. His hair and beard he arranged by the aid of a mane-comb, which he carried in the pocket of his flannel shirt, and then entered the kitchen where the tea was awaiting him. As soon as he was seated, his little niece Florence mounted his knee, and received a kiss through that great shaggy beard, which tickled her into laughter. Though Lucy—Mrs. Warner—was present at the table, its honours were performed by an elderly person who had held that position for the eight preceding years, ever since Warner had been in the colony, having come with him, old as she was, from her native England. She was called Nurse, and it was difficult to say who loved her most of that desert family. She did no household work now, but patched and mended when her old eyes would let her, and looked after the idol of the house, Florence, when Lucy was engaged in other domestic duties. Mr. Warner had gone down to the new town of Bathurst on business, and was not expected until late in the evening; so we shall have time to say something of him, and of what he has done since we parted with Gerard Norwold eight years ago, and when we learned that we should never hear of that dishonoured name again except in connection with the past.

George Warner had inherited all the good or evil pertaining to that banished son, and had vowed that his father's home should never more be his, but that in this new land he would raise up a house that should outvie in honour and repute any that could be found in England, although title should be wanting. To achieve this, he did not hesitate to accept the assistance of his mother's friend, his devoted nurse; so together they had come to this distant land, and had made a resting-place which God had blessed, until one poor exile's spirit wandered day and night back to his native land, and hovered round the dwellers at the Elms, growing bolder and bolder from the blessings which came every day, and at last it wrote down the earnest, passionate words to which Lucy had listened, and which made Jack Spraggatt part from all that bound him to the home of his fathers, so that he might bring two loving hearts together, and make all their lives happy for a time.

Lucy had not come undowered to her husband, and Jack had brought into the partnership not only money, but willing labour, and farming knowledge, and was one of the first in the colony to discover that gold could be really gathered from the backs of sheep, though the breed did not come from Colchis. He had brought with him two of the choicest animals of his herds, and their produce had helped to enrich him beyond his expectations. It was he who had worked about the log-house, and laid out the garden to resemble in some degree the one at the Elms, though there was no yew hedge to bring back the remembrance of past sorrows. But there is to be no more a Paradise upon earth, and occasionally thoughts of the old time and a love of the old land would come back to all, and for a while sadden each in turn.

The barking of the dogs announced the return of Warner, and all were glad to see that he was accompanied by a young man, evidently a stranger to the Bush. There was no mistaking the military air of the new-comer, and none were surprised, therefore, to learn that Lieutenant Hammerton was stationed at Bathurst, and had come over, on leave, to stay a few days at Ararat, as the location was called.

"I have been fortunate enough to discover in this gentleman the one who was so kind to me on my arrival in the colony," said Warner. "Nurse, you recognise our friend in Lieutenant Hammerton."

"Ah, bless me, yes!" replied Nurse; "we have spoken of you a hundred hundred times."

"I am sure you are very kind to remember such a small service," said the young man. "I assure you, madam," addressing Lucy, "I merely performed the commonest civility to a stranger."

"Not so," answered Warner. "You thought us poor and destitute of friends, and would have supplied both, my good fellow. Let me introduce you to my wife, who will be glad to entertain a civilised gentleman as long as his leisure or inclination will permit him to remain."

Lucy spoke a few earnest words in corroboration of her husband's invitation, and an ample supper was soon prepared. Jack had charged himself with the care of the horses, and having seen them carefully stabled and groomed by one of the men, joined the party. Of course the conversation went to the Old Country, and the young lieutenant did not hesitate to confess that he cared not how soon he returned home again.

"It is all very well for you, Warner, who are employed in making your fortune, to live in this desolate place; but I long, I confess, for the comforts and elegancies of a more advanced state of civilisation," said Hammerton.

"I can well understand," replied Warner, with a very small sigh, "that you miss much to which you have been so long accustomed that it has become necessary to your enjoyment of life; but we have projected our own future, and are happy and contented to work it out."

"For my part," said Jack, "I would not exchange our

free and independent life in the Bush for all the shams of what
is called society at home. One feels a sort of king in this
new country, and only regrets that it is necessary to slaughter
so many of one's subjects annually, even after shearing
them."

"I can believe *you*, sir," replied Hammerton ; "but when
a fellow has nothing but his pay to exist upon, and no prospects of increasing it, I would rather enjoy some of the privileges of my red coat, and take a little out of society."

Hammerton then recalled some of his pleasant experiences,
and dined again with hospitable mayors, and danced once
more with their pretty daughters, as he had done when his
first uniform was untarnished.

Jack Spraggatt would have taken exception to much that
Hammerton described as human felicity, but he was too considerate to say anything which might be distasteful to their
guest; whilst Lucy was pleased with their young friend's
good spirits and grateful remembrance of such small enjoyments as he had described.

"I think you and Mr. Warner are brave people," said
Hammerton, quite omitting Jack, " to squat down here, and
live as though you had been always used to such hard lives.
I know you have not—I see it—and I hope you may never
feel your life irksome. By Jove ! I don't think any amount
of gain would reconcile me to such an exile. I should look
at little missee there sitting on papa's knee, and think what
she might be in Old England, and what she must be in this
wilderness. There she would have access to all the refine-
ments and accomplishments which make a lady; here she
will be obliged to vegetate into the wife of some colonist,
like——"

"Me," said Jack, finding Hammerton's eye rest on him as
he paused.

"Well, without offence, yes—and a very good husband
you would make, no doubt, for a colonist," replied the lieutenant.

Lucy looked at her husband, and saw there was a shade upon his face as he gazed earnestly at little Florence. Perhaps she had seen it there before, as she rose instantly, saying, "Flory must go to bed now, it is long past bed-time; but she was promised to sit up for papa, and promises to little girls must not be broken." So, taking the child in her arms, she held its rosy lips to be kissed by the dreaming father, and to be tickled once more into laughter by Uncle Jack's big beard.

The conversation then turned upon the new discoveries made by Blaxworth, Wentworth, and Lawson, and the future prospects of the colony, occasionally varied by some of Hammerton's experiences with the convicts, and the remarkable prosperity of some who had worked out their term of servitude, and become men of wealth and character.

The party retired to rest early, and in the morning Jack started before the others had assembled at breakfast to attend to their distant stations, where they had large flocks under the care of hired shepherds, so that Hammerton was left to Warner for entertainment and amusement.

Throughout the two succeeding days their conversation frequently reverted to the Old Country, and Hammerton produced an effect on Warner's mind which for awhile disturbed him, and required the exercise of a strong will to control, if not to subdue, altogether; and it was well, perhaps, that the regiment to which Hammerton was attached was ordered home before much further intercourse took place between them.

The order of recall came very unexpectedly, and would have placed Hammerton and a young ensign in considerable pecuniary difficulty had not Warner proved his sense of the lieutenant's former kindness more substantially than by words. The time came when Warner was strangely reminded of this parting.

Lucy, with the eyes of love, had seen what was often present in her husband's mind, and, as Florence grew older, sought diligently to impart to her as much knowledge as she herself possessed; but the child was self-willed, and being petted by every one, was induced only with great difficulty to apply herself to her studies. Her chief delight being in music, Uncle Jack, by the aid of his fiddle, made her acquainted with the rudiments of that delightful science, and then by degrees she learned to sing from notes, and added greatly to the few amusements of the home in the Bush.

Lucy met with an unexpected adversary to her watchful care and endeavours to ensure contentment to her husband, in no less a person than old Nurse. As she increased in years, her mind became enfeebled, and, like most old persons, she would wander back into the past, and dwell upon the remembrances of her youth. She was never happier than when so employed, narrating to Florence stories of great people and grand doings, until the young girl began to contrast her own unvarying mode of life with the changeful and pleasurable existence of those whom Nurse had conjured up, as it were, like living things before her.

Lucy had often gently chided Nurse for this imprudence, but the forgetfulness or wilfulness of age made her a frequent transgressor. The consequences which Lucy foresaw, her brother Jack feared also, and at last their mutual anxiety led them to take counsel together frequently on a subject so deeply interesting to all.

As Lucy never encouraged Florence in a repetition of these recollections, she soon ceased to speak of them to her mother, but as she was continually the companion of her father in his rides about the location, she found in him a willing listener to the disguised legends of his own forsaken family, and much of his pleasant life began to assume the restraint of exile, and the regret of a forfeited position.

Jack was one day surprised as he sat at the kitchen window, making artificial flies for his favourite sport of angling, to hear old Nurse describe—though without using names—the family story, and to find little Florence had been crying from sympathy with her own representative. Jack was very angry, and later in the day was remonstrating with Nurse, when Warner joined them. Jack freely told him what had occurred, and urged him to request Nurse to be silent upon such subjects for the future. The appeal came too late, the seed was sown and grew slowly, very slowly, in the lonely Bush; but it was destined to blossom and bear fruit in a more congenial place.

From that day Warner was a changed man. Not much changed either; and had he been less beloved, it is possible that the alteration in him would have been unobserved. But the love which had left home and kindred, and had regarded five thousand miles across the sea but as a day's journey, to unite itself to another love which had come forth out of sorrow and injury, could not be deceived for a moment, and Lucy remembered her compact with her brother, and came to him to share her sorrow.

Poor Jack had a great, but not a quick head, and it required some days before he could devise a plan which appeared to meet all the difficulties of the case. He hit upon one at last, and it needed all his brotherly love to propose it for the consideration of Warner and his wife.

Warner had had one of the moody fits to which he was now frequently disposed, and had only recovered his usual good-humour when supper was over, and old Nurse had retired to bed. Lucy had given a slight preliminary yawn, indicating her bedward intentions, when Jack filled his pipe, and requested another glass of grog, having, he said, a matter of importance to speak about, and which he wished both of them to sleep upon before they gave him an answer.

Lucy's heart beat quickly, for she surmised that what Jack was about to say, had reference to the subject they had so often discussed in secret.

"I have been thinking, George Warner," said Jack, "that the time is come when we ought to extend our business, or dissolve partnership." Jack would not observe the surprise this announcement occasioned, but giving two or three puffs at his pipe, he continued—

"Our flocks are numerous, our other stock flourishing and productive, but most of our profit goes to the middle-men at Bathurst and Sydney, and that, I think, ought to be avoided."

"What do you mean?" asked Warner, as Jack took a sip of grog, and then drew one long breath at his pipe, and blew the smoke in a wreath towards the ceiling.

"My meaning is very plain," continued Jack. "I have seen for some time that our darling Florence," a slight pause here, "is growing out of Lucy's teaching, and that you both are aware of that. Now I propose (puff), taking that into consideration (puff), as well as the great amount for commissions we pay to the brokers and others (puff), that you, George Warner, should open a merchant's store either at Bathurst or Sydney (puff), and leave me to manage the location for the benefit of both." Jack puffed now so vehemently, that even his great bushy beard was lost in the clouds he emitted.

"Leave you here alone?" cried Lucy.

"Alone!" said Jack from his cloud.

"Oh, impossible!" said Warner. "Our life is dull enough as it is, but to live here alone—impossible."

"Not in the least," said Jack; "I shall prefer it. I want to see you and Lucy perfectly happy, and Florence (puff) properly educated, and that I have long seen can't be done here in the Bush. If you can persuade old Nurse to stay with me, so much the better for me and for Floey, and——." The smoke, or something else, got into his throat, and he coughed rather violently for a minute.

Lucy put her arms about his neck, and kissed him; and when she could speak, she said—

"Dear, dear brother, your clever plan will not do. Neither I nor my good husband would consent to such a proposal. To leave you here lonely——"

"I'm never lonely now," interrupted Jack; "and when my duties are increased a little, I shall not have time to think about myself. Now, go to bed, both of you. To-morrow is Sunday, so you can take an extra hour to talk it over; and if you don't come to my way of thinking, you don't deserve to have the care of such an angel as God has given to your keeping. Good-night; and go along, and don't leave out the grog bottle!"

Jack spoke so authoritatively, that there was nothing to do but to obey him, and he was soon left alone with his pipe, for which he felt a growing affection, believing, as he did, that parental love would overcome any scruples of Warner and Lucy, and that he should soon find himself like Alexander Selkirk, the monarch of all he surveyed.

He was quite right in his conjecture; but he did not succeed to the throne of solitude until many fireside parliaments had been held, and great firmness had been displayed upon his part. Old Nurse, strange to say, elected to remain in the Bush, fearing, as she told Jack, that if she should be taken where there were any old women to talk to, she should be disclosing the family secret, and so defeat an object for which such sacrifices had been made.

It necessarily required some time to make arrangements for the new state of things, and it was surprising what a deal of business Jack found for himself abroad. He was evidently schooling himself for the life which was before him, and seeking to accustom himself to absence from those whom he loved so dearly.

And this continued until within a few days of their departure, and then, poor, simple heart! he seemed not to be able to bear Florence out of his sight. He played to her the old tunes upon his fiddle over and over again, making her sing to him the songs which she had learned by his rude teaching, and which she promised never to forget—no never! He gave her a rude drawing of the station, which he had made, and showed her upon it where he should live and sleep, and asked her to look at it sometimes, and blow a kiss to Uncle Jack, which he was sure some good angel would bring safely to him in the Bush.

He was very merry, nevertheless, for he had calculated well all the consequences of their separation, and knew that to secure happiness to those for whom he was surrendering so much, he must not allow them to believe they had left behind them a sorrowful, because a lonely man.

When the drays and waggons which bore away those he held dearest in the world, had started for Bathurst, Jack ran to a little eminence which commanded the most distant point of the road, and stood there, waving his hat, until the last of the departing train could be seen, and then he threw himself upon the grass, and uttered words of prayer and thankfulness before returning to his own house; feeling, when he entered it, more desolate than he had ever done in his life before. His nearest neighbour lived some forty miles distant; and before Warner reached *his* home, twice that space would be between them. But they should meet again very often; for what were the eighty miles or more which would lie betwen them to such hardy bushmen as they had become. They would be with him again before a year had passed, and he would take a holiday when he could, and pay them a visit, to witness the happiness he had procured for them at some sacrifice of his own.

Old Nurse should now have a free use of her memory and her tongue, and he would live with her in the times that were gone, and with those who had had their joys and sorrows in them. And so it came to pass, and Jack sat a patient listener night after night, until he could repeat all the old stories word for word, although when Nurse was most fluent in speech and clearest in recollection, he would often let his thoughts wander miles and miles away, sometimes to the colonial town where Lucy, Florence, and Warner were; and sometimes over the sea, to the graves in the churchyard, and to the homes of living friends, tarrying longer, perhaps, with one fair woman, whose presence would have filled all his heart and lonely home, had it been decreed that their lives should have been passed together.

The Warners were faithful to their engagement, and came every year to pass a month at least with Uncle Jack, but not to listen to old Nurse's stories longer, for she soon passed away, and Jack laid her under the shadow of a large tree, but still where the setting sun could throw its parting rays upon the green turf which hid her dust. Faithfully had she discharged her trust, and a small marble stone bore testimony to her faithfulness, placed there by "her foster-son."

Matters prospered well at Bathurst with George Warner and Company; as time went on their names were known in the London markets, so that wealth came fast, so fast that the small colonial town was not large enough for its display, and the doting father thought of scenes more fitted to his child, of companions more worthy of her—station—yes, that was the word that ever and anon he heard in his waking dream.

CHAPTER XIV.

A BLUSTEROUS day in August was drawing to a close, and
the distant plains and surrounding forest-trees looked cold
and cheerless in their snowy covering, as Jack Spraggatt sat
down to his lonely meal of tea and damper. Strange contrast
to his early life, when it was a rare day that did not find some
two or three friends at his hospitable board, and rarer still to
have no familiar face to look upon,—no familiar voice to bid
him welcome. The rude kitchen of his log-house would often
fade before his eyes like pictures in a magic lantern, and
change to the snug parlour of the Elms; and shadowy forms
would glide about the room, and for awhile—a little while—
supply the places of realities. And then all would pass away
again, and he realised the place he occupied in this new land,
and almost wondered how he had come to have a part to play
there, so far away from all which had made his early life. He
often found most cheering answers from an approving conscience, which told him he had fulfilled at his own self-
sacrifice a duty imposed upon him and sanctified by death,
and that he had striven hard and successfully to leave his
father's name as honoured in his own land as when it came
into his keeping. It needed this approving voice, and something more, sometimes, to keep a good heart in the bosom of
the lonely settler, and Jack never refused to welcome any
comforter that came into his thoughts. "Lucy is happy, and
Warner is happy, and my darling pet has the promise of a
bright future, and I have helped them all a little," he would

think. "And I am, or ought to be, without a care, so prosperous as we are at present. I have buried that hideous
skeleton of debt, which made my life nothing but bitterness
—thank God for that—never to rise again to haunt me and
drive me almost mad. It is somewhat lonely, I confess, but
then I can command companions at my will, and read the
thoughts of such immortal men as Shakespeare, dear Oliver
Goldsmith, and Robbie Burns. Have I not the Warners'
visits to look forward to? Though there is the parting also,
when the house seems to have had a joy removed that may
not come again. Pshaw! I must put such a thought as that
in my pipe and blow it away in smoke. Now, Hephzibah,
bring another log or two, lass, and let us have a good fire.
Tell your husband to learn what the dogs are barking at, and
mind that the two shepherds who came in to-day have good
suppers and warm beds. Poor fellows! they've a rough time
of it in the plains."

The cause of the dogs' barking was not an unusual one at
that time in the colony. It was a convict who had obtained
his ticket searching for employment, which was not to be had
so readily now that the winter had set in. Jack had ordered
the man into the house, and more wretchedness than was
wrapped up in the rags and scraps of leather which composed the covering of the poor fellow, it would have been
difficult to have found, even in New South Wales. The snow
still clung to his matted hair and beard, and fell from him in
flakes, as he sought with his benumbed hands for the document which entitled him to be at liberty.

"Never mind your ticket, man," said Jack; "thaw yourself first, and then we will know more about you."

The man muttered his thanks, and almost crept into the
burning logs piled up in the chimney of the outer kitchen,
whilst the shepherds, themselves old convicts, eyed him with
curiosity, as though expecting to discover a former comrade.
The eagerness with which the fellow ate his food, told plainly
enough that his fast had been a long one, as no word was

spoken by him until he had satisfied his hunger, and then it
was to utter the briefest thanks, as he produced his ticket.
Neither of the shepherds could read, and as Jack was content
to look at the pass at a distance, not caring who the poor devil
was that had sought food and shelter at his house, the man
remained as much unknown as he was before the production
of his papers, and appeared to be thankful when Jack ordered
one of his shepherds to show him to his sleeping-place.

"If that wretched being could be paraded as he is, through
every town in broad England," thought Jack, "it might
deter the hesitating thief from risking such a life, and perhaps
frighten the boldest into a course of honesty. Transportation
is only a word meaning a sea voyage and long absence to the
prosperous rogue at home. Here it has other significations—
bitter misery, deprivation, lingering death! Terrible expia-
tion for violated laws which have been transgressed as often
from ignorance as intention. It will be well if Society, that
guards itself so carefully, can hold up a clean hand and say,
'I have done my duty to these children of sin, and so claim
a right to punish the offenders.' It is a noisome task to dress
the festering sore, but the good surgeon would try the experiment before he felt justified in amputating a limb. I fancy
there is room enough in this colony to make half the future
thieves of England into decent men, if Society would send
us the very young, and let us train them to be honest.
Poor devils! born thieves, bred thieves, believing detection
the worst thing in this life (and they know of no other),
what can await them but the gallows, the prison, or transportation? And there's no one to blame for all this—only
Society."

As Jack was not oppressed by any superfluity in that way,
he may be excused for this long soliloquy, the more so as
he knocked out the ashes from his pipe, and went off to
bed and slept all the better for his odd thoughts and his
good deeds.

The snow fell fast in the morning, and no man with a

heart in his bosom would have turned a wild dingo abroad if it had sought shelter at his hands. How could Jack, therefore, dismiss the poor wretch who had come to him the night before, although he had no need for his labour? He bade him stay, and saw logs in an outhouse, the interior of which could be seen from the kitchen window. As Jack sat opposite to it eating a warm and substantial breakfast, the convict pursued his work; but at intervals he would pause and press his hand upon his side and beat his breast as though to deaden pain.

"Bless my heart!" said Jack; "the poor wretch may be ill, and we've set him to earn his breakfast of scraps at work that may be torture to him. A pretty sermonising humbug I am." So he rose, and, opening the window, called the man to come to him.

The convict made haste to obey the summons, and again involuntarily, it seemed, pressed his hand upon his side.

"Tell me, my man," said Jack, "are you in pain?"

"I am, sir," answered the man; "in great pain."

"Then why the devil didn't you say so?" asked Jack.

The man shook his head to and fro mournfully, as he replied, "Ah, sir, for eight years I have had to bear pain both of mind and body, and know that I must continue to bear it without complaining. I might have told you, though, had I given it a thought."

"Why me," asked Jack, "more than any one else about here?"

"Because Mr. John Spraggatt is not known to me now for the first time. I knew you in the Old Country," replied the convict.

"Knew me?" said Jack. "I have lost all recollection of you."

"No doubt, sir; and no wonder," replied the man; "for what I have undergone must have made me more like a beast than the man I was. O Lord! what I have suffered during the last twelve years! It will be only transportation,

I used to think; *only* transportation! Better have swung twenty times, I have thought since I have been here."

"What is your name, man?" asked Jack, rather sharply.

"I have come many miles to see you, Mr. Spraggatt. I am Ray—the miller Ray, whom you knew at Morden."

Jack fairly staggered from the open window, he was so shocked at the alteration in that wretched schemer.

Ray saw the action, and, shrugging his shoulders, said, hoarsely, "I don't wonder at your surprise, Mr. Spraggatt, if it is that which makes you recoil from me. If it is from remembering my offences, you must think that I have paid a terrible penalty for them."

"It was surprise, Ray—it was surprise," said Jack. "I have no reason to cast a stone at you."

"Perhaps not,—perhaps yes," replied Ray; "but I have come here to see you, and to die, I hope; for I think there is that at work within, which will set me free again."

"Come into the house," said Jack; "come in here, and let me hear what you have to say."

"First of all," said Jack, when Ray had seated himself, "what can I do to ease the pain you seem to suffer continually?"

"Nothing, I have been told—nothing, I hope; for I do not wish to live," replied Ray. "I have been dying, I believe, for these eight months past; and I should not have made the long journey I have done, but hearing from a pal that you had settled here—your name is somewhat singular —I could not rest until I had seen if you were the same as I had known at Morden. It seemed that it would be like having a glimpse of home again."

"And have you still the desire to return to England?" asked Jack, rather surprised that such a wretched creature should have any other wish than the one he had just expressed; namely, to die out of the world.

"Had I such a desire?" cried Ray. "It has been the one hope that has sustained me through all the dreadful sufferings of my convict life. I have dreamed of it waking and sleeping, and have been made very nearly mad when I have fancied it to be an impossibility. When I despaired of it at last, this gnawing, killing pain came ; and I care not how soon its work is over."

The man evidently spoke with difficulty, and Jack proposed that he should rest himself for an hour or two ; in the mean time some more decent clothing should be found, and then he would see what could be done for the future.

Ray merely said "Thank you, sir," and followed the person who had been called to show him to a room in the house, where he could comply with Jack's proposed arrangements.

When Ray had left, Jack threw himself into a chair, and stretching out his legs to their full length, commenced an earnest investigation of the fire—that wondrous camera, more wonderful than the conjuror's boasted crystal, and wherein may be seen the mouldering relics of times gone by grow into life again among the glowing embers.

The business transaction at the mill, and the burglars' visit, Gerard's disgrace and the burning of the great house, all came back to him ; and he could not help a presentiment that much of the perplexity of the past was about to be removed by the death-stricken convict beneath his roof. Under this conviction he became very restless, going to and fro between the stock-yard and the house, almost regretting the sleep permitted to the wretched man who could reveal so much which affected his dearest friend, George Warner.

Ray was greatly benefited in appearance when he again entered the kitchen, where Jack awaited him, and very few words passed between them before Ray became absorbed in deep reflection, as though uncertain how he should commence to unburthen himself of the "perilous stuff" by which he was oppressed.

"I have sought you out—" he said at last—"I have sought you out as much for my own sake as for that of

others, whom I never intentionally injured, but who have
suffered very grievously from my silence, when a word or
two from me would have made justice a little more even-
handed. I did speak once under a promise which has been
shamefully broken to me. It matters little now when the
journey's so nearly over."

Ray then ran over so much of his early life as we already
know, and do not care to hear again, and until his appearance at Morden, as tenant of the mill.

"At that time I had resolved," he said, "to live an honest
life, having been bred a miller; but temptation came in my
way, and I could not resist the prospects of easier gains to
be obtained by a confederacy with other rogues."

"How came you to select Morden for your residence?"
asked Jack.

"Jasper's wife is, or was—for sometimes I think her dead
—my only sister; and when she left London to live at Morden,
I could not rest away from her, for she was the only one that
ever loved me in the wide world, except my poor mother.
Bless you, Barbara, dead or living!"

He paused for a moment or two and then went on.

"Jasper married her for the money she had, not caring how
it had been obtained, or from whom. He was always a lucky
man, and matters throve with him. He lent me money to
carry on my business as 'receiver,' taking a large share of my
gains, I need not say. He suspected, I fancy, that all was
not honestly come by, but he kept a quiet conscience by
asking no questions. That he thought I was playing a dangerous game I am satisfied, for one day he proposed that I
should execute a deed giving him power of sale over all I
possessed. I consented conditionally." ·

Ray paused, and a smile passed over his face, and his eye
twinkled for a moment at some pleasing recollection.

"Well, you know all that happened; how he claimed
priority of the Government, and succeeded in obtaining possession, although at that time I did not owe him a farthing,

having repaid all which he had lent me. Now comes one of my great grievances. Before I was sent to the hulks, I had an interview with Jasper Jellifer, and it was arranged—solemnly arranged, that Jasper should transmit to me, whenever I required it, the money due to me under that bill of sale. As soon as I obtained my ticket—three years ago—I wrote home to Jasper; but after waiting many weary months, no answer came. I wrote again to Barbara, and as yet no answer. I can't believe that Jasper would play me false, or that my sister, if she be living, would allow him to do so; and I have sought you out, Mr. Spraggatt, to learn if you know anything about my relatives ?"

Jack was sadly disappointed at this termination of Ray's communication, and therefore he briefly replied by telling him of his last visit to the mill, when he thought he had found Jasper with the Bow-street runner Higgler.

"Higgler!" cried Ray. "Curse me if I have not thought that possible, often—very often."

"What do you mean?" asked Jack.

"That Higgler was put up to much that he knew by some close friend of mine, and it might have been Jasper! If I were sure of that!"

Ray paused, and a dark shadow overspread his face, dark as the black thoughts in his mind. Jack cared little for this roguish conspiracy, if there had been one, his whole desire was to learn what Ray knew of the story of the bracelet.

"Ah!" said Ray, "I am glad I made a clean breast of that matter before I was lagged, although Sir John has not acted fairly by me."

"How so?" asked Jack.

"It was a bargain between us, that he should use his influence with the big wigs at home and out here to get me some respite from my convict labour; but when he had learned my secret, he dropped me altogether."

"Sir John died before you were sent away," said Jack, "the day after his interview with you at Newgate."

"What!" cried Ray, starting up. "Died! I remember well that when I had told him that Gilbert, and not Gerard, was the thief, he left my cell suddenly, and—died the next day! Good Lord! perhaps I killed him."

Jack had risen also, and, seizing Ray's arm with the grip of a vice, said: "Gilbert, and not Gerard, was the thief! and this you proved to Sir John."

"Yes," answered Ray.

"I see it all," cried Jack. "The old father's heart broke when he knew the injustice he had done to the noblest, best of sons. And did Jasper know of this?"

"Yes," replied Ray.

"The old scoundrel!" exclaimed Jack, quite beside himself with rage. "I'll go back to England, drag him into the market-place, and make him declare the truth upon his knees! Why was he silent?"

"Because he thought it his interest to be so. Jasper only knew the truth from me, and after the mischief had been done. You do intend to go to the Old Country again, then, some day?" asked Ray.

"Well, perhaps," replied Jack.

Ray paused, and then said abruptly, "Are you certain it was Higgler that you found with Jasper at the mill?"

"Nearly so," replied Jack. "Why do you ask?"

"Because I could never guess how he got so closely on my track, unless—unless Jasper Jellifer betrayed me. No, I won't believe that either—for Barbara's sake, I won't believe that."

Ray was evidently much moved, and walked up and down the long room some moments before he could continue to speak.

"Do you remember the night I bought your wheat, and the night after your sister's wedding?" asked Ray.

"Distinctly," replied Jack, "and that a burglary was attempted on each occasion. You kept watch the last time. I could swear it now."

"Quite right, sir, I am sorry to say; and on that occasion Jasper put the thought into my head by wondering some one did not attempt such a robbery. Higgler was put up to both the jobs, and would have grabbed me for them had we been successful. He told me so—and who told him, I wonder?"

Both Jack and Ray ceased speaking, each busied with the thoughts which this retrospect had awakened; and both continued silent until Ray was seized with an acute attack of pain, and, begging to be taken to his resting-place, the two shepherds were called, and assisted him from the room.

Jack was glad to be left alone, being perplexed as to the course he was to pursue. It was easy to take horse to Bathurst and communicate all he had heard to Warner, but what good was to come of that? Ray might not care to repeat what he had said, if he conjectured that it could be used to the disadvantage of his sister, for whom he had expressed such strong affection, even in his present degraded position; and it might therefore only reopen a wound in Warner's heart, which it was to be hoped had healed long ago. And yet, Sir John had known the truth before he died, and the knowledge of that circumstance would necessarily be a satisfaction to the injured son. So Jack resolved to find some business in the morning to take him to Bathurst, when he would seek an opportunity of communicating what he had learned to his sister Lucy.

The snow fortunately had ceased to fall, and a sharp frost succeeding, Jack resolved to make tracks for Bathurst, giving orders to his household that Ray should be cared for and left to his own discretion.

Jack was always a welcome visitor at Bathurst, and more so, if possible, when he came unexpectedly; and he was never so happy as when his darling Florence was by his side, combing his rough hair or singing one of the songs he had taught her in the Bush, or playing in the clumsiest way imaginable upon the only piano known to exist at that time

N

in Bathurst. He had hitherto found no opportunity of speaking to Lucy alone, and when he looked upon the happy group
of husband, wife, and child assembled in their pleasant home,
he feared he might prove the serpent that was destined by
his fatal gift of increased knowledge to destroy their paradise.
However, he had come nearly one hundred miles to tell Lucy
his story, and he could not return with it unsaid. So one
day, when Warner was to be absent from morning till evening,
Jack repeated all that Ray had told him, leaving her to determine what course should be pursued.

Lucy was greatly affected at her brother's communication,
and her reasons for being so were wifelike enough. Hitherto,
they had lived peacefully and contentedly in the rough,
young colony, desiring no other distinction than what their
own character and success procured for them, and Warner
appeared to have forgotten almost that he had had an ancestry
or could have claimed to be its head, had he not foresworn of
his own free will its advantages for ever. Might not this
tale make the past appear less dreadful? Might it not revive
desires which yet slumbered in her husband's breast, although
long thought to be dead ashes, making him regret the position
he had abandoned and stimulating him to regain it?

Her course of duty, however, was clear as light. Whatever
the consequence, Ray's story must be told to her husband,
and the result be left to that Providence which had never
failed her hitherto.

When Jack returned to his home in the Bush he found his
convict guest much weakened by an increase of pain, which
received but slight mitigation from the sedatives which he
had considerately brought from Bathurst, where he had had
the opportunity of consulting a surgeon.

Ray had been writing a great deal during Jack's absence, and
usually destroying one day what he had written the day
before. He said this, and declared it to be consequent on
what he had heard concerning Jasper's apparent intimacy
with Higgler, and which had disturbed him greatly.

"It is a dreadful thought, Mr. Spraggatt," he said, "to have on your mind, that all I have suffered should have come from the treachery of the man I did trust with my life."

"I might have been mistaken," replied Jack; "I only saw the person I thought to be Higgler for a moment."

"You only saw me for a moment in the moonlight, and yet you knew your man, Mr. Spraggatt," said Ray. "I wish I had never had these doubts of Jasper, but the more I think of the past, the more I suspect that he has sold me, or why no answer to my letters?"

"They, or the answers, may have miscarried," observed Jack.

"Yes, they may, and Jasper shall have the benefit of the doubt; but if he be not a true man, I may reach him in England from my grave, here in the Bush."

The business of the location called Jack abroad for some time, and when he returned, Ray had written over several sheets of paper which he had divided into two packets bound about with string, and fastened with knots. One was addressed

"No. 1.   Jasper Jellifer,
            England.
Which I shall never see again, R. R."

The other packet was superscribed, "If Jasper Jellifer, on the receipt of the packet addressed to him and numbered '1,' hands to you 200*l.* for your care and kindness to me in this time of great suffering and death, then this packet No. 2, is to be delivered to him also. Should he not comply with my rightful demand upon him, then this packet is to be opened by you, Mr. John Spraggatt, or by any one whom you may appoint."

"Keep these packets apart, sir," said Ray, "and should you ever return to the Old Country, honestly try what No. 1 will produce. If he does not do what I have requested, open No. 2."

Jack believed there was as little chance of one event occur-
ring as the other, when he locked up those packets in his
bureau, nor thought for one moment how the living and the
dead would be brought again together by the conjurations
written therein.

The disease which was at war with Ray's life marched on
slowly, silently, and surely to its ultimate conquest, and the
quietude of the sufferer's present existence made him more
sensible of the approaches of his grim enemy.

How lightly had he spoken and thought of death when
engaged in the whirl of pleasure, or in his struggles with the
mad misery of his suffering consequent upon his life of crime!
But now, when subjected to no exciting condition, except
physical pain, and left in the great solitudes which surrounded
him, to commune with his guilty self, how terrible appeared
the conqueror who was to lead him captive into the realms of
the unknown future. His early years had not been without
some religious training, and as it has been justly said:—

"Man is a religious being. He is everywhere a worshipper.
In every age and country, and in every stage, from the
highest intellectual culture to the darkest stupidity, he bows
with homage to a superior Being; be it the rude-carved idol
of his own fabrication, or the unseen divinity that stirs within
him, it is still the object of his adoration."

Ray was no exception to this teaching, and he began to be
anxious concerning that future which he felt to be as true as
the light and darkness of every day, and the growth and the
decay of every season.

Jack Spraggatt was a simple, earnest man, who had received
the divine truth as a little child, and his faith had grown with
time and all the changes brought by it; and so he strove to
be a teacher and a comforter to the miserable man who had
sought him out, to lay bare his miseries before him.

"Your last resting-place on earth is to be here," Jack said
one day when Ray had suffered greatly in mind and body,
"and death ought to be made welcome. It should be regarded

as the angel which releases our souls from the trammels of mortality, and opens the gates of a world where peace is eternal."

The struggle was long and difficult before Ray would acknowledge the truth of Jack's simple teaching, but conviction came at last, and when most needed.

It was Christmas-day, and the heat within doors was stifling and most oppressive, especially to the dying man, therefore Jack had had a couch carried out under the verandah. Ray had remained some time without speaking to the boy who had been appointed to attend upon him, and his breathing became more difficult every minute. At last he started up and with great effort requested that Mr. Spraggatt might be brought to him. Jack was sitting under the shade of the gum-tree which grew by old Nurse's grave, and anticipating that Ray's dying hour had come, instantly joined the sufferer.

"All is over, sir,—but I could not pass away without thanking you—that I die in peace." Ray had spoken with great difficulty, and a fit of coughing which succeeded, left him much exhausted.

"Those papers," he gasped at length—"I gave you—destroy"—he could say no more.

"I understand all you desire, and if I return to England, will endeavour to fulfil your wishes." Jack addressed a deaf ear, for Ray was dead. In the time to come Jack remembered all that had passed at this closing scene, and believed that the last words of the dying convict had had a better meaning than the construction which he had then given to them.

Jasper Jellifer, far away over the sea, in England, kept that Christmas morning in his counting-house (he had grown to be a thriving man, and finding Morden too small a place for his money-making ability, had settled himself in London) and there he counted his gains, and no windfall had prospered better or borne goodlier fruit than the produce of the goods and chattels and other effects of Raymond Ray, the convict miller then dying in New South Wales.

Jack Spraggatt had returned to the Bush some days before

Lucy had had an opportunity of speaking to her husband on the subject uppermost in her mind, as Warner had requested her never to allude to the past, unless at times when he himself reverted to it, and for a while she hesitated to disobey his injunction. Warner was greatly excited when Lucy told him the revelation made by Ray, and he uttered words of thankfulness on hearing that his father had been made cognisant of his innocence of the cruel charge which had driven him forth a wanderer. Again and again he asked Lucy to repeat the story which he connected with the account Jack had given him of his father's death-bed, and his anger against Gilbert and Lady Norwold, whom he presumed to have been acquainted with her son's iniquity, broke forth in more violent expressions than Lucy had ever heard from his lips before, and he more than once regretted the solemn vow he had taken to forego his claim to the inheritance and title of his ancestors.

Lucy avoided remonstrance, trusting that time and reflection would restore that contentment which had hitherto made their lives so peaceful and so happy. She thought that her expectation had been realised after a few days, and then she ventured to say, " Dear husband, have not our lives been such as we should choose to live again, if we had the power to recal the years which are gone ? What have we to regret ? Honoured as you are by all who know you, beloved by those who know you best, what more could inherited wealth bestow than that which you have achieved for yourself?"

"True! true, my dear Lucy," he replied. "There is nothing to regret in what I have abandoned. A new name in a new world is better than an inheritance tainted as it would ever have been in the old, for men are prone to remember evil of each other, and

> 'Calumny
> Will sear Virtue itself.' "

Gladly would she have believed that that conviction was ever in his thoughts ; but a love so complete as her own was far too watchful not to discover the slightest indication of any disturbing influence, and Lucy found many. They were only like passing clouds, but they served to cast a shadow upon the stream, although for a single minute. When Jack first told him of the destruction of Norwold Hall, Warner appeared to be gratified that the scene of his disgrace should have perished; but now, he spoke of the loss of the old place regretfully, as though he had latent hopes which might have found realisation in the home of his fathers, had the fire spared it. Sometimes, when they were alone, he would speak of what his daughter might become, could she take her place with her own lineage, until Lucy almost feared that he would in time repent that he had wedded her, so lowly born compared to the one he would have selected had he been less unhappy. Then came the remembrance of all their married life, when love was everywhere, and she reproached herself for allowing such an unworthy thought to have possession of her mind for a moment.

CHAPTER XV.

FLORENCE was now seventeen, and her character beginning to develope its tendencies to good and evil. She had much of her mother's firmness and gentleness, marred by a wayward-ness which sometimes became unamiable. Like most over-indulged children, she appeared occasionally to be deficient in affection to those who had claim to her most devoted love, and would rarely confess to the wilfulness which her own reflec-tion generally condemned. There were none to censure her —neither father, mother, nor Uncle Jack,—for to all she was ever the most faultless being in the wide world. Had she claimed the place which her father at times regretted she had lost, she could not have been more commanding, or more readily obeyed, than as the daughter of the colonist, George Warner. Poor child! she was not to blame for the infirmities of her character, petted and caressed as she had been. There was a little dross among the gold which the fire of adversity might some day refine away.

It was not surprising that Warner should have occasional discontents, the offspring of his early training and associa-tions, and he had been brave indeed to set them aside as he had done, until the provocation to their indulgence became very strong.

Florence one day ran into the room where Warner and Lucy were sitting, holding in her hand a newspaper from England, the possession of which she had secured by inter-cepting the clerk on his way from the counting-house.

"Look, mamma," said Florence, seating herself on her

mother's footstool, and spreading out the English newspaper on her lap. "Here is a story so like the one old Nurse used to tell me frequently, that I should not wonder if the persons are not the same, for she never could remember their names. It is called the 'Court of Chancery before the Lord Chancellor, *in re* Norwold,' whatever that means. 'This was an application by Gilbert Norwold, Esq., of Norwold Hall, in the county of ——, to be permitted to assume the title and entailed estates of his late father, Sir John Norwold. It appeared by the affidavits put in, that Gerard, the elder son of Sir John, shortly before his father's death, twenty-two years ago, was discarded by him for some cause not set forth, and that no tidings of Gerard had been obtainable from that time until the present, although diligent search and inquiries had been made in England and elsewhere. At the time of the said Gerard's departure, a coat and waistcoat, known to be his, were found on the banks of the river' (just as they were in Nurse's story,) 'and were thought to have been placed there in order to mislead the friends of the fugitive. It is now assumed that the said Gerard committed suicide, and that his body was carried out to sea.' In Nurse's story, the young man, you know, went abroad, and was married to a beautiful lady, and had a lovely little daughter. Do you think, papa, they could have been the same persons?" but Florence found that her father had left the room, and that her mother's face was pale, and that she was greatly moved.

"Papa gone? What is the matter, mamma? You are not well, dear!" said Florence, rising and placing her arms round her mother's neck.

"I shall be better, love, in a few moments; the weather has been so warm; and—please fetch me the smelling salts from my bed-room."

Florence hastened to obey her mother's request, and Lucy hastily seized the newspaper and read rapidly all that Florence had been reading. It was true! Gilbert Norwold was seeking his brother's birthright. Not waiting the return of

Florence, Lucy hastened in search of her husband, and found
him in his own room at the counting-house, reading the report
in one of the other London papers, and, as she expected,
greatly agitated by the knowledge of his brother's proceedings.

"The hardened villain!" exclaimed Warner; "with the
knowledge of the wrong he has done me, he has dared to seek
the reward of his infamy by supplanting me in my birthright.
How knows he that I am not biding my own time to claim
my rights, or that I may have children whom his perfidy has
not reached? He has not repented of his sin against me, or
he would have avoided rather than have sought to bear a title
which must always remind him of his crimes."

"It is always difficult for me, dear husband," said Lucy,
"to speak to you upon this subject, remembering as I do,
that by your love I have been raised up, whilst you, by what
has passed, have been driven from your higher place, and
that must be hard to bear."

"No Lucy, no. It was not hard to bear until now that I
know my dishonourable brother has sought to reap advantage
from his damnable treachery!" exclaimed Warner.

"That has only made endurance more difficult, dear
husband," replied Lucy, placing her arms around his neck;
"for I have seen, dear, again and again, that old feelings,
old expectations, old ambitions, come back to you when you
thought none could guess the cause of the clouded brow and
the heaving bosom, and the fixed eye that was looking back
into the past when you bore another name, not more honourable than the one you have made honoured; but still it was
yours by birthright, a legacy from a noble ancestry."

"Well?"

"What prevents you claiming again that which you regret
so much to have abandoned?" asked Lucy, calmly.

"Lucy!" cried Warner, looking at her with surprise;
"you, also, wish to have your true place in the world? You
wish me to claim my own?"

"Your words seem to upbraid me, dear husband, because I would have you consult your happiness, not mine. What should I gain by the exchange? Nothing, for hitherto I have been a most happy wife, a most happy mother. The yeoman's daughter would not be so regarded as to have her happiness increased. With you it might be otherwise. You might realise some of the bright dreams of your youth, you might take your place among your equals, and add new lustre to a name known already in the annals of our country. Take counsel with yourself, and if you decide that duty requires you to press your claims to distinction, or if you believe that your life would be made happier by the change, be resolute, and do at once what you elect to be the better for your peace."

"And do you counsel this, Lucy?" asked Warner.

"I counsel only contentment."

"And you, should I resolve upon this change—are you prepared to give up all which has hitherto made the happiness of your life?" he asked.

"All!" replied Lucy, and kissing his forehead fondly, she left him to his own reflections.

They did not meet again until supper-time, and then Florence resumed the subject which had been occupying her mind all the evening.

"Do you think, papa, those are the people old Nurse spoke of? And if so, will the elder son not claim his title and fortune?" asked Florence.

"I think not," replied Warner, in a calm, grave voice. "Nurse did not tell you all. Nurse did not tell you that once upon a time, when the devoted wife believed that her husband regretted his lost position, that regardful only of her husband's happiness, she urged him to regain what he had so long abandoned, although she believed, and truly, that those who would then have been her husband's friends would have looked upon her coldly, perhaps contemptuously, as an intruder amongst them, and that her place might have been apart from his, for whom she had left home and kindred, and shared the privations of a struggling man. Self-sacrificing, truly loving, she forgot all that pertained to her own future in her regard for him and his unsettled fancies. And it was not until he saw all this, and reflected how they had hitherto made their two lives one, hoping, loving, sorrowing, and rejoicing always together, that he crushed out the last spark of those old remembrances which might have been fanned into a flame, and burned out the record of an oath solemnly sworn and hitherto faithfully fulfilled."

Florence noted not the love that was in her mother's face, or the tears which flowed from her mother's eyes, but said—

" You are a very naughty papa to defend such folly. I am sure if I were the young girl, I would never forgive those who prevented me being a lady."

Miss Floey then went to her piano, and played away with more emphasis·than was consistent with proper expression. Possibly her energetic fingering proceeded from inefficiency, possibly from a little ill-temper.

Uncle Jack had been expected to make one of the family party on Christmas-day, but he was, as we know, away in the Bush, keeping Christmas like a Christian man, by the side of a dying sinner. The Warners were disturbed at his absence, the more so, as there had been one of those terrible droughts which, at intervals, visit New South Wales, decimating the flocks and herds of the settlers; and it was feared that Jack was detained by home anxieties. Warner had disposed of his share in the location to his brother-in-law, and the loss would, therefore, have to be borne solely by Jack. Warner sincerely wished it had been otherwise, as he had done so much to increase the value of the property, that it seemed ungrateful to sell him a loss; but he found when Jack arrived that he had taken his disasters very easily, and looked forward to the next year to compensate him, repudiating, with a hearty laugh, Warner's offer to bear a share in his ill-fortune.

"Not a shilling, my dear boy, not a shilling," cried Jack. "Next year I will have the stock-book as full as ever. Next year I have two or three new experiments to carry out that will astonish, not only the natives, but surprise the 'cutest of settlers. Next year I shall build a new location, with some European improvements, which have become necessary since Floey has grown a young lady, and prefers a piano to Uncle Jack's old fiddle, when she comes to visit him."

And so the next year was to bring many changes, and one or two that Mr. Spraggatt did not contemplate when enumerating his own projects.

There were letters from Madame Letty, sister Letty, who married Mons. Fichard. They usually came twice a year, and were always welcome, seeming to bring with them a breath from the Old Country. Her husband had been fairly prosperous; and though she was childless, her married life had been pleasant enough.

"Mons. Fichard had," she said, "been not in the best of health of late, and had resolved, therefore, to return to his native Paris, where he had a manufactory, and be content with an agent in London."

Letty was very pleased with this arrangement, as she had spent a month or two every year in that gay city, and coveted its pleasures. All this is small news, but "trifles make the sum of human things;" and Letty's contributions were destined to produce greater results than she had contemplated when inditing them. Aunt Letty was a great favourite with Florence, who often expressed her wish to know her, and to hear from her own lips about the gay balls, the plays and operas, accounts of which usually occupied some pages of her long epistles. These letters Floey would carry to her own room, and read over carefully, contrasting their vivid descriptions of Letty's amusements with the humdrum existence she led at Bathurst.

Thus, as small birds carry little seeds from which grow great plants, Aunt Letty's letters implanted desires and fancies which cast a shadow for awhile over more lives than one.

The postscript of one of Madame Letty's communications contained her new address in Paris, and concluded with these memorable words:—

"And, oh! my dear Lucy, if I could only see you, and your dear husband, or my darling little niece, whom I love so much, or dear, old Jack, whom I love more than all of you, in my *maison*, I should be *so, so* happy."

Florence loved her aunt more than ever.

Florence rarely spoke with her mother, though loving her very dearly, of her girlish interest in these pleasant descriptions of Aunt Letty, as their conversation generally terminated in a little maternal sermonising, which was not always agreeable to the young lady. With her father it was otherwise. He listened to her "pretty prattle" with a smile, and would often entertain her by recitals of his own early experiences; until Florence wondered how he could have abandoned such pleasant society for a lonely home in the Bush, or the little less dreary residence in the money-grubbing town of Bathurst.

But Uncle Jack was even a better listener than papa, as he not only had recollections of similar events, but sometimes spoke as though a time might possibly come when the Old Country should be revisited again, and all the fairy tales they had told to each other be realised. Had the postscript to Aunt Letty's letter put that into Uncle Jack's head? and into Warner's also? for as the three elder people sat together one night, after Florence had gone to bed, the conversation turned upon it.

"I almost wish it were possible——" said Warner, thoughtfully.

Lucy and Jack awaited elucidation.

"I mean, that I wish it were possible for Florence to have for a short time, and when she is of an age to profit by it, the opportunity of better studies and better society than she can have here."

Lucy thought that the old story contest was about to be resumed, and shook her head reprovingly, smiling as she did so.

"No! no!" said Warner, understanding her meaning. "Never more, I have said that. Nevertheless, as I do not promise to spend all my life in the colony, I should wish Florence to be equal to any European society we may choose to cultivate."

Poor Lucy's heart sank within her, and she looked towards Jack for comfort. None came, however, for he said——

"I have thought the same, Warner, very often, and could never see my way to the accomplishment of such a desirable state of things." Lucy's spirits revived, only to be more cruelly depressed, as Jack added—"until now."

"Good gracious, brother," Lucy always called him brother when he was a little out of favour. "You must be mad to think of such a possibility."

"Nay, nay," said Warner; "let us hear what he has to suggest. Hermits, like Jack, have bright revelations made to them, and more time for reflection than we busy town-folk. Florence is now rather more than seventeen, and a voyage to Europe would bring her nearly to eighteen. She is a clever girl, and would know how to profit by example and instruction. Letty has expressed a wish to see us——"

"Letty," cried Lucy, colouring deeply, "Letty is a kind, loving woman; but surely you would not infer that she is a better instructress than myself?"

"Of course not," replied Jack, taking a long pull at his pipe. "Not *herself*; but living as she does now in the most refined city in the world, she could procure the best masters and mistresses, and so have Florence instructed."

Lucy, like most other mothers on similar occasions, declared that she would not hear of such a proposal; and Warner, like

most married men under like circumstances, entreated her to
talk calmly over the matter, as he had had thoughts in the
same direction.

"Your sister," he said, "is in a good position, we know
something of her husband's family, and if she would undertake the charge of Florence, it might—mind, I only say it
might—be desirable to let the child have the advantage that
Jack hints at."

Jack had done more than hint; and if ever Lucy had felt
a real anger against her brother, it was at that moment.

"I really cannot consent even to discuss such an absurd,
such a cruel suggestion. Florence is neither ignorant, nor
ill-mannered; and for the station she is *now* expected to
occupy, will be accomplished enough. Pray, say no more."

"Very well," replied Jack.

"Indeed," continued Lucy, in spite of her own injunction
to silence—women rarely know when it is dangerous to pursue
a defeated enemy,—"indeed, if such an arrangement were
desirable, how could she be sent to Europe? Not alone,
surely? I am the only person who could be sent with her, if
you thought me sufficient protection on such a voyage."

"True," replied Warner; "I had never thought of that!"

"Nor I," said Jack, again adding—"until now."

"Very well. Then such being the case, it is useless to
continue the subject."

Lucy could not help it. "I should be glad, very glad, if
Florence could have the advantage of better teachers than I
am. It might possibly be agreeable to her in after life,
especially should papa determine to return to England; but
women of moderate acquirements are generally equal to the
occasion, and rise with their position, and I have no doubt
but Florence would do the same."

Jack puffed away at his pipe, and Warner stirred his grog,
allowing Lucy time to regain her usual composure.

Jack saw that she had accomplished what to her was not
a very difficult matter, and he then ventured to say:

" My dear Lucy, as you seem to have acknowledged that what I suggested was rather desirable than otherwise, had it been possible of accomplishment, you don't think me mad, and are not angry with me?"

" No, you dear old goose," replied his sister,—" not now, but I own you did vex me at first. You men are so inconsiderate where women are concerned, and you would have shipped poor Floey off like a bale of wool, and put her down in an invoice."

The two men laughed good-humouredly at their defeat, and the matter was at an end—so Lucy thought.

The long-looked-for rain came at last, and Jack Spraggatt was in great spirits, although it kept him a prisoner indoors during the greater part of the day. He employed himself in writing to his sister Letty, preferring the counting-house to the parlour for the operation, and never told any one what he had done, or why he had posted the letter himself.

Nothing more was said in open council about the educational project, although Warner and Jack, it must be confessed, meanly discussed the subject at odd times when they were together; but Lucy had mentioned such a formidable obstacle to its fulfilment that it seemed to be impossible of realisation.

Jack's Christmas holidays were at an end, and despite the rain, he set off for his lonely home in the Bush, being more excited at parting than was customary with him. No doubt the welcome rain had something to do with it, as every hour's fall was worth a head or two of cattle, and they were not to be neglected after the losses occasioned by the long drought.

When he had been fairly gone some four or five hours, Warner was surprised to receive by a messenger a letter, directed in Jack's handwriting. That stupid Bushman had a great objection to personal communication whenever he had to ask a favour or to offer a service, and as he now wanted to do both, he had had recourse to pen, ink, and paper.

o

The letter ran thus :—

"MY DEAR WARNER,—The conversation which we had on the subject of Florence's education has never been out of my head. I have thought of it night and day, until I have come to the following conclusion and determination.

"Lucy, you, and I are all of opinion that there could be nothing more desirable for our darling's advantage than the suggestion *we* made; but Lucy very properly mentioned a difficulty, which I now fancy can be overcome. This bountiful rain will make the matter easy. I reckon that I am worth at least 8000*l.*, and as I have no debts (thank God!) I am an independent man for the rest of my days. My next neighbour is my old townsman of whom we used to talk in days gone by, and, as you know, one of the richest men in the colony. Now as this glorious rain will put him into good spirits, as it has done me, I intend to call upon him in a few days and offer him my location just as it stands—stock and block, and I know he will be glad to purchase. Having completed that bargain to our mutual satisfaction, I AM DETERMINED to go to Europe; and if you will do me the favour to entrust our darling Florence to my care, I shall be the happiest Uncle Jack in the new world or the old. My own DETERMINATION nothing shall change. I shall communicate all my great schemes for next year to the purchaser of my location, and so nothing will be lost to the colony by my secession.

"Now, dear Warner—dearest Lucy, consider over again our talk concerning the future of our darling, and make a parental sacrifice for her life-long benefit. I know I am a selfish old fellow in asking this, because I shall not have to part with her as you will have to do; but I am sure if I were in your place I could bring myself to the separation, knowing how much she has to gain by it.

"I wrote to Letty when I was at Bathurst, proposing that *we* should come over to her. She will be delighted no doubt, and by the time her answer arrives in the colony all can be prepared for our departure by the next ship.

"I have nothing more to add than I have already said to you, so with love to you all,

"Believe me your affectionate Brother-in-law,

"JOHN SPRAGGATT."

There was an end of the great difficulty! There was the little one with Lucy to be surmounted; but as all her life she had made small sacrifices for those she loved, this greater one —the greatest she had then been called upon to make, either as sister, mother, or wife, was accepted also—and humbly putting her trust in the One who had supported her through other trials, she consented to part with more than half her heart.

Letty's letter came in due time; it was full of loving welcome, and Jack sold himself up a second time to gratify a love which had grown stronger than common, because of an earlier one which he had known years ago. Florence was delighted at times when anticipating the approaching change; at others she thought it would be impossible to part from those dear ones who had made her life so happy. Nor were Lucy and her husband without their alternations of joy and sorrow when contemplating the separation from their child; and when the parting hour arrived, and Florence was gone, they were dearer to each other than ever they had been throughout their wedded lives.

O treacherous sea! that smooth as a mirror hides beneath thee unfathomable deeps, and dangerous shoals, and hidden rocks to make wreck of so many, many brave ships, less treacherous art thou than the sea of life, where there are deeps, and shoals, and rocks, but where shipwreck is often nearest when the sun shines brightest, and the breezes sigh odorous with the breath of flowers.

CHAPTER XVI.

GILBERT NORWOLD PROVES THAT A BAD SON MAKES A BAD FATHER.

THE events which occurred in England from the time that Gilbert Norwold attained his majority have now to be regarded. The property he inherited under the will of his father, and the settlement of his mother, was not very considerable, although it was sufficient for the moderate requirements of an English gentleman. Gilbert was what is termed a man of pleasure, but he combined with his own unrestrained enjoyments, an almost miserly care of his money, and bought his selfish pleasures as cheaply as possible.

He made no friends, and sought few associates among persons of his own station in society, nor was his morose and selfish disposition likely to invite advances from others. The few persons of his acquaintance were, therefore, somewhat' surprised when it was announced in the *Morning Post* that Mr. Gilbert Norwold had married the only daughter of a country banker, reported to be very rich, and possessing considerable county influence. The marriage had been one with which strong affection on either side had had little to do, as the lady had given away her first love to one whom her father had rejected, and who paid the penalty of his presumption, for loving in his poverty the rich man's daughter, by the abandonment of his native land, and hard service in India. So, having parted with the great treasure of her maiden love, there was only left a gentle, amiable woman, who passively yielded up her future hopes to the will of her father, and he had decided to entrust them to the keeping of Mr. Gilbert

Norwold. What Gilbert's consideration was in seeking this union, it is very easy to guess, and to express by one word, "Money;" and as that could be obtained with no particular objectionable contingency, by his union with Laura Ravenshaw, he married her. Ready cash and formal settlements supplied the want of mutual love; and gay dresses, merry bells, and great feasting, made the wedding-day appear a happy one; and there were lookers-on, struggling with many of the difficulties of life, who silently envied the more prosperous fortunes of the young bride and bridegroom, as their neat travelling carriage rolled away from the banker's door.

For some time this union proved to be, not a happy one certainly, as some doting men and women estimate wedded happiness, neither was it altogether unhappy, as neither husband nor wife had brought much expectation of affectionate recognition from each other. Gilbert went his way as it pleased him best, with no regard or inquiry as to the pleasure of his wife, and she, too indifferent as to the pursuits of her husband, was rarely disturbed by a course of conduct which a more interested woman would have construed into neglect. When her son was born, she felt that a blessing had come into her home, although his birth had brought her loss of health, and consequently greater estrangement on the part of her husband. It was well for her that she had found this comfort, as an unexpected cause of great sorrow and disunion came with the death of her father.

The settlement which had been made at her marriage provided for the payment of certain moneys, when the banker had no further use for his wealth, but as an elder son would inherit from his father, the money thus secured was to pass to any second child living at the time of the mother's death, and failing such issue Gilbert became sole inheritor, provided he should survive his wife. The old banker had been a clever schemer and manager, a driver of hard bargains, and a bold speculator during his lifetime; but like many other sharp adventurers, he had ended in failure so complete, that

simple men wondered how he had contrived to die in the
odour of respectability.

The compact, therefore, between Gilbert Norwold and
Laura Ravenshaw—they had called it marriage—was at an
end, at least so far as he was concerned. All the promises
which he had made at the altar were cancelled in his mind
by the failure of the banker to keep the covenants of the settlement, for which he had sold his liberty, and there was in
no corner of his heart one hidden love to whisper a word of
kindliness or consideration for the mother of his child. He
had been wronged, deeply wronged, where he could feel
injury the most, by the dead father of his wife, and he
revenged himself upon her by as much domestic tyranny as
he could exercise without interfering with his own convenience. He made ostentatious retrenchments of expenses,
and dismissed one or two servants immediately necessary to
the comfort of his wife, whose declining health required
more than ordinary attention. "This great loss," he would
say, "must be met by economy, and if that is disagreeable to
you, you must only blame the old rogue, who has occasioned
it." This was a bitter thing to hear, as Laura loved her
father, despite the one cruel act, which had seemed, at its
committal, sufficient to cancel all her former obligations; but
she remembered that she had known a happy childhood, and
a girlhood when money had been lavishly expended with the
desire to compensate for the sorrow which he had occasioned
by the rejection of her first lover. She could not understand
the chicanery of which he was accused; but believed that he
was subjected to the injustice which usually is meted out to
the unfortunate; and so she loved his memory still, and
trusted that when the first hour of disappointment had passed,
her husband would forgive, if he could not forget, the injury
he had sustained.

She was mistaken in Gilbert Norwold. The world, he
thought, had revenged itself upon him for his own misdoings,
and having suffered persecution, alas! for him, and those con-

nected with him, he had "not learned mercy." Day by day,
whenever they had been together, he left her with some new
taunt to bear her company through the many lonely hours, of
which her life was composed, and, but for the companionship
of her little son, her lot would have been miserable indeed.
As her health continued to decline, he declared his intention
of giving up their house in town altogether, and arranged
that she should have a simpler home at a watering-place, thus
removing her from the very small circle of visiting friends,
and which had grown less since the disclosures at her father's
death, and the more limited expenditure permitted to her in
consequence.

She went, therefore, into the solitude of a populous watering-place, where she had no acquaintance, and as Gilbert's
business matters—so he said—kept him much employed in
London and elsewhere, she rarely had other companionship
than her own small household supplied. It was not wonderful, therefore, that Edward, her little son, became invested
with all the love of her whole woman's soul, and in her plans
for his future she forgot the sorrow and the sickness which
surrounded her. As his growing intelligence found utterance, she seemed to need no other society, and her days
ceased to be wearisome, except when some childish ailment
made her associate with it the dreadful possibility of death
stealing away her precious treasure. How she would watch,
then, that little face, as though seeking to learn from the
pallid cheek or the fevered lip, the approaching danger, and
by her silent prayers seek to preserve to her the only solace
of her almost widowhood. With what thankfulness and
increased love, it seemed, did she receive him back again
from that perilous chance wherein his life had been engaged,
and hardly came to laugh at her own fears when experience
had taught her how slight had been the peril. But one was
at hand who would prove to her as cruel as death, and do
his work in part.

The boy grew into a fine sturdy fellow, and received such

mental culture as he was capable of obtaining at a small
school devoted to children of his age and condition; and
Laura would watch his going and returning with a glad
heart, for she knew that he would be a bright man, and
would fight as bravely for his place in the world as he did at
school, for he brought home evidences of his class victories,
and upon one occasion, a swollen nose and a reddened eye,
obtained in a gallant skirmish in the playground.

Laura, for a moment or two, hated the little hero who had
left those marks upon her boy, but forgave him heartily when
she learned that "he was the best fellow in the school, and
had given in after the tenth round, and was coming to tea the
next evening, if mamma pleased to let him."

Why chronicle such simple instances of a mother's love,
when the maternal eyes which may honour these pages with
their regards have read them in their children's lives a
hundred times, and never thought them worth recording?
They are here set down in sorrowful remembrance of her,
who, having known them to the full, had the pretty book
wherein they were to be found torn away so rudely, that her
eyes grew dimmer daily from her tears, and until she closed
them for ever.

Gilbert Norwold had been away in Germany for some
months, and on his return to England came to his family,
bringing with him nothing which made them happier.
Edward had been studiously taught to love and honour his
father, but children are stubborn learners in the matter of
the affections, and remember no lessons that have not been
practically illustrated. A cold kiss, short questions, and curt
replies, were all that Edward received when his father came
or left him, and the boy soon lost all recollection of such
brief courtesies, and returned the love of his father in the
same proportions as he had received it. He was to receive
a proof of his father's care, which, as it might be conducive
to his after good, produced in the mind of the boy a sense
of injury undefined, yet poignant, which never was entirely

effaced, but did its evil work in time to come. This would not have been the case had after-reflection been able to trace in the severity of the act, the hand of parental love seeking to direct the growth of a cherished object, and had he known that a mutual pain must have been inflicted in the process. It was not thus, however, that Gilbert Norwold did his fatherly duty. It was harshly, coldly—even brutally accomplished, and it did the work it was, perhaps, intended to do.

"He had," he said, briefly, "made arrangements to send Edward to school in Germany."

"Alone?" asked the terrified mother.

Of course, to be left alone, although he would make the journey in care of the proprietor of the school. The father had made every inquiry as to the treatment of pupils and course of education, by which the boy would have the chance of becoming a scholar, and of learning that self-reliance which made more than half the success of a man's career.

If this dreadful resolve had been only hinted at a little—a very little time before, so that Laura might have realised the prospect of such a separation by degrees;—if it had then been named as a project to be acted upon hereafter, when her reason could have held some conference with her love, and been brought to acknowledge the necessity for the sacrifice which was asked of her, there might have been some hope that the proposal would have been heard with patience, and possibly assented to with resignation. As it was, she repelled the outrage, and drawing her boy to her side, she said:—

"Gilbert, you cannot have the heart to do this thing! You have been a cruel husband to me for years past, but I have borne all—have I not?—patiently and obediently. You have shut me up here away from the few friends who cared for me, and left me to pursue your own courses unrestricted and un-questioned. I have not complained. You have told me you have suffered great wrong at my father's hands, and you have weighed your conduct to me, and to this child, against the lost money. I said let it be so! If that will expiate my father's wrong, let it be so! Throughout that time I have had but one consolation, and a great one it has been truly. My love for this boy has sustained me when nothing else could have done so, and I should have died, I doubt not. You would now take him from me for no justifiable reason. You would send him away, and I—and I am never likely to see him more on this side the grave."

She paused from exhaustion, whilst Edward clung to her, never removing his eyes from her face, and never forgetting to his life's end the sorrow he then saw in it.

"Have you done, madam?" asked Norwold, apparently unmoved.

"No! I have not told you all I have to say. I see, at once, that I am complaining to a heart of stone, and shall not move you to show me and this child any compassion. Let that pass. The law gives you no right to take my child from me, and nothing but brute force shall separate us. If you will resort to that, I will appeal to the law, and make public the wretched life I have led at your bidding, to be made utterly miserable by what you propose to do. Now I have finished."

"I am glad to hear it," answered Norwold; "and now listen to me. If you think to deter me from following any course which I think it my duty to pursue, you are mistaken, madam. I believe it to be my duty to send that boy from your teaching and your indulgence, and to have him brought up as a man and a gentleman. I shall take the course I consider best for the accomplishment of my views, and to-morrow morning Edward goes with me to France, and thence to Germany. Now I have finished."

He placed his hat upon his head, deliberately arranged his cravat by the glass, and then walked out of the room, closing the door gently after him. His footsteps were heard in the street marking slow-time, as though he were perfectly composed, and Laura saw from the window that he was proceeding to the beach. She saw that he sat down upon the shingle, and after a few moments began to cast stones into the sea, as though he had no grave thoughts in his mind, and was satisfied with that childish amusement.

Laura then carried her terrified boy into her bed-room, and having kissed him passionately, removed the traces of tears from his face and her own. Taking from her jewel-case its valuable contents (her father's gifts), and placing them in her reticule, she proceeded with much deliberation to dress Edward as for walking, and then put on her own bonnet and shawl, and all this without speaking a word. When their *toilettes* were completed, she kissed the boy again, and said :

"Come, my child."

"Where are we going, mamma?" asked the lad.

"I don't know, dear," replied his mother. "I have not quite decided. God will guide us."

They went out into the busy town, and made their way to the coach office, where they learned that the afternoon coach to London started in an hour. Laura secured two inside places, giving the name of Lauriston. Nothing could have been more calm and collected than her manner, even when she saw Norwold pass the shop where she was waiting the departure of the coach, and enter the hotel nearly opposite. She accepted that incident as an assurance that her flight to London was less likely to be discovered by her husband. The coach started at last, and it was with difficulty that she could reply to the boy's inquiries concerning the objects they passed on the road, until the second change had been made, and she fancied they were secure from pursuit. Until then she had feared that Norwold might have returned to her house, and been curious as to her absence. She needed not to have disquieted herself, as that gentleman was quietly taking his dinner, and remained over his wine until late in the evening; when, having a regard for his digestion, he slept where he had dined.

When Laura arrived in London, she ordered a hackney-coach and proceeded direct to the house of her husband's agent, Mr. Jasper Jellifer, to the utter consternation of that self-seeking person. He had, as we know, left Morden, and was now engaged as a commission agent, and dealt in everything that promised to yield him a profit.

"Mr. Jellifer," said Laura, "you are, I see, surprised to find me here; but I have come to town very unexpectedly, and, having been away from London so long, I venture to intrude upon you."

"Oh, no intrusion, madam," said Jellifer. "None in the least. Does Mr. Norwold know of your coming?"

"Not at present," replied Laura, curtly. "I must trespass upon your kindness for a bed, and to-morrow I will tell you my business in London."

Jellifer was in a quandary. He knew pretty well that his employer, Mr. Norwold, and his lady, were not the most attached couple in the world, and he was fearful of placing himself in some difficulty by receiving the wife unknown to her husband. He, therefore, stammered out how much pleasure he felt at being of service, and retreated to consult Mrs. Jellifer, who, with the quickness of her sex, instantly surmised that there had been some domestic difference, and with natural curiosity, was anxious to know all about it, especially as she could see no damage to Jasper from affording a night's shelter to the lady and child of their excellent and honoured employer, Mr. Norwold. Besides, Jasper would become master of the situation, should there be any mystery on foot, and she knew enough of her worthy help-mate to be certain that he would find a way to turn such a position to his advantage. Laura, however, was provokingly uncommunicative, as her only purpose in seeking Jellifer was to obtain a shelter for the night, intending in the morning to ask the assistance of a friend of her late father, and whose place of business only was known to her, as it was there she had been taken when she signed her marriage settlement. In her terror and her simplicity, she had overlooked the danger she had incurred by carrying her dove into the nest of the hawk.

During her sleepless night this thought occurred to her, and she became impatient for daybreak, when she might redeem the mistake she had made, supposing the Jellifers to be base enough to betray her to her husband, should they suspect that she had left home without his consent or know-ledge. The morning came at last, but with it the con-sequences of the excitement of the previous day and night, and the poor fugitive, exhausted in mind and body, was incapable of further exertion. Fever succeeded, and then as Mrs. Jellifer sat by the bed-side, she listened to mutterings and delirious utterances which told her almost all the truth of Laura's flight and intention.

The course of Jasper Jellifer was clear enough to him when he had heard his wife's revelation. He started instantly to Mr. Norwold's chambers in the Albany, arriving there shortly after that gentleman, who had posted up to London directly the flight of his wife and son came to his knowledge. The face of Gilbert had almost a fiendish expression as he listened to Jellifer's communication; and without staying to partake of the refreshment which he had ordered, he returned with Jasper to the house, where his wife was lying unconscious even of her own suffering. When Gilbert stood beside the bed of the fever-stricken woman, whom he had sworn to love and cherish, it is only the truth to record that he looked upon her unmoved, and without a feeling of pity. His stubborn, selfish nature felt no remorse, and he found his justification in the reflection that her own act had produced the result he now witnessed. Jasper was ordered to procure the needful medical aid, concealing the patient's name and condition, and then conduct the boy to the Albany, where some person should be waiting to receive him.

For some days it was thought that Mrs. Norwold would succumb to the fever, as her weakened constitution was adverse to her recovery; but she improved at last, and when consciousness returned, her first inquiry was for the boy.

She listened to Mrs. Jellifer's reply without any visible

emotion, and when the physician came again he shook his head despondingly, and said, "Something is very wrong indeed."

For days and days the poor patient continued to lie almost in a stupor, and when at length "the shadow of death" passed away, she appeared to have forgotten all things, even her child. At last, when death, the merciful, came to release her spirit, the cloud over her mind seemed to pass away, and with her saddened face turned heavenward, she murmured the name of her boy, and died.

In due time Gilbert Norwold took his son to Germany, and as there was no longer a dear mamma at home, Edward was contented enough to remain with the really kind schoolmaster and his wife, who, knowing something of the history of the past, strove to win the love of the little fellow: and as children are grateful receivers of kindness, they soon succeeded in their pious object, receiving, in return, almost filial affection and obedience, through the twelve years that Edward remained under their charge, as he continued to reside with them after he had entered the University.

Norwold saw Edward occasionally when he paid holiday visits to Germany, and their correspondence was regular and at appointed intervals—that was all which passed between them—so that the father gained no place in the heart of his son, as he never sought it, but left him to remember always the miserable day when he clung terrified to his mother's side, and looked up into her face, and noted the agony, fear, and sorrow then depicted upon it. When Edward grew to know the meaning of all that he then saw and heard, remembering his mother, his mind became filled with angry thoughts which he never tried to restrain.

The incision made in the rind of the sapling grows into a scar as time progresses, and nothing can efface it.—WAIT FOR THE END.

CHAPTER XVII.

THE *diligence* from Havre was half-an-hour behind its time,
and as Madame Letty and her husband had anticipated the
hour appointed for its arrival by full thirty minutes, their
excitement was intense when the loud cracking of the driver's
whip, and the thundering rumble of the stupendous convey-
ance, announced that the long-looked-for had come at last. The
expectation depicted in the faces of M. and Madame Fichard,
however, gradually faded away when · the *coupe, banquette,*
and *rotonde* disgorged themselves of their passengers, and no
one resembling Jack Spraggatt and their unknown niece presented themselves. Unless, perhaps, the rough-bearded man
who was speaking most execrable French, and claiming a
multitude of packages partly by words and partly by muscular
demonstration, could be he, and the pretty slender girl who
seemed to have lost herself in wondering at all she saw,
could be Florence Warner.

"Il est à moi, I tell you!" said rough-beard. "Re-
gardez-vous mon nom on the trunk, you fool. John
Spraggatt!"

It was he!

"Mais non, M'seu," replied the porter. "Il est Mademoiselle Warner!"

That must be Florence.

"Tout le même! Tout le même!" cried Jack. "Je
suis Mademoiselle Warner aussi—that is, I'm her uncle;"
and turning round to corroborate the assertion by an appeal

to Florence, he was surprised to see her folded in the embrace
of a plump lady, who was supported in her turn by the
arm and large cotton umbrella of a pursy Frenchman, who
waved above their heads a white beaver hat of considerable
dimensions.

" Good gracious!" thought Jack; "Letty can't have
grown to that size, nor can M. Fichard have swollen to
that figure in twenty years!"

In a moment his doubts were removed, as Madame and
M. Fichard transferred their embraces to his own portly
figure, and when Monsieur impressed a brother-in-law's kiss
upon the sunburnt cheek of the colonist, his blushes fairly
illuminated his beard and whiskers.

Jack's first impulse was to knock down his affectionate
relative; but, remembering that it was the custom of the
country, he contented himself with rubbing his face, and
giving in return a shake of the hand which left the receiver's
fingers powerless for a few minutes.

Letty carried off her niece forthwith in a *fiacre*, leaving
her husband and Jack to follow with the luggage, and to
satisfy the host of clamorous porters, who had all done
nothing to assist in its transfer from the *diligence* to the
voitures, which were now driven away to M. Fichard's
residence in the *Champs Élysées*.

The route from the *Messageries* was through some of the
best streets in Paris, and Florence was entranced with the
wonders which she saw on every side. The grand houses,
the beautiful shop, the stately public buildings, the noble
Places, the gay dresses of the people, all combined to fascinate
and surprise her, She was indeed in the Fairy Land of
which she had dreamed so often; but oh! how unmeasurably
it exceeded all that she had conceived of this abode of pleasure! What she had heard of it was true, then! and how
she loved that dear Aunt Letty, who had, like the good
godmothers in her fairy-books, called her over the sea from
that drowsy Bathurst, to share in the delights which abounded

everywhere in this happy city. And then, when she was almost dizzy with succeeding novelties, how grateful was the change to the green trees and flower-beds of the *Champs Élysées*, and the groups of happy children keeping long holiday under their shade—now filling the swings and roundabouts—now spending countless *sous* in lemonade and gingerbread, whilst their white-capped attendant *bonnes* plied their needles, or chatted to some gallant soldier, who, released awhile from his duty to Mars, was devoting himself to the service of Cupid, until lured away by some eloquent mounte-bank or juggler, or *primâ donna* of the *café concerts*.

The *fiacre* stopped at one of the lofty houses near the *Rond-Point*, and Florence could hardly believe that she heard cor-rectly when she was told that there her home was to be so long as she pleased to make it so. There was a shop for the sale of furniture on the ground floor, and M. Fichard occupied the *premier* and *deuxième*, a domestic arrangement which some-what surprised the young colonist. The other apartments were distributed, as they usually are in French houses, among lodgers, who rarely have any intercourse with each other. The only person with whom the Fichards were acquainted was Herr Dortz, an old Teuton, who professed to teach French, English, and German, to any one desirous of acquiring those languages at 3 frs. a lesson. He lived in the capital of this domiciliary pillar, and which would have been called the attic in this common-place England.

There was no doubt how welcome the visitors were to their hospitable relatives, and Jack had a long battle with the Fichards before those kindly people would consent to make terms for Florence's future residence with them. They pro-tested, entreated, resented, but all to no purpose. Jack was firm as a rock, as he had promised Warner to make a fair arrangement, and if M. and Madame Fichard refused to allow him to fulfil his mission, why he should take Florence to England, and place her in some boarding-school. This idea was positively revolting to M., Madame, and Ma'amselle, and

P

so the Fichards accepted the hard conditions on which they could retain their niece, and Jack Spraggatt had his way. The delayed recognition of this delicate treaty had not been permitted to interfere with their enjoyments, and Florence had been taken to more wonders, and had heard and seen more pleasant things than she had ever believed the great world contained. Letty was an admirable *chaperone*, as time had not destroyed her own relish for such agreeable excitements; and some staid guardians might have paused to consider, whether she was quite the right person to be entrusted with the charge of a young impressionable girl, whose mind had to be directed and formed, coming, as it were, from the nursery life of the new world into the dazzling fascinations of the Pleasure metropolis of the old.

If Letty were not the most proper guide and teacher, Jack Spraggatt was the last man to discover it. The long years of absence from each other had made him love Letty more than he had ever done before, and to see Florence so happy in her new state blinded him to any dangers that might lie hidden among the flowers about her path. Such reflections might have come to him had he been permitted to have remained a looker-on for any length of time, but the first mail which followed him from Bathurst brought news that Warner had met with a serious accident, and that he requested Jack to return by the next ship in case of need. This painful intelligence—so far as her father was concerned, had to be kept from Florence, and she parted from Uncle Jack, believing him to be a very unsettled naughty old fellow.

"Ah, Florence! dear Florence!" said that maligned individual, "when next we meet it will be to put the great sea between us no more, I trust. May God guide and guard you until that good time comes, and ever afterwards."

A good ship and a skilful mariner left little to fear for Uncle Jack in his long voyage back to the new world; but who could say with such a frail bark as Florence Warner, and with such a pilot as Madame Letty, what course would be steered, or what haven they would make?

Florence soon perceived her educational deficiencies, and therefore set to work with a will to acquire the French language, not, however, under the tutelage of Herr Dortz, but assisted by one of the best masters of Paris. The old German was content to teach her his own language, and his report of her capacity and assiduity was equally favourable with those of her music and dancing masters, so that when the letters of Florence were read aloud in the home in the distant colony, Warner and Uncle Jack were delighted at the wisdom of the course they had advised and followed, and Lucy endeavoured to be satisfied also. She was not always successful, for she feared that her love and watchfulness might still be wanting, to chide with gentleness, or to direct with prudence her susceptible and wayward child. They barter to a disadvantage who exchange for the loving care of a perfect mother any other earthly promise, though it may lead to a throne.

Time mowed among flowers, and Florence gathered them up for a long summer year, and until she was nineteen—sweet nineteen. To keep her birthday, and to give poor Herr Dortz an opportunity of taking baths for the obstinate rheumatism which afflicted him, it was determined to spend a week at *Enghein les Bains*, six miles from Paris; and because it was a very pleasant place in summer time, when balls and *fêtes* were of frequent occurrence. The change of scene from the white glare of the streets of Paris to the beautiful valley of Montmorency was acceptable to all, and the numerous amusements of *les Bains* moderated the transition from the gaieties of the city, and left nothing to be desired or regretted.

In one of their morning strolls, Herr Dortz had the pleasure of meeting a former pupil, one who had benefited by his instruction some six years ago in Germany, and this chance recognition was evidently gratifying to both.

"My bubil M. Edward, my dear bubil Edward," said Herr Dortz, speaking what he was pleased to consider English.

"He has com to *les Bains* for a day of pleasure, and he has not found it. Shall we not help him to find what he has com to seek? and ask him to be of our barty?"

The Fichards were not the churls to reject such a proposition, so M. Edward was invited to join in an extemporised pic-nic, and a visit to the *Hermitage,* where once resided Jean-Jacques Rousseau. The little party had been increased to nearly a dozen, by the adherence of some acquaintance of the Fichards, and as they all brought good spirits and easy tempers to the sylvan *fête,* the day passed away so merrily that Florence was surprised to find the daylight going. It is true, that for nearly all the latter part of the day, she had been listening to M. Edward's jokes and stories, and snatches of song in French, German, and English; for, as in duty bound, he had been the cavalier to Aunt Letty and herself. All the way back to Enghein the German and M. Edward interchanged old pleasantries with each other, as though the pupil had so much youth in him that he had lent part of it to his old master. To dissolve immediately such a pleasant union as the little party had made that day, would have been folly, and therefore it was resolved and carried unanimously, that they should all meet at the ball later in the evening. All were faithful to their tryst—the ball commencing at the rational hour of eight. Mr. Edward proved as good a dancer as he had been a talker, and Florence could not refuse him when he asked her for the third time to become his partner in a *quadrille.* As every one had come there to dance, and all carried out their intention to the full, they were satisfied when the clock struck eleven, and the tired band followed their example. Oh, what a moon shone forth that night to light the happy revellers to their homes, and the chaste goddess would not have looked down thus benignly had there been anything to censure in mirth harmless as theirs. Would that cold moonlight ever change to an unextinguishable flame consuming all remembrance of duty, and of willing sacrifices made through years of love?

M. Edward's day of pleasure had been so satisfactory—of course, because it had renewed his intimacy with dear Herr Dortz,—that he resolved to continue for the rest of the week at Enghein, and try the baths also, in case, at any future day rheumatism should be his portion. A bad reason, says the adage, is better than none ; or so lame an excuse, M. Edward, should have condemned you to solitary confinement, until all but your old preceptor, had departed. Three short—how very short ! happy days passed away, and then M. Fichard being compelled to return to his business in Paris, the little party embraced where permissible, and otherwise made their *adieux*, going their several ways, and taking with them some of the sunshine of the past to brighten many a shadowy hour in the time to come.

The next lesson which Herr Dortz attempted to give Florence should not have been charged in the account, as Aunt Letty came into the room and continued all the time usually devoted to study, talking over the events of their pleasant holiday, and commending Herr Dortz for having introduced such an agreeable addition to their party as M. Edward, whose surname, by the way, had never been mentioned. Herr Dortz could not for the life of him recollect it, as he had always called him Edward when he was under his tutelage, but he would ask him when he called again, if Madame wished it.

He had called, then ?

No doubt of it, and had even proposed for a course of reading, in order to refresh his German. There was nothing surprising or unusual in such an incident, and yet Florence felt the blood mount into her face, as she said involuntarily, "Indeed!" Herr Dortz was proud of his old pupil, grateful, perhaps, for the proposed employment, and he talked so glibly and earnestly of his good qualities and acquirements that, as we have said, the German lesson was forgotten, although the whisperings of a new language was possibly heard by one of the listeners.

As M. Edward descended the stairs after his next visit to Herr Dortz, he stopped at the *premier* landing-place, and rang the bell at M. Fichard's door. The ladies were abroad, and therefore he left a card inscribed Mr. Edward Norwold, No. 6, Rue St. Honoré.

Aunt Letty was vexed not to have been at home, the more so as the name—not a very singular one—set her wondering whether he was any connection of the Norwolds she had known years ago. But for that circumstance we question whether she would have pressed M. Fichard so earnestly to call the ensuing day, and ask M. Edward to favour them with his company to dinner.

À la bonne heure! The young gentleman was luckily within, and the invitation was one of the most agreeable that could have presented itself. Herr Dortz, too, was invited— poor fellow! he ·had rarely any engagements—to meet his pupil, and at six o'clock the party of five sat down to a small, well arranged dinner, made additionally agreeable by the interest all had in each other.

"The sight of your name," said Aunt Letty, as the dinner and conversation progressed, "carried me from France to England, as I was born at Morden."

"Morden! Morden!" said Edward, "I rather fancy I have some recollection of that name—but it has been my father's pleasure to allow me to visit England once only, and that for a very short time, since I left for Germany. I was then quite a child."

"There was a family of your name living at Morden," continued Letty, "and I thought you might have been a connection."

"Possibly I am," replied Edward; "but for some unexplained reason I have been kept away from all my family connections, and having only very painful recollections of my childhood, I have been contented with my exile, and shall be more so since you have admitted me to the pleasure of your friendship."

Aunt Letty acknowledged such a compliment with the sweetest smile and most graceful bow, although she felt that Mr. Edward Norwold did not care to be questioned, and that the subject was painful to him. Yes, he had said so. The conversation, therefore, went upon other subjects, and it was evident that Mr. Edward Norwold had known a great many good people wherever he had travelled, and was well-received in Paris. He was a gentleman—no doubt of that. When he was leaving later in the evening, he asked permission to call occasionally, as it was more than probable that he should continue in Paris for another year, until he was of age and at liberty to choose his own career for the future. "I hope I shall find," he added, "that I am connected with your old friends."

"Oh! they were not friends," said Letty.

"Well then, with Moreton."

"Morden," said Letty, correcting him.

"Morden, Morden, I shall not forget the name again, as I have done, if it was ever known to me before," and then having bade them all good night, he went his way.

"He is a very nice fellow," said Aunt Letty, "but not one of our Norwolds, evidently," and having this conviction, and not seeing so plainly as we do, what was looming in the future, she continued to call him Mr. Edward, and never mentioned this meeting to her sister in any of her letters, for how could the Warners in New South Wales care to know that she had met a stray Norwold in Paris?

Florence had, we fancy, received another lesson in that language of which she had heard the whispering, when Herr Dortz was the teacher, as she sat long at her window peopling the Elysian Fields with creations of her own, long after the lights of the *cafés concerts* had disappeared among the trees, and the hum of the adjoining streets had given place to silence.

A worn goose-quill, telling of long labour accomplished, is not the instrument wherewith to trace the bright hopes and the sweet words of a pure first love, and we have none other. Yet we must record, that insensibly, undesignedly, as we pass from youth to age, the pleasant companionship of Florence and Edward Norwold grew into love.

Great mystery of our nature! who can define it? Some speaker's voice long lingers on the ear when the lips which breathed the words are hushed and absent. Simple phrases that may have been heard a hundred times before, when uttered by that voice, live in the heart, and come like recurrent echoes. A form pursues the thought, and will not be denied, until it becomes the constant companion of our waking hours and our dreams, making no pleasure perfect where it is not. Then grow within us a great charity which blinds us to all faults, and a liberal fancy which conceives perfections until a willing faith receives them as realities. All self-love dies, and our strong desires, whether for wealth, fame, life, or honour, must be joined to a hope that one will share the blessing, or they stimulate no more. The mind becomes subservient to its idol, and trains itself to make its worship perfect. And more——

No! the words we have written shall remain, but they do not describe what love is—what love should be—nor what it was in the young pure hearts of those whose fate it was about to influence so materially.

CHAPTER XVIII

A DAY's holiday at Meudon having been arranged by the Fichards, a pleasant drive of some five or six miles brought them to the *château*, Edward riding upon the box, as the old German was, as usual, of the party. After an inspection of the house and beautiful gardens, which occupy an elevated situation, commanding an admirable view of Paris and the meanderings of the graceful Seine, the little party took their way to the adjoining forest, the gentlemen carrying the baskets containing the materials for their repast, whilst the ladies carried M. Fichard's great umbrella and fluffy white hat. There was no difficulty in finding a fitting resting-place in the forest, and a snowy cloth spread upon the green-sward was soon covered with *pâtés*, salads, chickens, and strawberries, whilst M. Edward went to the house of one of the keepers for fresh water, and a jug of cream. Three or four bottles of wine completed the arrangements for their simple meal, which was heartily enjoyed. As on all occasions, M. Edward's attentions were equally divided between Madame Letty and Florence, and therefore the other gentlemen had little to do but enjoy themselves.

The day was beautifully fine, and there was a laziness in the air which soon overpowered M. Fichard, until he fell asleep, leaning his back against a tree, whilst his wife, equally affected, laid her head upon his shoulder after covering her face with her handkerchief, and added, it must be recorded, a gentle treble to her husband's *basso profondo*. Herr Dortz had a passion for mushrooms, and was generally seized in

season and out of season with an irresistible desire to search
for them, and upon the present occasion he wandered away
in pursuit of his coveted delicacy. Florence and Edward
were left therefore to amuse themselves as best they could,
and desired no additional society. Their conversation had
been about Paris and its gaieties, and Edward had inquired
how long Florence intended to remain among them?

"I believe for another year at least," she replied, "and
I shall leave France with regret."

"You are not affected then with the *maladie du pays*," said
Edward, smiling.

"I am not, I confess, although my life at home was a very
happy one. Were it not that I am apart from my dear, dear
parents, I should have no wish to return. As it is, I would
rather go back to Bathurst—dull, dreary Bathurst, than to
any other place in the world."

"Indeed!" said Edward, looking her in the face, surprised to see it so suddenly saddened, and her eyes filled with
tears. "Do you love your parents so very much?"

"Love them so much! I should be ungrateful indeed, did
I not love them from the depth of my heart," replied
Florence. "If you knew dear mamma, you would not
wonder, as you seem to do, at the strength of my affection.
So gentle, unselfish, and forbearing, never wearied by the
waywardness of her naughty child, never chiding her but
with the tenderest words. O mother, dear mother, when
shall I be with you again!" Florence clasped her hands
together, and raised her tearful eyes, as though she sought
her mother's face in the bright blue heaven above her head.

"And your father," said Edward, after a short pause—
"do you love him as dearly?"

"Yes—quite, quite as dearly! When I had little griefs, so
insignificant, that they are forgotten now, he used to soothe me
with such caressing words, that I fear I sought occasion to be
troubled that I might hear them. Such a noble, brave man
he had been! Mamma has said again and again. He had

suffered great wrong, when he was very young, and had neither repined nor despaired, but went to New South Wales, and made his home in the lonely Bush, and worked himself up to wealth and position. His injuries had purified his heart, mamma said, but had not cankered it, and all the goodness of his nature was cast about our lives, and made us the happy household we were until——" Florence paused.

"May I ask you to go on?" said Edward.

"Yes, until I fear their love for me brought the first great sorrow home, and there it will continue until I return to them. And I will return and strive to do so contentedly, whenever Uncle Jack comes to take me home again."

"Uncle Jack?" asked Edward. "Is he in Europe?"

"No, dear soft-hearted, loving Uncle Jack was recalled back to Bathurst after he had placed me with Aunt Letty. I knew not at the time that it was an accident to my father which made his return necessary, or I should have gone with him. What think you, M. Edward? He sold his location in the Bush in order to bring me here, because his wayward niece had fancied that the colony was not good enough for her. Oh, you would so like Uncle Jack!"

M. Edward was sitting with his knees clasped in his hands, looking thoughtfully before him. At length he said slowly, "Father, mother, and Uncle Jack, and all loved, and all loving so very dearly! I had a mother who loved me very dearly, Miss Warner, although I never saw her gentle face without the trace of sorrow, even when it seemed most happy. She died when I was very young, died as I believe from cruel neglect and wrong at the hands of one who should have cherished and protected her. I see her very often, see her now, and love her as a child would do—for my love has grown no wiser, no stronger since she died. Would it were otherwise." The speaker paused, and again looked thoughtfully before him.

"But your father, M. Edward,—you have a father still?" said Florence, at length.

"In name only! In name only! I was not eight years old when he took me to Germany, and left me in charge of a schoolmaster and his wife. Dear good souls, they faithfully discharged their trust, and in a measure filled the void in my infant heart. But my father,—*you* will hardly believe me,— I have not seen him, excepting during a short stay in England—twenty times since my mother died. He put me away from him during her short life. He has left me to the care of strangers, contenting himself that his duty was done by paying money. He has defrauded me of the exercise of my affections, and has cheated me of the happiness of my childhood, for I already see that manhood brings its sorrows, and that life has its phases of struggle, victory, or defeat. I should have rebelled, uselessly rebelled years ago, but for the kindly remonstrance and advice of my dear old schoolmaster. Remembering his teaching, I have brought myself to bear with patience, and to perform with obedience whatever my *father* requires of me—until the time comes, another year only, when I shall be free to choose my own career. But the the past will remain with me until my life's end—the cold, cruel, bitter past wherein since my mother died, I have found no outlet for the love which God has planted in our young hearts; because my father would not let it flow, but dammed it back by his own selfishness and pride, and wicked indifference!" Edward again clasped his knees, and rocked himself to and fro, as though in bodily pain.

"Poor M. Edward," said Florence, her eyes once more filled with tears, "how much—how very much—I pity you. I am sorry that I spoke of your father."

"No—do not regret it, I beseech you, dear Miss Warner," he replied. "It is a relief—an unutterable relief to have told you this—to you who, so blessed in your own home relations, can feel for me, so lone and so deserted. The most pleasurable moments of my life have been those which I have passed with you—and these kind friends; and, I know not why, I cannot divest myself of a belief in your aunt's impression, that we are connected some way by old times or place, and I feel that I am not quite alone in yonder great city, as I was before I knew you. I bless Herr Dortz every day that he has made us known to each other."

Florence, as he spoke, could not keep her eyes fixed upon his, as had been her wont, but her long lashes drooped slowly down, and with some difficulty, she said :—

"Was Herr Dortz your old schoolmaster?"

"No; he was an usher in the school, but pitying the poor lonely English lad, he showed me many kindnesses in his quiet way. I am glad to be his pupil again, as he so much needs one." He paused, and then continued. "I see him yonder among the trees, coming towards us. Before he disturbs this strange, yet to me most happy meeting, allow me to ask you a great favour—a very great one."

Florence would have spoken, but she could only smile most sweetly, and bow assent.

"Let me—" said Edward, looking intensely in earnest— "let me for the time to come call you Florence."

Another bow, another smile, but the face was all over blushes as she assented now.

"O thank you, Florence!" (Her name had never sounded so musical before!) "One more request, one more—a greater still! Call me Edward. I will only believe that it is a sister speaking; but call me Edward."

How could he press her with his earnest eyes to answer, when he saw her full bosom rise and fall enough to stifle sound?

Thus implored, she made one effort, and murmured only—

"Edw—. No, no! I must say M. Edward; but—you will call me Florence!"

He seized her hand, and the involuntary shriek she gave made M. Fichard start from his stertorous slumber; and as Madame Letty was, very properly, leaning upon him for support, the portly lady rolled upon the grass.

A merry laugh from Herr Dortz, who had arrived; a merry

laugh from M. Fichard, who had awakened, and from M.
Edward, who could not help it; but such a confused bewildered look from pretty Florence, that her aunt would have
been amazed had she regarded her.

There was nothing more to be done at Meudon but to dis-
tribute the fragments of the feast to the forester's children,
pack up the *matériel* in the hand-baskets, and then return to
Paris. Herr Dortz was a great admirer of sunsets, and
Edward tried to persuade him but in vain to ride home on
the box, in order that he might have a better view of Paris
under departing daylight. No! the good old scholar would
not deprive his generous pupil of such a pleasure, and insisted
on re-occupying his seat next to Florence. Edward was
ashamed of his own duplicity, as he read sincerity in the
puckers and wrinkles of the old German's smile, and only
forgave himself when he saw how beautiful was the one
other face whereon he had looked, and found a sister's
sympathy. The ride home was quickly performed, and M.
Edward made his *adieux*, holding Florence's hand for a
moment—only a moment longer than he had ever ventured
to do before.

Only a moment! but we have ceased to measure events by
time, even in less material things than nerves and hearts.
The electric current makes "its circle round the earth" in
time that is uncomputable; and why should not the invisible,
impalpable influence that is to encompass a whole life perform
its function in a moment.

As M. Edward had told Madame Letty of his compact with
Florence, and as that lady saw no objection to it, especially
as she herself was entreated to confer the same favour, and as
M. Fichard and Madame had heard from their niece so much
of the conversation in the forest of Meudon as Florence could
or would remember to repeat, M. Edward's attention and
visits were received without alarm or suspicion by all except
the real object of them. Grateful as Florence felt them to be,
they were not altogether without alloy, as she had at times a

vague conviction that she was pursuing a clandestine course of conduct which was neither just to her unsuspecting and confiding aunt, nor to her absent and devoted parents. True, Edward had never said one word to her in secret which might not have been repeated without exciting a suspicion that it had a meaning far deeper than the words ordinarily conveyed; but there were looks and tones unheeded by all but her, which could not be mistaken by her pure and susceptible heart, and which were to become either balm or poison to its peace. It was not possible for her to reject this knowledge, and so she came to believe that he loved her, even as she knew she had learned to love him. Her mother's quick affection and jealous eye would have discovered the great secret, hidden in her daughter's heart, seeing that there were pensive moments when Florence neither heard nor saw what was taking place around her.. She would have noticed a flushing cheek and a sudden silence when some common-place was uttered, or some ordinary civility was performed. She would have observed an expressive smile or a downward glance, when Edward came or went away, and would have suspected the cause which made Florence so late a watcher, when she should have been sleeping peacefully. But between that dear, watchful mother, and her loving child, thousands of miles of water intervened, and she could only seek to guard her beloved one by her prayers and her written counsels.

The slumbering fire would surely find a breath to blow it into flame! It came from Edward's father.

Sir Gilbert Norwold—he was a baronet now—wrote to his son a formal dictatory letter, such as his communications to Edward had always been, reminding him that he would shortly be of age, and that as the family—he had married again some years before—were going to Switzerland, he would defer keeping the day until their return to London. Edward cared little for this indifference on the part of his father—he had been too long accustomed to such neglects; but there was, however, one passage in the letter which, for

a time, stirred his indignation. Without consulting his son
in any way, Sir Gilbert had arranged, he said, for Edward's
early departure to India, where he was to enter the Civil
Service, and provide for the future by the exercise of his own
talent. This course would not have been objectionable,
perhaps, had Edward been consulted; but he resented this
despotic disposal of his life, and resolved at once to decline
compliance.

The cooler counsels of M. Fichard obtained a hearing, and
he was persuaded to wait the completion of his minority, and
to avail himself of this ungracious offer, unless some fairer
prospect was open to him.

"In India," said M. Fichard, "you will find your place,
my dear young friend, and none that know you can doubt but
it will be one of the foremost. You have no ties to break in
this Europe of ours, so go to the land of the sun and become
a Nabob."

No tie to break in Europe! Those words had convinced
him for the first time, perhaps, that there was one united to
his heart-strings—which it would be death to separate. To
part from Florence! Never to hear the music of her voice
again! To put the space of his whole life between their
meeting! Such thoughts had never entered his mind before,
and now that they came crowding in, he grew bewildered.
There she sat, her sweet face almost as bloodless as his
mother's when he looked upon it for the last time as she lay
in her grave-clothes.

As motionless as though that which she had heard had
been words of grammary changing her into marble, sat Florence. She too had never thought that there could be a
parting hour, but had trusted all to the happy deceitful
present.

Could he have been a living, loving man, and not spoken
then? No!

"What have you said, M. Fichard?" he cried. "What
have you said, that in a moment I seem to be changed from

an apathetic clod into the most daring of mankind? No tie in Europe! No tie in this very chamber that I could break from and live! Oh, my dearest only friends, forgive me if I have unwittingly betrayed your confidence; if I have, without consideration, perilled the peace of one who is more dear to you—more dear to me—than any other that loves her, be he who he may. Yes, I must speak—I cannot be silent now; I love her! I love you, Florence; and as you are a truthful, honest, loving woman, confess that you return my love."

He had thrown himself at her feet, and as he spoke, she fell back into the arms of her aunt as though his passionate words had killed her. It was, however, but the similitude of death—the shadow of the king of shadows—and it soon passed away.

A nature less honest, less loving, or more schooled in worldly feelings, might have resented   ch a sudden onset to surprise her into a confession of the secret of her heart; but with the truthfulness to which he had appealed, she threw her answer into her face, and then fell weeping upon the neck of her kneeling lover.

All that followed was confused, painful, and pleasureable; each felt in turn that some great catastrophe had overtaken them, and that the last hours which had passed would be memorable as long as they should live.

Such a trying scene was not without its effect upon Florence, and for some days she had to keep her chamber. During this time, she and Aunt Letty had many conferences, and it was resolved that letters should be dispatched by the next mail to Bathurst, narrating all that had transpired, and asking the parental approval of what chance, and not design, had made necessary to the future happiness of Florence.

As for Aunt Letty, it must be confessed that she was rather satisfied than otherwise with the course of events, now that she knew that Edward was the son of Sir Gilbert Norwold;

Q

and considering herself *in loco parentis,* she did not hesitate
to allow the lovers free access to each other, planning, indeed,
many pleasant excursions, and contriving other opportunities
of meeting, believing that she was consulting the present and
future happiness of her niece by so doing.

"It was very naughty of you, Florence," she said, "to
fall in love without giving Aunt Letty notice of your intention
to do so, and had it been with any unworthy person, I don't
know what I should have done. Brother Jack, to say nothing
of Mr. Warner and Lucy, would never have forgiven my
want of foresight. It was very sly of you."

Florence could only smile, and declare the truth. That the
act had been unpremeditated, and that no unworthy object
could have won her regard—of that she was certain. But
when all Edward's claims to be loved were considered, was it
to be wondered at that she had given him her heart as soon
as he had asked her for it?

"No, it was not to be wondered at," replied Letty; "and
I am sure that your dear mamma will be delighted at the
selection you have made. Only to think! Not only is he
the most amiable, accomplished dear young fellow I know,
but he is the heir to our native baronetcy, and must some day
succeed to the Morden property and Norwold Hall, ruin that
it is. They say the course of true love never does run smooth,
but I see no reason, my darling, why yours should do otherwise, and therefore you have Aunt Letty's permission to love,
and be as happy as two silly fond creatures can be."

Was Aunt Letty to blame? Not very much, looking at
the case from the plaintiff's side of the question.

Edward had also written to Mr. Warner, detailing his
family connections and future expectations. Had that letter
reached its destination it would have been read as though
traced by the hand of a destiny that sought to annul the deep
injustice of the past, and to restore to Florence the advantages
of her birthright, despite the abnegation of her father.

All the letters had been dispatched to the distant colony

before any one thought of Sir Gilbert and the acceptance he was likely to accord to these arrangements for introducing Florence Warner into the proud family of the Norwolds as the wife of its future heir. M. Fichard was the first to speak of some possible difficulty, and Madame Letty turned pale at the thought.

Florence, also, when made to understand the importance that some persons attach to the distinctions of birth and connections, became conscious that her reception might be unsatisfactory, and her natural pride becoming alarmed, she resolved to speak to Edward on the subject.

"My dear love," he said, in reply, " I have not overlooked the possible consequences with my father, but I have been silent, as any surmise that you were not worthy to take rank with the highest, would have been an insult from my lips. Now that you have spoken, I will confess frankly, that I anticipate objections on the part of my father, which I may find it difficult to overcome."

" 'Your mother, sir,' he wrote to me, when announcing his second marriage, ' was *only* a banker's daughter; but I had then political aspirations, and I married her to secure her father's local influence. Our name commands a higher alliance, and I have therefore united myself to the Lady Clara Normanton.' Pshaw! My German student life has discouraged the growth of such old world absurdities. I seek for my happiness in virtue, truth, and love, and I have found them in my darling Florence." He kissed her pretty cheek, and then continued :

"All my life long my father has treated me as some encumbering thing that he was compelled to recognise, and has never endeavoured by act or word to win my affection, or even my esteem. He has doled out to me, as it were, education and maintenance, because I am known to be his son, and I have repaid him with obedience, cold obedience. So much for the past. Our accounts are fairly balanced, and there is an end. For the future I will make my own conditions. He has promised to procure me an appointment in India, and he

will do it, I am sure, because it will provide for me without
encroaching upon his own pocket. Let me have one foot
on the ladder, and do not fear but I shall mount, and with
such a stimulus to exertion as you will be, dear Florence,
I shall ascend more quickly. If my father receive my choice
with the honour which is her due, well—we are friends.
If he pause in according her one jot of her just right, we
part—not enemies, I trust. It will be only to continue our
old relations again. No love, no reverence—no sympathy on
either side. Your love, dear Florence, will be all-sufficient
for me. May I deserve it always."

Florence rested her head upon his shoulder, and was silent,
although, when this matter had been thought over by her,
she resolved that she would urge Edward to consider if the
love she had given him was a fair equivalent for the sacrifice
he might have to make, and whether he was sure in the
time to come, he would never feel regret that he had abandoned so much for her sake. What he had said had made
her silent, and she was glad not to have had occasion to
urge those questions, for had he answered " No," her heart
would have broken.

The family council was satisfied in part with Edward's
view of the difficulty, but this dark cloud in the shape of
Sir Gilbert Norwold, which would ever and anon cast a
passing shadow on their happiness, at last threatened storm
and thunder. Sir Gilbert wrote to Edward announcing the
receipt of the appointment, and requiring him to return to
England in six weeks, and then to be prepared for an early
departure for India.

An early departure for India ! Florence thought.
Away for ever from father, mother, Uncle Jack, even as
Edward's wife was a condition which Florence had never
realised until that moment. Five thousand miles could not
keep her love from the old home, and thither it went the
moment such a separation appeared to be possible. Whenever they had spoken of India, which had been very seldom,

it had had no other effect than was produced by the mention
of England, London, France! She had never thought otherwise than that she should be with the distant loved ones
again, sharing with them the new happiness she had found
in her love and its object!

And could she part with him who had created the new
life? Could she send 'him away alone to fight the battle of
life, and whose conquests were to be shared by her, knowing
how he had reckoned upon her companionship, to sustain him
in the struggle?

What was to be the result?

Aunt Letty could not answer her, neither could M. Fichard.
They had not contemplated such difficulties — they had
imagined that they had only to await letters from Bathurst
never doubting but that the absent authorities would ratify
the treaty, and then to abide the usual culmination of such
wooings. In a few days the mail would arrive, but matters
would then be no better than they were at present. What
was to be done?

Edward—when did a true lover hesitate to cut the
Gordian knot, which perplexes and baffles the less interested
lookers-on?—Edward suggested a bold solution of the difficulty.

"Florence, my beloved," he said, embracing her slender
waist, and pressing her sweet head to his bosom, "I will be
your guide from this labyrinth of hopes and fears. To part
from each other is impossible. It would be to part from life,
for neither could sustain the separation. Such a trial is not
demanded of us. In a few days at most we shall have your
parents' approval of our love, and then—and then, dear
Florence, let me make you my wife—let us be so united that
no one can divide us. We will then go together to your
distant home, and you shall justify, if you can, the choice
you have made in me."

This was cutting the knot undoubtedly, and Aunt Letty
and M. Fichard were long in debate as to the advisability of
permitting it.

Ah! news of the Mail at last!

Aunt Letty trembled as she prepared to read aloud the paragraph in *Galignani* headed—

"*New South Wales—The Mail.*—We regret to record the total loss of the mail-ship *Josephine*, when within two days' sail of Bathurst. Part of her crew and passengers only were rescued, but none of her mails, and——"

Letty could read no more, as she saw at once that the whole responsibility of Florence's love-matters rested still with her and her husband.

No reply to their anxious inquiries could be obtained for months, as in Letty's subsequent letter she had merely expressed a hope that the important news which had reached them by the former mail had been favourably received, and that they should soon have occasion to congratulate each other. Florence had been reticent also, upon the one great subject, and had not even mentioned Edward's name in any way, fearing to do so, in case an objection had been taken to the engagement which she had formed so unwittingly.

What was to be done? The question pressed for a reply, as Edward had received a peremptory call to London, and all the hopes of love seemed imperilled by his departure.

What was to be done?

O! Aunt Letty, weak as a kindly woman! O! M. Fichard, submissive as a tender easy husband and a benevolent man! O! Edward and Florence, trusting, hopeful, daring as two young loving hearts should be, why do you all wear those wedding garments, and what have two of you vowed to each other in that little chapel of the Avenue Marbeuf, in the Elysian Fields, which never were visited by happier spirits than those which occupy those hackney *voitures* on their way back to the apartments of M. Fichard?

CHAPTER XIX.

"THE COCK," in Fleet Street, has been sung by Tennyson, and henceforth stands on classic ground. The student in Lemprière knows that the cock was of old dedicated to Esculapius, but the golden bird in Fleet Street more properly belongs to Themis, for on its mahogany shrines, flocks of sheep in the shape of chops and kidneys, herds of bullocks, cut up into large and small steaks, and tons of cheese converted into Welsh rarebits, have been offered up time out of mind to that legal deity, whilst libations of stout and every other alcoholic compound have been freely poured down the gullets of his priests and acolytes; as the Temple is on the opposite side of the street, and law, like love, requires to live on something more than the flowers of rhetoric. A long narrow passage brings you at once to a low-roofed dining-room, divided on each side into boxes supplied with the narrowest of seats and tables, the latter covered not at all times (we write of times past) with the cleanest of table-cloths; and a superstition prevailed formerly—mind formerly—that by removing the crumb-strewn damask and shaking it, the "coming" had lost all traces of "the parting guest!" The spacious fire-grate, amply filled in winter time, gave a cheerful welcome, and on hot summer days, from its capacity for ventilation, combined with the pervading gloom of the place, made the heat more endurable. A young Templar had given his orders—as the phrase runs—and was preparing to wile away the time necessary to execute them, by a perusal of *Crabbe's Digest*, when his studious intention was interrupted by the entrance into the same box of a *quasi* military person, who with a smile and a bow took his seat composedly.

Having deposited his hat and gloves carefully beside him on the seat, he said, with another smile and a bow—

"Mr. Elliott, I believe?"

"Yes," replied the Templar; "am I known to you?"

"I had the honour," answered the new-comer, "to be subpœnaed—although I was not called—in the case of Baxter *v.* Hammerton, and in which you held a brief as junior."

"O yes," said Elliott,—rathered flattered to find that in the only case in which he had been engaged he had made such a lasting impression; "I presume you are Captain Elmsley, and had to prove, if I remember rightly, the hand-writing of the defendant."

"Such was to have been my evidence; but the other side admitted, and I was spared appearing against an old, although unprincipled friend. Waiter!"

"Coming, sir," replied that functionary, making his exit through a door at the upper end of the room, and bawling at the pitch of his voice, "Two lamb-chops to follow mashed potatoes, pint, steak, very well done!"

"Extraordinary class of persons are waiters," said Elmsley, "never can speak the truth, even in their reckoning. Why could not that fellow have said, 'Yes, sir—or coming directly, sir,' without adding mendacity to neglect?"

"'Coming,' I presume, is according to waiter-craft, and has supplanted the 'Anon, anon, sir,' of the old drawer," replied Elliott.

"Ah, Shakspere!" said Elmsley, again smiling. "I am glad you are a reader of the immortal Swan! Waiter!"

"Coming, sir."

"When, sir, when?" exclaimed Elmsley, rather testily.

"Beg pardon, Captain!" said the waiter, flicking off a few crumbs with his soiled napkin. "What'll you have, sir—chops and steaks, sir—potatoes—no peas, all gone, sir."

"That's provoking," said the Captain. "I had fully calculated upon peas—Well! say a small steak—no potatoes, and half a pint of stout."

"Yes, sir," and bawling, "Coming," in reply to another summons, the waiter disappeared as before.

"I find it advisable to live sparingly this hot weather," observed Elmsley, "and therefore wander into this locality, as they understand the art of small cookery better here than at the West-end."

To this latter proposition the young Templar agreed, although he had given a more substantial order for his repast than his *vis-à-vis*, and he now proceeed to devote his attention to the materials placed before him.

"Has it been demonstrated ever," said the Captain, giving a hasty glance at Elliott's well-cooked chop—"why waiters generally are flat-footed, and wear linen that appears to have been rinsed in pot liquor?"

"I never observed those peculiarities," replied Elliott.

"Do, and you will find my observations are correct," said the Captain. "They also appear to clean the cuffs and lappets of their coats with black-lead, which is not always pleasant to look upon. Why they will not imitate the French *garçon*, with his neat jacket and clean white apron, is a mystery to me. A very small steak this, Edward, very, and no fat. Find me a piece of fat, and—yes—you *must* bring me potatoes."

"Yes, sir," replied the man to whom these latter observations were addressed. "Point steaks are small, sir—Coming! and potatoes directly, sir."

Elliott began to feel a kindly sympathy for his new acquaintance, suspecting that there were other reasons than the heat of the weather for the limitation he had placed upon his appetite.

"You quoted Shakspere just now," said Elmsley, after a short pause.

"I did?" asked Elliott, rather surprised, and then

added, "Oh, I remember! Master Francis and his anon."

"Quite enough to show me that you have been a careful reader of the immortal Swan," said Elmsley. "I, too, am a disciple, and never lose an opportunity of paying my devotions. To-night there is to be a new *Juliet* at 'The Lane,' and I shall spare her an hour or two."

Elliott was relieved at finding the Captain's abstemiousness was not enforced, and he finished his dinner more pleasurably than he had begun it.

"I presume you are fond of a play?" said Elmsley, when the waiter, having cleared the cloth, furnished the Captain with a tooth-pick, and Elliott with a glass of hollands, for which The Cock enjoyed a celebrity.

"Yes—I am—very partial to a good play well acted, and I consider I am honestly pursuing my studies when witnessing both," replied Elliott.

"May I venture to offer you the opportunity of doing so this evening?" said Elmsley. "I am a friend of Elliston, and he has kindly sent me an order for two to the boxes."

Elliott was convinced that his former conjecture respecting his new friend's limited dinner was the correct one, and he had not the heart to refuse the acceptance of the proposal, resolving to acquit himself of the obligation by asking the Captain to supper. It was not a wise thing, certainly, to take up so readily with a tavern acquaintance, although he had appeared in a brief, but there was an independence about the man's poverty, and a certain gentlemanly bearing, which disarmed suspicion. The waiter evidently knew him, and though he was only a poor customer, treated him with a respectful deference, which one of that knowing order of men would not have accorded to a questionable visitor.

Having discharged their reckoning (which, to the honour of Edward, the waiter, was scrupulously correct, so far as Elmsley was concerned, however seventeen-pence might have been transmitted into one shilling and seven-pence, in the computation of Elliott's account of sundries), the Captain and the Templar—the Sword and the Gown, proceeded on their way to Drury Lane.

Captain Elmsley was evidently well-known to the officials in the front of the theatre, as his order was not examined, and might have been a piece of waste paper for what care they took to examine it. The box-keeper knew him, also, and passed him in the lobby, with a slight bow of recognition, and the assurance that every place was let.

"We must give these fellows a shilling, I suppose," said Elmsley, proceeding to unhook his frock coat very deliberately. "'They must make profit of their place,' as Ben Jonson says."

"Oh, that must be with me, Captain! if you please," said Elliott, and a shrug of remonstrance was the reply.

"Jones—here Jones!" cried Elmsley, rather authoritatively to one of the box-keepers, after this considerate offer of the Templar, "Two good places, mind—my friend wants a bill."

Jones understood the Captain. The box-list was examined, and by great good luck two places on the front row, in the bend of the house, were found to be vacant.

Ah, those were playhouse times, when our grand old drama was not too slow for the lovers of good acting, and which will survive the neglect of the present, as it has done that of the past. When "the play was the thing" for which men and women fought, struggled, and endured, under the old Piazza of Covent Garden or the less commodious entrances of Drury Lane, good-naturedly for hours, undeterred by the well-remembered cry of, "Take care of your pockets, Ladies and Gentlemen."

A good seat in the pit was worth contending for, when Kean, Kemble, O'Neil, Young, Munden, Elliston, Dowton, Liston, and many others, now in the land of shadows, were to awaken tears or laughter, both excellent soothers of the real sorrows and carking cares, which have so large a share in the life of man.

We will leave Elmsley, to observe and criticise the new Juliet, as the Templar had found "metal more attractive" to occupy his attention in the centre compartment of the dress circle.

The object which so fascinated him, was a young girl, about twenty, whose beautiful face showed the deep sympathy she had in the mimic scenes she was witnessing. Her features were regular and expressive, and her full dark eyes showed in their tears or laughter the ready susceptibility of her nature. She was dressed in slight mourning, which contrasted favourably with the gaudier attire of the two elderly ladies accompanying her, and who—so Elliott surmised—could not be nearly related to her. The young Templar did not remain many minutes together without looking at that beautiful face, and an undefined feeling stole over him, which you, dear reader, may have known once or twice in your younger life. It was only between the acts of the play that those beautiful eyes sought for other employment than what the scene afforded them, but during those intervals they more than once encountered the earnest, respectful gaze of Elliott, and received no offence, as he instantly withdrew his regards, as though he were abashed at being detected in such admiring scrutiny. It became evident, however, at last, that the fair object of his admiration was conscious of his persistent observation, as her lovely cheek coloured deeply and her eyes sought his no more.

"Oh, beautiful being," he thought, "I wonder where you live, and to whom you belong! Not to that ponderous woman in the yellow turban! Nor to that attenuated mummy in an auburn crop! Have those lovely eyes looked favourably on some money-grubbing cit, or is your maiden heart as yet untouched by love? In what utter folly am I indulging? Losing all interest in the play, I care nothing who marries yonder love-struck Juliet, so that I can contemplate that beautiful face, and perhaps imprint its features on my heart. Bosh! I *will* attend to the actors."

And so he did, until Juliet said :

> " This bud of love, by summer's ripening breath,
> May prove a beauteous flower when next we meet."

Elliott listened no longer, but again looked towards the beautiful unknown, and continued to be thus occupied until the curtain fell to the loud plaudits of the audience.

Elmsley was delighted at the success of the young actress, and was rather disappointed at the coldness of Elliott, and his apparent indifference that a new star had been—as the Captain said—" added to the dramatic hemisphere."

Elliott was much more interested in the movements of the three ladies in the front of the dress circle, and as they prepared to leave the theatre without waiting for the farce, he proposed to Elmsley to depart also.

" Certainly, certainly ! " said the Captain. " The farce is nothing without Liston, and he, you know, is at the other house. I saw it on the first night, and believed it would have been damned but for the exertions of myself and umbrella. A judiciously applied umbrella has saved many a dramatic trifle. Like the bell-wether in a flock of sheep, your umbrella can very often lead the ignorant or doubting public the way they should go. What a night ! Why, it is raining a deluge."

Elliott, calling one of the watermen to him, slipped a shilling into his hand, and bade him secure the only disengaged hackney coach, in the fond expectation that the three ladies following him down the stairs, might be without a carriage. His boldness was rewarded, as the two elderlings began to lament their situation, and wondered how they should ever reach Billiter Square.

Almost before Elmsley could realise what was in progress, Elliott had politely placed his coach at the service of the ladies, and in the most respectful manner handed the yellow turban into the creaking vehicle, and though the young lady

stiffly declined his attention, he extended the same civility to
the mummy with the crop.

"How shall we get away from here?" said Elliott to
Elmsley, when the coach had been driven away. "I want
you to be my guest at supper somewhere, but there is no
facing this rain."

"I know of an odd place close at hand," said Elmsley, "if
you are not very particular; and I think you will be amused
if you have never been at The Lyre."

"I have never been there, although I have heard of the
place," replied Elliott. "How can we get there?"

"Follow me," said Elmsley, turning back into the theatre,
and passing through a sort of corridor known little to the
public, they were soon at one of the pit entrances which faced
the hostelry he had mentioned. Then crossing the road they
passed through the bar of the house, and entered a room at
the back. It was not very large, but its decorations were
remarkable. It was divided by partitions into four compartment, or wards, as they were designated, Elmsley told Elliott,
at the same time directing his attention to the paintings
which distinguished one box from the other.

JUNIPER WARD was set apart for the neophytes of the Lyre,
and the design upon the wall represented, somewhat after the
manner of Hogarth, the gin-drinker's career in all its painful
gradations.

The next compartment was called appropriately POVERTY
WARD, and the picture which distinguised it was illustrative
of the miseries of penury produced by an indulgence in
drink.

The grimness of the ornamentation increased as the frequenter
of this strange place graduated higher or lower, and the next
division was named INSANITY WARD, with its appropriate
illustrations, coarsely, but truthfully rendered.

The last compartment was inscribed SUICIDE WARD, and
the incidents pertaining to that sad termination of many a
misspent life were faithfully depicted.

" And is this place devoted to social enjoyment?" asked Elliott, in surprise. " It seems better calculated to frighten men into abstinence and the doldrums. It is a sort of public-house 'La Trappe.' "

" It was the strange fancy of a poor lost scene-painter to decorate this room as you now see it," said Elmsley, in reply, "in the belief, perhaps, that others might be deterred by these grim pictures from pursuing a course which he himself could not abandon. Poor fellow! he laboured in vain. It is now more frequented than ever, after the theatres are over, by certain actors and their friends, who are given to late hours and potations 'pottle deep.' See, there is some one asleep in Poverty Ward." As he spoke, a shrunken pale-faced man, dressed in a drab overcoat, although it was summer time, roused himself from his uneasy slumber, and regarding Elmsley for a few moments with his large staring eyes, said in the intervals of a racking cough :

" Ha, Captain Elmsley! why you are quite a stranger here !"

" Good gracious!" cried Elmsley, involuntarily, as he recognised the man. " Why, you are Mr. Brownley?"

" Yes," answered the man, "jolly Tom Brownley, but changed a good deal for the worse, owing to this infernal cough."

As the paroxysm which succeeded this brief response lasted some time, Elmsley whispered to Elliott ! " As fine a fellow as you ever saw twelve months ago. Sang a capital song, too, poor fellow !"

As soon as Brownley could speak again, he said, " I can't master this torment sometimes — hot rum-and-water only keeps it quiet—and the landlord here is an ungrateful brute —quite forgetting the pounds I have spent, and the pounds I have brought him for years past."

As the man said this, Elmsley had unhooked the front of his coat, and taking a shilling from his waistcoat pocket— after directing Elliott's attention to one of the pictures on the wall—quietly slipped the money into Brownley's hand, motioning him to silence.

The man nodded his thanks, and instantly summoning the waiter, threw, with an air of offended dignity, the money upon the table, and ordered the stimulant he required, and then coughed again. As soon as he received the liquor, he contrived, steaming as it was, to swallow it off in two or three gulps, immediately dispatching the waiter for another supply, and then was penniless again. The next glass he husbanded with more care, and the effect was such as he had asserted it would be, as he was able to talk with much less interruption.

"Why, Captain, it is many years now since we first met in this room. Ten, or more. We were made Buffaloes on the same night, if you remember.

> 'Through the wild woods we'll wander,
> And chase the buffalo.'"

His effort to sing this couplet brought a return of the cough, and during its continuance, Elmsley informed Elliott that the Ancient Order of Buffaloes was a club organised for the purposes of good fellowship and late hours, more to his shame to acknowledge it.

"Ah!" said Brownley, when he had recovered, "my singing days are over for the present, that's certain. I must keep quiet until I can get rid of this troublesome complaint. Unless it masters me as one did poor Bill Basely. You remember him? A stout, jolly fellow, that used to sit in JUNIPER WARD long after he had come to POVERTY."

"Yes, I remember him very well. I saw him when I was here last. And so he is dead?" said Elmsley.

"Yes, Captain, he died from drinking—wasted away to a shadow," answered Brownley.

"There was a friend of his a capital story-teller—Mr. Grayson—where is he?"

"Grayson! Oh! he's dead likewise. He died from drinking. Very sudden death his was," replied Brownley.

" There was a comic actor who came here sometimes," said Elmsley, thinking to get a more pleasant account of his old friends; " he gave promise to become a metropolitan. Where is he now ? "

" He's with the others we have mentioned," answered Brownley. " He came to London, and played one or two short engagements; but Juniper Ward did for him. He got into yours," pointing to Insanity Ward, wherein Elliott and Elmsley were seated, " and there he died. He brought it on by drinking."

The cough again intervened, and Elliott said :

"Let us hasten our supper, Elmsley; for I really feel as if we were in a charnel-house, and your friend there were the sexton. If you think more drink will do him no injury, let me order him some, for that cough is terrible."

" He is past further injury, I fancy," said Elmsley, so when the waiter brought their supper of broiled kidneys, Mr. Brownley was prescribed the mixture as before. The effect produced upon the man was surprising when he had drunk again, and his figure, hitherto shrunken, as we have said, expanded, and he appeared the wreck of the fine fellow Elmsley had described him to have been.

"If I could only get some employment," said Brownley, " and earn money enough to buy medicine—for this is medicine to me—I should get round again, I am certain. Well! enough of my complaints, and don't let me spoil your supper. No, thank you. I couldn't eat now if I had turtle and venison. By the bye! we shall have a full room presently. Rupert has promised to come to-night."

"Indeed!" said Elmsley. " I have not seen him, except on the stage, for these two years."

The person thus familiarly spoken of by Brownley was a popular actor of the day, and who, unfortunately, forgot what was due to his position, and indulged too freely the vices and the virtues of a liberal disposition. It is lifting no veil from

R

the memory of any dead prototype of Rupert Merville to
narrate what follows, as similar examples of prodigality and
folly were too common at The Lyre; and the renewal of his
acquaintance with Elmsley is necessary to our story. Elliott
had often seen and admired Merville on the stage, and the
desire to meet him overcame his objection to the place, which
was now beginning to fill, as actors and their friends, released
from other duties, came in, seating themselves indiscrimi-
nately in any of the wards which suited their fancy. The conversation turned chiefly upon the new Juliet, and Elmsley, who
seemed to be known to most of the actors, spoke in terms of
approval, which he occasionally asked Elliott to confirm. The
young Templar had very confused notions of what he had
been supposed to have seen, and he confined his criticism to
mere exclamations. "Oh! certainly! very good in parts—
very good, and gives promise."

Rupert Merville at length entered the room, and was
received with rapping of tables, jingling of glasses, and vociferous demonstrations of welcome. When this clamour had
subsided, a gentleman in Poverty Ward rose up, and holding
his glass above his head, said : .

· "Welcome to Elsinore!"·

"Bob Bentley, or I do forget myself?" replied Merville,
adopting the "humour" of the moment.

"The same my lord, and your *poor* servant ever," replied
Mr. Bentley, emphasising the word poor rather too strongly
for perfect elocution.

"And what brings you from Whitstable!" asked Merville,
"as I saw your name in the bills."

"A truant disposition, good my lord ; and the bursting up
of the concern. The ghost did not walk for three consecutive
weeks."

A laugh followed this statement. Actors are prone to laugh
at the misfortunes of themselves and other poor fellows : they
are wise in doing so, as they have plenty of them, and the
non-appearance of the ghost, Elmsley explained to Elliott,

signified that the treasury of the theatre had not been opened during the time specified.

Rupert Merville having taken a seat set apart for him, rang the bell, and a waiter entered.

"Ah! Tom," said the great actor, in a pleasant tone of recognition, "I am glad to see you here still.".

Tom ducked and rubbed his bald head—not bald from years —and thanked Mr. Merville for his kindness.

"There is a sovereign, Tom. Bring in twenty glasses of brandy-and-water—ten hot—ten cold," said Merville, and his speech was received with "*Cheers*" from all parts of the room.

"Yes, sir; twenty glasses of brandy-and-water—ten hot— ten cold. Yes, sir; but David will take the money. David is head-waiter."

"Why not you, Tom? You have been here long enough," said the kindly actor.

"Bad chalk-head, sir. Haven't got a chalk-head, and can't keep score," replied Tom, hurrying out of the room, being conscious that delay would subject him to what he described as " bushels of chaff, and a peck of personalities."

Merville's order was well understood at The Lyre, and very soon the landlord, attended by two waiters, appeared, carrying trays of glasses, containing brandy-and-water, some steaming, some cold, and then ranged them in rows on the mantel-piece.

It was understood that those who chose to avail themselves of the privilege were welcome to help themselves; and the quickness with which the mantel-piece was cleared, proved how well the hospitable intention of Merville was estimated. The conversation now became general, the subjects being universally professional, and, in a great part, unintelligible to Elliott, who was surprised at the interest they excited in the other auditors.

Some time elapsed before Merville recognised Elmsley, and then he instantly rose and came towards him. The other rose also to meet him, and they shook hands most cordially, Merville apologising for not having observed him when he came into the room, excusing himself as being near-sighted. Before Merville resumed his seat, he said :

"Gentlemen, do me the favour to drink the health of my old friend, Captain Elmsley; for when I was a poor actor in the country, he generously lent me a guinea, much to the relief of an excellent landlady and myself. Captain Elmsley's health ! "

The toast met with a hearty response; and Elmsley, in reply, assured every one that the circumstance had been forgotten by him, as the money had been honourably returned; and he was under so many obligations to actors, for the pleasure he had derived from their talent, not to say anything about their "orders" (every one laughed at this), that he was happy to have been of the least service to one so distinguished as Mr. Merville. Such a neat and appropriate speech was honoured, as it deserved to be, by a spontaneous chorus of "He's a jolly good fellow," and which nobody did deny.

The spirit of harmony thus awakened was not to be put to sleep again; and Rupert Merville set a good example, by singing, in a clear, sweet voice, the once popular ballad of "Sally in our Alley."

Of course, his health was drunk, and toasted in a relay of twenty more glasses of brandy-and-water, provided from the same open purse. Other songs succeeded; and Elliott intimated to Elmsley his desire to leave. The Captain assured him he had only waited his pleasure, and the two rose to depart. Merville would not let them go without again rising to shake the Captain by the hand; but, as he crossed the room, his step was unsteady, and his bright eagle eye appeared to be clouded by the depth and strength of his potations.

"Good night, gentlemen," he said; and then, addressing Elmsley individually, added: "I hope, my kind friend, that you will make use of me on all occasions when I can be of

service, and you shall find, I promise you, that want of
gratitude, or forgetfulness of past kindness, are not among the
feelings of Rupert Merville.   Bless you, old boy!"

The day was to come when Elmsley would remind him of
this promise, and find that he had spoken truly.

The two new friends parted at the door of The Lyre.
Elliott, after thanking the Captain for his novel evening's
amusement, went off to his chambers in the Temple, and
Elmsley to his home—where?   Few knew beside himself.

CHAPTER XX.

BEFORE the happy honeymoon of Edward and Florence
Norwold had waned, Aunt Letty and her husband, M.
Fichard, left to themselves, without their tenderest sympathies
being excited by their daily intercourse with the two loving
beings whom the Church had made one, began to see more
clearly the consequences likely to arise from this unauthorised
marriage. Aunt Letty had endeavoured, more than once or
twice, to write to her sister; but the confession, as it were,
which she had to make, appeared so formidable upon paper,
that she laid down her pen in consternation at the act which
she had not only sanctioned, but actually counselled. In
this dilemma she resolved to avail herself of her connubial
privileges, and transferred the burthen of revelation to the
shoulders of her helpmate, M. Fichard, and succeeded, though
not without the exercise of all her womanly arts of persuasion,
in obtaining an unwilling compliance. M. Fichard found an
equal difficulty in communicating the events which had taken
place, and it was not until he had consumed nearly a quire
of paper in unsatisfactory attempts, that he resolved on
adopting the briefest form possible to announce the fact of
the marriage, leaving their distant relatives to take what view
they pleased of the part he and his wife had had in the
matter. M. Fichard was less concerned than he would otherwise have been, had he not succeeded in obtaining a snug
government post in Algérie, where he would be out of the
reach of any personal reproaches with which Uncle Jack or
Mr. Warner might feel disposed to visit him, as, long before

either could reach Europe, he would have wound up his affairs in Paris, and be installed in his new home. Aunt Letty, always fond of variety, was rejoiced at the change of position, and, contenting herself with the assurance that they had all acted for what they believed to be the best, soon became indifferent to the effect of her husband's communication. There was one trifling error in M. Fichard's letter, and which Letty detected when the rough draft was shown to her, a few days after the departure of the mail. M. Fichard, in his brief statement of what had occurred, always spoke of M. Edward, and had omitted entirely the name of Norwold. He was a stupid pig, no doubt, as he said he was, for such an omission; but what was to be done? Nothing! They had been foolish throughout the business, and this last act was only a continuation of their folly. Why had they consented to the marriage? Why had they acceded to Florence's entreaties that they should communicate its occurrence, and not have left the task to her, or to M. Edward—that is, to M. Norwold? Bah! They had both been pigs, no doubt of that.

The time arrived when Edward and his new wife must proceed to England, unless he was prepared to abandon the appointment and trust to his own resources. What were they? None; truly none! M. Fichard therefore advised and entreated him to go to England, and accept the appointment—and so it was determined. When the time of parting came, Florence felt that she was separating from true, kind, and loving friends. M. Fichard generously supplied many things more or less useful in her new state, and Aunt Letty gave Edward an introduction to one of her oldest friends in London, and thither the young couple repaired on their arrival in England. In a few days they had lodgings of their own, and Florence realised more and more the isolation of her position, which would have been painful had she not possessed the fullest trust in him who was her husband.

How much was comprised in that single word, husband!

The arbiter of all her future life, decreeing that each coming
day should bring the renewal of affection, peace, contentment,
or converting all succeeding years into sorrowing for the love
that was dead, and for the dazzling hopes changed into dark
regrets.   She never doubted what he would prove to her, and
in that unswerving faith she found her happiness; for she
was largely happy, and would be entirely so, when her beloved parents and her dear Uncle Jack again held her to their
hearts, and gave her, and her other soul, their blessing.

When Edward Norwold stood in the presence of his father
—his cold, unloving father—he felt how difficult was the
task he had to perform—how almost hopeless the expectation
of any kindly result arising from it.   He had been met with
a formal greeting that chilled the blood in his veins, and made
his heart almost pulseless.   His lady mother-in-law, whom
he had not seen before, received him far more kindly, and
simulated, if she did' not feel, a pleasurable interest on his
return to his family.

"You have been a truant too much, Mr. Norwold," she
said, "and we must make home so pleasant to you, that you
will not indulge in such long absences again."

As though he had been allowed any choice in the time
past, poor fellow !

Edward thanked her briefly, as his father's coldness and
the thoughts which had arisen consequent upon it, made the
utterance of common-place difficult.

"I trust I may dispense with all formalities and call you
Edward," said Lady Clara, after a 'pause; "and that you
will call me Mamma.   I should be quite proud of such a
son."

"Oh, certainly," he replied; but he felt his reverence for
the memory of the one whom he had called by that sacred
name, often in his dreams, would render compliance with the
last request impossible.

"You must be introduced to my little fellows," said her
ladyship, ringing the bell.   "I hope you will not consider

them as intruders in this illustrious family. Let Master
Horace and Master Gilbert come to me," addressing the servant who had answered the bell. "They are boisterous
monkeys, as you may know by the noise they are now making,
but their nurse spoils them."

Two fine, handsome boys ran, laughing, into the room, but
paused in their merriment when they saw Sir Gilbert was in
the room reading the newspaper.

"Come here, my dears, and let me introduce you to your
elder—brother may I say? Your elder brother, Edward,
whom you must love very much and always obey."

Edward felt strangely as he took first one and then the
other of the boys upon his knee and kissed him. "One touch
of nature makes the whole world kin," and as in their veins
his own ancestral blood was mingled, they soon found a place
in the young man's heart. The sooner, as he saw that they
had less than was their right in the heart of their father, for
he rose and left the room without exchanging an embrace or a
word with the little fellows.

When the evil influence had departed, the restraint of the
children vanished also, and they soon made a confidant of
Edward as to their horses and carts, and drums and guns,
upstairs in the nursery.

"Brother Edward will be shocked to hear that we do
nothing but play in this said nursery," said Lady Clara, "and
that Horace, who is more than five years old, spells cat with
a k; and that Gilbert, who was four last birthday, has only
just made acquaintance with big A and bouncing B."

The two dunces were not in the least abashed at this
denouncement of their ignorance, but looked up into Edward's
face with sparkling eyes and smiling lips. Edward could
only smile in return, and express his conviction that, some
day or other, they would be bright men and Lord Chancellors.

"We are going to make a beginning very shortly, when I
can find a governess to my satisfaction," said her ladyship,
"and then they will be good boys, and learn to read about

'Jack the Giant Killer,' and all the other heroes of the story-books. Now, my dears, go back to your nurse."

Edward had made himself so agreeable to his little relatives that compliance with this request was disputed, and submission only accorded on the promise of receiving a Big Box of Bricks that very afternoon.

"We have a little dinner to-morrow, Edward, which I have arranged, so as to introduce you to our most intimate friends, and make you some society. On Tuesday, in the next week, we shall have an evening party, when you may extend your acquaintance if you desire to do so. I will now show you your rooms, which I have had arranged under my own superintendence, and I hope you will find all to your wish; if not, pray name it to me or to the housekeeper."

Lady Clara rose, and her fine stately figure showed to advantage as she walked across the drawing-room wherein this conversation had occurred, and the side-glance or two which she cast at herself in the great looking-glasses, was evidence enough that she was not unconscious of her personal endowments. She was ten years younger than Sir Gilbert, and had succeeded, since her marriage, very unexpectedly, to a legacy of nearly three thousand a-year, and the scandal-mongers of her set did not hesitate to declare that, had she anticipated this windfall would have tumbled into her lap, Sir Gilbert would have wooed in vain.

It was his wife's accession to this large income that made Sir Gilbert desirous to recover the Baronetcy dormant since his father's death, and which he succeeded in obtaining by a rather strong affidavit of Jasper Jollifer, in which the death of Gerard appeared to be more than problematical. Her ladyship now led the way to two rooms on the second floor of the mansion—one appropriated to a bedroom, with a dressing-closet adjoining, and the other to a snug bachelor sitting-room opening on to a lead flat, and commanding a view of St. James's Park.

"I have placed you here, Edward," said Lady Clara,

" so that you might take advantage of this outlet, to indulge at your ease your continental habit of smoking, as Sir Gilbert *affects* to be disturbed by it, and we never disoblige him if we can help it." There was a slight change in her ladyship's tone as she said this, which made Edward conclude, that his noble father was not the most agreeable of husbands; and he therefore was touched the more by the anxiety displayed for his comfort, as it appeared that his lady mother was desirous to compensate by her own attention for the indifference of Sir Gilbert. He thanked her very heartily, and expressed his satisfaction at all which had been done for him.

" The adjoining room I shall presently appropriate to the boys and their governess, and as they will only occupy it during the hours of study, you will not be disturbed by them unless you are too good-natured, and encourage them to be riotous. Poor little fellows! they have not much gentleman's society—and boys, I have observed, always prefer it to that of ladies."

" Until they come to years of discretion," said Edward, " and then——"

" They laugh at their former teachers," said Lady Clara, " and make fools or slaves of them, if they can. I hope my sex will find a kinder friend in you than others have done in some of your name "—adding, after a slight pause—" that is, if report may be trusted, which it may not. You had better order your luggage to be sent home at once, as we dine at seven."

Edward had thought of Florence a hundred times during this interview with Lady Clara, and wondered when the necessity for leaving her would become imperative; but he had not anticipated such an immediate desertion.

" I will not occupy these charming rooms just at present," he said, " as I have promised a friend, who accompanied me from France, to stay a few days, and——"

. " Oh! pray excuse yourself to your friend," Lady Clara said, earnestly; " you had better do so, I assure you. Sir

Gilbert will expect you at dinner I am certain; and it may be as well to consult his wishes, as he goes to Homburg either to-morrow or the day after, or the day after that—I know not which—and until he departs, I would advise you to place yourself at his disposal."

Edward was little inclined to yield anything to please this exacting unamiable father, but Lady Clara continued, in a tone of entreaty: "To oblige me I am sure you will not disturb the serenity of your papa;" and so he promised to dine with them, stipulating to return to his friend afterwards.

Edward, as he walked to the house where Florence was staying, reflected upon the difficulties of his position, and·saw how impossible it would be for him to refuse residence in his father's house, without creating suspicion of some strong motive for so doing; and when he had related to Florence all that had passed, she also acknowledged that the course of their true love was getting among rocks, and was ceasing to run smoothly as it had done hitherto. It seemed so strange to separate at the hour when they had been most together; that he should be going to a home which was not her home also; and that friends were waiting to receive him and give him welcome, who would, it was surmised, refuse her admittance to their ranks, even when presented as his wife, his loved, his honoured wife. Both had these thoughts, though when he kissed her, and bade her adieu! she smiled as though her heart was full of joy—and not of her first wedded sorrow, which spent itself in tears when he was gone. She chided herself for this weakness, and then endeavoured to reason herself into endurance, knowing, as she thought, that the time must come when they should be apart for days and weeks, perhaps; and as her parents had been when her father was striving to make a home for them at Bathurst, and in the Bush. She would school herself to bear these separations as her noble mother had borne them; but then, this was her first experience, and it was not altogether free from mortifying accessories.

Edward returned thoughtful and depressed. His father had obtained an exchange of appointments, to his advantage it was considered, but it delayed his emancipation from his present thraldom for five or six months. At first, Edward was glad of the postponement, as he had hoped to make Lady Clara a friend, and, perhaps, an intercessor with his father. But as he walked homeward to his lodgings, he had seen that the delay increased the danger of discovery; and that in his anger his father might cast him off at once, and for ever. Further reflection had shown him how few outlets there are into the world of honourable labour for the gentleman and scholar only; and though genius will pluck its reward sooner or later, honest mediocrity too often perishes in the struggle —the annoyance of failure increased by witnessing the success of the lucky empiric, or the subservient knave. Had he stood alone, the chances might have been risked; but now that the dearest fate on earth was united with his own, he was bound to accept—nay, to secure, if it were possible, the legitimate advantage which would arise from keeping on terms with his father. Florence agreed with him in all that he had thought and told her: and having much of her mother's hopeful nature, she bade him look the present boldly in the face, and trust to God to direct him in the future.

The next day was the little dinner of which Lady Clara had spoken. It was limited to twelve persons, all the best of the Norwold set, and aristocratic, exceedingly. Edward was received with the kindness and amenities pertaining to good breeding, and was surprised to find how so many persons bent upon their own selfish enjoyment could manage to fulfil the business of their lives, and be so agreeable to each other.

Lady Clara strove earnestly to bring out her young relative; and if the interest which all professed to feel in his welfare was sincere, she had succeeded in making for him many earnest friends.

Will he ever learn the truth of their professions? and if so,

will he find that the earth "hath bubbles as the water
hath ?"

Florence was delighted to hear how Edward had been
received, and forgot all the lonely minutes she had passed in
that strange room, which became, hour by hour, less like
home when he was absent.   They both, poor worldlings,
believed that they had now a host of friends, and that in the
event of Sir Gilbert proving the stern and cruel father
they expected to find him, there might be some door
opening a way to independence, and whose golden key
was in the keeping of one of the new friends who had
professed so much interest for the young cadet of the
house of Norwold.   Go sleep, and dream the brightest of
visions—fond, loving, trusting pair, until an unkind hand
awakens you !

The next day Edward had an appointment with his father,
and the interview was, like all that had preceded it, productive of no kindly feeling in the breast of either parent or son.
Edward learned that his father was going to Homburg for his
health's sake, and that during his absence he required Edward
to be in attendance upon Lady Clara, and to occupy the
rooms set apart for him.

Edward was to be prepared to leave England on Sir Gilbert's
return from Germany, and until that period an allowance
should be made to him in accordance with his proper requirements.   That was all.   Good bye.

Edward's spirit rose in rebellion, and it was only by great
effort that he did not resent the manner in which these
favours were doled out, as though to a bedesman and not to a
deserving son.

Edward carried home this heavy news to Florence; and
who will wonder that she had no word of comfort ready at
her lips, but that silently she laid her head upon her husband's
breast and wept bitterly ?

The morning brought no alleviation of Edward's perplexi-
ties, and he was almost prepared to abandon his determina-

tion to await the course of events and at once to learn the worst.

Not so Florence. Her woman's wit had discovered, she believed, an escape from some of the embarrassments which beset them; and as Edward stood despondingly, prepared to make confession and take a formal farewell of his father, she said:

"I have thought, my darling, how some of this painful trial may be avoided, and if you will think over what I am about to say, and approve of what I am about to suggest, I think you will return to me with a lighter heart and a less gloomy face. Lady Clara, you tell me, is a kind gentlewoman, and has shown herself mindful of your peculiar position, and it is therefore right to infer that she would be considerate to any other who might be under her control, although that other might be only—" she paused and looked in his face for a moment, smiling so lovingly, so hopefully—"might be only the governess of her children."

Edward started at the suggestion, but she laid her finger upon his lips, and continued:—

"I could undertake such a charge, and so the same roof would cover us, and we should be near each other and ready to go forth or to remain as your father should elect hereafter. Do not dismiss this proposal without consideration, but think it over until you come back to me, and as you decide, so we will act, dear husband."

He could not have replied to her, had she not uttered this injunction to silence, for his heart was too full for words; and pressing her to his bosom and kissing her fervently, he left her with a smiling face and tearful eyes.

As he walked along he pondered over what Florence had said, and the scheme of his clever, loving wife took form and substance in his mind, and ceased to be the shadowy thing it had seemed at first.

Why should she not assume this charge which appeared created on purpose to alleviate the most painful condition of their position? Lady Clara would obtain an opportunity of knowing her, and how worthy she was of all love and honour, and when the hour of trial came she could the better plead for a recognition of her virtues, and obtain for her that place which she had a right to claim as his wife, and as due to her own unquestionable merits. Yes, it was an inspiration which had suggested this course of action, and it must not be rejected.

This special pleading satisfied all his doubts, and he entered his father's house with a lighter heart than he had ever done before. He found everything prepared for Sir Gilbert's departure, and was witness to an outburst of temper occasioned by some overt act of one of the servants, which spoke well for the stamina of the invalid, who was about to seek the restorative air of the baths at Homburg. In what consisted the ailments of Sir Gilbert no one appeared to have discovered, for beyond his habitual moroseness and irritability, he seemed to have the full enjoyment of all his functions. He could have enlightened the world had he been so disposed. Nearly three hundred years ago the mighty mind which had searched into the heart of all nature, had declared that none could minister to that disease which Sir Gilbert Norwold was destined to carry with him to his grave!

When Edward returned home, he told Florence the reasoning to which he had subjected her proposals, and the conclusion at which he had arrived. She had not doubted but he would do so, she said, and therefore she had written to her Aunt Letty, entreating her to provide her from among her London friends the necessary references and recommendations, should they be required.

It was well that she had been thus thoughtful, for Lady Clara had only waited Sir Gilbert's departure to carry her plan into execution, and having mentioned her intention to many persons, she was not surprised to receive an application from a stranger soliciting an interview, and enclosing a letter from Aunt Letty, and a list of references of good respectability. The interview was granted, and the impression made by Miss Florence Warner was so satisfactory, that after due inquiry she was entrusted with the important duty of instructing the two little rebels of Lady Clara in the first rudiments of education.

This reads sadly like romance, but our lives are all made up of such unlooked-for events,—as we should know did we examine every incident of our daily life, and note how strange and inexplicable most of them have been.

CHATEPR XXI.

THERE was enough of deception in the notable scheme of
Florence to make it dangerous and not altogether satisfactory
to those concerned in its development. As these convictions
acquired strength in the minds of both Edward and Florence,
they almost regretted not having borne their separation
patiently, rather than have earned for themselves the self-
reproach which occasionally oppressed them. It was true,
also, that though they resided beneath the same roof, their
relative positions kept them almost entirely apart, and Edward
had occasionally to witness the small humiliations to which
Florence was exposed, as Lady Clara, with the good-nature
of her class, possessed also much of its selfishness and dis-
regard for the feelings of dependants. Edward's opportunities
of meeting and conversing with Florence were restricted
almost entirely to the early morning in the library, and then
those interviews had to be most guarded to escape the prying
eyes and sensitive ears of the domestics. Careful as they had
been, they were not quite as successful as they had hoped,
for love, like the violet, is betrayed by its own sweetness;
and their bearing towards each other had been discussed
more than once at the servants' table.

The governess in a large family occupies an ambiguous
position, unless her honourable service is carefully recognised
by the heads of the house, and she is received with the
equality to which she is entitled on every consideration except
her comparative poverty. When her duties are otherwise

regarded, and she is received and cared for rather as an upper servant than the trusted guardian of our children, to whom is transferred a mother's privilege to form the infant minds of those so very dear to us, the ignorant and conceited persons whose low minds are clothed in livery, are always glad to ignore the distinction between themselves and the one of gentle nurture whose mission has come to be among the holiest in the whole range of womanly duties.

Lady Clara was too busy with the world and her own pleasures to give much thought to the comfort of her governess, whom she had engaged to relieve herself of her maternal anxieties, and considered her acknowledgments made by the liberal terms of their contract. Encouraged by her treatment of Miss Warner, the servants were not too respectful in their conduct towards her, and their occasional impertinence, combined with Florence's own consciousness of wrong done to her absent parents, caused her many, many sorrowful moments.

Six weary weeks had passed away, and Sir Gilbert was expected to return daily. Florence had been out for an early walk with the children, and was returning homeward, as Gregory, Sir Gilbert's footman, was indulging in a chat with the under-butler at the next house.

"You seem to have been going it lately at your house, Mr. Gregory; three 'evenings' and four dinner parties in six weeks is pretty well, I think," said the under-butler.

"Why, yes, Mr. Hoggings," replied the footman. "Her ladyship has made the most of her time since Sir Gilbert's been at 'Omburgh. I shouldn't stand it much longer, I can tell you. I shall have a *quid per quod* or give warning, unless we have a dickey put to our carriage, for I'm regularly spiling my ankles. My calves is a hinch less since I jined this family."

"I must say," remarked the under-butler, "that you are hard-worked, and no mistake. Fortune must have given Lady Clara the picking of her plate-chest, and a precious large spoon she selected."

"Why, yes, we are dusty, I believe; and so we ought to be," replied Gregory; "for I see her ladyship drop a trifle or two, I can tell you, at cards lately."

"Plays, does she?" asked the under-butler. "I hate gaming in a family. Not that people hasn't a right to ruin themselves if they pleases; but gamin's no good to us, as there's no discount to be got off debts of honour as they call 'em. Ain't that your governess a-coming? Miss What's-her-name?"

"*Miss*, indeed!" said Gregory, with a sneer. "I do 'ate governesses from my 'eart, that's the fact. Miss, indeed! They ain't better paid than we are, and they don't call us misters."

Florence and the boys had reached the house, and were waiting for admittance, as Gregory continued, in a low whisper —but the words reached her ear—

"If I ain't mistook in my hobservation, Mr. Hoggings, our youngster, Mr. Edward, has a 'ankering in that quarter."

The door opened, and Florence nearly fainted as she crossed the hall, but the children scampering up-stairs allowed her to enter the library and recover herself.

Edward had been watching for her return, and hearing the boys pass to the nursery, immediately sought the old trysting-place, the library, and found Florence in tears.

Instinctively he embraced her, unmindful and regardless of observation, and pressed to know the cause of her distress. Florence told him briefly what she had heard, and for a moment he was angry at the fellow's impertinence; but, seeking to sooth her, he said:

"What matters what such a brute as that imagines? A few days more, and I will make my father acquainted with our marriage. What does it signify what such a fellow thinks of us?"

"To you nothing, dear husband," replied Florence. "To me it has the painfulness of shame, almost. A woman's honour is like a polished glass—an infant's breath can cloud it."

Edward entreated her to dismiss the doubt that any thought unworthily of her—even the fellow whose coarse words had given her so much pain.

As further conversation might be fatal to the scheme for which they had endured so much, Florence promised to think no more of what Gregory had said, but to wait patiently, cheerfully through the few days which intervened between them and the knowledge of their fate.

Sir Gilbert had returned, as had been expected; and the next morning, when Lady Clara, accompanied by Florence and the two boys, entered the breakfast-room, they found him engaged in the study of a small volume neatly bound in Russia leather, and which her ladyship shrewdly guessed was his banker's book. Sir Gilbert closed the volume, placing it beside him on the table; and then coldly kissed the two children, as though he had not been absent from them an hour.

Her ladyship was evidently mortified at his indifference, but contented herself with inquiring for the morning paper, adding, "That will do, my dears; I will send for you again by-and-by."

The boys appeared glad to escape, as they almost ran out of the room, followed by Florence, to whom Sir Gilbert had accorded only the most solemn of bows.

Edward had, as usual, breakfasted in his own room, and Florence went to the library, expecting to find him there. She was disappointed, as Mr. Gregory was seated in one of the reading chairs, occupying himself with the newspaper, which James, her ladyship's footman, had just declared not to have arrived.

"Are you aware, Gregory," said Florence, anxious to send him from the room, "that her ladyship has inquired for the newspaper?"

"Yes, Miss," replied the fellow, continuing his reading.

"And is it not your duty to take it to her?" asked Florence.

"No, Miss; I am Sir Gilbert's footman, and have nothing to do with my lady," answered Gregory, impudently.

"I think her ladyship would entertain a different opinion, were she acquainted with your present behaviour."

"Will you tell her ladyship, Miss?" asked Gregory, rising.

"I am no tale-bearer," answered Florence, indignantly. "I will trouble you to take this letter to the post in the course of the morning."

"Is it her ladyship's?" said Gregory, examining the direction.

"No! it is mine," replied Florence.

"Then I decline to post it, Miss. I am only engaged to wait on Sir Gilbert, and my lady occasionally, and not on any of the upper servants, except· as a favour," said Gregory, throwing the letter on to the table.

"I am not a servant, sir, and you know it," replied Florence, reddening at the indignity conveyed by the fellow's speech.

"Well, I don't see the difference, Miss," he continued; "you attend the children, and go into the drawing-room when you are rung for. You receive wages, and I do the same; so I don't see such difference between us that I'm to take your letters to the post, except as a favour."

Gregory's back being towards the door when he made this impertinent comparison, he had not perceived that Edward had entered the room and been a listener to his rudeness. He was startled when his young master confronted him, and said—"Take that letter, sir—take it instantly."

Gregory, although flurried by this unexpected appearance, answered stubbornly, "I have made Miss Warner acquainted with my views, Mr. Hedward, and I'd rather carry out physic for a doctor than be servant to your ——"

He paused for a moment, and then added "governess."

Florence hid her face in her hands, and uttering a faint scream sank into a chair.

Edward's anger overcame all restraint, and following the insolent fellow, who had hastily quitted the library, gave him a sound thrashing in sight of his fellow-servants.

Sir Gilbert having finished breakfast, resumed the study of his little volume, and Lady Clara sought for all the information she desired to obtain of the world without in the columns of the then fashionable *Morning Chronicle*.

Sir Gilbert, after much sighing and figuring on the envelope of a packet which he had received during breakfast, paused, as though to compose himself to speak without temper, and said—

" I am sorry to find, my dear Clara, that you have greatly exceeded the sum I named as the limit of our expenditure during my absence."

" Have I, dear, indeed ? " replied Lady Clara, without discontinuing her perusal of the *Chronicle*.

" Yes, indeed, very much ; and I am really distressed to observe that my account at Messrs. —— and —— is considerably overdrawn."

" They are good souls," said her ladyship, smiling, " and will consider it an evidence of your friendship ; rely upon it. They know that you would not condescend to borrow of any but friends."

" My dear, I assure you I do not consider such a matter a subject for jesting. In the first place, it should have been perfectly unnecessary, and in the next, it has incurred an obligation which I shall be distressed to acknowledge. Is it not so ? "

" I am very sorry to hear what you say," answered Lady Clara, turning the newspaper about, " the more especially as I wanted money rather particularly."

" Want money ! More money, Clara ? You perplex and astonish me. I was about to ask you whether we could not reduce our expenditure," said Sir Gilbert, becoming rather excited.

"As far as I am concerned," replied Lady Clara, "I don't think it possible."

"Surely we might dispense with one of the carriages. The *vis-à-vis* is useless now, except to keep Jackson and a pair of cobs in idleness; and the Richmond villa might be sold as the season is nearly gone; and I think your present stock of jewellery need not be increased for a year or so. These retrenchments would amount to—how much?" and Sir Gilbert resumed his figuring.

"I'm not clever at arithmetic, Sir Gilbert," said her ladyship, coolly.

"Pray be serious a minute," replied her husband.

"I was never more so," answered my lady. "Shall I tell you what these retrenchments would produce?"

"That is what I am trying to arrive at."

"They would produce a great deal of inconvenience, a great many unpleasant remarks, and a great domestic quarrel between ourselves. So, if you please, we will break up this committee of ways and means," said her ladyship, throwing down the paper and walking to the window.

"But we must not live as we are doing, Clara, or we shall be ruined," bawled Sir Gilbert.

"Ruined!" repeated her Ladyship, laughing merrily. "Ruin is better than retrenchment. Let us fall with three carriages: they will at least make the auctioneer's catalogue look respectable! Ruined! My dear Sir Gilbert, you are not talking to a child. Ring the bell for me, like a good husband: you want to see Mr. Edward, do you not?"

"Yes."

And a servant answering the summons was despatched for the young gentleman. Edward soon came into the room, his face flushed, and evidently excited. The cool reception he met with from his father did not serve to allay his irritation.

" Shall I leave you gentlemen together? " asked Lady Clara.
" You have business, I believe."

" No," replied Sir Gilbert, " nothing particular—I mean,
nothing which you may not know. I have here, Edward,
your appointment," and he held up the packet on which he
had been figuring. " It ensures you 300*l.* a-year to commence
with, and your own ability may increase it to 3000*l.* I
will provide you with an outfit, so that you will commence
life .without debt or any of those incumbrances which frequently paralyse the efforts of young men, and enmeshes
them, as it were, in a web of difficulties from which they
never entirely escape."

Edward briefly thanked his father, his brain confused with
the sense of his own position, and the effort he was about to
make to disclose it to Sir Gilbert.

At that moment, Florence entered the room, having been
sent for by Lady Clara; and the sight of her—his wife! his
beloved, insulted wife!—restored his manliness, and he resolved to make the avowal as soon as she had retired.

Florence had been greatly agitated by the events which
had recently occurred, and no less moved by the idea that
Edward was with his father for the one great purpose.
Therefore her voice was sad and tremulous when she replied to
Lady Clara's desire to take the elder boy with her for a drive.

Lady Clara was not in the best of tempers. Sir Gilbert
had annoyed her greatly, and she remarked, when Florence
had spoken,

" Surely the separation from Master Horace for a few hours
can't be so painful as to require such a very mournful answer.
Are you ill, or out of humour? "

" I am not well, my lady," replied Florence, her cheek
reddening as she answered.

" Then I am sorry for you! " said her ladyship, tartly ;
" I am afraid that an infirmity of temper is sometimes
mistaken for indisposition of body. I will take both the
children."

Edward himself would probably have betrayed his secret prematurely, had not Gregory entered the room at the moment.

"I beg your pardon, Sir Gilbert, and yours, my lady, for hintruding, but there are circumstances that'll make a ser-vant come up without being rung for," said that person.

"Well, well, what do you want?" said Sir Gilbert, petu-lantly.

"Will you please, Sir Gilbert," continued Gregory, "to look at them marks on the back of my coat. Them marks is from a cane."

"Nothing very serious in that," remarked Lady Clara.

"True, very true, my lady; but when I tell you that they was made when I was inside the coat, I hope your ladyship will alter your opinion."

"Who caned you?" said Sir Gilbert.

"Mr. Edward Norwold—"

"Yes, I did," interrupted Edward; "and his insolence to this lady deserved a much severer thrashing than he received."

"Indeed!" exclaimed his father.

"Miss Warner was fortunate," said Lady Clara, with a sneer, "to have found such a champion."

"Why were you insolent to my governess?"

"Oh, my lady!" whined Gregory, "don't ask me for explanations; ask the servants generally; ask—"

"No one but me, if you please, madam," said Edward. "Leave the room, fellow!"

Gregory was too glad to escape, as he foresaw a tempest was about to commence, and he might be the first victim to its violence.

Florence had thrown her arms around her husband's neck, and clung to him for support.

"What is the meaning of this?" cried Sir Gilbert, astounded at what he saw, and Lady Clara was equally scandalised.

"Be not surprised, sir, that this lady has sought my protection. She has the right to do so."

"What!" exclaimed Sir Gilbert, the dark fiendish look peculiar to him when greatly excited spreading over his face; "you will not dare to say that woman is your—"

"My wife, sir—my faithful, loving wife," answered Edward, drawing Florence closer to him as he spoke.

"Yes, his wife," sobbed Florence. "My love has been selfish, not criminal."

"Not criminal!" cried Lady Clara. "Have you not deceived me?"

"Pray, madam, spare your reproaches. This matter concerns myself only and my father," said Edward, bowing respectfully.

"You are right, young man, it is between us only. Who was this person?" said Sir Gilbert, hoarsely.

"The daughter of a distinguished colonist."

"The daughter of some liberated convict, doubtless," said Sir Gilbert; "and worthy to be one in such a beggar's match."

Edward's nostrils dilated with indignation, and he was about to reply, when his father checked him by a motion, and then said, as deliberately as though nothing had occurred previously to move him—

"Edward Norwold, you have chosen for yourself, you have forgotten all the claims your father had upon you, and have made your own election for the future—of course not without due calculation; that I have a right to conclude to be the case. It is well that I have known it in time to lessen my own obligation to my friends and yours to me."

As he said this he tore up the appointment into several small pieces, and opening the window threw them into the street.

"You see, sir, what I have done with your appointment; —and where I have thrown that paper I desire to leave you. You and your wife will quit this house as soon as possible— to-day at the latest; and I trust that I may never look upon you, ungrateful wretch, again, whilst I am spared to live."

Other words followed which must not find a place in these pages, and then, with a steady step and upright carriage, he walked out of the room, Edward never removing his eyes from him until he had passed out at the door.

Edward then kissed Florence tenderly, most tenderly, and said: " Our doom is spoken, my beloved one. Come, let us submit to it."

" Oh, no, no ! Edward, you must not go without one effort to recover all that you are losing for my sake. O Lady Clara, you will not let him be driven from his father's house without interceding for him—without an effort to revoke this dreadful sentence."

" Ask me to interfere, Miss Warner, or rather I should say, Mrs. Norwold ? " said Lady Clara. " You are asking impossibilities. In the first place I am not disposed to have an altercation with my husband; and again, the deception you have practised upon myself is not so easily forgiven, I assure you."

" Come Florence," said Edward, " we have only ourselves to befriend us; ' the world is all before us where to choose,' —is it not so, Lady Clara ? "

" I conclude as much," replied her ladyship. " You people who make these romantic marriages are always prepared, I suppose, for the consequences. They form part of the charms of the situation, I believe. I really could do nothing, if I would. Mr. Norwold knows that his father is not easily influenced by any one, especially when he conceives that he is injured; and I must say he has some cause in this instance. But I will promise this, that if at any future time I find an opportunity for attempting a reconciliation, I will do what I can."

" Thanks, my lady," replied Edward, " but there will be always two to reconcile, two to forgive injuries, and the attempt would fail. For your kindly consideration to myself and to this dear lady, accept my warmest thanks. I can say no more."

Lady Clara held out her hand, which Edward pressed gently, and then, as she looked at Florence, her woman's heart spoke out, and she exclaimed, "Poor child! poor child!" and kissed her.

That one display of womanly sympathy was remembered to her advantage when fortune had betrayed her to the usurer and his treacherous ally.

On the evening of that eventful day Mr. and Mrs. Norwold were once more installed in their former lodgings, which fortunately were unoccupied. They found a letter from M. Fichard awaiting them, announcing his departure for Algérie, and telling them that he had arranged with a friend in Paris to forward at once to London all letters from Bathurst, whether directed to himself or to Aunt Letty, or to either of themselves. He promised to send them his address as soon as he was informed of it himself, and begged to hear all concerning themselves and their fortunes.

"I wish dear Aunt Letty had remained in Paris," said Florence, with a sigh.

"Why, my love?"

"I should then feel we had one friend in this great Europe on whom we might rely," answered Florence.

"We must trust only to ourselves, darling," said Edward, drawing her closely to him. "I can brave all, overcome all, but the feeling of dependence. So long as I knew that I needed no one's help or favour, I was ready to accept of both; but now that I must win for myself whatever is needful for us both, I should feel any courtesy almost an act of charity. No. I must work; and He who feeds the ravens and the sparrows on the house-top will find me work to do."

Florence had no fear—no misgiving now, for the future; and both felt relieved that the crisis they had dreaded so long had arrived, and was decided.

CHAPTER XXII.

WHEN the letter of M. Fichard to Mr. Warner reached its destination, the effect it produced was painful in the extreme, and the part which Letty and her husband had taken was in no way excused by the loss of the letters which had been written before the marriage. Warner was greatly distressed that Florence should have been guilty of—he could hardly say disobedience, but the want of that filial reverence which it had been his dearest joy to believe she entertained for him and her mother. To have taken such an important step as she had done, without their positive approval or consent, appeared so monstrous, that at first he was disposed to close his heart against her, and to have no further interest in her welfare. And then her mother, as deeply stricken as he was, became the advocate of their child, and reminded him of her youth and loving nature, and to what fascinating temptations she had been exposed, with no wiser head or colder heart to guide and remonstrate with her than Aunt Letty's. That, although they knew not who this M. Edward was, they had strong assurance that he was not unworthy of the love of their child; and as their own lives had been made so happy by the trust and affection they had mutually known, it was their duty to hope—nay, to believe, that their prayers had not been in vain, and that the happiness they had supplicated for their beloved Florence had been accorded to her. There was gentle chiding and strong comfort in what Lucy said, which soon won forgiveness from a father who from the hour of his daughter's birth had known no limit to his love or his indulgence.

As for Uncle Jack, he blamed no one so much as himself, not even Aunt Letty. Certainly not Florence, nor the bold young fellow who had carried her off so gallantly. It was he that had coaxed his pet away from her mother's watchful care and simple teaching, and had been blind—stone-blind—to the weakness of the thoughtless guardian to whom he had confided their precious treasure. Lucy might not reproach him with words—Warner had no right to do so, as he was nearly as criminal as himself—but Jack fancied that every sorrowful look she wore, every sigh she gave, were registered against him somewhere, and that she thought him her cruellest foe, although he loved so very dearly. Lucy was quick at reading such honest books as the face of Jack, and her husband and she soon deciphered what was rankling in the heart of her good old brother, and resolved to remove it. There was much womanly skill displayed in the process.

She told him it was true that, only for his ready sacrifice of his own interest, Florence could not have gone to Europe, but that he should remember also, that had he not been recalled to Bathurst, by Warner's accident, this marriage could not have taken place without their knowledge and approval; —Jack would have discovered the threatened danger, and stood between his niece and matrimony. And then, as there was no recalling the past, it was well to seek out any good that might have come with the evil, and there was a very welcome blessing in the wake of this sorrow. Warner had not recovered the shock of his accident, and his health had been uncertain and failing for some time. He had been advised, as he had amassed a considerable fortune, to return to his native land. This advice was repugnant to him of late, ever since Gilbert had claimed the title, and he had hesitated to adopt it, until this news reached him, and then—well Lucy had pressed it—he determined to wind up his affairs in the colony, and bid it farewell for ever.

Jack threw his hat into the air when Lucy communicated this resolve of Warner, and declared it to be his honest belief that all would turn out to have been for the best if they would only wait for the end.

Kind, loving letters of forgiveness were therefore written to Madame Florençe and M. Edward, and to Aunt Letty and M. Fichard, and despatched under cover to that latter gentleman at his place of business in the Rue Rivoli, Paris. The Fates, alas! were adverse, and the comfort those letters contained never arrived to solace those by whom it was most needed, until it was too late, and the first battle of their lives was ended.

When Warner's determination to leave the colony became known, it occasioned a general feeling of regret, as his ability and enterprise had done much to increase the prosperity of the community. So many had profited by his advice and assistance, whilst others had come to look upon him as a man to be trusted in every relation of life, that his departure assumed the character of a calamity. Indeed, he was subjected to so much solicitation, and even remonstrance, to re-consider his determination, that his resolution might have given way before a sense of duty, had not the consideration for his child been admitted to be a paramount obligation that could not be forgone for any other interests, and therefore Lucy had been right when she declared that their present sorrow was not all evil.

It was not without great pain that Warner bade farewell to that land which had received him when almost an outcast from his own, and where his early toil had been rewarded with such bounteous gains, that he had been able to call to him those he loved the dearest in the world, and who had made his life almost too happy for continuance, until the sorrow came which was to carry him back to the old world, where he would be a stranger among his own kindred, and in no less solitude than when he had a home in the lonely Bush. His regrets were not of long duration, for he was strong in faith, and believed that he could trace in this enforced separation the hand of Providence.

The voyage was made in safety, and now that the old land was gained, and there was no longer the great sea between him and his child, he had no other feeling but of utter thankfulness that they should be again together, to be separated, he prayed, by no other accident of life.

No happy omen, however, was to welcome back the wanderer. The London agent had no letters from Florence nor Aunt Letty, nor M. Fichard, although Warner's business communications had been duly delivered. What could this disappointment imply? What was to be done? Jack Spraggatt was alert, as usual, and he proposed that he should start instantly for Paris, as Warner had many business matters claiming his attention. And Lucy would accompany him, and take with her those words of love and forgiveness which the post had failed to convey, and which would be so much more welcome to their darling Florence when spoken by her mother than by Uncle Jack; and Paris could be reached in three days at most. Therefore it was decided that they should start the next morning, and in the meantime endure the suspense with patience.

Warner busied himself with his affairs as much as possible, and thus kept his hopes and fears in abeyance; but the nights which intervened between Lucy's departure and the receipt of her first letter were almost without sleep. Neither did this letter help to allay Warner's anxiety, for she said:—

"We were much distressed to find that Letty and her husband had left Paris some months for Algérie, where M. Fichard has a civil appointment, and that the person who owned the house could give us no information respecting Florence. A packet of letters had arrived from the colony, and which they had been instructed to forward to England, but the French post-office authorities refused to deliver them unless by the written authorisation of M. Fichard, to whom they were addressed. The people of the house had taken no

T

further trouble in the matter, as M. Fichard had left at the worst season of the year for letting their apartments, and after giving the proprietor a very short notice.

"My distress being very apparent the proprietor's wife became more anxious to assist us, and remembered that a German tutor, Herr Dortz, who formerly occupied the *cinquième*, or garret, in their house, had been very intimate with the family, and usually made one of their parties during the time a young lady was residing with them. From her description, I recognised our darling Florence, whom this kind woman declares to be most amiable and beautiful. I dare not trust myself to say more. To trace Herr Dortz was our next difficulty, as he became too poor to retain even his attic in this popular neighbourhood; but Jack succeeded, after many hours' search, in discovering his last lodging in Paris, and then only to learn that he had returned to his native place in Germany. I forget the name of the town, but Jack has it written down correctly. To-morrow, therefore, we start for Germany; and my heart is full of hope that we shall gain tidings of our darling, and find her in England, as the *propriétaire* is certain that they left Paris some time before M. Fichard went away."

Then followed expressions of her wifely love, and such consoling and encouraging words, that Warner, when he had read them, resolved to imitate her courage and hopefulness.

Warner wisely concluded that occupation was the best solace he could find, and therefore he kept himself fully occupied throughout the day. Among other trusts which had devolved upon him from his brother colonists, was that of executor to the will of a prosperous settler who had bequeathed over £15,000 to Marian Mayley, a niece in England, at the same time appointing Warner her guardian, should he ever return (as it was said he would do) to the Old Country. He had written to the young lady, requesting an interview, and one was appointed to take place at the residence of an aunt in Suffolk Street, Pall Mall.

London had altered greatly since last Warner had looked
upon King Charles' statue at Charing Cross, and he would
hardly have recognised the locality, but for that equestrian
effigy of departed royalty. He soon found himself at Suffolk
Street, and was evidently expected by Miss Mayley and her
aunt, as the elderly lady was arrayed in full state to receive
him. Miss Mayley was strikingly beautiful, and appeared to
be not altogether insensible to her natural advantages (what
pretty woman can be?), and she shook back her long, dark
curls before she advanced to receive Mr. Warner. Her aunt
had evidently migrated from the city — say from Billiter
Square, and gave a most singular sweep of her head in
acknowledgment of Mr. Warner's bow, making the bird of
Paradise on her yellow turban quiver again. Like many
other odd people, she had only to be allowed to be natural to
discover a great many good qualities, of which she gave no
outward promise; and Warner soon found that, making certain
allowances for want of early education, Mrs. Gregson was a
very agreeable old lady. She was very proud of her niece and
her niece's fortune, and evidently considered that with such
an excellent recommendation, combined with Miss Mayley's
beauty, the family had a right to look up, and to find itself
"somebody" in the course of a short time. When Mrs.
Gregson heard that Warner and his wife had no settled habi-
tation in London she peremptorily insisted that he should
make his home in Suffolk Street until such time as he had
decided upon his future arrangements. This request was
made with so much heartiness that Warner could not refuse
the hospitality, nor could he decline an invitation to dine there
that day, when Cousin Martha would be of the party.

Poor Warner was too glad to escape from the society of his
own thoughts, and was also desirous of learning something of
the young lady committed to his care. Before dinner Mrs.
Gregson herself conducted him to the chamber, which she
desired he would be pleased to consider his own for the future,
and promised to have another arranged by the morrow for a

study, or counting-house, or anything he liked to call it; and Warner began really to admire the yellow turban, which, at first sight, he had thought the most odious head-dress he had ever seen upon a woman. When he returned to the drawing-room before dinner, he was introduced to Cousin Martha, who had arrived during his absence. She had evidently been considered a beauty in her youth, and had out-stood her market, although it appeared that she did not despair of an offer, as her rich auburn hair was cultivated into a crop, and her shoulders were exhibited in a state of nature. Whether matrimony could have plumped her out to satisfactory dimensions was questionable; but as she was presented to Mr. Warner, there was only the frame-work of a fine woman, which evidently required covering.

The dinner was very bountiful, and combined several reminiscences of Mansion House banquets, at which Mrs. Gregson had assisted, when the late Mr. G. had been in the flesh and the Common Council. The hospitable hostess was profuse in her regrets that there was no gentleman present to assist Warner in passing the bottle, but, possibly doing violence to her own feelings and habits, she certainly contrived to be a moderate substitute for such a companion. She was very curious about New South Wales, and asked a number of questions, from which it might have been inferred that she set the colonial civilisation at a very low point, and conceive that tailors and milliners were not the most prosperous amongst the settlers.

Warner was at some pains to correct these erroneous notions; and gave such a favourable account of all matters colonial, that the New World appeared to the excited fancy of Mrs. Gregson to be overflowing with every blessing except marriageable ladies; and this conviction induced her to exclaim:—

"Why, Martha, dear, what a place for you!"

The lady of the crop did not appreciate the suggestion as complimentary, and replied that Mrs. Gregson had thought of nothing but matrimony all her life, and would marry again before she was sixty!

There was so much acerbity in this remark, that Mr. Warner was not surprised at the sharp shoulders, nor the sharp, red nose, nor the auburn crop, and the ringless fourth finger of the left hand.

Miss Mayley was disturbed by the little exhibitions of ignorance and vulgarity on the part of her relatives, and Warner sought to change the conversation to subjects more agreeable to her. Miss Mayley acknowledged the obligation by chatting freely on matters within her knowledge; and Warner gathered from their colloquy that the young lady had a little vanity, and rather high expectations, but was at heart a kind, maidenly creature, who might in skilful hands be moulded into an excellent woman; and he resolved to make her and Lucy—perhaps his dear Florence also—friends, and so discharge his trust faithfully. With this thought upper-most in his mind, Mr. Warner took his leave, promising to return on the morrow, and avail himself of Mrs. Gregson's very liberal hospitality.

He had been domiciled in Suffolk Street three days before he received a letter from Lucy. His hand trembled as he broke the seal, for his heart foreboded evil. Yes, bad news! Herr Dortz had returned to Paris, so the hunters must hark back!

He was glad to find, therefore, on his return to Suffolk Street from the City, that the ladies had arranged to go to the Opera, which now was near its close. He would be, therefore, left to himself, as his mind was out of tune, and jangled melancholy music.

He retired to rest very early, and soon fell into an unquiet sleep that brought strange dreams. He dreamed that he was at Norwold Hall, blackened and charred as he had often thought of it at times, but the snow fell, and hid the traces of the fire until it appeared one whitened heap. He turned away into the old avenue of Elms, and some reflex of his

sufferings, when he was driven forth by his father, came over
him, and he hastened on to reach the open space beyond. As
he did so, his feet became entangled in briers and other under-
growth, and he tried to cry for help, but could not utter a
sound. At last he paused in his effort to proceed, and saw
standing beside him Raymond Ray, half miller, half bushman,
and who showed him, by the light of the moon, the diamond
bracelet. He was not moved by what he saw until the
miniature of his father grew larger and larger, and every
feature of the face became distinctly visible. He thought it
smiled, then grew overcast, and then it smiled again. His
dream became confused after this, and he fancied he was
once more upon the sea, great waves rolling by the ship, and
by his side his daughter Florence.

The driver of the hackney-coach, containing the returning
opera party, knocking at the door awoke him, and he tried
for some time to piece his dream together as though he
imagined it was a revelation sent to him in his sleep. His
father's face, with its smiles and its displeasure, was recalled
so vividly, that his heated fancy connected it someway with
the abandonment of his name and inheritance, until the line
of Hamlet came to his remembrance,—

"Do you not come your tardy son to chide ? "

These thoughts disturbing him greatly, he rose and, opening the window, looked out into the street. As he did so he
observed a man in a cloak walking up and down on the opposite side of the way, occasionally looking towards the windows
of the houses and continuing his observation until Warner
heard the servant close the shutters of the drawing-room,
when Mrs. Gregson and her niece retired to rest. The man
paused opposite their house for a moment, made a frantic
gesture, and left the street. This incident had the effect of
changing the current of Warner's thoughts, and he retired
again to rest, sleeping soundly until the morning.

When assembled at the breakfast table Mrs. Gregson gave

expression to some very original criticisms on what she had heard and seen the preceding evening.

"I was quite ashamed of my sex," she said, "when I saw Norma and the other young woman running after that soldier-fellow; and by moonlight too, in the middle of a wood, that put me in mind of Epping Forest, where the Alderman and me went one Fairlop Fair. If it had not been for those two unfortunate children, who were certainly rather tall to have been only just shortcoated, I should have been very pleased when the old clergyman in a long beard gave her up to the police-officers."

Mrs. Gregson said much more, and quite as little to the purpose; but Miss Mayley was more silent and thoughtful than a young lady ought to have been who had been listening to the music of *Norma*, with Pasta for the interpreter of the ill-fated Druidess. "The glare of light always made her head ache," she said; although it certainly did no damage to her complexion, for she blushed like roses when Warner, for want of something better to say, mentioned the mysterious promenader he had seen from the window, and at which Mrs. Gregson laughed, and said it must have been an admirer of Cousin Martha, as she had been of the party, but had returned to her own house in Billiter Square. The joke was so good that Marian actually put her cup down with a bounce, and ran out of the room coughing very loudly. Mrs. Gregson laughed more than ever, and as she wore in the morning a black turban covered with bugles, upon which a stray sunbeam now played, her head appeared coruscating with witticisms or electric sparks, like those a cat emits when her hair is rubbed the wrong way. In this high state of hilarity Warner left her, and went to his agents in the city.

Three more weary days came and passed before Warner received another letter. It was from Jack this time, having been written at the room of Herr Dortz, in order to save the post to England.

"Hooray!" it began. "Herr Dortz is bagged at last, and appears to be a very stupid old German, but I have made this out of him. He will take me to the church or chape where they were married, as he can't remember its name, or that of the street, and then we shall know who Mr. Edward is, for Dortz is evidently in a muddle upon that point. He thinks also he can find from his pocket-book (which he has mislaid) where they went to in England—for they did leave Paris. .

"Be patient, my dear old boy, and all will come right at last. So prophesies your devoted

"JACK SPRAGGATT."

Here was some relief at last, and so he would wait patiently and hopefully.

In the meantime he will not be unemployed—what with his shipping agents, and his stock-brokers, and his pretty ward. Nor has he seen the last of the strange man in the cloak, nor of one whom he knew only by name in the far-off colony, when Lieutenant Hammerton did him the honour to accept an obligation and forget it.

CHAPTER XXIII.

SINCE the days of the Merry Monarch, as it has been the fashion to call the licentious Charles the Second, the enclosure in St. James's Park has had a peculiar attraction for the votaries of the love-in-idleness, and thither they have resorted to catch a glance of the fickle deity. The ducks which have inhabited those waters since Mr. Storey was the King of Duck Island, are supposed to be Rosicrucians, permitted to assume those ornithological shapes, and thus revisit the scene of their former pleasures. Rochester, Buckingham, Cheffinch, Portsmouth, Castlemaine, may all be there for what we know, and one old drake that is usually well-conducted, and sober enough, until he breaks out occasionally into water antics, standing on his head, and then skirling over the surface of the lake in pursuit of two Muscovy ducks, is supposed by the learned in such abstruse matters of transmigration to be old Samuel Pepys flirting with Mistress Knibb and Mistress Pierce. Be this as it may, the enclosure has been long known as Cupid's garden, and Hymen has enlisted many followers as they emerge from its gates on balmy summer evenings.

Here, then, on the morning after Miss Mayley's visit to the opera had Vincent Elliott come, neglecting his own pleasant Temple Gardens and their historic memories, to cast himself upon the sunburnt turf beneath the shade of a wide-spreading beech-tree, or some other umbrageous giant.

He looked at his watch at short intervals, and at last muttered to himself:

"There never was a punctual woman : they are either too

fast or too slow, like a Dutch clock. They're as uncertain as a tavern bill, or a coach fare, and the force of simile can no further go. Twenty minutes past ten! The park will soon be like a nursery ground. Maids and babies will be as plentiful as small salad in June. Why don't she come?"

He sat up to make a better observation, but his eyes wandered round about, and evidently saw not the object of his search. He recognised, however, his eccentric acquaintance, Captain Elmsley, and the discovery was not pleasurable.

"There's Elmsley!" he thought, "by all that's unlucky. That fellow's course is as eccentric as a comet's!" His next thought was flight, but perceiving that Elmsley had observed him, he concluded to remain, and get rid of him as soon as possible.

"How do? How do, my boy?" said the Captain, little imagining what was passing in Elliott's mind—"Like myself, eh? Out with the ducks."

"Yes," was Elliott's answer.

"Nice place this," continued the Captain. "I often spend an hour here watching the Muscovies, and the dab-ducks, and the other things paddling about, 'till I fancy I see the rascals swimming in a lake of brown gravy; when I take out a biscuit and devour them in imagination."

"Indeed!" replied Elliott.

"Indeed!" said Elmsley—"why, you are as laconic as a pauper's epitaph! What's the matter, my boy? you are either anxious for me to go, or for somebody else to come."

"Somebody to come, or you to go?" asked Elliott, confused, and wondering in his own mind if the Captain could really have a doubt as to the true state of the case.

"Are you fond of children?" said Elmsley, evidently anxious to be taken into confidence.

"Yes—for a bachelor," replied Elliott. "What do you mean by that question?"

"Nothing," said Elmsley, "only I have known some frequenters of this spot find the society of children particularly interesting, but then the nurses have not been remarkably ugly."

They both laughed, and Elliott saw that the Captain had a shrewd suspicion of the object which had brought him to the Enclosure, and feeling convinced that he would not leave until his curiosity was satisfied, determined therefore to make him his confidant.

"Captain!" said Elliott, "it is not easy to deceive a man of your experience; and I am here, having fallen in love, and become anxious to get married."

"O la!" cried Elmsley, "not so bad as that, I hope! There must be a matrimonial epidemic raging, as you are the fourth fine healthy bachelor that has shown alarming symptoms of the disorder this week—How did you take it?"

"Naturally enough," replied Elliott, not caring to speak seriously to his friend the Captain. "The first symptoms, I fancy, developed themselves when we were at Drury Lane together, and were increased last night at the Opera——"

"Oh, oh!" interrupted Elmsley, "merely an affection of the eyes, I thought it had been an inflammation of the heart; your case is not dangerous."

"Doctor! Doctor! you are wrong in your diagnosis. I am in love, honestly—truly. I can neither study, eat, nor sleep," said Elliott, with a sigh.

"Exactly my case years ago," remarked Elmsley, "but brandy saved me. It first rushed into my head, and then got me into the watchhouse. I should have been married then, to a certainty, only when I ought to have been at the altar of St. James's Church I was at the Bar of Bow Street."

"You are right to laugh at me," said Elliott, a little piqued; "but if you remember—but you are not likely to have been impressed as I was with that lovely face."

"Not I! not I!" replied Elmsley. "Ha! ha! I thought you were seriously touched; but you're not!"

"But I am!" said Elliott, with emphasis, "and as though

Nature had not done enough for her, Fortune must be her godmother. She is an heiress!"

"An heiress!" said Elmsley, seating himself beside his prostrate friend,—for Elliott had stretched himself at length on the grass, and covered his face with his hat while he made this odd confession.

"An heiress, eh? I don't believe it. They are so scarce now-a-days. No brown beauties from Bombay! No golden Venuses from Wapping! India consumes its own produce, and the city seems to have lost the art of making them. However, let me hear what you have to say."

Elliott then recalled the circumstances which attended their visit to the theatre, the rainy night, and the sacrifice he had made in placing his hackney coach at the service of three ladies. O yes. Elmsley remembered well the carroty crop, the yellow turban, and the girl with the black eyes.

For two days Elliott had been so possessed by the young girl's beauty, that he thought he would lay the ghost which haunted him by a visit to Billiter Square, where he might chance to see her in her every-day life, and so break the spell. He remembered the number of the house, and thither he went to discover, to his great gratification, that John Mayley, who resided there, was a Ship Chandler and Dealer in Marine Stores. That knowledge would be sufficient to smother any fancy which had possessed him, he was certain, and so he turned his steps westward, but he had not left the street when the beautiful face came back to him, and his feet moved more slowly until they stopped at last, and he thought he would, from mere curiosity, endeavour to learn something more concerning its possessor. As he stood looking towards the dingy shop, a lad came forth carrying a bulky parcel, and Elliott resolved to question him. The lad was not reserved, and soon related all the family history.

"There was a Miss Mayley as wore her hair a crop; was it she? And there was a Miss Mayley as was a deal younger, and dark eyes, and such nice hair; was it she? Oh, it was,

was it? Ah—she only came on a visit with her aunt, Mrs. Gregson, a widow, and they was gone back again to their own home in Suffolk Street, Pall Mall. A prime street that was—all among the gentry at the West-end. *That* Miss Mayley had been brought up by her aunt, and was to have all the money some day. Not as she wanted it, for an uncle as went abroad and died there, had been and left her fifteen thousand pound, if he'd left her a penny, it was said."

Elliott rewarded his informant with half-a-crown, and went straight to his chambers in the Temple. They were excellent rooms, overlooking the garden and the river, but they appeared so dull and cheerless now, that he had resolved to abandon his studies and his boating, and dedicate every hour of his life to obtaining an introduction to this beautiful angel.

"No—call her heiress," interrupted Elmsley; "it is a better term; it sounds more substantial."

Elliott preferred his own designation, and then went on to say, that he had kept a respectful watch upon her house, and had more than once passed her in the street, and was certain that she had recognised him. Last night he had seen her at the Opera, and by her manner he was convinced that his respectful admiration was not unfavourably received. An introduction' to the family appeared to be impossible by the usual means, and he had therefore bribed the milkman, from whom he had learned the name of her lady's-maid, to convey a letter to that person, asking a meeting here in the Enclosure, and had obtained an appointment, although the time was somewhat past, and he almost feared that the maid had been laughing at him.

"Look," said Elmsley, " yonder comes the damsel; there's intrigue in every plait of her petticoat. Pretty foot, and she knows it, or she would not have shown her ankle in stepping over that little boy's hoop-stick."

Mrs. Digby justified Elmsley's description; for she was a bold, scheming woman, whose main business was to make money, and cared little for the means by which she increased her gains. She had noticed Elliott more than once sauntering near the house of Mrs. Gregson, and was not surprised, therefore, at receiving the communication from the milkman, and instantly discovered, in the possibility of a clandestine correspondence between her young mistress and this admirer, certain profit to herself, whatever might be the consequence to Miss Mayley.

"Have I the honour of addressing Mr. Vincent Elliott?" she said, with a slight curtsey.

Elliott acknowledged that he was that gentleman, and the presumptuous sender of a letter and enclosure to Mrs. Digby.

"Your object in making this assignation, I presume," said Digby, smiling, "is not on my own account, and I am glad of it"—she added, as both the gentlemen expressed by their action that she had arrived at a correct conclusion—"I am glad of it, for I am plagued to death with offers."

"I trust Miss Mayley is not as amply provided as yourself," said Elliott, not caring if Mrs. Digby had been proposed for by the whole household brigade.

"Miss Mayley," said Digby, "is, in my opinion, a deal too fastidious. Lovers shouldn't be looked at like French cambric; you are all a little faulty. I've broken the ice for half-a-dozen young fellows, who thought nothing of a five-pound note."

Elliott understood the hint, as his enclosure had been only a sovereign, but he merrily said:

"And were such valuable young gentlemen all rejected?"

"La! bless you, sir, she wouldn't hear of one of 'em," said Digby, opening her eyes widely to convey her disgust. "The fact is—that is, it's my belief—that she has made up her mind to marry a title, or die a spinster."

"There is an end to my hopes," said Elliott, addressing Elmsley, sotto voce, and then taking a turn on the grass.

"I don't see it," replied Elmsley; and leading Mrs. Digby a little apart, he said in a whisper, "Mrs. Digby, you are evidently a clever woman, and can manage this matter if you like. My friend here is very anxious for an introduction to Miss Mayley; and as his lordship is very unhappy, the sooner the auspicious moment can be brought about the better."

The word "lordship" had struck upon Digby's ear, and Elmsley allowed her to place her own construction on a phrase common enough in ordinary conversation.

"He's a lord," thought Digby. "He only enclosed a sovereign. Not wanting money himself, he thinks nobody else does. Desires to be *incog.*, I suppose. That's very like having a best gown and never wearing it."

Elmsley did not interrupt her reverie until Elliott had again joined them, when the Captain said:

"I am sure Mrs. Digby may count on your liberality if, by her means, we can be introduced. Eh? Vincent."

Elliott rather started at the Captain's familiarity, but did not hesitate to make the most liberal promises to Digby, pressing upon her a note for five pounds, as an earnest of the future.

"Well, gentlemen," said the experienced negotiator, "I see only one way of doing it. Miss Mayley has a favourite Pomeranian dog—a brute—I hate it, and I will contrive, now she is out, to carry the little beast to our milkman's; there will be a rare fuss, you may be sure, when they come home to lunch. Hand-bills, and all that—a sovereign reward, I shouldn't wonder; and then, gentlemen, I must leave the rest to your ingenuity, as the Pomeranian wretch shall be delivered up to you, if you so desire it. Our milkman is a poor man, with a large family, and will expect—"

"Of course, of course," interrupted Elmsley, "two sovereigns—you may promise him two sovereigns from us."

"Certainly," said Elliott; thinking, however, that the Captain was a most generous fellow with anybody's purse but his own.

"We don't dine until half-past six to-day, as the party as is staying with us cannot get home from the City before.

There's the clock striking twelve, and we lunch at half-past one, so there's no time to spare, and consequently, gentlemen, I wish you a very good morning, and thank you, for me."

Having made her very best curtsey, the vulgar *intriguante* took her way homeward.

"All's fair in love, I hope," said Elliott, "as I feel a little shabby at what I am proposing to do. Nor after what that woman has said, do I see much chance of success."

"We will not fail!" cried Elmsley, theatrically. "I shall not leave you until I can take you by the hand and say, Bless you my boy, take her and be happy."

"Aha! then I shall have the pleasure of your society for a few days, I fancy," replied Elliott, smiling.

"Don't name it," said Elmsley, "I will inconvenience myself to serve you. Decision is everything in such matters, and that is a military accomplishment."

"Billeted," thought Elliott; adding, "By the bye, Elmsley, as we are to be chums, don't you think it will be as well— not that I am curious, but in case I should be asked the question—that I should know something about you?"

Elmsley was apparently surprised, and said, "Something about me?"

"Ay!" continued Elliott. "You seem to know everybody: you shoot forth in the morning, and coruscate during the day, and vanish at night. You appear to be a gentleman, but you may be Asmodeus or Commissioner Lin, for what anyone knows to the contrary. I suppose you do come from somewhere, and are related to somebody."

"My dear boy," replied Elmsley, rather moved, "I consider your questions particularly impertinent; but as I like you, I shall endeavour to gratify your curiosity."

"I really meant not to be offensive," said Elliott.

"I conclude not," answered Elmsley, "as you are a gentleman, and I am the youngest son of one. I entered the army at sixteen, and served in New South Wales. I then returned to England, quitted the paths of glory for the shady side of Pall Mall, and, am bold to say, the service lost an ornament. You now know who I am." When he had finished, the Captain, as though to bring the conversation to an end, made a low bow.

Elliott returned the salute, and was fain to acknowledge, in his own mind, that he was as much in the dark as ever respecting his friend of The Cock. We may have to record another biography of the Captain, if we wait for the end.

As Elliott found it would be useless to return to his chambers for any useful study, during the time that had to elapse before Mrs. Digby could put her scheme into execution, and as he became more reconciled to Elmsley's companionship in this rather questionable invasion of the domestic dominions of Mrs. Gregson, he proposed to his new ally, that they should occupy part of the time in a quiet stroll to Westminster Abbey, and there, as Elmsley said, look out the site for the tomb of the Lord Chancellor Elliott. As they proceeded in the direction of the Abbey, a sudden turn in the path brought them upon two ladies, one engaged in reading a book, whilst the other was listening to her, resting her hands on the handle of a very formidable parasol. Elliott stopped, and checked the progress of his friend, by placing a hand upon his arm, and whispering "Stay! she is there!"

Miss Mayley's eyes had for a moment wandered from her book and rested upon her persecuting admirer, whilst Mrs. Gregson, surprised at the sudden cessation of the reading, looked up, and was about to turn her spectacles in the same direction she found her niece's regards had taken, when Miss Mayley suddenly exclaimed, "Oh, dear aunt, don't!"

"Don't what?" replied Mrs. Gregson, and, as a matter of course, staring with all her eyes in the forbidden direction.

"What an unlucky *contretemps*," Marian thought half aloud: "the man will think I am the fourteenth daughter of some unpopular family, and wish to attract his attention," and forthwith she proceeded to read with much energy, but corresponding incoherence.

U

Elliott would have retreated, but Elmsley insisted upon taking the enemy in front, and, as they advanced, poor Marian Mayley was horrified to hear her aunt exclaim—

"Why, my dear, I've seen that young man's face before, I'm sure and certain. Of course I have! Isn't he the polite person who gave up his hackney-coach to us, when we were catched in the rain at Drury Lane Theatre? If he looks this way again, I shall certainly give him a bow."

As the Fates would have it, this chance introduction did not take place, Elliott, fancying that he and his friend were the objects of Mrs. Gregson's attention, passed by, apparently unconscious of the presence of either of the ladies, and Marian was very grateful for her escape; continuing, however, to make so many blunders, as she attempted to read on, that her aunt came to the conclusion, that the glare of the sun was hurting her eyes, and suggested a walk to the gate, where Mrs. Gregson usually invested a penny in curds and whey, to the great scandal of her niece, and the amusement of other fine ladies.

The Abbey was not open that morning, as the Dean and Chapter were whitewashing the poets, or cleaning the waxwork, and therefore the two conspirators were compelled to seek some other occupation. The milk-shop was in a little street leading out of Leicester Square, and Elliott remembered that it was faced by one of the *restaurants* peculiar to that quarter. Elmsley knew it well, he said, "and I go there whenever I want an order—I mean whenever I desire to visit the Opera, as the place is frequented by many of my professional friends, both native and foreign."

"Then we will lunch there; and as one of the windows commands a view of 'the dairy,' we shall be prepared to act as soon as Mrs. Digby affords us the means of doing so."

Elmsley considered Elliott's suggestion worthy of all commendation, and a walk of a quarter-of-an-hour soon found them seated at "Paravini's."

Having called for the carte, the dishes for selection appeared to be numerous, and had been named after very distinguished prototypes; but Elmsley's experience led him to recommend some of the homeliest preparations, and those least subject to sauce. Whilst their lunch was in preparation, Elmsley recognised, at the other end of the room, a theatrical friend, named Ranton, and one whom he was particularly glad to meet.

Apologising to Elliott for leaving him to the contemplation of the red cow over the milkman's door, Elmsley joined his friend, and after certain civilities had passed between them, said:

"Have you read the drama I sent you?"

"Yes, Captain, and I like the piece very much," replied the actor. "I think I could do something with the part of the brother, although the woman is certainly the stronger of the two."

Actors, as a rule, never admit their own part in a piece to be the best, and therefore Elmsley bowed to his friend's criticism, at once expressing his pleasure at what he heard.

"I am greatly indebted to you, Mr. Ranton," he said, "for the trouble you have taken for me; and may I ask you to increase the obligation by putting the drama into the hands of your manager?"

"I would," said Ranton, "if I thought it would serve you; but it would not, strange as that assertion may seem to you. Managers are very jealous of all their prerogatives, and ours, though the best fellow in the profession, would resent any interference with his duties, and your piece would be rejected."

"I am sorry to hear that," said Elmsley, "as I know how difficult it is to get a piece, by an unknown man, read by a manager."

"You would not be surprised that it is so," replied Ranton, "did you know the crude—nay, unmeaning rubbish that arrives at the stage-door under the name of dramas. No;

I should not serve you. You must know some one who has influence with our governor."

"Would Rupert Merville's recommendation have any weight, think you?" asked Elmsley.

"Rupert! dear old Rupert! No doubt of it, and he would think it no trouble—in one of his moods—to read and write about your piece," said Ranton.

"I am greatly obliged," replied Elmsley; "I think I can obtain his assistance."

"I have left the piece out in case you should call," said Ranton, "as you would not let me send it back—so, tat-ta! I have only run out during a carpenter's wait, as we have a long rehearsal of a certain failure. Look here," showing some soiled sheets of paper, "this is my part; not seven lengths for a man who has played Hamlet, and that is thirty-two."

Mr. Ranton made his *exit* with this piece of professional grumbling, and Elmsley returned to Elliott, and the lunch, which had been placed on the table.

Elliott told him that during his absence he had seen Mrs. Digby hurrying into the milkshop, carrying something bulky concealed under her shawl, and which she had left behind when she returned into the street.

"Then the Pomeranian beauty is in captivity," said Elmsley; "and we have but to await the announcement of the sum offered for her ransom to present ourselves to the Princess of the golden money-bags."

The Captain's thoughts were evidently in the theatre, and it was to be hoped that he was not quoting from the drama which Rupert Merville was to read and recommend.

Paravini's wines were to be treated both with respect and caution. They professed to be natives principally from La belle France and the banks of the Rhine, and it was quite evident to those who made their acquaintance that they never would have been admitted again to the land of their birth, so much had they suffered from becoming naturalised in England.

They were not, also, entitled to be received with unlimited confidence, as, like other foreign exiles, many of them had assumed names which they were not entitled to bear in their own countries, and much that was "Ordinary" had called itself Lafitte, and the most plebeian of hocks had assumed the princely designation of Metternich. The two plotters, however, sought "Dutch courage" rather recklessly, and a quiet stroll in the Park was decided upon before opening the campaign in Suffolk Street.

Elliott paid the bill, and then went forth with the Captain.

The fresh air by the lake-side soon dispelled the feeble fumes of Paravini's wine, and the two returned slowly, but confidently, to the scene of action.

On a street-post they read as follows :—

"STOLEN OR STRAYED,

A POMERANIAN DOG.

Answers to the name of 'FLORETTA.'

Wore a blue ribbon, to which a locket was attached, containing nothing particular.

Whoever will bring the same to No. —, Suffolk Street, Pall Mall, shall receive (no questions asked)

ONE SOVEREIGN REWARD."

CHAPTER XXIV.

MRS. GREGSON and her niece returned home punctually at one, according to the custom of the elderly lady, as an excellent luncheon worthy of her civic experiences was always prepared as a mid-day prop to a rather hungry constitution. The two ladies had reached the drawing-room, preparatory to making a slight toilet, when Digby intercepted their ascent, and with looks of terror and a voice of woe announced the abduction of "Floretta." Miss Mayley was quite as distressed as she ought to have been at her loss, but to Mrs. Gregson the shock had been nearly productive of very disastrous consequences, for "hitting her," as she said, "just as she had arrived at the second landing after a sharpish walk home, as Marian had been very fidgety all the morning, it fairly took the breath out of her body, and spoiled as nice a little appetite as she had had all the summer."

Digby had anticipated some of these consequences, and with a forethought which did her great credit, had prepared, by the assistance of the foot-boy (who had had the advantage of a parish education, and been weaned as it were in livery), the hand-bill which had attracted subsequently the attention of Elliott and Elmsley. Digby advised the immediate printing and circulation of the announcement of the loss the family had sustained, and the foot-boy being despatched to a neighbouring printer's, delivered the "copy," and then abandoned his afternoon duties to search the neighbourhood for the lost Floretta, in the hope of securing the reward as some compensation for the trouble she had occasioned him in washings, combings, and constitutional promenades.

As Digby was in attendance on Miss Mayley, the conversation turned naturally on the lost Floretta, and Digby detailed how she thought she should have dropped when she first missed the dog, and had it not been for her bottle of smelling salts, she never should have done what she had done, which was to run out into the open streets with nothing on but her cap, and without a bit of shawl upon her shoulders. So strange she looked, that two gentlemen—quite gentlemen, who were standing at the corner of the street—asked her what was the matter; and when she told them, one of them, the younger one, exclaimed, "Miss Mayley's dog! Captain, let us scour the neighbourhood."

"Yes, your lordship," replied the older party; that is, Digby was almost sure that he said "your lordship," but she was too confused at the moment to take her affidavit of the exact words.

Why did Marian's cheeks flush, and her full bosom rise and fall more quickly, as Digby told her this lady's-maid's fib, and read its effects upon her mistress, as she looked over her shoulder at her form reflected in the glass?

As Marian did not speak, Digby thought it advisable to make an observation.

"It was very kind, Miss, wasn't it, of two strangers to take so much interest in poor Floretta?"

"Very," replied Marian, "though I fancy you were mistaken in imagining one to be a lord. He is a gentleman evidently—that is, I mean from his politeness, he must be one."

"O yes, certainly; that is, if we mean the same person," said Digby, artfully, having observed Marian's recent confusion.

"I mean no one in particular, how should I?" replied Marian, in a little pet. "My poor dear Fioretta, I shall never be happy again if I lose you!" she added, after a pause.

"Oh, yes, you will, Miss. You'll get married some day, and want no other pet than your husband. See what offers you've had, and refused already."

"Offers, Digby! I hope you do not consider those offers, as you call them, which I ought to have entertained for one moment."

"Oh, certainly not; though Mr. Hardman, the wholesale tobacconist, was very rich, and kept a beautiful phe-aton, Miss—"

"And patronised the horrors in which he dealt," replied Marian, inflating her fine nostrils to express her disgust.

"I don't think Mr. Richards such a very disagreeable man," said Digby, slurring the words a little.

"Digby!" exclaimed Marian, "the man called himself an upholsterer, but I do believe he sometimes performed at funerals."

"You don't say so!" said Digby, although she knew well enough that Mr. Richards performed the necessary duties of undertaker to the Corporation of London.

"As for that Mr. Ruffles—a broker, was he not?—I never saw him without some unpleasant association. I always thought him one of those cruel men in possession of whom I have read, and fancied he was making our furniture up into lots."

"La! Miss. Mr. Ruffles was a stockbroker, not a furniture one. But I see how it is," answered Digby, "the City must give up the hope of having you for a lady-mayoress."

"If they would make the position permanent, I might be tempted," said Marian, with a smile.

"Well! if I didn't think so!" cried Digby. "Excuse me, Miss, but I have often said to myself, again and again, Miss Mayley will never marry under a title. And why should you, Miss? There are plenty of remnants of nobility that may be had at a bargain."

"Digby, don't talk such nonsense," said Marian. "You are always thinking of matrimony."

"But not on my own account, Miss; do me the justice to say that;" and feeling that she had sufficiently prepared the mind of her young mistress to receive any favourable impression that her employers could make, she left Miss Mayley to her own reflections.

The foot-boy was not successful, and had returned rather depressed and exhausted, to be soundly rated by the cook, with whom things had gone wrong all that day, as things will go sometimes; and when he, in the plenitude of his own tribulation, ventured "to give her as good as she sent," at a moment when she was particularly hot, she administered to him a succession of cuffs which reminded him of his parochial beadle, and sent him howling to his only place of retirement —the boot-hole. Pain and disappointment, combined with brick-dust and blacking, had made him totally unfit to be seen when Elliott and his ally arrived with Floretta; and Digby, having been on the watch, was therefore enabled to open the door, and admit the conspirators.

The sound of the knocker roused Mrs. Gregson, who was sleeping off the effects of the shock her feelings had sustained by the loss of Floretta, and her appetite; and going to the glass (a feminine habit all over the world) she discovered to her horror that, in the agitation occasioned by the events of the morning, she had put on her bugles and not her bird of paradise.

To retreat up-stairs was the instinct of the moment; and Miss Mayley was left to receive the visitors.

Digby entered the room with mouth and eyes open, exclaiming as she did so, "O my dear Miss, here's Floretta brought back—"

Marian rose up instantly, and as she advanced towards the door, exclaimed, "Where is the darling?"

"Hush, Miss," said Digby, interposing herself, "who *do* you think has brought back the pet?"

Marian could scarcely say Who? as she was instantly anticipated by Digby's answer.

"No other, Miss, than the two gents that spoke to me this afternoon. They have found her, and are on the landing outside, waiting to present her."

"O Digby, how could you invite them up, and my aunt not in the room?—they will think it so rude to be kept there."

"Then I had better show them in;" and without waiting for a reply, Digby introduced the two male conspirators, and then ran up-stairs to attend upon Mrs. Gregson, whose bell had been jingling in vain for some minutes.

Marian suspected some *ruse* when she saw Elliott—her unknown persecutor, as she was accustomed to consider him —and had long thought he would one day do something desperate. Her beautiful face was therefore rosy with blushes, and her eyes brilliant, not with pleasure, yet scarcely with anger; so that poor Elliott's confusion was complete, and he could only stammer out, "I—that is, we have to apologise, madam, for this intrusion; but understanding that this little—little——"

"Pomeranian beauty," chimed in Elmsley, seeing Elliott in difficulties.

"Yes—Pomeranian—belonged to you—I—we—I could not be satisfied until we had placed it again in your possession."

Was he a barrister? Had he eaten terms for such an exhibition as this?

Marian was relieved by his embarrassment, as she had expected to have met, perhaps, a brazen fellow, who would have astounded her by his impudence. She had, therefore, courage to reply, saying, "I am greatly—very greatly obliged for the trouble you have taken about such—a trifle"—and then she paused. Elliott would have given anything for his wig and gown, feeling that he was called upon to say something more, or to withdraw. A glance at Elmsley decided him.

"Some physiologists," he said, leaning one hand upon the

table, "have asserted that these lower animals are really guided by reason, and not influenced simply by instinct. I think— I think, this little——"

"Pomeranian pet"—again Elmsley came to the rescue.

"Yes—pet—the conduct of this pet destroys the hypothesis."

"I don't quite understand you, sir," said Miss Mayley, speaking very sincerely.

"I mean, madam," continued Elliott, placing one hand under the tails of his coat, and the other in his bosom—his favourite attitude when addressing an imaginary jury in the solitude of his chambers—"I mean, madam, that being an object of solicitude to you, had he been directed by reason, he would never have grown tired of captivity, and sought for freedom in the streets of this metropolis."

Marian knew not what to answer in reply to such eloquence, and so she said, "You flatter me, sir."

"Indeed not," continued Elliott, "for I consider flattery another form of insult; and if I dare——"

The opportune arrival of Mrs. Gregson prevented Elliott making a greater exhibition of himself than he had done already, and relieved Marian from a position which was becoming very embarrassing.

Digby had possessed Mrs. Gregson with the business of her visitors, and she therefore was prepared with a profusion of thanks when she entered the room. They nearly choked her, however, as she recognised at once the young gentleman to whom they had been indebted for the hackney-coach, and whose civility she had been so anxious to acknowledge in the morning.

"Why, deary me, Marian!" she exclaimed, "if it is not the gentleman we were talking about this very morning in the Park, before I took my curds and whey." (O Marian Mayley!)

"Pray sit down, gentlemen; for I am sure, and so was Marian, that you, sir," addressing Elliott, "was so very good when we went to see 'Romeo and Julia' at Drury Lane, as to give up your hackney-coach when it was raining cats and dogs, as you may say."

"You are very kind to remember such a slight civility," said Elliott, recovering his self-possession.

"O dear, no; if you hadn't, sir, I should have spoiled my new turban, and the bird of paradise in it, which cost me two guineas and a half, wholesale price, I assure you."

Elliott seeing how much Marian was annoyed by her aunt's conversation, rose to leave, and this consideration was not lost upon Marian.

"And now," continued Mrs. Gregson, "only to think that you should have brought back our darling little Floretta, of which Marian, dear, you'll now be fonder than ever, having known her loss. I've got a sovereign somewhere, I know"—fumbling in a capacious netted purse, "and I am sure we're more obliged than money can pay."

"O, my dear madam," said Elliott, "pray do not ask me to cancel the pleasure I have received in restoring your favourite, by compelling me to accept your promised reward. [How considerate, thought Marian.] But if I might dare to ask permission to make your acquaintance——"

"Oh, not the least objection, on my part," said Mrs. Gregson; "but Miss Mayley, my niece, is no longer quite at her own disposal or mine."

Elliott's heart sank within him, as he instantly saw (Love is so readily jealous) a rival who had already been accepted.

Elmsley guessed what was passing in his friend's mind, and resolved to set that matter of doubt at rest.

"Ah, ah!" he said, cheerily, "some happy fellow, I presume, has *veni, vidi, vici*'d it. Lucky dog—luckier than Miss Floretta, here."

Marian's eyes flashed angrily, but Mrs. Gregson, having no reason to be disturbed, continued coolly: "O no, not a sweetheart, sir; if that's what you call being 'vidivicied.'

O dear, no—it's her guardian to which I referred, Mr. Warner."

Elliott had moved towards the door, being anxious to spare Miss Mayley; but Elmsley was less considerate, and noway inclined to evacuate his position.

"Mr. Warner?" he asked—"Mr. Warner! I once served with a fine fellow, named Warner. · I wonder if it is the same."

"I don't know," replied Mrs. Gregson; "but you might have served with him. Pray, what was your line of business?"

Marian uttered a little cry, which both the gentlemen were too considerate to notice, and Elmsley bowing, said:—

"I was not so fortunate as to be brought up to commerce. I was in the army."

"Oh," said Mrs. Gregson, not in the least disconcerted, "I remember now.

'Who'll serve the King? cries the sergeant aloud.'

Deputy Baffer used to sing a song about it. No, sir; you could not have known Mr. Warner in that capacity"—and a knock at the door led her to add—"but you can now make his acquaintance, as that's him, I should not wonder."

An introduction to a male guardian was more than either the conspirators had bargained for; but Elliott was quite prepared for any emergency likely to arise from contact with such a formidable personage as a guardian of real life.

"You have company, ladies," said Mr. Warner, bowing.

"Yes, Mr. Warner," answered Mrs. Gregson, whilst Marian blushed deeply and looked at the carpet. "These gentlemen have kindly brought back our Floretta, who, naughty little dog, ran out of the house this morning in search of its mistress."

Elliott waited calmly to ascertain what Mr. Warner might have to say, and resolved to shape his own course accordingly.

Not so Elmsley, who, presenting his card—a ceremony neither had thought necessary, or remembered to be so until the present moment—said :—

" I shall always feel grateful to the little wanderer, since she has introduced me to—Mr. Warner."

Warner bowed very stiffly, and having read the name on the card—there was no address—looked Elmsley hard in the face, and repeated his name very slowly.

"Do you know the Captain ?" asked Mrs. Gregson, with an expression of pleasure.

" I remember the name, I fancy," replied Warner, placing the card in his waistcoat pocket.

" He recognised yours the moment I mentioned it," said Mrs. Gregson, " and thought you had served together under the banner of His late Gracious Majesty ? "

" Hem ! "

Warner gave a short cough, and then added :—

" You have thanked these gentlemen, I presume, for their politeness, and therefore, Captain Elmsley, and you, sir, will not think me rude "—he rang the bell—"in wishing you a good day, as I have business with these ladies."

The situation was embarrassing enough, but the foot-boy having been listening on the landing outside the drawing-room door, their probation was a very short one. They, therefore, would have bowed their *adieux* and departed, but Mrs. Gregson insisted upon shaking hands with both, to the annoyance and amusement of Marian and Mr. Warner. Was Elliott deceived, or did those lustrous eyes glance upon him once, and for a moment only, as he left the room ?

"Have you met those people before ?" asked Warner.

"This morning, in the Park," replied Mrs. Gregson; "but Marian wouldn't let me notice them. I've no doubt they thought us rude, as the young gentleman gave us up his coach one night at the play.".

"Do you know that one of them is little better than a swindler, and has been so for years ? "

"Oh, you must be mistaken, sir," said Marian, colouring deeply.

"In Captain Elmsley?" asked Warner. "No, no; such men are not to be mistaken or forgotten."

"But the other, sir," said Marian, hesitating before she added—"I have some reason to believe—is a nobleman."

"Who told you that, my dear?" asked Warner, and before Marian could have replied, had she been inclined to have done so, Digby entered the room, and Warner made a bold guess, saying:—

"So, Mrs. Digby, you have been in league with the persons who have just left the house?"

The go-between, with all her tact and coolness, was taken aback by this sudden accusation, and became so' confused, that Warner waited for no further confirmation of his suspicion, but requested her to leave the room at once, and the house to-morrow morning. Digby soon recovered her self-possession, and was not one to retire without firing a shot.

"Well, sir," she said, "I don't care a great deal about the place. Miss Mayley is certain to be married in six months, and then the lady's-maid would degenerate into a servant, and that wouldn't suit me." The noise she made in shutting the door set Floretta barking, and her poor young mistress was grateful for the temporary diversion.

"My dear Mr. Warner, what an escape we seem to have had! Do you really think that nice military gentleman is a what's-a-name?" asked Mrs. Gregson.

"And the other no lord! Yes, my dear Miss Mayley," Warner added, taking Marian's hand, and looking at her sadly and kindly. "Wealth and beauty are dangerous possessions—they have ruined the happiness of many a heart. You have both, my dear; let this morning's adventure be remembered."

The young maiden's face reddened, as though she rebelled at this unaccustomed schooling.

"It is a father that speaks to you, dear Marian,—one

whose own heart is bleeding at this moment from a wound inflicted by a daughter's thoughtless act, and who has no other
desire than to clasp her to his bosom and forgive her."

Marian had kept her eyes fixed upon him as he spoke, and
when he had ended she rose and kissed his forehead. Nothing
more was said, no more words were needed, and Warner left
the room, to return at dinner-time with a pleasant face and a
cheerful voice, as though to assure his pretty ward that he
was not always disposed to play the schoolmaster.

The next morning, when Warner arrived at the office of
his agent in the City, he found there Lucy and Jack Spraggatt.
With tearful eyes and a smiling face she met him as he
entered, and having said, with a choking voice, " All is well,
dear love," laid her head upon his bosom, incapable of
further utterance. Jack Spraggatt—who, unfortunately for
himself, inherited " much of his mother's weakness "—dared
not trust himself to speak, but proceeded to open his large
black pocket-book, and then produced from it the certificate
of the marriage of Florence Warner to Edward Norwold, and
which he read aloud as distinctly as he was able, merely
adding : " her cousin—your brother Gilbert's son."

Warner's face became pallid at the announcement, and he
would have fallen had not Lucy placed a chair for him, and
Jack blamed himself for his indiscretion in making him
acquainted so abruptly with the knowledge they had obtained,
and he was only relieved when Warner had asked him for
the paper.

Warner read it over twice, as though he doubted the
correctness of what his eyes assured him was there written.
When he had satisfied himself that he comprehended the
meaning of the words, he said, in a low voice, " Mysterious
Providence ! Is it decreed that the vow I made, in the agony
of my affliction, should have been fulfilled in vain ! "

" Even so, dear husband ! " and Lucy knelt down by his
side, and took his hands between her own. " Nor must
we regret that it has been so ! Our sorrows are not to be

cast from us impatiently or absolutely, for no grief, however great, is sent to us without its purpose. Endurance, humbleness, and sympathy for all mankind, are what we are taught by sorrow. You—and we who have shared your life—resented the affliction which came upon you, and said: 'This shall not be borne, but as we choose to bear it.' And so we have lived and planned and determined until two have been joined together, and by that union we are compelled into submission and obedience, but by a hand of gentleness and mercy."

"You are reproaching me, Lucy," said Warner; "and yet when I have sometimes wavered in the course I was pursuing, you have always urged me to continue in it."

"Do not think my words reproaches, dear George," Lucy replied. "You will not do so when you have recalled them. Nor do I wish or counsel you to abandon the name you have made so honourable, through the many happy years we have passed together. No. I would have you see, dear husband, that no common chance has restored your child to her just inheritance, although we had reared her in the lonely Bush, and placed the ocean between her and the home·of her forefathers."

"And would you have me forgive all that has passed, and take her, and the son of my bitter, unrelenting enemy to my heart, Lucy?"

"I would! I would!"

"O Lucy, can you doubt it?"

They embraced each other for some time, whilst Jack Spraggatt was snuffing and blowing his nose violently at intervals, at one of the windows which looked out upon that most depressing spectacle in London—a City churchyard.

We know how Lucy and Jack had journeyed about, until they had come to a check in the little chapel in the Avenue Marbeuf, and why no letter had reached Florence. Jack advised that the next call should be made at Sir Gilbert's house, as it was nearly certain that the whereabouts of Mr.

x

Edward Norwold would be known there; and as Warner considered it to be his duty now to pursue the inquiry, he dismissed his wife and brother-in-law to their hotel, and proceeded to Gilbert's residence in St. James's Square, almost unconscious of all around him from the tumult of conflicting feelings by which he was agitated.

The lamp in Mr. Vincent Elliott's chambers, in Pump Court, Temple, had been noticed burning late into the preceding night, and the shadow of that gentleman parading the room had led his opposite neighbour to fancy that he was training for a walking match, so rapidly and continuously was it observed to appear and vanish. Elliott was, in truth, utterly dissatisfied with the past day's proceedings; he could not rest in his easiest chair, and a retirement to bed was ridiculous. He had been a party to a shabby deception, which, now that he was alone, neither his love, or whatever his feeling was for Miss Mayley, nor the excitement produced by Paravini's obfuscating liquids, could justify. No—he had done an ungentlemanly act, and Miss Mayley and the turbaned lady, and Mr. Warner, had doubtlessly come to the same conclusion, hours ago. What a horrible thought! and one for which neither brandy and soda, nor cigars, were palliatives.

Walking! perpetual walking, was his only relief, and so, like Douglas Jerrold's "Jack Halcyon," who declares, "Let a man have any trouble he will, and he has only to walk—walk—walk, to get rid of it"—he kept striding about his chamber until the person in the rooms under him protested by vigorously thumping against the ceiling with a poker.

Elliott was too much of a gentleman to continue an annoyance, and, therefore, as St. Clement's clock struck four, he rolled on to his bed, and nearly strangled himself in his sheets during the first restless doze which exhausted nature perpetrated.

In the morning, after a most unsatisfactory breakfast, and

several futile attempts to read the newspaper, he came to the
conclusion that the proper thing to be done, was to make a
call in Suffolk Street, and apologise to Mr. Warner, and
through him to the ladies.   He arrived too late, as Mr.
Warner had left for the City, and thither Elliott went,
having been furnished with his direction by Jacob the foot-
boy.   He had scarcely turned out of Suffolk Street, when he
saw the very man he was in search of approaching at a quick
pace, and evidently much disturbed by his thoughts.

"Why, here comes Warner," thought Elliott, "and not in
the best of humours, I fancy.   Something's 'up' in the
market which he hasn't got—or something is 'down' that
he has!   I don't care.   I shall stop him.   Good morning,
Mr. Warner."

"Good morning, sir!" replied Warner, continuing his
course, not regarding, even if he had recognised, Elliott.

"I beg pardon for detaining you"—which he did not, as
Warner walked on.   "I wish to say a word or two in explanation of what occurred yesterday.   I was then an
intruder in your house, sir!"

"Oh!   I remember you," said Warner, still walking
forward—"A bold venture, sir! but the prize was worth
trying for."

"Oh! hang the money, sir," answered Elliott, "it was
not that which induced my impertinence."

"Pardon me," replied Warner, "if I am incredulous."

"You are quite right to be so," said Elliott.   "I am, now,
utterly surprised at my own conduct, I assure you.   It was
shabby, as well as grossly impertinent."

"You are a specious fellow," observed Warner, pausing
for a moment, and looking Elliott full in the face; but that
gentleman did not avoid the scrutiny, and replied—

"I am an honest fellow, if you'll only take the trouble to
inquire."

"I am afraid I cannot spare the time, my lord," said
Warner, with a sneer.

x 2

"Lord!" cried Elliott. "I am no lord. There's my card, sir. Vincent Elliott, Pump Court, Temple. I am a barrister."

"Then why allow your friend to represent you other than you are?" asked Warner, sternly.

"What, Elmsley! That fellow's cleverness has ruined everything," said Elliott.

"Your special pleading won't avail with me," said Warner, coolly. "I know you, sir, I fancy."

"If you do, sir," replied Elliott, his anger making him rather emphatic,—"if you do, you must be aware that I am incapable of the dissimulation with which you charge me."

Warner stopped, and, after a pause, said:

"And Captain Elmsley?"

"I knew how it would be," cried Elliott. "I knew I should suffer from my connection with that enigma. I picked him up at The Cock, in Fleet Street, and, like the old man of the mountain, he has stuck to me ever since. You misunderstand my character."

"No, I don't," said Warner, very coolly.

"Yes, you do," replied Elliott. "You think me a fortune-hunter—a swindler—a sneak; but you shall make inquiries. I insist upon it. There's my card."

"At present," answered Warner, "I have more important business on hand."

"Than repairing an injury done to a gentleman, and an honest man?" said Elliott, almost confronting Warner, who again regarded the barrister with a stern, fixed look, saying:

"You seem in earnest, sir?"

"I should think so," replied Elliott. "I have acknowledged that I have been guilty of a great rudeness—perhaps something worse, and I am anxious to apologise. You think me a rogue, and I must ask you to disabuse yourself of that impression.'

Well, sir," said Warner, taking the card, "I will make some inquiries."

"I thank you," replied Elliott; "and I will call to-morrow in Suffolk Street for my character, if you will kindly name an hour."

"If you please," said Warner, almost mechanically, as they had now arrived at the house of Sir Gilbert Norwold, and the thoughts of one were busy on another theme.

Elliott was surprised at the suddenness with which their conversation had been brought to a close, and more so when he saw Warner ring the servants' bell of the house before which they had stopped, and not make use of the knocker.

No less a personage than Mr. Gregory opened the door in full livery, his head plastered and powdered *secundum artem*, whilst his breast was decorated with a shirt-frill not unlike the fin of a stage demon.

"I wish to speak to Mr. Edward Norwold," said Warner, mildly.

"He doesn't abode here," replied Mr. Gregory. "We know nothing of him, and it is not likely. Sir Gilbert has cut him off, I believe. Howsever, we know nothing of him," and Mr. Gregory slammed the door rather unceremoniously.

Warner, in his consternation at this intelligence, beat upon the door with his closed hand, and cried, "Open the door! tell me where my child has gone!"

Gregory unfastened a little window beside the hall door, through which letters and small parcels were received, and said loudly, "If you don't go away, I'll call the police!"

The window was again closed, but Warner called out—
"Here, young man; here is money for you—only tell me the address of Mr. Norwold."

Elliott was moved by Warner's evident distress and excited manner, and found himself irresistibly compelled to interfere.

"You want some further information," he said; "we'll have it!" and then applied himself with considerable power to the knocker.

"Hallo, you sir!" said Gregory, opening the door—"are

you aware that that knocker makes a deuce of a row inside the house?"

"Yes," said Elliott, seizing him by the collar, and pulling him out on the door-step. "Now, answer this gentleman."

"Leave go off my collar!" replied Gregory; "don't you see I am dressed to take up lunch!"

"Answer, sir! answer!" said Elliott, in his excitement shaking the well-powdered flunkey till a little white cloud hung over the empty head.

"Use no violence, I pray," said Warner. "Young man, here is a note for five pounds—take it, and tell me where I can find Mr. Norwold—my daughter is his wife."

"Ah! sir," said Gregory—"thank'ee, sir—I can understand what the feelings of a father is when he pays for them in this way—and so, sir, you must know there was a great blow-up about three months ago in our family, and Sir Gilbert turned his son and your daughter out of doors—bang! —without a day's warning."

"And they went!" said Warner, with great effort—"they went where?"

"Well, sir, as it was no business of mine in particular I didn't make no inquiries, specially as Mr. Norwold insulted me in the most grossest manner that one gentleman could do to another. However!"—looking in through the door— "here, Baxter. Did you hear where the coach was told to drive as took away Mr. Edward's things?"

"Well, I did hear certainly, but the circumstance is gone out of my mind," replied Mr. Gregory's second in command, and to whom he had appealed. "I knowed the coachman as drove 'em though, by sight. He used to live helper in our stables, and went by the name of Chelsea Bill."

"Well there, sir," said Gregory, "Chelsea Bill is all we know, and as I hear my child a-crying" (referring to a bell, which was ringing), "I wish you good-day, and thank'ee for me."

When the door closed, Warner stood gazing at it, as

though he would read upon it the knowledge he so much
desired.   .

"Pardon me, Mr. Warner," said Elliott, "if I venture to
press my services upon you, but I am sure the man he has
mentioned—this Chelsea Bill—can be found; and, if so, the
discovery will be easy enough.   If not, an advertisement in
the paper is almost certain to obtain the information you seek.
Take my arm, sir.   Pray don't despair!   Keep up your
spirits; and if we fail to-day, we'll move for a new trial to-
morrow."

Warner grasped Elliott's hand warmly, and so Mr. Vincent
appeared to be in a fair way of making himself useful and
agreeable to the guardian of Marian Mayley, and of arriving
at that very desirable state of affairs without fraud or
conspiracy.

CHAPTER XXV.

WHILST Warner and Elliott and other friends were exerting themselves for the discovery of Edward and Florence, Jack Spraggatt had paid a stolen visit to Morden, in the expectation of finding Jasper Jellifer, from whom he hoped to obtain some valuable information respecting the lost ones. There was a railway then to Morden, and as Jack had not the heart to look up any of his old cronies—so anxious was he concerning the fate of his niece and her husband—he took up his quarters at the Station Inn, as a place where he was less likely to be recognised, than at any of his old haunts in the town. He needed not to have been concerned about himself, for the changes which time had made in him and in the dwellers in Morden would have enabled him to have passed anywhere without question, or even observation. The railroad had converted Morden into a busy place, and the presence of a stranger was not the event it had been twenty years before.

He found, as we know, that Jasper had gone to reside in London—although, as Sir Gilbert's collector, he paid occasional visits to the old town; but as his business was to collect money and arrange difficulties, he was not over-welcome at any time. His residence in London, Jack learned, was in one of the streets of the City, and at no great distance from the office of Warner's agent. The up mail-train passed through Morden about midnight; and therefore Jack, having some time upon his hands, made his way to the churchyard, which stood just outside the town. How many times had he revisited it in his dreams and his waking hours, since he had been away a lonely dweller in the Bush! It was the only spot which had remained unchanged, it seemed to him, and he was glad that it was so. He made his way through the old lych-gate beneath whose covering so many of the dead had halted on the way to their places of rest, leaving behind them for ever the busy world, in which they had played their parts for good or evil. On one side of the churchyard was a row of almshouses, their doors opening into it, as though the poverty of the indwellers had made death and its memories no longer terrible. As Jack Spraggatt approached the graves of his parents he was moved almost to tears (poor Jack! his woman's heart was always ready to well forth) to see that some friendly hands had been employed upon them during the day, and had clipped away the long grass and weeds. The pious task was not completed, and the worker's basket and well-worn shears were left behind, to be again employed before the sun went down. Jack felt interested to learn who had such grateful remembrances of the departed; but being desirous of keeping his visit to Morden unknown, he placed a bright new sovereign on the blade of the shears, and withdrew to another part of the churchyard. He had scarcely done so, when an old woman came from one of the almshouses to resume her self-imposed employment; and he was gratified to observe that her wonder and delight were extreme when she discovered Jack Spraggatt's gift. As she turned her face about in search of the good fairy that had made her so rich and happy, Jack recognised in her his nurse, whom he had left a buxom woman of forty. Pleased with what he had observed, but still desirous of keeping his visit unknown, and remembering that a footpath in the adjoining field led nearly to the Elms, he felt himself impelled to take it, and visit, as it were, another burial-place, where so many of his young hopes were lying. The dear old home was changed indeed! It had followed the fortunes of many other yeomen's dwellings when the temptation of higher rents added farm to farm, dispersing their happy households to seek fresh fields and pastures new, or compelling them to exchange their free out-door country lives for the monotonous toil of the pent-up city. The Elms farm, by Jasper's advice, had been united to an adjoining one, and the house was now let to labourers, who had neither time nor inclination to keep the once trim garden in decent order, but were content to grow their potato patches and cabbage rows where Jack remembered only flowers. Many graver sorrows give no sharper pang than such a sight, so witnessed. Jack cared to see no more of Morden and its neighbourhood, so hastening back to the Station Inn, he endeavoured to smoke himself into a happier state of mind; but the experiment was not successful, as he could not avoid remembering that the time had been when he could not have visited the old town without having a score of good friends to keep him company. There are many lonely vigils passed in inn parlours, made more lonely from the associations with which such places are beset; and the recollection of old days giving Jack the heart-ache, he was glad when the railway-bell summoned him to take his seat in the train for London.

On the following day, Jack started on a visit to Jasper Jellifer, and had nearly reached the house of our old acquaintance, before he remembered the letter which Raymond had confided to him. It was some time before he could recollect where he had deposited it, but as he had given a promise to deliver it, he was sure he had it safely somewhere. After rummaging certain boxes, which had not been disturbed since his return to England, he came upon the forgotten letter No. 1; but as No. 2 principally concerned himself, he did not continue the search.

Jasper Jellifer's place of business was gloomy enough, in all conscience. The street itself was narrow, having no outlet at one end, as though to exclude half the daylight that struggled into it, for the sun only had a fair chance for about an hour during the day. Jasper's lower windows were carefully whitewashed, so that he might have been engaged in forging bank-notes, or sweating sovereigns, or distilling without a licence, or some other illicit proceeding, without detection from any passer-by. His name was written in a fair black letter, on each side of the doorway, and beneath it he was described as "Commission Agent, &c.," whatever that ambiguous designation might have signified. Jack, however, entered boldly, and was received by a rough straight-haired head and a pair of spectacles, which popped up, like a Jack-in-the-box—it was quite as ugly—from behind a square curtained desk.

"Your pleasure, sir?" asked the head.

"I want to speak with Mr. Jellifer, sir," replied Jack.

"On business, sir?"

"Of course on business, sir."

"That is quite sufficient, sir," said the head. "Mr. J. is at dinner, but if it is on business, he doesn't mind being disturbed in the least. Oblige me with your name, sir."

"Mr. John Spraggatt," replied Jack.

"Mr. John—Spiggott, did you say?" asked the head, again bobbing up.

"S-p-r-a-g-g-a double t," replied Jack, not in any way disconcerted by the mistake in his name.

The head disappeared like a flash,—the simile being suggested by the glitter of the descending spectacles.

In another minute the whole of the Jack-in-the-box came forth, and it was not surprising that he should have contented himself, generally, with exhibiting the only part which nature had clothed, as some experimentalist had been evidently trying to ventilate him, so cracked and seam-broken were his garments. Jack Spraggatt put his salary at six shillings a week, remembering Jasper's character for liberality.

The clerk's message soon brought Jellifer down-stairs—as he lived in the house, to be ready for any job on an emergency, he said, and had not invited Jack Spraggatt up, until he—with commendable prudence—had satisfied himself that

he was in good case, and not likely to require assistance of a
kind which would not pay a commission.

As Jack looked well-to-do, Jasper received him with the
utmost cordiality, and expressed his regret that his visit had
not been made an hour earlier, and in time for dinner. The
truth was that Jellifer had had instructions to detain Jack in
the office, until Mrs. Jellifer could clear away the fragments
of their very limited meal, in case hunger might have tempted
him to covet the uninviting morsel which remained.

The Jellifers had grown rich, and loved their money-hoards
so well, that they cared even for the farthings.

Mrs. Jellifer was, of course, delighted to see Mr. Spraggatt,
as he had come upon business, and, therefore, as there was
no necessity for any hospitable display, she considerately
placed upon the table a bottle of ink, pens, and writing paper,
and then, having a due regard for commercial proprieties,
withdrew into an inner chamber.

Jack knew Jasper well enough, to be certain that, unless his
own interests were to be served in some way, he was not
likely to trouble himself with the affairs of other people ; and
Mr. Spraggatt, after briefly referring to his colonial experiences, inquired how far Jasper was in a position to dispose of
certain produce which had accompanied him to England, and
as to the rate of commission to be charged for agency.
Jasper was tickled at once, and after a few pertinent questions, he formed very enlarged opinions of Mr. Spraggatt's
wealth, and saw such a profitable accession of business, that
he even invited Jack to take a glass of wine, a proposal
which was respectfully declined.

"And, now, a word or two about old acquaintance," said
Jack, who then inquired after many of the old burghers of
Morden, and learned how some had died, how some had left
the place, and how others had become bankrupt, whilst a few
lived and thrived, as Jasper had done.

"The Norwolds," said Jack, carelessly— "they have
almost deserted the old place, have they not?"

"Entirely, you may say," replied Jasper. "I never can persuade Sir Gilbert to pay his people there a visit, and, consequently, I have to see to everything."

"His second marriage brought him a large accession of property, did it not?" asked Jack.

"Some ten or twelve thousand pounds at first," replied Jasper, "and her ladyship succeeded after her marriage to about 3000*l.* a year, which she had cleverly secured to herself by her marriage settlement. This money she spends."

"And not quite to Sir Gilbert's satisfaction, I conclude, from your tone, Mr. Jellifer?" said Jack.

"I do not say that," answered Jellifer, cautiously; "of course, her ladyship spends her own as she pleases; but I have reason to think that she does not confine herself to that amount."

Jack was rather surprised at this confidence on the part of Jasper, and felt satisfied he had a motive in giving it.

"Now, here," said Jasper, taking a paper from his side-pocket—"here is a note from her ladyship, and not the first I have received, asking for money—for an immediate loan, in fact, of three thousand pounds, as though I had three thousand pounds! The money would be safe enough, and the interest would be considerable, and some of the old family jewellery would be lodged as security. So the investment would be safe enough—if I had the money."

Jack could not quite see his way through this labyrinth of words; and so he said, "Very true."

Jasper paused for a few moments, and then continued: "I have just been thinking that, possibly, Mr. Spraggatt, it might suit you to make this advance until such times as you can find a permanent investment for your capital. You see her ladyship would give 20 per cent. for the loan, and—does it seem feasible, Mr. Spraggatt?"

Jack was not a quick thinker, but a vague notion came into his mind that some advantage to Warner, or Florence, or her husband, might come out of such a connection with Lady

Norwold, and he resolved not to decline entertaining the proposal without consultation with his brother-in-law.

"Your proposition," he said, "is unexpected, and I hardly know what answer to make. Three thousand pounds on Lady Norwold's security, and your own. Hum!"

"Not my own," replied Jasper, quickly. "I make it a rule never to become security for any client, however responsible, as I might be tempted by the practice to involve myself with a bad one. No. The jewels—diamonds, I believe—are valuable, I am certain, and Lady Norwold dare not risk the consequences of non-payment. The interest, remember, is larger than it would be if the transaction were an ordinary commercial one."

"Very true," said Jack, looking profoundly usurious. "I had forgotten that. You must give me until to-morrow to decide."

"That will do," replied Jasper; "and as it is as well to be clear upon all matters of business, I shall look for a commission of, say one per cent., from you, and so we will leave the affair for the present."

"Certainly," said Jack. "And now tell me what has become of Sir Gilbert's son, Edward. He has married, I hear, against his father's consent, and been discarded. Is it not so?"

"It is, I believe," replied Jasper. "All I know of the matter is this: Sir Gilbert, before he went away to Rome, three months ago, desired me to stop his son's allowance, which I had formerly paid. That is all I know of the matter."

"And you have never heard from young Norwold?" asked Jack, earnestly.

"Yes; I think I did once," replied Jasper, looking furtively at Jack. "Why do you ask?"

"Because I am anxious to see him," said Jack.

"On business to his advantage?" asked Jasper, peering from under his eyebrows.

"Yes; I have no doubt but it would prove so."

As Jack said this, Jasper stroked his chin, and then rubbed his nose with his hand, as though he could say something more than he had done, and was considering the prudence of doing so. The two men sat silent for a few minutes, and then Jasper spoke.

"It is not altogether impossible that I might be able to find a clue to the young gentleman; but it would take time and trouble to accomplish it."

Jack thought quickly enough now.

"Mr. Jasper, if you will furnish me with any address of Mr. Norwold after he left his father's house, I will give you fifty pounds."

The offer almost took away Jasper's breath, and its magnitude made him hesitate to accept it, not on account of the amount, but because he thought that information so valuable might possibly be turned to better account. As he did not see how it could be at the moment, he followed Jack's example, and promised to see what could be done by the next day.

"Having disposed of those two matters of business, I have another communication which I should wish to make in the presence of Mrs. Jellifer, as it refers to one who died at my location in the Bush—Raymond Ray, the miller."

Jasper turned deadly pale, and placing his finger on his lip, glanced anxiously at the door through which his wife had left the room.

"I think we had better speak on this subject first in the office, if you please," said Jasper, rising; but the moment he had done so the chamber door opened, and Mrs. Jellifer entered the room.

It was her custom to mix in all business transactions, and consequently, when absent as a matter of form, her ear was at a hole in the wall, and nothing which was said escaped her.

"Didn't I hear you call me, Jasper?" she asked; "I thought I heard my name."

"I was *about* to call you," said Jasper, forcing a grim smile, "as Mr. Spraggatt had requested to see you."

Mrs. Jellifer muttered some words in reply, and then sat down with her back to the window, whilst Jasper endeavoured to appear as unconcerned as possible. Jack Spraggatt, then, with more than his usual circumstantiality, narrated his meeting with Raymond Ray, and as he described the wretchedness of the convict's appearance, the miseries he had known, the unceasing suffering which ended only in death, Mrs. Jellifer sobbed aloud. Jasper's features became so rigid and dark, they seemed to have turned to iron.

"A day or two before Raymond's death," continued Jack, "he made me promise that, should I return to England, I would look you up, Mr. Jellifer, and place this letter in your hands. I do so now. Please read it while I am here."

He rose, and walked to the window, in order that Jasper might not feel himself observed.

The letter was rather a long one, and Jasper read it over to himself rapidly. When he had ended, he folded it again, and put it away in his pocket, saying:

"You know the contents of this letter, I presume, Mr. Spraggatt?"

"Not a word," replied Jack, "although I remember he said that it might concern me in some way. Does it?"

"Not in the least!" said Jasper. "It merely relates to his unfortunate condition, and contains his remembrances to me and my wife. I am sure we are greatly obliged by the trouble you have taken to bring it so far, and for your kindness to—him!"

"Yes—very grateful, Mr. Spraggatt," added Mrs. Jellifer, her voice full of tears. "He deserved a better fate, poor fellow! poor Raymond!"

Jack had no desire to continue his visit and remain a spectator of the grief of Mrs. Jellifer, as it was evidently sincere—and therefore he took his leave, promising to see Jasper on the morrow.

As Jasper did not return up-stairs, after showing Jack out through the office, Mrs. Jellifer went in search of her husband, and found him in his little room, again reading Ray's letter, which he folded up at her approach, and replaced in his pocket.

" Let me see that letter, Jasper, please," said Mrs. Jellifer, her voice made almost musical by her grief.

" You had better not read it, my dear. Its contents I have told you—only omitting one matter, and which, I am sure, you will not blame me for concealing. The poor fellow, no doubt, was very weak before he died, and was thankful for Spraggatt's kindness, and all that, and so he requests me to give that gentleman 200l. Why, Mr. Spraggatt would have felt insulted had I offered such a thing; for, as you heard, he has made an enormous fortune!—an enormous fortune!"

What a strange conflict went on in the mind of Mrs. Jellifer! Her love of money contended with her love for the dead man, and a desire to fulfil his last request; but Jasper continuing to set before her their own interests against the sentimentalism of Ray's letter, Mammon prevailed, and she gave a silent consent to her husband's reticence.

" It is strange that he never wrote to us before, Jasper, is it not? So often, too, as you urged him to do so. Poor Raymond! I should like to read the letter—the last I shall ever see of my only brother!"

" Not now, Barbara—not now! You had better not— indeed "—continued Jasper, as his wife urged her request. " I shall not let you read it now. I am going out this evening, at eight o'clock, on business, so let us have tea as soon as you can, as I have accounts to prepare before I go."

Mrs. Jellifer merely replied " Very well," but it was apparent from her look and manner that her purpose was unchanged, and that she would see that letter, as she was now convinced it contained something which Jasper wished to conceal from her. Such a conviction would have stimulated

Y

inquiry in a less unscrupulous woman than Mrs. Jellifer, who had, upon more than one occasion during her married life, resorted to very questionable means to obtain her own ends and gratify her curiosity. She had as a rule always endeavoured to know "the movements of her husband's various games," and although he professed to conceal nothing from her, she had more than once suspected him of keeping papers and other matters secret, and discovered afterwards that her suspicions were justified. The means she employed to obtain information were very simple, and not altogether dangerous; but Jasper would have protested strongly, most strongly, had he known how frequently the deep sleep which sometimes overcame him was attributable to a narcotic imbibed in the most innocent of his bibations. When he was rendered thus secure, Mrs. Jellifer did not hesitate to pry into all his secret doings, and Jasper was often surprised at a knowledge which seemed to be intuitive. Jasper's afternoon meal was hastened according to his request, and prepared after a recipe peculiar, let us hope, to Mrs. Jellifer. The cup neither cheered nor inebriated Jasper, but induced a sleep both long and sound. When the narcotic had produced this effect, Mrs. Jellifer took from her husband's pocket the letter from Raymond Ray. The sight of her brother's handwriting affected her for some moments, and she could hardly distinguish the characters, but this weakness soon passed away, and then she read as follows :—

"In the Bush, Australia,.
"Near Christmas Day.

"MY DEAR SISTER AND BROTHER,

"Before these lines can reach you, I shall have found a grave in this great wilderness, and terrible as death is, come when, and where it may, my present misery will make it almost welcome. Twelve long wretched years of suffering have passed since I came here a convict, and during all that time no word from home has reached me, not one single line of comfort from any one, until hope has often left me, and I have been made so desperate, that I could have braved anything but death to have escaped from my miserable thoughts. Hope, however, came again, and I went on trusting that the next mail would bring me some line from you, some means of lightening the load of wretchedness, which left me no rest day or night. None came. Why has this been? My fellow-convicts' had letters from home, why was there not one for me through all these miserable years? I wrote and wrote. Surely one of them must have reached you, unless, as I sometimes thought, you were dead, for I have never believed, after all which has passed between us, that you could have forgotten or abandoned me. If you have, let me tell you what torture you have inflicted upon me, and be your own consciences my avengers! Jasper, had you received my letters, you would have learned, that by keeping your solemnly sworn faith with me, you would have saved me from living the life of a beast, and given me the means, which were my own, of making myself a place in this country, as hundreds have done before me, wherein I should have held up my head again as a man, and been as happy as my crimes and my remorse would have allowed me to have been. Of that twelve hundred pounds of mine which you had in trust for such a chance as befel me, if you had sent me even a half—a quarter, I could have rescued myself from the misery I have undergone. You would have done so, would you not, if my letters had reached you? I will not believe otherwise, even now, when I should have died like a beast in the forest, but for one Christian man. I will not believe that either of you would have kept back what was mine by right and solemn swearing, had you known that it could have bought me a release from cold and hunger, blows and bitter words, which have done their work at last, and begotten disease which is eating away my life minute by minute, and has to be borne under the hardest toil that degraded men are driven to do. At times the thought has beset me, that I have been sold—yes, sold by you for the money you obtained by the deed of sale, and I dare not write what I said then—no, Jasper; no, Barbara! I am going to my grave, and I will try to forget all my savage anger.

"Barbara, dear sister, the only one I ever loved, except my mother, you would not have left me to this misery, I am certain. Our lives have been unhappy—guilty and unhappy—and we alone in all the world can find excuses for each other's errors, for we only know who were our early teachers, and to what privations and temptations we were exposed. All the good that was in us was crushed out long before we knew its value; no, not all, one true feeling was left in us—our love for each other. That has never gone from me—and at this last day, perhaps, of my miserable life, I will not believe that it has left you! Dear Barbara! I kiss you with my heart.   *   *   *

"It was a happy chance that made me resolve to go to Mr. Spraggatt, hoping to hear some news of home. He will tell you the wretched being that crawled to his door, and whom he has sheltered, and fed, and taught to die like a human creature. If ever this letter reaches you, he will bring it, and it is my dying wish that you give to him 200*l.* of *my money*, to buy some trifle which shall remind him of my gratitude, and, perhaps, induce other honest men to remember that the wretched convict—outcast as he is—is still a man.   *   *   *"

The letter went on to describe much more that Spraggatt had done for him, and concluded with earnest words, and lofty hopes, which had too solemn a meaning to be lightly read. They were unregarded by the worldly woman to whom they were in part addressed, although the rest of the letter was not.

As Mrs. Jellifer looked upon her sleeping husband, it is truth to own that she would not have grieved if his slumber had been eternal, so bitterly did she resent his treachery to herself, and to her brother Raymond. Jasper had told her, again and again, that no letter had reached him from Ray, and that he concluded her brother was dead, as one of his (Jellifer's) letters, and been returned to him unopened.

It was clear to her now, that she had been deceived, and much as she had loved money, living only to heap it up for no defined end, but to reckon its increase, she resented her brother's wrong and suffering as though she had been the victim.

From that hour Jasper became to her an object of mistrust and loathing, which needed only one other confirmation of his treachery, to be converted into hatred, that was strong enough to evoke revenge.

CHAPTER XXVI.

WHEN London was busy migrating northward, covering the country and pleasant fields with villas of every denomination, certain long-standing houses, deprived of their gardens and little meadows, became tenantless, or, until the builders razed them, were let to persons who set a low rent against the many discomforts of young streets growing to maturity around them. Many of those condemned houses had been occupied formerly by wealthy people, and commanded a certain respect by the evidences of their former condition, which could be traced on their walls and ceilings, displaying gilded cornices and florid mouldings, whilst without, the weed-grown carriage drives, and lofty iron gates and railings, showed their decadence from a former respectability.

In the dining-room of one of these houses, a neat, plainly-attired woman, of between thirty and forty, was ironing what are termed, we believe, "light things." Seated by the open window was her husband, reading a newspaper, borrowed from the neighbouring public-house, and smoking at the same time a meerschaum, almost black, its owner said, "with its burnt offerings of the nicotian weed." He wore slippers, and a dressing-gown, carefully patched in many parts, but free from stain everywhere, and altogether his appearance and employment were those of a person who might have lived in the old house in its better days, and decayed with it.

As the ironer paused for a moment to test the temperature of her iron, by holding it near her cheek, she said, in a sweet, pleasant voice, "I wish, Joe, you would step into the next street, and buy the potatoes."

"Elizabeth, my love," replied Captain Elmsley—for it was he,—"Elizabeth, my love, how often am I to request you not to call me Joe ? Joseph is my name, and nothing is so vulgar as Joeing, and Tomming, and Billing."

"Vulgar !" and Mrs. Elmsley sighed—"I'm always doing something vulgar ! Heaven knows what would become of us if I was as genteel as you, Joseph ! There ain't many officers' ladies as would do what I am doing now."

"My love," said Elmsley, tenderly, "I am not blind to your good qualities; you know how foolishly fond, how ridiculously proud I am of you, Elizabeth."

"Proud !" retorted Mrs. Elmsley, with a slight pout, "not much of that, I am thinking. We've been married three years, and you've never crossed the threshold with me half-a-dozen times in the day-time."

"You must not blame me for that," said the Captain, "indeed you must not. Blame society. It's a fashionable axiom that no man now-a-days can be seen with his wife !"

"Fashion !" cried the lady, drawing down the corners of a rather pretty mouth—"What have we to do with fashion on a little more than a hundred a-year !—or if we have, why don't I go shares ? No, I'm a slave, I am."

"I wish you hadn't said that," replied Elmsley. "Are you not the centre of my affections ?—the ivy that has entwined around my heart till it has become part of it ?—in fact, are you not my wife ?"

"And I might as well be a maid-of-all-work from what I get by it !" answered Mrs. Elmsley—and it really seemed as if she were in the right.

The Captain, however, placed her position in another point of view, by saying: "My love, don't repine; you know nothing of this hollow world—I know too much of it. I love you, Elizabeth, and cannot let you mix in that society which I have proved to be worthless. Your beauty would only excite envy, your virtues detraction, your conjugal affection ridicule. But now, surrounded by your flat irons, clothes horses, and culinary appurtenances, you look the embodiment of domestic felicity."

"Ah! none of your flowery speeches, Mr. Joe, I've had too many of them," said the wife. "Usen't you to tell me about your country-house?"

"Here it is!" replied the Captain—"there is Primrose Hill—yonder Chalk Farm."

"Your Parks, too!"

"Regent, Hyde, and Green! They're public property, and we are the public," said Elmsley.

Mrs. Elmsley only replied with a contemptuous "Pshaw!" Though we question if she were really angry, for there was a shadow of a smile on her face as she listened to her husband.

"The fact is, my dear," continued the Captain, "you are like a great many other people; you are discontented from the want of a perception of the advantages of your own position."

"My advantages!" cried the lady, with a scornful laugh. "Well! I do like that."

"Are you not the mistress of this mansion?" asked Elmsley.

"Mansion! a ruinous old house that nobody else would live in," answered the wife.

"Never mind, it is yours. Don't you do your own washing?"

"To be sure I do; but what's the advantage of that, Captain Elmsley?"

"Ah! I thought you did not see it," said the husband; "I'll show you. Your linen is always right, nobody wears your stockings but yourself, the basket is always home on a Saturday, and there is no washerwoman's bill to pay, when you have deciphered it."

"Well!" replied Mrs. Elmsley, "there is something in what you say now."

The Captain, thinking to improve his advantage, continued :

"You've the happiness to be your own cook—your own housemaid."

"As I know to my sorrow," was the rejoinder.

"Because you won't perceive the benefits of your situation. Go where I will, every one is grumbling about their domestics. One lady is going out of her mind through Susan : another's driven mad by Mary ; no comfort anywhere; for there seems to be an intestine war in every kitchen of the metropolis. You know nothing of this, and is not that a satisfaction ? "

Mrs. Elmsley was driven into a corner by this heavy charge of the Captain, and so she deployed a little, and said, "Well, but you might take me out sometimes with you, Joseph ? "

"Ah, how little do we know in what our real happiness consists ! " sighed the Captain. "Were we always together, that beautiful, that ecstatic feeling which we now experience, would be no longer ours."

"What feeling ? " asked the wife, in surprise.

"What feeling ! " cried the Captain. "The pleasure of meeting after absence. Were we always together, we should hate each other."

"La, Joe ! " exclaimed his wife, alarmed.

"True ! What gives people the yellow fever, and destroys their livers in India ? The blazing perpetual sun ! Nothing but sun won't do. You see what I mean ? Kiss me ! Take my word, Elizabeth, you're a happy woman, though you don't know it."

Fort Elizabeth surrendered, and saluted the Captain, who thought it generous to change the conversation in which he had obtained such a splendid victory; and, therefore, he asked, "Have you seen our lodgers this morning ? "

Mrs. Elmsley replied, that she had not spoken to them, but had noticed the gentleman go out rather early, adding, "They seem to be very respectable, though poor. Ah ! Joe, we are not the worst off in the world, are we ? "

"No, my love; and I am glad you believe me at last—
There! Go, my darling, and buy your potatoes."

"Well, I suppose I must," said the Captain's lady, laughing, and putting on her bonnet; "for I never see a man
hate to do any thing useful as you do."

"She is quite right," thought Elmsley, as his wife left the
room, "and my progenitor ought to blush in his grave for
the smallness of my annuity. Poor Elizabeth, she is a very
good wife, and much more economical than a servant."

He was interrupted by a knock at the door, and on desiring the applicant to come in, Florence Norwold entered
the room.

Elmsley instantly rose, and received her with much politeness and without embarrassment, as they had frequently met
since she and her husband had been tenants of the old dilapidated rooms up-stairs. They had occupied the lodgings
nearly a month, and their introduction to the Captain had
been simple enough.

When Edward left his father's house, he returned to his
wife's former lodgings, which were fortunately vacant, and
there he remained for some time vainly endeavouring to find
occupation by which he could earn an independent subsistence.
It had been easy to say, "I will depend upon myself;" but
none know, save those who have passed through the depressing ordeal, how difficult it is to emerge from respectable
poverty to respectable independence. The honest labourer
finds many uses for his brawn and sinews, but the poor name-
less toiler, who has only his bright intellect to offer in the
market-place, finds often scanty employment and small reward.
Edward Norwold was no exception to this too common condition of the mental workman, and he soon determined to
husband most carefully the little wealth he had, so that the
struggle might be prolonged to the utmost, as he was convinced that the parents of his wife had resented the step she
had taken, and abandoned her to the fate she had chosen. He
tried manfully and hopefully to find some way to competency,

but without success, and at last he determined to risk the rejection of a drama which had been the work of his former leisure. Unacquainted with the usages of a theatre, he put his little manuscript into his pocket, and proceeded at once to Mr. Weaver, one of the most popular managers of the day.

He was puzzled to find an entrance to the spacious theatre, and was rather disappointed at discovering that it had to be made through a small door, in a back street, around which were men in faded wardrobes, grouped idly, it seemed, but who were waiting to be summoned to the performance of their duties, as the rehearsal, then in progress within, proceeded.

Edward was rather abashed at having to face this group, as those comprising it eyed him with undisguised curiosity, and observed a profound silence when he requested to see the manager. A man occupying a dingy corner just within the entrance, from which the reek of some savoury mess came forth provokingly, assured him that Mr. Weaver was engaged, and would continue to be so all day; but if the gentleman would leave his business, it should be communicated in due course.

Edward was embarrassed. He was ashamed—he knew not why—to declare himself an author, seeking an interview with so great a man as the manager of the —— Theatre, and therefore he replaced his manuscript in his pocket, thanking the man, and promising to call again in a day or two.

Whilst he had been thus engaged, a gentleman had looked in at the door, and asked, "Anything for me, Jackson?"

A small piece of paper was handed to him, with somebody's compliments, and Edward would not have noticed him again, but for a vague fancy which beset him, that he also was an author, as he looked so gentlemanly, and yet so faded. When they passed out into the street together, their eyes met, and Edward's face must have betrayed the anxiety that possessed him, as Captain Elmsley felt compelled to address him.

"A thousand pardons, sir," he said; "but I am about to be impertinent enough to ask, if you are not an author?"

"I have no reason to deny that I am aspiring to such a position," replied Edward, glad of any sympathy, and there was kindness in the Captain's tones.

"I fancied I saw a MS. in your hand when I looked in at the stage-door just now. It was a piece which you are anxious to submit to the manager, I suppose?"

"Yes," answered Edward, "you have surmised correctly."

"My dear sir, you have set yourself a task for Tantalus," said the Captain. "You will wear out your boots, and your patience, however large the stock, before your desired end can be obtained by the means you are proposing for its accomplishment. No blame to the manager. A thousand calls a week are made at that stage-door. Rely upon it, without a friend at court, or a letter of introduction, you'll find all to be 'labour lost.'"

Edward looked very grave at this statement, the truth of which he had no reason to doubt, and he would have returned home, sorrowful enough, had not Elmsley said, "I'm afraid I'm an impertinent fellow, but as I read Gentleman in your face, and perhaps something else, which interests me, I shall be glad to be of service to you, if you will allow me. I am known to a great many persons connected with the theatres, and it is not improbable but I might find one or two to concern themselves for you, as they are a good-natured race, and never hesitate to do any one a good turn when they can."

"I am really greatly obliged," replied Edward, "and most willingly accept your kind offices."

"I am compelled to add a condition, which I trust will not be objectionable. It is proper that I should know something of your piece, and I will gladly meet your convenience to hear it read," said Elmsley. "I cannot ask you to my chambers—as at present they are out of repair."

"Pray make no excuse to me," replied Edward, "my lodgings are close at hand, and if I might beg such a favour, will you come at once and allow me to inflict my tediousness upon you ?"

Captain Elmsley cast his eye up to the clock of St. Martin's church, and, after a brief calculation of the time and his own obligations, consented to accompany the young author and sit in judgment upon his first-born.

Florence was delighted to see the cheerful face of her husband, and received the cause of it so genially, that the Captain's interest increased considerably. A slight luncheon, and then the reading of that great work, to whose eloquent scenes of passion, love, and pathos Florence was never tired of listening, or of repeating ; for she so loved the minstrel, that every touch of his had become a memory. At least, so Florence said, when Edward had left the room, and Elmsley was desirous to recall some passage which had pleased him, and which Florence quoted instantly.

Elmsley was honest in his criticism of what he had heard, and whilst commending it very highly, he pointed out a few imperfections which had reference principally to its construction for the purposes of the stage, and for which his experience readily suggested a remedy.

Before the Captain took his leave, Edward had informed him of his uneasy position, and his desire to earn and economise. Elmsley said nothing then of the accommodation of his suburban mansion, as he was always careful to conceal his place of residence ; but when he became better acquainted with Edward and Florence, and more interested in their fortunes, he confided to them his own peculiar state of life, and advised them to share his seclusion and its economical advantages.

The Captain's proposal was readily accepted, and Edward having invested a very few pounds in the purchase of some additional furniture for the two rooms, which Elmsley usually let, made them, by the aid of Florence's good taste, soon resume something of their old appearance under more prosperous tenancy.

"I am somewhat late to-day, Captain Elmsley," said Florence, with a smile, placing some money on the table; "but I have been watching the return of Mr. Norwold, until the business of the morning escaped me. He left home with great expectations of obtaining a clerkship in the city."

"Really, madam," said Elmsley, covering the money with his hand, "I am almost ashamed to receive this sum."

"Why so, my dear sir?" replied Florence, smiling again, "no gentleman need be ashamed of his rent-roll, however small; and we are happy to have found such a very considerate landlord."

"Well, my poverty and not my will consents," said Elmsley; "but should Mr. Norwold find his balance at his banker's inconveniently low at any time, I trust that he will consider me a friend, and make this poor house his home until brighter days return."

Florence was touched by this rhetorical flourish of her needy landlord, and thanked him with "nods and becks, and wreathed smiles," as she felt it difficult to find words at the moment, and then left the room.

When she had departed, and Mrs. Elmsley had returned from her marketing, the Captain completed his toilet, and having ascertained that a shoulder of mutton was to be added to the potatoes, promised to return to dinner at five o'clock. As he left the house he saw Norwold approaching, his eyes bent upon the ground, and his step slow and hesitating. Elmsley, therefore, conjectured that his morning's expectations had not been realised; and having no consolation to offer him, the Captain made a detour and avoided him.

"No success, Florence," said Edward, as he entered the room. "My want of experience again the objection. It is really disheartening. Very."

"It must be, dear boy," replied Florence, placing her arms around his neck, and kissing him; "but we must hope on, and strive on, as you used to say when we anticipated this struggle. No evil has come but what we have thought possible; and all that we have hoped may follow—will follow, I should have said—if we strive patiently."

"There is some comfort in what you say, darling," said Edward, "and I will not despond, but take new courage from this bright face and loving look, and believe that to-morrow will bring us nearer to the end of this 'hope deferred.' Aha!" he continued cheerily, when he had gone to his writing-table, "so you have been copying for me, and really made pleasant reading of what, in my abominable scrawl, seemed to be detestable nonsense. I wish the editor could have seen the pretty hand tracing these lines, its beauty might have dazzled him and hidden the poverty of the thoughts which are attached to these pot-hooks and hangers."

A little box on the ear and a kiss on the forehead were his punishments for such nonsense, and, had it been possible, he would never have talked more wisely, but have continued to deserve such reproofs. There was work to be done, however, and so putting by his walking-coat carefully, and assuming one less presentable out of doors, he sought, by the aid of pen, ink, and paper, to coin his thoughts into drachmas.

An hour or so had passed, when Elmsley entered his house and surprised his wife by the pleasing excitement which was depicted in his countenance.

"Elizabeth, my dear," he said, not regarding her mute wonder, "is there a sheet of note-paper in the house?"

"Dear me, Joe, I don't think there is," replied the lady; "but what has happened?"

"You shall know presently—but I want some note-paper. Ah! here is a sheet," said the Captain, rummaging the pocket of an old writing-case; "and now, my dear, I am going to invite the Norwolds to dinner. We have a baked shoulder of mutton, four silver forks and a gravy-spoon. Whilst I write the note, you ask Mrs. Jackson at the next house to lend us her little girl to deliver it."

"La! Joe, what nonsense!" cried Mrs. Elmsley. "Ask them to dinner and welcome, but what need of a note and Mrs. Jackson's girl, and all that fuss?"

"My dear," replied the Captain, "I wish the Norwolds to be assured that we know the rules of polite society, and are not neglectful of the usual *etiquette*."

"Then you'll dine without me, Joe," said the lady. "If there is to be any of that *ettyket* as you call it, I shan't be able to eat a morsel, and I won't sit at my own table looking like a goose. If Mr. and Mrs. Norwold will take me as I am, well and good. I shall be delighted to see them, but if onion-sauce is not good enough for them with shoulder of mutton, why I shall leave you to serve it up with *ettyket*."

The Captain knew his lady well enough not to perceive that she was in earnest; and whenever she arrived at that condition of mind, he had found from long experience, that it was conducive to domestic harmony to allow her to have her own way.

"Be it as you please, my dear Elizabeth," said Elmsley; "you shall deliver our compliments to our lodgers, and say that as I hope to have an important and pleasurable communication to make to Mr. Norwold, we shall be delighted if they will honour us and our shoulder of mutton with their company."

"Oh, I can't remember all that rigmarole, Joe, I'm sure; but I will run up and ask them to dinner, and you can make as many flowery speeches as you like afterwards," replied Mrs. Elmsley.

The Norwolds made but slight objection to dining with their friends, and the Captain's lady returned to make the necessary preparations for their reception, resolved to convince Joe that her onion-sauce was better than his *ettyket*.

It was as good as a transformation scene in a pantomime to see with what rapidity the shoulder and its attendant potatoes were transferred from the brown pan and the baker's tray to the cleanest of blue dishes, and placed on the pure white table-cloth, which glittered with the family plate. And then it was equally surprising to observe how Mrs. Captain Elmsley disappeared through the bedroom door with a somewhat heated face, disordered cap, and slightly stained dress, to return "in a brace of shakes," as she promised she would do, decked in the smartest of caps and the neatest of gowns, ready to do the honours of her humble hospitable table, after the Captain, in a playful manner, had bawled, "Dinner is served! Coming down, Mr. and Mrs. Norwold!" So the dinner, beginning with a simple jest, was made a merry one by the pleased and contented guests reciprocating from the bottom of their hearts the truthful welcome and friendliness of their entertainers.

When Mrs. Elmsley had cleared away, Florence helping her, though under much protest, and a jug of cold punch of the Captain's brewing had been placed upon the table, Elmsley rose with great apparent solemnity, and spoke as follows:—

"Ladies, before Mr. Norwold and myself proceed to tobacco, which delicious weed, I understand, one lady admires, and I know that the other adores, I wish to mention a fact which I think will make the incense more agreeable, and the punch more acceptable. I now produce a missive of some importance, which reached my hands to-day, but whose contents I did not communicate to any one at the beginning of our limited banquet, fearing that it might take away the breath of some of us, and the appetites of others. With your permission, I will read to you a note from that distinguished actor, and my esteemed friend, Rupert Merville, who writes from the Theatre Royal Drury Lane, and is pleased to address me as my dear old friend and captain:

"'I have more pleasure than I can express in the few moments I have at command between the acts, in communicating to you that Mr. Weaver is as much delighted with your friend's drama as I was, and will see you both to-morrow evening, if you will call upon him during play-hours, as he enacts'——"

z

The Captain did not over-estimate the importance of his communication, as poor Florence uttered a little cry, and fainted quietly away into the arms of Mrs. Elmsley, and Edward was so bewildered that he sprinkled his darling's pallid face with the cold punch, making her eyes smart for some minutes after her recovery.

And was it not a dream? Florence thought. Was her dear clever husband about to become famous, to proclaim to the selfish father that had discarded him what a noble son he had never sought to know and appreciate? To tell to those so dear, the dearest of all but one in the wide world, that she had not chosen unworthily, nor forgotten her proper course of duty without the great excuse to be found in the excellence which had enthralled her. Father, mother, Uncle Jack! would read of his triumph, and take her to their hearts again, and him also! Success was so certain.

Such was the estimate that silly Florence entertained of her husband's genius, now about to dazzle the world by aid of the footlights of a theatre. So the Captain was right. The incense and the libation were more acceptable for the revelation of the oracle.

CHAPTER XXVII.

JACK SPRAGGATT and Warner sat long in conference in the agent's gloomy office in the City, after the former had detailed the particulars of his conversation with Jasper Jellifer. Warner had always such loving faith in Florence, that he could not believe she had married anyone that was not worthy of her; and now that Herr Dortz had been so lavish in the praise of M. Edward, his pupil and his friend, he had forgiven his beloved child long ago, and craved with all his heart to call her home. Hitherto his search had been in vain, but he was strong in hope, and was, therefore, most desirous to restore her husband to his proper place again, in despite of the bad man with whom they both claimed such close kindred.

The sense of wrong, which in his own case he had endeavoured to extinguish by all the means that Christian men employ for such a charitable end, returned to stimulate him to do battle for his children, and he resolved to compel restitution at any sacrifice almost.

But how to proceed? His long absence from England, his change of name, and his brother's possession of the hereditary lands and title, made the task most difficult. He was, however, convinced that an outlet would be found, or this strange union would not have been brought about by such an unlooked-for accident. Was this extraordinary want of Lady Norwold's to be a means to the great end? It might be. Might she not fail to repay the money she sought to borrow, and so become a compelled agent to work in some way, unseen at present, the accomplishment of his desires? The security she offered—diamonds—Jasper said, might comprise the tangible evidence that the past had lied and done a wrong which was to be atoned for in the present.

The links of the chain might have been severed, but not lost; and Jasper and Gilbert's wife and himself were destined, perhaps, to unite them again! The money would be as dross to such a consummation.

Jack Spraggatt, therefore, called again upon Jasper, and gratified him greatly by confiding to him certain merchandise to dispose of on "commission;" for our honest friend could not consent to break faith, even with such a man as Jasper Jellifer. He then said:—

"I have been talking with a friend over your other proposal—I mean the advance of money to Lady Norwold. The interest she would pay, I think you said, would be twenty per cent."

"Less my commission. Yes," said Jasper.

"Well, it can be done, provided the diamonds are of adequate value; and that you vouch for—?" asked Jack.

"No, no! I vouch for nothing," replied Jellifer. "I believe the diamonds are family matters, and therefore I conclude of value, or they would not have been preserved."

"The family diamonds," thought Jack; "that sounds well for Warner's purpose."

"The interest, as I said, is large," continued Jasper, fearing that some difficulty was presenting itself; "and the pledge must be redeemed very soon, as her ladyship always gives a great party on Sir Gilbert's birthday—nobody knows why but herself. Then they would be missed by her husband, who has a sharp eye for such matters."

"Well, it shall be done, Jellifer!" said Jack. "If you and her ladyship will call on me to-morrow at this address"—(he gave him a card of the agent)—"a friend shall meet you with the money."

"Is the presence of her ladyship necessary?" asked Jasper. "She is a proud woman, and would perhaps decline such a visit."

"Then she may keep her diamonds, and we will keep our money," replied Jack. "The matter is in your hands, Mr. Jellifer. At twelve o'clock to-morrow I shall expect you, unless I hear from you before that time. Good day, Mr. Jellifer."

When Jack reached the street he gave himself a rough shake, as though he had been in contact with some unclean thing and was fearful of contagion. He had never in the days of his innocency liked Jasper, and now that he had some experience of the world and its wickedness, he more than doubted that Jasper Jellifer was a great rogue, and one, too, that he was destined to unmask, whenever it was worth the trouble of doing so.

As Jasper conjectured, Lady Norwold was very indignant when she heard of Jack's requirement, and vowed for some time that she would not go, and that Jasper must find other means of meeting her necessities or lose Sir Gilbert's favour. He had none, he protested again and again, and succeeded at last in reconciling her ladyship to the indignity of personally receiving the money in the City. It had been · so arranged with Warner, who felt a strong desire to be a witness of the humiliation of his brother's wife; but when the hour approached for the fulfilment of this wish, Lucy's better nature prevailed over him, and he deputed Jack to receive her ladyship—an office which that gentleman accepted with the utmost reluctance.

A note from Jasper announced Lady Norwold's acceptance of Mr. Spraggatt's terms, and that her ladyship would be in the City about twelve o'clock. Jack waited impatiently long past that time, until the neighbouring church clock chimed the hour of two; and then, as he was preparing to leave the office, her ladyship and Mr. Jellifer were driven up to the door in a hackney carriage. Nothing could exceed Jasper's obsequiousness as he ushered Lady Norwold into the little counting-house, and it was evident the haughty lady was not in the most amiable mood. Jack was glad of that. He did not mind a woman in her rough temper; but he had lived so much alone in the Bush, and in such easy society when out of it, that he would have been embarrassed had he had to have encountered a lady of fashion in her superfine manners.

"What a dismal hole!" said her ladyship, as she surveyed the little room where Jack was standing to receive her. "I had no idea that money was made in such a gloomy dungeon. 'Pon my word, I excuse your twenty per cent. Well, sir," addressing Jack, "are you the person who has put me to this inconvenience?"

"I am here, my lady," replied Jack, "at the request of Mr. Jellifer, to lend somebody three thousand pounds on certain jewels."

"Well, am I to stand throughout the business, Mr. Jellifer? Or am I to mount upon that pedestal?" said her ladyship, pointing to one of the high office-stools; for Jack had omitted to provide a chair.

"Oh, dear me!" cried Jasper; "how very inconsiderate, Mr. Spraggatt! Her ladyship never can mount that stool."

"Her ladyship can do anything she pleases, Mr. Jellifer," replied her ladyship, seating herself on the high stool, and displaying her pretty feet and ankles. "Now, sir, as this position is neither comfortable nor graceful, let us proceed with our business. Where are the diamonds, Jellifer? Have you made a list of them?"

Jasper produced the various jewel-cases from a blue bag, and he had made a list.

"There, sir, are the most valuable of my jewels, and I beg that they may be kept in a secure place, as some of them are heir-looms, and very much prized in the family. Jellifer, get me a glass of water, whilst Mr. What's-his-name counts out the money."

Jasper went in pursuit of the water, and Jack counted over

the crisp bank-notes, their music seeming to have a soothing effect upon the high-seated lady. Jasper returned with the water, and her ladyship having slaked her thirst, received the money, which she reckoned with facility and correctness, proving that she was not unused to such calculations.

. "Quite right, sir," she said; "and I hope these notes will bring me better fortune than some I had of Mr. Jellifer lately. I am afraid, Jellifer, your money comes from low people, and is anxious to get out of good society as fast as it can; for of the two thousand pounds you advanced to me on my next year's dividends, not a pound remained after a week at *piquet.*"

So Jasper had lent her ladyship two thousand pounds; he was rich enough for that, thought Jack. On her ladyship's dividends, too, the cunning old fellow!

"Well, sir," continued her ladyship, addressing Jack, "as I have the money and you have the diamonds, permit me to inquire why I have been dragged, at this unreasonable hour, into this dungeon of a place?"

"Your ladyship must sign, if you please, this bond, in further acknowledgment of the loan," said Jasper, producing a written form.

"And your character stands so high with Mr. What's-his-name, that he required to have it signed in his own presence. Eh! Mr. Jellifer? Here, help me down from this bad eminence." But without waiting for the solicited assistance, her ladyship regained the floor.

As she was signing the acknowledgment, the words she had addressed to Jellifer came back into the mind of Jack Spraggatt, and he never got them out again; no, never!

. Having completed the bond, Lady Norwold, after giving Jack a stately "good morning," left the office, preceded by Jasper, who returned, however, for a moment, to pop his head in at the office-door, and say:

"I'll call in the morning for my commission, Mr. Spraggatt, if you'll please to leave it out for me;" and then he disappeared to escort his imperious employer through the wilderness of the City.

Jack hastened to Warner with the coveted jewels, and displayed them before him. There were necklaces that had been at many Norwold bridals, encircling round white throats which had grown wrinkled within their embrace until death unloosed the clasps, and then another bride perhaps, and another crone became possessors. Bracelets that had enclosed wrists long since pulseless, but not the one for which Warner sought, and against which all the other glittering stones were reckoned worthless. No, not all—for there were some one or two ornaments which he remembered, or fancied he remembered, his mother to have worn. Old Nurse Bland had made him familiar with them perhaps, and he looked upon them as memorials of the mother whom he had lost so young, and who had bequeathed her maternal love to one who left home and kindred in the hour of his great need, to pay it back to him. As soon as he had overcome his emotion and disappointment, he insisted upon Lucy putting on the ornaments which had been his mother's, so that for an hour at least she should be my Lady Norwold. He then told the legends connected with many of these family relics, and Lucy saw how closely his heart still clung to the honours of the house which he had abandoned so recklessly. She foresaw that the storm which had shown itself "no bigger than a man's hand" in the distant colony, was coming up slowly but surely, gathering its rain, its thunders, and its lightnings from all that passed around it. She dreaded sometimes that it would destroy the happiness of their domestic life, frightening away the content and peace which had been their household gods so long; but then she knew that the destroying fire of heaven could be turned aside by skill and forethought—and so she prepared herself to baffle the tempest when it came, and to shield those whom she loved from perishing in the strife.

When Warner had gathered together the family heir-looms which had come into his possession so strangely, he left the room to put them in some place of security. Lucy instantly approached her brother, and laid her hand fondly on his shoulder, as he sat with his arms crossed on the back of his chair and looking out of window. Jack cocked up his ear, as he guessed some important question was about to be raised.

"It is most unfortunate, Jack," said Lucy, "that no tidings can be gained of our children; most unfortunate at this crisis, for I foresee one."

"So do I," replied Jack.

"I am certain that man, Jellifer, could put us upon their track if he would."

"So am I," answered Jack.

"He will not do so without he is paid for his information," said Lucy.

"He wont," replied her brother.

"Now, you must go to him at once, Jack, and make terms with him at any cost."

"Just what I was thinking when you touched my shoulder," replied Jack. "I am to see him to-morrow."

"To-morrow is a very long way off, my dear brother," said Lucy, "now that we are measuring years of our future destiny by every tick of the clock. Try and find him this night; buy from him the least hint that he will sell you, as I fear his own interest is so connected with his bad master that he will not risk much for us at present. Hereafter he may be ready to give himself away. You will go."

"At once," said Jack, rising. "Bid Warner good day, as I shall not return until to-morrow should I hear no satisfactory tidings from Jellifer."

Jack, it will be remembered, had already made Jasper an offer of fifty pounds; but of this he had said nothing to Warner or to his sister, fearing to awaken hopes which would not be realised; and he now, in accordance with Lucy's wish, went direct to Jasper's house, resolved to buy whatever the commission agent might have to sell.

Jasper was at home, and apparently no way disturbed by the absence of his wife, who had gone, as she sometimes did, as his representative, to receive certain rents due at Morden. Had he known what that journey was to cost him, he would have sat upon red hot coals rather than have rested calmly on the easy chair which he occupied, when Jack-in-the-box introduced Mr. Spraggatt to him.

Jack went at once to the subject which had brought him to Jasper's office so late in the afternoon, and saw, short-sighted as he was at times, that Jasper could sell information of some sort.

"Mr. Jellifer," said Jack, "I have now told you my business, and I am sure you can be of service. Will you?"

"He-he-m-hem!" grunted Jasper.

"Don't he-m-hem with me,'" said Jack; "you will make a better bargain by speaking out. What is it sticks in your throat, man?" as Jasper repeated his impediment. "Out with it. If it is an increase of reward, and you feel ashamed to ask it, write it down; the ink won't turn red, I'll be bound."

"The same man as ever, the same man," said Jasper. "You will have your joke, Mr. Spraggatt, although we are upon business. Well, sir, I can give you a clue to those imprudent young people, but I run a tremendous risk in doing so."

"How much?" said Jack—"100*l.*?"

"Say 150*l.*" replied Jasper, "and I'll risk it."

"A bargain," cried Jack.

"Although, mind, I cannot assure you that any good will come out of my information, I shall expect to be paid all the same," said Jasper.

Jack dived into the side-pocket of his coat, and producing a roll of notes proceeded to count them into two piles of seventy-five pounds each.

"There, Mr. Jellifer," he said, "I know there are certain

men who very properly are distrustful of other men's words, and you seem to be one of them. Take that lot of notes, put them into your pocket : now button it up. You have them safe, have you not? Now open your lips, tell me what you like, and I shall be satisfied. Tell me anything about Mr. Norwold, and this lot is yours also. That's fair, I hope?"

Jasper called it not only fair, but liberal in the extreme ; and he then ventured to tell Jack that he had learned from the man who saw the governess and Mr. Edward out of the house, that the hackney coachman was told to drive to some number in Colchester Street, Manchester Square, and that was all he had to communicate.

"It does not seem much, Mr. Spraggatt, for 150l.," said Jellifer, as he received the other half of the notes, "and would not be worth the money, but for the risk I run of offending Sir Gilbert, who has forbidden anyone connected with him directly or indirectly to mention the name of his son."

Whilst Jasper was delivering himself of this excuse, Jack had risen, put on his hat, and reached the door of the room.

"Mr. Jellifer, you are quite right. You have not communicated a great deal of information for your money, but I am satisfied, and much good may your gains do you. It is by such shifts as yours that some men grow rich, and then, remembering the price they have paid all their lives long for their money, they get to love it, and sometimes to die for it. Good evening." *Exit* Jack.

"Love it!" cried Jasper, clutching the remaining pile of notes in both hands. "Love it! What else is there worth loving? What else does not change or leave you as you grow old? But money increases more and more the longer we live and use it wisely. Die for it! That depends upon circumstances." Jasper did not quite like that figure of speech as well as the other—but he added, after a pause, "Yes—I think I could die for it—that is, I would defend what I have with my life, and I should die to lose it."

It is said that as the doomed man passes beneath the headsman's axe the metal becomes sentient, and rings, as it were, the first notes of his knell. So, as Jasper thought this, he discovered he had a hole in his pocket, through which a bad half-crown stole down to the knee of his breeches, and fell with a dishonest jingle upon the hearthstone on which he was standing.

Jack Spraggatt having reached Colchester Street commenced his inquiry by knocking at Number One, and continued unsuccessful in discovering any clue to Mr. Norwold until he had arrived at Number Twenty-seven, when he learned that about two months before a gentleman and his wife had occupied the drawing-room floor at one guinea and a-half a-week, kitchen fire and boot-cleaning extra, but had left, it was supposed, from motives of economy; as comfort they confessed to, and every attention that the most fastidious could desire. They appeared to have expected the arrival of some letters from abroad, and it was not until two mails had arrived without bringing the looked-for communication that they gave a week's warning, and went away to some place near Primrose Hill; the exact address was forgotten, which was unfortunate, as a letter, post-marked Algeric, came soon after their departure, but the postman took it away again when he found that Mr. Norwold had left Colchester Street. A party had called the night before to make the inquiry after Mr. Norwold, and given the name of—" Jellybag."

" Jellifer?" suggested Jack.

" Yes, Jellifer; that was the name. And said he was a friend of the family."

So, then, Mr. Jasper could have given Mr. Spraggatt a more definite address than some number in Colchester Street; and it was unwise in him not to have done so, as he set Jack thinking earnestly what his motive could be for trying to keep him and Mr. Norwold apart.

The information Jack had received was valuable, however, so far that it narrowed the circle of inquiry, and he resolved

to take counsel in the morning with his new ally, Vincent
Elliott, before he communicated what had transpired either to
Warner or Lucy. As he walked homewards, Jasper Jellifer
came continually into his mind, bringing with him all kinds
of unpleasant associations and suspicions of dirty dealings
with the Norwolds at home, and with the dead man in the
Bush. So often did these thoughts recur, and always to
Jasper's disadvantage, that when Jack reached home, he
resolved there and then to search for the second letter Ray
had given him, and ascertain its long neglected contents.
This resolution was not very easily accomplished, as two or
three large chests stowed away in the attic had to be un-
corded and rummaged; Jack having always considered that
letter No. 2 was a document to procure him some acknowledgment from the Jellifers, for his care of their relative, Raymond
Ray, and that he would not have accepted. The letter
was safe enough somewhere among the heap of papers which
had been tossed into the chests when Jack came to France
with Florence, but it required time and patience to find it.
It turned up at last, and a poor, faded packet it looked, quite
incapable of moving men's hearts, and stirring up strife, and
revealing secrets long thought to have been trodden under
the heel of time, and hidden from the sight of man for ever.

As Jack drew the lamp closer to him, and prepared to
unfasten the string with which the packet was secured, he
felt a slight tremor pass through him, remembering, as he
did, a death-scene he had witnessed in his lone location. The
ink was pale, and the paper musty and discoloured, and he
fancied that he was about to hear the dead man speak again
from his grave in the wilderness.

It read as follows :—

" As I write these lines, I am certain that I shall not live
to know who profits by them; and I have tried hard more
than once to act justly; but I have been influenced by old
habits and old feelings, and now leave it to be decided by
another will than my own."

" Rather misty," thought Jack.

" If faith has been kept with me, Jasper—if you have not abandoned me for the sake of that which you held in trust, then you will be rewarded.

" If you have been a cold, treacherous villain, then you will, by the means of this last act of my wretched life, be rewarded also, and as you well deserve to be."

"Aha!" thought Jack, "I was sure that Jasper was a scoundrel, and I am destined to expose the rascal."

"Now note particularly what I write," the paper read on. " In Morden churchyard, on the south side of the church, nearly opposite the chancel window, is the grave of Godfred Mason. At the back of his headstone I buried, years ago, a small box, containing certain matters which will repay anyone for the search. It is not likely that the box has been discovered, as there was only a small space between Mason's headstone and the footstone of the adjoining grave. The search had better be made secretly, as the contents of the box may be used for good or evil, Jasper.; and whichever chances to you, it will come by your own act and deed, and as yo have dealt fairly or foully with Raymond Ray."

Jack Spraggatt was fairly puzzled when he had finished this extraordinary document, and felt as though he were taking part in some terrific melodrama, and expected to hear chains clank, and bolts rattle, and to smell brimstone. There was nothing so singular after all, he thought, when he had read the musty paper again. Ray had been concerned in many nefarious schemes, and was not unlikely to have prepared for some contingency which might arise, and in which this buried box might be of service. So Jack determined to run down to Morden quietly very soon, and ascertain if this hidden treasure was to be recovered.

Mrs. Jellifer, we know, had started for Morden early in the day. She had taken her seat in a second-class carriage, divided into compartments, but open at the top, so that two men who were conversing at one end could be heard by Mrs.

Jellifer, who was seated at the other. They were evidently well versed in the criminal history of the day, and at last their conversation became so interesting to Mrs. Jellifer, that when the train stopped at two stations short of Morden, and the men got out, Mrs. Jellifer could not continue her journey, but left the carriage also, following them to their inn; and, after a brief conversation with one of them, invited them to a supper of roast ducks, so highly seasoned, that unlimited brandy-and-water was needful to stimulate and preserve the digestion of the partakers of this savoury banquet.

Jasper Jollifer, although he had added more than a hundred pounds to his hoard that day, supped off a crust of bread and a slice of Dutch cheese, and retired to rest at ten o'clock. Oh, Jasper! Jasper! what a hideous nightmare; a horrid, starveling demon should have sat upon the coverlet of your bed throughout that night. Mrs. Jollifer has mounted it, and will ride it home before your life has ended.

CHAPTER XXVIII.

About six o'clock one afternoon, a small doorway in a large building presented no inapt resemblance to the entrance of a bee-hive. Over it was painted, "Stage-door." The first to approach it were some twelve or fourteen men, apparently mechanics, more or less dusty in their attire, and who sauntered in leisurely, after extinguishing the pipes which some of them had been smoking. These were the stage-carpenters and gasmen. Then came about the same number of men and women, generally dressed in the left-off wardrobes of persons in a better station of life, and to which they seemed to have succeeded as perquisites of office : the " dressers," or attendants of the actors, no doubt. To them succeeded young girls, usually by twos and threes, each carrying a little basket, the contents of which it would be impertinent to analyse. There was no mistaking the ladies of the ballet and the chorus-singers, the more especially as they were politely recognised by sundry gentlemen who came at the same time, and were known as the gentlemen of the chorus and the " young men" of the establishment. At intervals other ladies and gentlemen arrived, all evidently of some importance, as many of the bystanders touched their hats, and made way for them to enter the little door. They resembled ordinary mortals, except that the men were whiskerless and the ladies generally had their faces concealed behind thick veils. In a little while they were to be converted by the fancy of the dramatist and the skill of the costumier into lords and ladies, patterns of virtue or villany; fairies or demons; men and women of fashion, or clodhoppers and vagabonds. The "principals" without a question, and whose names stood forth in bold type on the playbills. Others passed in, bearing musical instruments; these were distinguished from common men by the length of their hair, a certain poetry of costume, and a prevalence of moustache. They were not to be mistaken; they were the "gentle musicians," whose "dulcet strains" would contribute so much to the evening's entertainment. Sundry stragglers made up a hundred or more of human bees, who, in that dramatic hive, gathered honey every opening night, except when they were compelled into unwilling idleness, at the requirement of the State, having to represent the national grief or the national piety at their own expense, to the wonder and admiration of the followers of all other callings whatsoever in modern Babylon.

And there also, about eight of the clock, came Captain Elmsley and his young friend, Edward Norwold; but their progress was barred by a low wicket guarded by a proud old porter, who had, in happier times, borne the banners of many renowned kings and chieftains in their bloodless wars and grand processions, and who knew by rote the roll of dramatic celebrities. He could, if required, have recounted the victories and the defeats of the chivalry of the stage. He had fallen to his present low estate by the rapid development of sundry bunions, which produced unsteadiness in his march, and rendered his execution of a "charge" a ludicrous hobble.

Elmsley was a favourite with the porter, as the Captain always treated him with the military respect due to a decayed standard-bearer, and he instantly offered to send the cards of the two gentlemen to the manager as soon as he had left the stage, although such a proceeding was not customary.

Elmsley informed him that they were expected, or they would not have ventured to trespass upon the dramatic potentate at such a time, and on this assurance the porter opened the wicket and admitted the Captain and Norwold to the

A A

back of the stage, as a more agreeable waiting-room than the passage from the street.

Edward had never been upon the stage of a theatre, and all his notions of that unknown world behind the curtain were connected with the pleasing illusions he had witnessed when seated in the front. He was surprised and disappointed, therefore, to find himself surrounded by objects the most incongruous and unattractive imaginable. Rude daubs of colour, whose intention could hardly be defined, but whose artistic combination formed, when seen from a proper distance, those marvellous pictures which so frequently adorn the modern stage. Over his head were large rollers, and wheels, and ropes, giving assurance that hard labour was not unknown in this once seeming fairy-land. A lantern on a pole was doing duty, he was told, for the moon, whilst a grimy man, turning a windlass, over which a strip of blue cloth was strained, produced the waterfall which had elicited on its discovery the plaudits of the delighted spectators. The glare of light everywhere made the rough carpenters' work and the dingy canvas of the backs of the scenery strikingly apparent, and other objects which had conveyed ideas of costly splendour were rendered conspicuously worthless.

The appearance of the actors themselves was by no means improved by this closer inspection, and as they passed to and fro there was a steady business air about them that ill accorded with his preconceived notion of actors behind the scenes, and which could not have been exceeded by sober city merchants congregated on the Rialto. And so this world in little was more a representation of the great world without than it appears to be to those who are not permitted to test their delusions, and by so doing prove that, as in larger human experience,

> " Pleasures are ever in our hands and eyes,
> And when in act they cease, in prospect rise."

At the end of an act of the play then in progress, a messenger showed the way to the manager's room, and Edward was again surprised at being introduced to a venerable man, ragged as poverty, who received him with the ease of a man of the world and a gentleman.

"I must ask you, Mr. Norwold," said Mr. Weaver, "to excuse, as I am sure my friend Captain Elmsley will, my receiving you in this manner; but my time has been so fully occupied during the day, that I could not make a more convenient appointment, and as our interview is a matter of business, I have not hesitated to ask you here this evening."

Edward assured him how gratified he had been at his invitation, and Elmsley was profuse in his expressions of obligation.

"I have only a quarter of an hour's wait," said Mr. Weaver, "and therefore I will be brief. I like your drama, Mr. Norwold, and will produce it immediately, if agreeable to you."

Poor Edward's heart beat very fast as he listened to those words of hope, and he could bow only in reply.

"I have ventured to offer a few suggestions for your consideration, and which my experience of stage requirements make me think necessary. They are very few, and very easy of adoption, and I will ask you to look at them presently, when I am on the stage."

Edward thanked him for what he felt must be valuable kindness, and Captain Elmsley warmly approved, without knowing what they were, of any suggestions coming from such a distinguished authority.

"Presuming that no difficulties will arise," continued Mr. Weaver, "I will mention that I consider ourselves fortunate in my having engaged a *débutante* who comes highly recommended to me, and to whom I propose to entrust the part of your charming heroine."

Again Edward could only bow, and Elmsley was kept silent by a slight motion of the manager's hand, and a finger directed to the clock on the mantel-piece.

"I am asking you, therefore, Mr. Norwold, to risk a little

A A 2

upon my account as I do upon yours; but I sincerely believe it will be to the advantage of both."

Edward could only say how obliged he was for the opportunity of testing his dramatic powers, as more than his own personal gratification was involved in the experiment.

"I may be deceived," said Mr. Weaver, "for dramatic success can only be ascertained by representation; but I am strongly of opinion that you have not much cause for anxiety."

"Called, sir," said a boy, putting his head into the room without ceremony.

"That is my summons to the stage," continued Mr. Weaver. "There is your piece, Mr. Norwold. Pens, ink, and paper are on the table, and you may possibly decide upon rejecting or adopting my suggestions by the time the act is over. Captain Elmsley, there is some light claret, there is the cigar-box, and I must leave you to do the honours during my absence."

Edward could hardly believe, when the manager had left the room, that all which he had heard was real, and that he had been listening to Mr. Weaver, of the Theatre Royal ——, who had spoken to him like a kindly gentleman and a man of business. Yet before him were the sheets of paper he had worked upon so pleasantly, so earnestly, and which he had resorted to in his need as the means of achieving an independent position for himself and his beloved Florence. As he thought of her his heart beat quickly, and her dear face seemed to look up to him from the open pages upon the table. Elmsley did not attempt to disturb him, but handed him a glass of claret, which was a grateful draught to his feverish lips and parched throat. Edward then turned to the pages which Mr. Weaver had marked with slips of paper, and found the proposed alterations so judicious and easy of accomplishment, that before the manager had returned to the room all the verbal changes had been made.

"Captain Elmsley," said Edward, when he had finished

writing; "I cannot now express what I would say to you, and to this kind manager, but I will some day. If you could guess the relief I experience by the *hope* only of the success of this drama, you would understand my inability to thank you. Don't speak, please. When I wrote these pages, I did so to please myself with my own fancies, and to find employment for idle hours which would have been otherwise irksome. Of late I have read in these lines almost my future fate. I have recalled them night and day, and tried to estimate their value; now casting them aside as worthless dreamings, then reading them as words of hope that promised emancipation from the miserable doubts which beset the future. The truth is now to be pronounced, the coveted trial appears to be at hand. What will be the verdict?"

"Success! success!" replied Elmsley. "I am not a bad judge of such matters, and I'll stake my reputation upon success."

The gage was not of much value, but Edward accepted it at once, and met Mr. Weaver on his return with a smiling face.

"Well, gentlemen," said Mr. Manager, "thus far 'have we marched on without impediment,' and I am beginning to feel a little tired," pouring out a glass of claret, "and I will drink to you both, and success to our new drama, eh, Mr. Norwold?"

Edward gladly answered the pledge, assuring the proposer how readily he had been able to accept his suggestions and to take advantage of them.

"Very well," said Mr. Manager, "then we will have the parts copied to-morrow, and on Saturday morning you shall read the piece in the green-room."

"Read the piece?" asked Edward; "to whom?"

"To the actors concerned in it. Don't look aghast. It is nothing after the first plunge, I assure you. We are not such formidable critics that you need fear us more than the public," said Mr. Weaver, laughing. "As we are upon business, these are my usual terms. Are they acceptable to you ?"

He had written on a slip of paper, " 100*l*., payable after the twentieth night."

Acceptable! 100*l*.!

The young author had never placed a definite value upon his labours, although he had associated them with prospective gain; and now that it came before him so palpably, he was scarcely able to realise such a consummation. He was only in the 'prenticeship of authorcraft, and had not as yet been called upon to barter his daily life—like the much-quoted pelican—to rear his literary offspring.

" As I have short 'calls' during the next act," said Mr. Weaver, " perhaps you will come with me to the green-room and learn something more of our life behind the scenes. The Captain is an old *habitué*, I believe."

Elmsley had certainly been an occasional visitor in former days to the green-room of the Patent Houses when it was more the custom than it is at present for strangers to be admitted to them, and he expressed the pleasure he should have in being again indulged with such a privilege. The Manager led the way into a well-lighted room at the back of the stage. The walls were nearly covered with character portraits of the actors and actresses who had fretted their hours on the stage of that particular theatre, the other space being occupied by large looking-glasses, placed there for the convenience of the performers, and it was observable that no lady or gentleman entered or left the room without availing themselves of the opportunity to examine their personal appearance. Mr. Weaver introduced a few of the principal actors to Mr. Norwold, and left him in conversation with Mr. Ranton, after the call-boy had again summoned the actor-manager to his duty on the stage.

" I am glad to hear from my friend Elmsley, that we are to have the honour of producing your charming drama, sir," said Ranton. " I read it with great pleasure, and think

I can make something of the gamester, should you have confidence in my poor ability to entrust me with the part."

Mr. Ranton had selected the best character in the piece, and which was not likely to fall to his lot, unless at the particular request of the young author. His commendatory speech was, therefore, not without an object, and Edward could only say he was happy to have the favourable opinion of Mr. Ranton.

That gentleman having been "called" away, and Elmsley and Norwold left to themselves, the Captain took the opportunity to impress upon his friend the advisability of leaving the distribution of the characters to the manager, as he would thereby avoid giving offence to any sensitive lady or gentleman.

"I have known many long enmities arise from a fancied slight or an imaginary injustice in the distribution of the parts of a play," said the Captain. "Nor is it to be much wondered at when you consider that within the walls of the theatre is the actor's world, and it must be particularly mortifying to be displaying yourself every night to a disadvantage. Leave the *cast* to the manager, my young friend."

At that moment a lady entered who had (on the stage) been destroying the peace of mind of an amiable husband, and, in consequence, had been execrated by the feeling portion of the audience. She curtsied slightly to the two strangers, and then proceeded to arrange her head-dress, which the passion of the scene had somewhat disordered.

"You played that scene capitally to-night," said the gentleman who had been opposed dramatically to her a few moments before; "I declare I quite hated you."

"It is a very good bit," replied the lady; "the strongest situation in my part, which is a very up-hill affair."

"Oh, that is too bad," said her friend; "you have it all your own way to the end of the piece, whilst I have done really at the end of the first act. Nothing worth going on for afterwards."

"What nonsense, my dear fellow," answered the lady. "You know you are not speaking the truth—that independently of the business of the last scene but one, you have—"

At this moment another lady entered, attired for the after-piece in the most enchanting fairy costume, which glittered as though powdered with diamond dust. Her beautiful face was improved by the taste with which her auburn hair was arranged, and her bright eyes seemed to sparkle with the consciousness of her beauty. O happy fairy!

"Ah, dear," said the malicious lady, breaking off the conversation she was engaged in; "how did you leave your poor husband?"

"Out of danger, thank God," replied the fairy; "a favourable change took place this morning, or I really could not have played to-night. What I suffered yesterday was dreadful! I wonder I got through at all. I would not have attempted it, but I could not lose my salary."

"Who sat up with Mr. —— ?" asked the other.

"Oh, I did, of course; and I shall do so again to-night, as I have a horror of hired nurses," answered the fairy.

"And so have I, dear," said the malicious lady. "Now you know what sad experience I have had, and what a good nurse I am. You must let me go home with you to-night and take your place, or you will be ill also, and then—that castle-bell is my cue. I shall wait for you, mind that." And so saying, and having made the happy fairy happier by her sympathy, the malicious lady rushes on the stage, to be exposed before all her family connections and one of the best houses of the season, as a wicked monster who had nearly driven a husband to suicide and a wife into a lunatic asylum.

And such a double drama—one scene in the green-room and one scene on the stage—is played, with varying phases of joy and sorrow, crime and goodness, every night in a theatre.

As Elmsley and Norwold walked homewards their conversation turned naturally to the preceding events of the
evening.

"What do you think of your new experiences?" asked the
Captain.

"New, indeed!" answered Edward. "I was inclined to
consider the manager of a London theatre as an unapproach-
able despot, except by the favoured few. At least so run the
traditions of the grand days of the old drama. Our friend,
however, has been most kind and encouraging."

"Ah! Mr. Weaver is hardly an exception, I believe, now-
a-days. He has made his own position, and many of our
popular dramatists have had from him early recognition and
assistance; although some of them are too proud to acknowledge it, I am afraid."

"The actors seem to be a charitable and kindly community," said Edward, "judging by what we have seen and
heard this evening."

"They are in all matters except their professional opportunities," replied Elmsley. "Our friend Mr. Weaver has
spent much, both of time and money, in his endeavour to
make his brother actors provident and independent, and has
succeeded admirably. There are many actors, now, who are
examples of economy and foresight. Fine qualities! fine
qualities! But never much in my way. I owe to actors
many hours of pleasant enjoyment, and have done my best
to encourage them by using their orders largely. It gratifies
them to do so; it gratifies them!"

Edward had frequently patronised the theatres of late by
orders which the considerate Captain had supplied, and he
was relieved from some feeling of obligation to the different
managers by the knowledge just imparted by Elmsley. The
Captain's order-hunting propensity was well known, but as
he was an agreeable companion enough, and presentable at
all times, and never suspected of being overburdened with
money, he was generally supplied with free admissions by

one or the other of his theatrical friends. That he made
good use of them, occasionally, may be inferred from the
little incident at the Cock in Fleet Street, which led to his
intimacy with Vincent Elliott and a supper at the Lyre. The
world was his oyster, and as he had evidently failed to open it
with his sword proper, he now and then tried a stage dagger.

It was a lovely night, and the moon lighted up the old
house near Primrose Hill, hiding with her splendour all
traces of decay. There was a light in Edward's sitting-room,
and two figures at the open window were watching the return
of their two husbands.

As Elmsley waved his hat and sang, most inappropriately,
"Behold how brightly breaks the morning," one lithe form
left the window, and as soon as Edward reached the house
the door was opened, and Florence clinging about his neck.
Mrs. Elmsley had been married too long, and been too often
a watcher, to display any enthusiasm at the return of her
spouse, although she loved her Joe very much, and was proud
of her Captain.

It was Florence's turn to entertain on this auspicious
occasion, and she had arranged the neatest of suppers after
the manner of Aunt Letty, who had often distinguished
herself, even in Paris, by her elegant arrangement of such
pleasant matters. The furniture of the room and table was
scant enough, but the good taste of Florence made it appear
abundant. Flowers which neither gems, nor gold and silver,
and cunningest workmanship can ever equal, cropped up in
many places, and looked prettier than anything else could
have done, considering the humble fortunes of those who
were there assembled together. The hearts of all were too
mirthful to need other exhilaration than the events of the day
had produced, yet Florence, with Mrs. Elmsley's assistance,
had made a compound which Edward declared to be worthy
of a bacchante, and the Captain of —— No—there were
some recollections connected with the compotation which
made him and Mrs. Elmsley laugh exceedingly.

Florence could not refrain asking again and again the particulars of the interview with the manager, and seemed disappointed rather that he had not been more prodigal of praise—that this passage and that had not been remembered and commended, until the loving critic had praised almost every line from "Act the First" to "the curtain falls." Whatever was to be the future of that drama, it had had its one night of success, and won its wreath of honour; and when Captain Elmsley led forth his dear Elizabeth, he felt that they had left in their first-floor a glory whose rays would penetrate into their own particular parlours.

The next morning was not so cloudless as the preceding night had been. As the broad glaring sun showed cracks and flaws in the old house, and weeds among the flower-beds and the garden-walks, so Edward's mistrust of his own powers showed him doubtful phrases and feeble fancies where Florence had seen only excelling beauties. Had he coveted only fame, he would have retreated from the pursuit, and buried his books like Prospero; but there was a stake to be won, in which the one dearest to his heart claimed a share, and he was bound to run the race, though failure and contempt should howl at him when he reached the goal.

The day was long, and the night longer, which intervened between the merry supper and the " reading " of the drama to the company of the Theatre Royal. The green-room presented a very different aspect to what it had done two nights before, when the Captain and Edward entered it at twelve o'clock in the day-time. Around it were seated the actors and actresses, summoned to take their parts in the "new piece." The daylight struggled into the room, through the ground-glass windows, their opacity increased by the dust and rains of many days. A little table, on which reposed the author's manuscript, supported by a bottle of water and its attendant tumbler, was placed at one end of the room. A silence that was almost unbroken by anyone until Mr.

Weaver arrived, and formally introduced the author to the
company, gave Edward the notion that he was looked upon
as a culprit, who was about to read a confession of his guilt
preparatory to receiving condign punishment. Even Mr.
Ranton kept aloof, and seated himself in an angle of the
room where the shadows fell deepest. A gentleman whom
he had often seen on the stage as the low comedian, complained briefly of toothache, and settled down in a remote
corner; nor was there more animation exhibited when the
manager, having retired, returned again in a few moments,
bringing in the young *débutante* who was to supply the place
of a former favourite, that had given herself airs and thrown
up her engagement. The young actress was apparently as
nervous as the young author, and Edward could not help
regarding her with more interest than he would have done,
perhaps, had he suspected how much her want of confidence
was to affect himself.

The reading began, and Edward was annoyed with himself
at the want of expression he was giving to his own written
thoughts, simply because his auditors were strange to him;
for Florence had restored his confidence in himself, and told
him to continue brave for her sake. The silence, which continued as he read, did not aid him; the sentences he uttered
appeared to have no influence; his pathos was disregarded;
and his humour elicited no response except from the manager
and the prompter, who also applauded at the end of the first
act, and received very feeble support from Mr. Ranton and
the low comedian.

Edward was rather mortified at this reception of his work,
but it only gave him greater confidence in himself. He read
the second act much more satisfactorily, but the result, however, was the same, and Edward concluded that he had produced an impression not at all favourable to that success
which his friends had so unhesitatingly predicted.

The distribution of parts followed, and as each lady and
gentleman received his or her allotted task, their manner

was much the same. Each proceeded to ascertain the number of pages which had been set down for them, and then, with a glance or a shrug at some other performer, he or she left the room without any valediction. Except Mr. Ranton, who had been introduced to the author, had been consulted on the merits of the drama, and had stated his willingness to play the young gamester—the leading character—and had received the part of the gamester's friend, who was only second fiddle to the manager! The look of indignation which accompanied his curt "Good morning, sir," was worthy a more appreciating public than the prompter, the manager, and the offending author comprised at that moment.

The young *débutante*, who had remained in a distant part of the room, received her part, and kindly words of encouragement from the manager, with much meekness, and having curtseyed to Edward, took her departure quietly. Not so another lady, who had, in other days, trod the same boards as John Kemble and "the Siddons," but who now, from the combinations of faction and a succession of bad parts, had engaged to play anything, and of course never would without grumbling. She had been cast (as it is called in the language of the stage) a most interesting mother, of limited conversation, but whose maternal demonstrations were highly necessary to the development of the fable of the drama. With some remembrance, no doubt, of "the Siddons" floating in her mind, she advanced to the little table at which the prompter and author were still seated, and dashing down the offending leaves, exclaimed, "No, thank you, gentlemen!" and swept out of the room, a deeply injured woman; nor was Edward's distress at being the cause of so much suffering alleviated by the manager's emphatic rejoinder of "Won't you, Madam!"

When all were gone, Mr. Weaver came to Edward, and shaking him warmly by the hand, said: "I am more pleased with your piece now that I have listened to your own interpretation of it, than I was by my own reading."

" But the company appeared to condemn it by their silence," replied Edward.

" You must think nothing of that. It is a peculiarity of ours," said Mr. Weaver. " We are very selfish, very greedy about our parts—I am as bad as the rest, but having the right of selection, I am better tempered than I used to be. There must be bad and good positions in dramas, as there are in the world outside the theatre, but nobody likes to have the worst if he can help it. You will find them all loyal workers when we meet at rehearsal—even the contemporary of Siddons, who has had much to embitter her life both in and out of my dominions. At one o'clock on Monday we will compare parts, and on Saturday week we will invite the opinion of the public. Good day."

With what strange feelings Edward went forth into the broad daylight! The excitement of the past hour or two had been very great. Another step had been taken towards the dark, the important future. He was glad to have the Captain's arm to lean upon, and the Captain's chatter to excuse his own silence.

CHAPTER XXIX.

MRS. JELLIFER, as we have said, loved money as dearly as
her husband loved it. She had learned its value very early in
life, and had sold her small inheritance of virtue, in her
youth, for money. Although her skin was very fair at that
time, and no stain of Africa could be traced in her bright blue
eyes, she had been sold as she had been bought when her
master had grown tired of her companionship, and Jasper
Jellifer had purchased her with his respectable name and
position, she giving in exchange neither love, nor even regard,
only money. They had lived quietly together, their only bond
of sympathy being the love of gain, for Mrs. Jellifer had
determined never again to be at the mercy of the world for a
dinner. This resolve seemed like prudence and independence;
but as she and her husband prospered, her love of gain increased, and she always rejoiced when Jasper had added to
his heap, and asked no questions. Her brother, Raymond
Ray, had had his changes of fortune, and though Mrs. Jasper
could not, as the respectable woman she had become, approve
openly of the desperate courses he pursued, she condoned
them in her own mind, and always maintained towards Raymond the same sisterly bearing as she had done in the days of
their comparative innocency. They had proved to each other
the only unselfish, sympathising beings in the great world;
and so, whatever of love—the seed of Paradise—remained in
their hearts, although it grew with a rank growth, it was
intertwined, and so remained, through every storm of fortune.

The discovery, therefore, which she had made of Jasper's desertion, and of some other wrong, she knew not what, to Raymond, had begotten a feeling of dislike, although she believed that they—she and Jasper—had profited by the injury. A scheme of retaliation had already dawned upon her active mind, and it would only need slight further aggravation to induce her to put it into execution. This stimulus was supplied, very unexpectedly, by a conversation between two men in the railway-carriage, which Mrs. Jellifer overheard, when on her way to Morden.

The conversation was carried on in a peculiar slang, which proved to Mrs. Jellifer at once that they were either thieves or thief-takers, and as she was moderately acquainted with the terms employed, we will avoid, in transferring to our pages what occurred, idioms which would render a glossary necessary to the uninitiated.

"Have you been in these parts before, Jubilee?" asked the elder of the two men to whom we have referred.

"No—not that I remember," was the reply; "though I suppose you have, or they would not have dug you out of your retirement to help in this job."

"O, yes!" answered the first speaker. "I once knew every yard of ground we are likely to go over. I have not been lower down, though, than our station for some years—ay, a matter of two-or-three-and-twenty, I dare say, since I was at Morden."

"Indeed," remarked Mr. Jubilee.

"A pretty put-up case I had then," said Mr. Higgler (it was our old friend). "A very pretty case, and I worked it, I am proud to say, to a perfect success. The parties concerned had gone into partnership, I fancy, as receivers, but one of them took fright, and so, from information which I received, I came down here with little Cobby, who used to play on a box of wires which he called a dulcimer. I started in the higgling line, in case anyone should have known my name, you see; and so, after about five weeks on and off, I bagged my bird, with all the evidence in his possession. I wondered at the time what the other party had to gain by 'nosing' upon his friend, but after the principal was convicted, something turned up which made me suppose that the other party was afraid of being put in the hole some day or other."

"Was the other in good feather then?" asked Jubilee.

"Yes; he was a miller, and had got into good credit, though he had been on our books for some time. He was called *The Silver Eel*, because he had slipped through our fingers so often. Old Sir Richard Birnie gave him the name, but I hooked him at last. He was 'lagged' for one-and-twenty years, which was a good thing for other parties, I fancy, besides a tender relation!"

Mrs. Jellifer listened to this communication until her blood became cold in her veins, and she almost a statue. The noise of the carriage had made parts of it indistinct and disconnected, but she had gathered enough to suspect that Jasper —her husband Jasper—had betrayed to the avenging law her only brother, Raymond, and been the means of transporting him, subjecting him to all the after-misery he had suffered, and to the cruel death which had overtaken him.

Yes. That was the conduct of her husband, if she had guessed rightly; and if it were so,—She would not rest satisfied with this imperfect hearing, but when those two men left the carriage she would get out also, and question the one who had told the story, as to its truth, and obtain an answer if she paid gold for every word.

As men of Mr. Higgler's profession are rarely surprised at any adventure which comes in their way, the old Bow Street runner received a lady who wanted to speak to him at the Station Inn with calmness and courtesy. The more so as the lady proposed, before proceeding to business, to order some refreshment, and a bottle of sherry for herself and the two officers, and which the latter regarded as a promising indication of liberal treatment in other respects, should their services

B B

be required. The luncheon over, and the wine drunk, Mrs. Jellifer requested Mr. Higgler to favour her with a private audience. Mr. Jubilee was too much a man of business to be offended at this preference, and therefore rose to leave the room, simply intimating that he should take a stroll to look at the church, and be back again in half an hour.

"My object in asking this interview," said the lady, "arises from something I overheard you say in the train as we came down from London."

Mr. Higgler felt a little ashamed of himself at this avowal, as he considered he had been unprofessionally communicative, and might have compromised himself.

"I heard you mention a name which, I fancy, refers to a person I once knew—The Silver Eel. Was his real name Raymond Ray ?"

Mr. Higgler, having recovered his composure, was not to be caught napping, and therefore replied by another question.

"Why do you ask, ma'am ?"

"Mr. Higgler," continued the lady, "I am not unacquainted with the proverbial caution of gentlemen of your profession, nor am I ignorant that you are accustomed to consider your information valuable. There is a five-pound note at your service, and now I will proceed to explain myself. The Silver Eel, or Raymond Ray, was very much attached to me, and I to him. His fate is known to me up to the time of his departure from England. I wish to know if he is living or dead."

"That's a question I can't answer off-hand, ma'am," replied Higgler, "for after we have worked a case to conviction, we think no more about the party, unless he comes across us again in the way of business, when the sentence is out, and Ray hasn't done that at present."

"Thank you, sir," said the lady. "You brought his guilt home to him very cleverly and clearly," said the lady; "but I suppose your information was good from the first."

"Information goes for little in such cases, ma'am," said

Mr. Higgler. "It's getting the evidence complete—completing the chain, ma'am, link by link, ma'am."

"And making one now and then," said the lady, with a faint smile. "Mr. Jellyby or Jellyfy always said that you placed the stolen plate in the mill, as the connecting link between it and Ray was wanting."

"Jellifer said that?" cried Higgler. "Why the lying scoundrel knew——. I tell you what, ma'am, if I heard that said by Mr. Jellifer——. I beg, ma'am, you won't say that again to me or anybody; I don't like such mean actions attributed to me."

Mr. Higgler was evidently disturbed by Mrs. Jellifer's clever insinuation, and she had gathered enough from it to be certain that Jasper had been concerned in her brother's condemnation. Yet she must be certain, quite certain, before she proceeded to take action. She apologised, therefore, to Mr. Higgler, and begged him to forget what she had said, and as there was no train from the station until the morning, she hoped he would allow her to provide a supper as an atonement for her thoughtlessness. She had been an old campaigner, and should be sorry to give offence to one so celebrated as Mr. Higgler.

"Such a lady-like apology, and such a liberal offer," Mr. Higgler said, "quite made amends for any annoyance, and if he might suggest a couple of ducks with sage and onions, he was sure Mr. Jubilee would be pleased, and he, himself, delighted."

And so it was arranged, and at the proper time the savoury dainties shed their perfume throughout the Station Inn, and were then offered up a smoking sacrifice on the altar of Friendship. Strong meats and strong drinks usually go together, and Mr. Higgler and Mr. Jubilee were prodigal rather of brandy and water.

"Well, gentlemen," at length said the lady, "I must now bid you good night, and once more I thank you, Mr. Higgler, for so kindly accepting my peace-offering."

[B B 2

"Not another word, madam," said Higgler—"not another, I beg: but if that Jellifer ever says in your hearing that I laid a plant for The Silver Eel, you tell him from me, that a quiet tongue keeps many a wrist out of the darbies. But he was always a sneak, ma'am, and so I used him."

"I never doubted it," said the lady. "I always knew that it was he who 'nosed' upon Raymond."

The familiar word threw Higgler off his·guard, and he exclaimed :—

"He did nose on him, ma'am, and made a pretty penny by the job."

"Good night, gentlemen," said Mrs. Jellifer, with a pleasant smile, "and if I do not see you in the morning, good-bye !"

She left the room, and though the light of her candle fell full upon her face, every feature grew darker and darker as she walked up-stairs to her bed-chamber, and scarcely brightened when she had fallen into an uneasy slumber.

The next morning Mrs. Jellifer rose early, and paying her large bill without a sigh or a murmur, proceeded by the first train to Morden, some time before her guests of the preceding night had awakened from their sleep.

Mrs. Jellifer soon transacted her business in Morden, staying a shorter time than usual in her old house in the Market-place, and declining the proffered hospitality of her tenant, with whom she was in better esteem than Jasper. The thoughts then uppermost in her mind led her by the old church, and away down by the side of the mill-stream, and under the drooping trees, until she came in sight of the miller's garden. She saw that it was neatly kept; on the lawn several young children were at play, linked hand in hand, and singing in concert a simple nursery song, which seemed to Mrs. Jellifer like a hymn, and as she remembered who had lived there formerly, and what had been his life and death, she thought that some good spirit had driven out all the evil things which once abided there, and had peopled it with angels.

She turned away sorrowfully, and walked to the station, on her return to London. Before she had arrived there she had forgotten the glimpse she had had of Paradise, and had yielded to her evil thoughts, which had now but one direction, the accomplishment of a retribution from which nothing was to turn her aside, until she had pursued it remorselessly to the end. When she reached her London home, she met Jasper with a warmth of greeting which had been somewhat unusual with her of late, and he, a Samson in cunning, was beguiled, and in a fair way to be betrayed by his Delilah.

It was somewhat strange that two persons on the same day should have passed up and down the iron road between London and Morden, intent upon doing justice to lucky Jasper Jellifer; but so it was, as Jack Spraggatt had gone down to solve the mystery which had been so long in his keeping.

Jack had taken Vincent Elliott into a limited confidence (for he had carefully preserved Warner's secret), and after consultation it had been decided that, whilst Elliott followed up the slight clue which had been obtained to Edward Norwold's retreat, Jack should proceed to Morden at once, and disinter the unholy thing buried among the peaceful graves in the churchyard. It was decided that when Jack had discovered the resting-place of Godfrey Mason, he should wait until night, and then recover the long-buried box and its mysterious contents. Fortunately, this would be easy of accomplishment, as the old servant Stevens occupied one of the almshouses abutting on the churchyard, and with her Jack could remain without exciting observation, and obtain ready access to the object of which he was in search.

It was evening when Jack arrived at Morden, and avoiding observation as much as possible, he proceeded at once to the churchyard, not doubting for a moment, but the discovery of the tombstone indicated in Ray's paper would be easy enough. He began his scrutiny, therefore, carelessly at first, but after having continued it for some time without success, he became alarmed, lest some trick had been played upon his credulity by Ray, and that no such memorials existed. Again he searched carefully, and read all the inscriptions which were legible, but without finding the name of Godfrey Mason, and it then occurred to him, that he had better make himself known to Mrs. Stevens, his old nurse, and learn from her if she had any knowledge which could assist him.

Great was the joy of the old servant, when she held the hand of the dear young master once more between her own, and saw through her honest tears the face she had looked upon so often in years gone by. Every baby-trace had gone, but there were the mother's eyes, and the father's manly features, which she remembered so well, and it was some time before she was sufficiently calm to listen, so as to understand Jack's inquiries.

What a strange interest for him to take in the grave of a stranger, when those of his own kindred were so near at hand, and which she had tended with such care for so many years, out of the pure old love she had borne them, when sharing their daily bread.

Master Godfrey Mason? Surely his was one of the grave-stones that was broken down five years ago, when the parson's donkey strayed into the churchyard, and made more havoc there, than Time had done in half a century. Yes, she remembered now, it stood the fourth from the footpath, and the first from the church wall, as his grand-daughter, who was living then as her next neighbour, had grieved so at the disaster. There was a portion of the headstone left, which she could show him.

This was fortunate indeed, and Jack rejoiced within himself that he had come on his former visit to his parents' graves, and had waited to reward the humble friend, who had planted flowers about them, when she thought none would regard her, but, perhaps, the angels in heaven. He bade her keep his present visit a secret, and despatched her into the village to buy materials for supper, whilst he assured himself, that her recollection of the position of the gravestone was correct. There was a fragment at the spot she had indicated, and a few inches from it a footstone adjoining. With what interest did he regard that little patch of earth, believing that it covered some long-hidden secret, whose revelation was to effect a powerful influence on the lives of those who were now unconscious of the existence of its silent testimony. The setting sun, which made the west a bank of fire, deepened the shadow of the church upon the south side mounds, as though there was sorrow associated with that which was about to be revealed; but then overhead was the moon, now like a round of film, soon to be paramount in the heavens and over the earth, and by her light his work was to be done.

The intervening time would have moved wearily enough, had not Mrs. Stevens's memory been singularly preserved, and from its stores brought forth wondrous stories of Jack's marvellous childhood, wherein he performed such deeds, and uttered such clever sayings, that he would have been a prodigy, had not every child of Adam, since Abel stood at his mother's knee, been equally surprising.

Although Mrs. Stevens had satisfied the curiosity of her immediate neighbours, and accounted for Jack's presence by describing him as the son of an old friend who had called to see her, he insisted upon having her solitary candle extinguished at her usual bed-time, and continued their conversation by moonlight until the church clock struck eleven, when he sallied forth, carrying in his hand a table-knife and an old trowel. As he approached the place of concealment, the reverberation of the bell was still humming in the church tower; and no sooner had he knelt down to commence removing the turf and soil, than a loud laugh startled him by its distinctness. A moment's reflection enabled him to discover the cause. It came from the departing guests of the public-house, which stood near the entrance to the churchyard, and as he heard footsteps and voices approach along the pathway, he withdrew into the shadow of a buttress of the church, and commended his own prudence which had extinguished Mrs. Stevens's candle. He waited a few minutes before he resumed his task, and then found but little difficulty, even with his imperfect tools, in clearing away the earth and grass, which he trusted had remained undisturbed since Ray had placed them there. In about a quarter of an hour, he came to some hard substance, which he judged rightly was the long-buried box, and which, with a little more exertion, he brought forth into the moonlight. It had been covered with some kind of wrapper, which was now almost decayed, and crumbled in parts under his touch. Hastily filling in the hole again, he returned with the treasure to Mrs. Stevens's house before he attempted any further examination of it. He was so fearful of being watched—he hardly knew wherefore—that he would only examine it then by the light of the moon, and he could therefore discern nothing more than that the box was of some hard heavy wood, securely fastened by screws. With this knowledge he proposed to be content until the morning; and having, with some difficulty, persuaded Mrs. Stevens to retire to her own bed, he tried to compose himself to sleep in an arm-chair. The earthy smell of the box, the wonder which possessed him as to its contents, the half-hourly booming of the church clock, made sleep impossible for some time; and when he fell into an uneasy doze, his previous thoughts and occupation mingled in his dreams. With the first dawn of light he was astir, and then he renewed his examination. The wrapper had been a piece of tarpaulin, and was decayed, except where the folds had been doubled. This he carefully removed, and found, as he had conjectured over-night, the box was of oak, nearly an inch in thickness, and about a foot square, fastened together with large screws, now rusted into the wood, and promising not to be withdrawn without great difficulty. He was, therefore, compelled to wait until Mrs. Stevens was up, and able to procure him the necessary instrument to attempt

their removal. The earthy smell had become so powerful
that it nearly sickened him, owing to his want of sleep, and
the anxiety of the past night; and drawing aside the curtain,
he opened the window, which looked upon the churchyard.
His thoughts then carried him back to the time when his
parents were among the living, and he a happy boy, never
dreaming that a time would come when he should look upon
two green mounds, and call them Father! Mother! or that
he should be so near them, needing their friendly counsel,
and be conscious that they could not hear him. And then he
looked back upon the years which had intervened since the
last green graves had been made, and the many, almost
countless, miles which he had travelled away from them, to
make a home in a distant wilderness, never believing that he
should return to lay his bones beside them. Then he remembered the miserable convict whom he had known the pleasant
thriving townsman, and who had come to him in his wretchedness, to lay down and die, and to bequeath to him a mystery,
which he had dug stealthily out of the earth, as though he
were sharing in some crime committed long ago, and buried
for more than twenty years. There it was lying behind him
on the table, smelling horribly of the graves among which it
had been hidden so long, its secret unrevealed, and for the
present defying his efforts to disclose it. All these fancies
proceeded, doubtless, from his feverish pulse and heated brain;
but he could bear his solitude no longer, and called to
Mrs. Stevens to come down to him. She was already dressed,
and her presence soon dispelled the unpleasant feeling which
had possessed him; and as she bustled about to put her house
in order, and to prepare breakfast, he too began to talk of old
times, and joke her about certain love-passages, which made
the old lady smile, though the jests brought tears into her
eyes. They never knew true love who say that it can die.
The flowers which composed its garland may fade or wither,
or be exchanged for an *immortelle*, but it lives with us to the
last, be we wise or simple.

When breakfast was ready, so fragrant was the bacon, and so golden the yolks beside it, that Jack forgot his sentimentalism, and ate like the sturdy yeoman of thirty years before. When the meal was over, Mrs. Stevens was sent in search of that unromantic instrument, a screw-driver, and after nearly an hour's absence, returned with the most diminutive example. Jack thought there was a spell about the box, and that he was never to open it, for feeble as the screw-driver was, the rusted screw-heads broke under its pressure, and the stout oak lid remained as firmly fixed on as ever.

What was to be done? To call in the auxiliary aid of any one in Morden, would be to proclaim that Jack Spraggatt had returned, and found a box containing a secret that would be none by twelve o'clock at midnight, if Morden ale was the provocative to small-talk,—which it had been hitherto within the memory of the oldest inhabitant.

No, there was nothing to be done, but to confide the rotten wrapper to the safe keeping of Mrs. Stevens, pack up the box in an old newspaper, and carry it forthwith to London, despite his curiosity, which, now that it was broad daylight, began to be painfully tantalising.

CHAPTER XXX.

FLORENCE DISPLAYS A NEW TALENT.

THE rehearsals at the theatre progressed, and not much to the satisfaction or comfort of the young author. When he came to have his scenes dissected, as it were, and their continuity destroyed by the actors, who were necessarily imperfect, he grew mistrustful of his own conceptions, which appeared to have lost all point and force when thus presented before him. The frequent interruptions occasioned by changes of position, arrangements of the business of the stage, and trivial alterations of dialogue, made it almost impossible for himself to follow the succession of incidents, and their consequent connection with the passion and humour of the scene, so that he could not imagine how out of this apparent chaos would ever come "the perfect chrysolite," which his partial critics had declared to be waiting the acceptance of the British public. The nervousness of the young *débutante* increased, and although she had been well tutored in the art of acting, she was evidently deficient in natural feeling and that quick perception, which alone ensure distinction in the arduous profession she had chosen. Notwithstanding the manager's assurance, that "she would be all right at night," and that "few actors could or would rehearse with any earnestness," Edward could see nothing of the impassioned Gipsy girl his fancy had imagined, and upon whom much of the general success depended. He was accustomed, therefore, to return home dispirited by the morning's work, and it required all the cheerful hopefulness of Florence, and the assurance of the experienced Elmsley, to dispel his inquietude. In this they were only partially successful, as his distressing fears came back to him more strongly during the night, and he rose feverish and depressed. It was only the remembrance of how great would be the prize, if he were successful,—that the venture might bring independence, and open a happy future for his beloved Florence,—that stifled the anxieties which possessed him, and made him brave enough to dare the worst that actor or critic might be able to inflict. There wanted but five days to the eventful night which was to decide the fate of his drama, and he had passed a morning of great anxiety, owing to a preposterous request of Mr. Ranton, who had asked that he should be allowed to commit suicide on the roof of a house, roll down the tiles, and fall at the feet of his betrayer, feeling, as he did, that without some such striking situation, the piece would flag, and the result be more than questionable. Had Edward known that Mr. Ranton was thinking only of Mr. Ranton, and not of the ultimate success of Mr. Norwold, he would have made light of the doubt which had been created in his mind by the communication, and not permitted it to have sat so heavily on his heart, as he paced home through the rain, and arrived at Primrose Hill drenched completely. Elmsley laughed heartily when he learned the cause of Edward's excessive anxiety, and Florence scolded him with the prettiest words, and the most gentle voice, for not deferring to her opinion in preference to that of the interested actor. Edward pleaded for pardon, and obtained it, but the rain and the anxiety combined had produced their effect, and the poor author went shivering to his bed, to become in a few hours so feverish and restless, that Florence arose, and roused the Elmsleys, who soon agreed with her that medical aid was required. Their fears were justified by the opinion of the doctor, who pronounced the patient to be seriously ill, but in no positive danger, if quiet could be insured.

There would be the difficulty. Florence knew that his thoughts would be away always with the actors and their requirements, and such proved to be the case.

During the delirium consequent upon the fever, he was repeating sentences of his little play, and correcting the faulty readings of the performers, and entreating for more passion or more mirthfulness in the delivery of his words. Then he would speak of failure, yet uttered no regret, on account of his own wounded vanity or loss of literary reputation, but connected all his regrets with the future of his wife, of his Florence, now so utterly dependent upon him. When he became calm enough to speak rationally, almost his first inquiry was as to the progress of his drama; and Elmsley did not hesitate to give a most glowing account of what had been achieved during the last three days. Florence saw he mistrusted the Captain, and when the doctor came she told him what had occurred; and finding that such anxiety might renew the danger which Edward had just escaped, she obtained permission from her husband to accompany Captain Elmsley to the theatre, and observe for herself.

The courtesy and kindness of Mr. Weaver, and indeed of all at the theatre, soon removed any embarrassment which she had felt at her strange position; and as the actors were now perfect in their parts, she was gratified by what she saw and heard. A slight difficulty of situation had been discovered in the last act, and its alteration had been postponed until the author should again attend the rehearsal, but as that was not possible now, the manager suggested a device of his own. Florence, who had a complete knowledge of her husband's conception of the argument of his play, saw a discrepancy of idea in this suggestion, and with a modest rejection, and a readiness of device which surprised her kind adviser, she immediately removed the difficulty by supplying a more appropriate alteration.

"You must make the next ascent of our dramatic Parnassus," said Mr. Weaver, smiling; "for it is quite evident you have a natural genius for our business."

"Oh, dear no," replied Florence. "I derive my present inspiration from Primrose Hill. Besides, I have read, and heard this drama read, until I could repeat every line of it, and thus readily saw the way to overcome your difficulty."

For the manager's satisfaction the last act was rehearsed again, and when it was over he warmly congratulated Florence on the improvement she had made, and bidding her be of good cheer, promised her that success was almost certain.

Florence returned home, nearly satisfied with what she had witnessed; but Edward was right, she feared, as to the gipsy exponent. The young girl had been trained to act, and no doubt had been applauded by kindly friends; but now that she came to contrast her ability with the powers of more experienced performers, she appeared to feel her own deficiencies, and to lose confidence in herself.

The considerate Mr. Weaver, however, encouraged her in every way, and his experience in management had more than once shown him that the unpromising actor at rehearsal had frequently been the most successful when excited by the presence of an audience. On the day before the production of the piece, however, he had not been so satisfied as he had expected to have been; so after the business on the stage had ended, he called the poor girl into his room, and kindly spoke to her as to certain defects which he had advised her previously to correct, and then dismissed her with many words of encouragement. He thought, however, that she began to weep as she left his room, and fearing that such a display of feeling was an unfavourable indication of her success, he resolved to be prepared for failure. When he rejoined Florence and the Captain, who had waited his return on the stage, he frankly communicated his doubts, but added his conviction that the deficiency of the actors would not affect the reception of the piece.

This opinion was very alarming to Florence, who could not share in the manager's consolatory conclusion, and as she walked homeward she discussed with the Captain the propriety of communicating what they had heard to her husband.

Elmsley was disposed to do so, but Florence dreaded the effect which might be produced, in his present state, by any unfavourable intelligence; and she therefore proposed to call upon the doctor and be guided by his advice. It was well that she had taken this precaution.

"My dear madam," said the doctor, "it would not be possible to declare the consequences of such a communication at this moment. It is quite clear that his whole thoughts are set upon this event: his mind has been so occupied with it—so strained by constant meditation upon it, and for the important reasons which he discovered during his delirium—that any delay in removing the exciting cause might prove very, very serious to him."

"Oh, sir!" cried Florence, clasping her hands together, "is there so much to fear? Is there danger to his dear life in success or failure? Is this matter, for which we were so desirous, and at which we so rejoiced, likely to bring such terrible results? Oh, sir!"

"Pray calm yourself, my dear young lady," said the doctor, taking her hand. "There is no cause, trust me, for fear, if we act wisely and composedly."

"I will—I will be composed," and Florence sat down, her hand still retained by the doctor.

"There is nothing to be apprehended—that is, no great danger—from the failure of his play, and I believe such a result is not anticipated. Even if the reception of it is not all that we could wish, it will be quite possible to keep such a fact to ourselves. But I do believe that any delay in its production, any justifiable anticipation of failure, would produce more anxiety than would be beneficial, and therefore I advise your silence upon Mr. Weaver's doubts, or the young actress's deficiencies. Pray be hopeful, as I am, I assure you, of Mr. Norwold's speedy recovery, and I will make it possible for me to stay with him to-morrow evening during your absence at the theatre, and I trust you will return with such good news, that you may soon throw 'my physic to the dogs.' You see I can quote Shakspere as well as Celsus."

Florence resolutely accepted what comfort she could from the doctor's words, and returned—oh, how anxiously—to the sick couch of her husband.

Mrs. Elmsley, who had divided the duties of nurse with Florence, now reported that Edward had had some calm sleep, and was decidedly better than he was in the morning. He had twice inquired the time, as though he were watching the return of his wife, and a slight flush passed over his face when she had entered the room.

Florence affected a cheerfulness which appeared to gratify the sick man, and he listened with apparent pleasure at her account of the morning's rehearsal; but when Mrs. Elmsley had withdrawn, a sadness stole over his face, and he held out his poor white hand to be taken by Florence.

"I have been thinking since you have been away, dearest," he said, with some difficulty, "what would have been your lot, if death had come to me in this fever. I should have left you the most friendless woman in this great London."

"But that danger is past, dearest," replied Florence, "and you have now only to encourage pleasant thoughts and cheerful hopes, and we shall be happier for the few anxious days we have known; shall we not?"

She kissed his forehead, and was pleased to find it cool and damp.

"I trust we shall. Another night, another day, and another long evening, and our future will be known to us," he said.

"Only in part, dear! Only in a very little part," replied Florence. "If we win the prize we have reckoned upon, so much the happier we. If we draw a blank—and there are so many blanks in all the lotteries of life—why then——"

"I shall despair," interrupted Edward.

"And I shall not," said Florence; "nor shall you, dear boy, if I can help it. You must not forget that there are those who love me, and it is only for a time that they are estranged from us; and"—

"Help must not come from them at present," replied Edward. "No; I must meet them as an independent man, not as an object for their bounty. With you it should be different—you are their child."

"And your wife—your foolish but loving wife, who cannot talk wisely to you for having such fancies; but who loves you with all her woman's soul, and forgives you for hinting that she could have any fortunes apart from yours."

Edward lay silent for some minutes, and then said:

"It is strange, very strange, that my life should have been so unlike others born to my position and prospects. My childhood was unhappy very often, and from unusual causes; my youth was saddened by the consciousness of my father's wrong to me; and what my present manhood would have been had you not loved me, I know not. I have wondered, lying here, why my life has been so unhappy. Why has it been so, Florence?"

"Why should it not have been so?" replied his wife. "Sorrows are our teachers, and make us know that we are mortal, and surrounded by mortality. Without them, we should fancy earth was heaven, and live only for life and death, and not for eternity. We must

> ' Love our sorrows, for they bring
> Their own excuse in after years:
> The Rainbow—see how fair a thing
> God built up of tears.'"

This simple verse seemed to dwell in the ear of the sick man as he tried to repeat it, and when he had accomplished it, by the aid of Florence's prompting, he fell into a quiet sleep.

It was hardly to be expected that Elmsley would give up his old haunts and pursuits on account of his sick friend and lodger, and less so as he was now of some importance among

c c

his dramatic associates, being in possession, "behind the curtain," of the secret of authorship of the new piece, always a subject of interest to the theatrical world, or "the profession," as actors delight to call themselves. He had, therefore, been about town much as usual, and in the course of his perambulations had again met with Elliott at the old hostelry in Fleet Street. Vincent was not over anxious to renew his intimacy with Elmsley, as Warner, for some reason or the other, did not appear to entertain the highest opinion of the Captain, and it was therefore with some reluctance that he accepted his invitation to share the same table in the common dining-room; but having been so recently under some obligation to him, he sat down. The Captain was, of course, full of his great subject, but carefully concealed the name of the author, unfortunately, or Vincent Elliott, and the others interested in the discovery of Florence and her husband, would have been spared many hours of anxious search and painful inquietude. Elmsley, like a kind friend, had been busy everywhere endeavouring to secure the attendance of all upon whose good offices he could rely in favour of the author, and Elliott was glad to secure his retreat unaccompanied by the Captain, by giving a hasty promise to take a private box for the eventful evening, a promise which he redeemed early the next day.

Vincent Elliott was now an admitted visitor of Mrs. Gregson and Mr. Warner, but not an accepted suitor of Marian Mayley; as Mr. Warner had exacted a promise, after ascertaining, by the aid of his City agent, the true position of Vincent, that the wooing of the young lady was not to be considered conceded by their intimacy at present. Vincent had, however, made himself acceptable to Mrs. Gregson and Cousin Martha, and may have been considered, therefore, to have advanced considerably towards the main object of his ambition.

"What I like in Mr. Elliott," said Mrs. Gregson, "is his modesty and want of assumption. Why, though he is an

Old Bailey barrister, who, they say, has the impudence of the old gentleman, he never interrupts me when I am talking, and thinks no more of his horsehair wig, which he never seems to wear, than if he had been born as bald as a coot! He sits as silent as a beadle in church, and generally has the good sense to agree with my opinions. What do you say, Marian?"

That young lady declared that she had never taken any particular notice of Mr. Elliott's manner, but she thought, after his conduct in connection with Floretta, he could hardly be called unusually modest or unassuming. But Cousin Martha asserted, that she had come into the drawing-room one morning, and at a time when Marian was supposed to be engaged in her library, and found their niece watching from her window with great interest the approach of some person, who turned out to be Mr. Vincent Elliott, and that she saw Marian run to the looking-glass and carefully arrange her ringlets, before she was aware that Cousin Martha was looking at her.

Marian declared that Martha's story was nonsense.

Mrs. Gregson added also:

"Now I come to remember, he has always contrived to edge himself in next to Marian at the play; and somehow or the other there has always been room for him to do so, though I had complained before of being scrowdged, over and over again."

Marian was perfectly shocked at her aunt's insinuation, and was in the midst of an avowal that she never would go anywhere again with Mr. Elliott, when that young gentleman was announced, and presented himself on no other business than to beg Mrs. Gregson's acceptance of a box for the new piece on the following night.

"Well, now, that is kind of you, Mr. Elliott," said Mrs. Gregson, "and was the thing I was about to propose sending for; but money saved is money gained, and I thank you, sir. Keep down, Floretta, and don't dirty the gentleman's

trousers.   It is astonishing how fond that dog seems to be
of you, Mr. Elliott, though you did kidnap him.   Well! of
course, my dear Marian, I know we promised to forgive and
forget."   .

Vincent blushed sadly for a barrister, and poor Marian
was rosy as an autumn sunset.

Cousin Martha was evidently chagrined, as she had accepted
an engagement to tea in the City, and could not be of the
play party.   She therefore suggested, a little spitefully
perhaps, that it was a pity her seat should be lost, and that
it would be a good opportunity to ask Mr. and Mrs. Warner
to take an evening's diversion.

"Poor things, to be sure," said Mrs. Gregson, not regarding the clouds upon the faces of Elliott and Marian—"they
are as melancholy in their fine house as two canaries moulting
in a cage.   I am sure a little artificial misery will do them
good and make them cheerful, and the pieces at the what's-
a-name theatre are always very touching.   I never go without salts, and a good supply of handkerchiefs, for I do enjoy
a hearty cry when there's nothing really to cry about."

Marian affected to approve highly of this suggestion, and
as Mr. and Mrs. Gregson would fill the box, she would
remain at home, or, better still, go with Cousin Martha to the
tea party in the City.

Vincent wished secretly Cousin Martha had been at the
Mansion House, or any other distant locality, for her considerateness; for although he would have done much to have
lightened the sorrow which oppressed Warner and his wife,
he would have preferred some other mode of procedure,
especially as he had expended two guineas to secure, as he
thought, as many hours with a certain young lady, who was
not his betrothed—at present.

Of course, such an arrangement as Marian proposed could
not be permitted, nor was it necessary, as Vincent had
arranged to go with a friend—a terrible fib!   Cupid, like
many other little boys, is a sad story-teller, and if Jove really

laughed at all "lovers' perjuries," what a merry time he must have had of it when Juno was not at home!

Although Marian did not believe Vincent in the least, she was too good-natured to interpose further difficulty to her aunt's arrangements, and therefore it was settled that the Warners were to be invited.

Mrs. Gregson immediately set out for the Warners, and pleaded for nearly an hour before she could obtain their assent to be of her party, but her pertinacity was rewarded at last, Warner and his wife Lucy consenting to be present at a stranger drama than is oftentimes played even in the unreal world of a theatre.

Captain Elmsley had returned home somewhat earlier than was his custom, and Florence, from her window, seeing him enter the garden, stole softly from her room to meet him.

"I have been so anxiously expecting you, Captain Elmsley," she said; "I have received a note which has almost distracted me. Please read it."

The note was from Mr. Weaver, and was as follows:—

"My DEAR MADAM,

"I have just received a communication from the father of Miss * * (the new actress), and he informs me that his daughter, alarmed at some observations of mine—most kindly meant and communicated—has become so utterly alarmed at her responsibility, that she has left London with her mother, and therefore will not appear to-morrow night. What can be done shall be done, but I am certain that no one could get the part into her head, much less act it, by to-morrow night. For my own loss and disappointment I care comparatively little, but, after our conversation of this morning, I fear it may add to Mr. Norwold's indisposition."

"Yes," interrupted Florence. "Yes, that is the dreadful part of it! You heard what the doctor said! The disappointment may kill my husband. What is to be done?"

Captain Elmsley's head was not quite so clear as it ought to have been when he reached home, but this astounding news dispelled the effects of his previous conviviality. He had come from a knot of good fellows, who had been toasting to the success of his friend, and he had been eloquent on the anticipated triumph, and now the trophy of cards was blown down by the breath of Miss ——, the novice! After walking up and down the unkempt garden, bareheaded, for some time, he returned into the house, and Florence instantly went to him, looking at him with large wondering eyes, as though she would read the conclusion at which he had arrived before he could utter it.

"Elizabeth, my dear," said the Captain, addressing his wife, "go to Mr. Norwold's room, in case he should need anything; I want to speak a few minutes with Mrs. Norwold."

Elizabeth had been so long accustomed to do her husband's bidding unquestioned, that she went away at once, although her woman's curiosity to learn the end of this dilemma was consuming her.

"Madam," said Elmsley, closing the door which his wife had intentionally left open—"Madam, you are a brave, loving woman, I am sure—are you not? and would do much to save your husband—would you not?"

"Anything—die, if need be."

"There is one chance of overcoming this difficulty, and the only one which presents itself to me. If delay in the production were of no consequence, the matter would be easy enough. But it is of consequence, though only for a day or two, and no actress would risk her reputation to play the part in that time. Mr. Norwold might imagine that his own mistrust of success was shared by the manager, and we might not be able to make him believe the truth, annoying as that is."

"He would not believe us, I fear!" cried Florence, wringing her hands.

"There is but one person who could prevent such a catastrophe, but I am afraid she would hesitate to undertake the task," said Elmsley, slowly.

"No—she must not!" cried Florence. "I will go to her at once! She shall be paid! All that we are to gain she shall have."

"Would she do it, then?" said Elmsley, all that the world had left him of a gentleman filling his voice and manner. "I fear that she might say 'I am too inexperienced—I have never been subjected to the gaze of a crowded theatre, to speak the words of simulated sorrow or pleasure, and I might fail.'"

"She will not fail, dear Captain Elmsley! You mean myself; I am the only actress that would dare to face such a trial, and I will do it—to save my husband."

A plenteous flow of tears came to allay her painful excitement, and when she was calm again, she said:—

"There is still a difficulty. Will Mr. Weaver consent to our plan? Will he risk the chances of such a desperate trial?"

"I cannot believe that he will hesitate to accept our proposal, and to promise the utmost secresy until the trial has been made. The actors are all perfect, and no rehearsal need take place to-morrow, excepting of your scenes, and those can be gone through with the knowledge of the officials of the theatre, who can be as 'close as death,' when it so pleases them. I will go to Mr. Weaver at once.".

The church clock struck one before Elmsley returned, and then he brought the welcome tidings that the experiment was to be made. Florence was to be the *débutante*. Who were to be her auditors?

CHAPTER XXXI.

On the following morning three conspirators had assembled in the parlour of the old house at Primrose Hill. The Captain, the doctor, and the wife of the sick man up-stairs. Mrs. Elmsley had not been admitted to the conference, as the Captain knew, from past experience, that his lady had not the gift of reticence; her stores of knowledge being limited, she was prone to make much of any domestic mystery which came in her way, and it was very necessary, therefore, that she should not be tempted to make any revelation to Edward, whose nurse she was about to be for the entire day.

The conspirators decided that Florence and Elmsley should leave, ostensibly, to superintend the last rehearsal of the piece, and that they should be understood to dine somewhere near the theatre afterwards, and not return until the great event had been decided. The doctor promised to call in, not professionally, but for a chat, as it were, and so keep his patient as much at rest as possible, whilst Elmsley was to despatch an *aide-de-camp* to report progress.

Florence found only Mr. Weaver, the prompter, and the stage-manager, waiting at the theatre to receive her and Captain Elmsley. She rehearsed so perfectly the scenes in which she was to take a part, and accepted the stage directions so readily, that the manager and his professional officers were astonished at what appeared intuition, but which was in reality her own plain sense stimulated into action by affection for her husband, whose life seemed dependent on her compliance with the extraordinary demand now made upon her.

They had just concluded the rehearsal when a lady came upon the stage with a quick step and lively play of the head. Before she had reached the group about the prompter's table she said, in a pleasant voice—

"Well, Mr. Manager, what's the matter, that I am dragged away in this peremptory manner from husband and child, and my bathing machines, and all that? Eh? what's the matter?"

"My dear Stella"—[Managers always call their pet actresses "my dear," and the lady addressed was a general favourite. She was usually called by her intimates, after a part which she had made famous, in and out of the theatre, and so we will also designate her, Stella.]—"My dear Stella, we are in a great difficulty, you may be sure, or I would not have interfered with your well-deserved holiday."

"There, there, I understand what all that means," interrupted the lady. "What—is—the matter? What am I wanted to do?"

"You have seen, of course, that we have a new piece announced for to-night; also that a young lady was to have made her first appearance."

"And, if successful, to have cut me out of all the pretty young ladies for the rest of my engagement," said Stella, smiling. "Well, I don't care much for that; I've looked lovely long enough."

"And look lovely still, dear," said the manager, with a stage manner. "Well—the young lady has taken fright and eloped with her mamma, and so I want you "—

"To read the part to-night? I won't!"

"No, my dear, your kind old manager is not so inconsiderate as that. But he wants you to study the part and play it on Wednesday next—to oblige a young author whose wife I beg to introduce to you," said Mr. Manager, presenting Florence.

"Really this is not fair," replied Stella, curtsying at the same time. "I can't say No, bluntly, to this lady's face, but without knowing what the part is, or—— What do you do to-night, then ?"

"The new piece, my dear."

"And who plays the part?" asked Stella, in great surprise."

"This young lady—the brave young wife of the sick author, whose life is thought to be imperilled, should any accident delay the production of this, his first essay." Mr. Weaver then told how it chanced that Florence was able to perform the arduous duty she had undertaken for her husband's sake.

"Oh, you dear, good creature," cried Stella, throwing her arms around Florence. "I will do anything in the world to help such a good wife, and such a good husband, as I am sure he must be."

"I knew you would, my loyal Stella," said the manager. "And now I will tell you what you must do. I will have dinner sent into your room for you and my young friend here, and you must take charge of her for the rest of the evening."

"With pleasure!" exclaimed Stella, clapping her hands. "I will go over your part with you! I will see to your dresses, and initiate you into some of the frauds which we practise upon the noble British Lion when he pays his money at the doors, and believes in all he sees, and wags his tail accordingly."

Florence thanked her new-found friend sincerely, for she felt how much she should be sustained by the sympathy and assistance of this kind, warm-hearted actress. The Captain and the manager then left them together.

Poor Florence ate little, and would have taken nothing but for Stella, who "kept her courage to the sticking-place" by cheerful counsel and encouraging praise. At Stella's suggestion, the dresses were tried on and little alterations made, which improved their effect, and Florence grew braver, from the consciousness that she had a friend whose experience had already removed some of the misgivings which had beset her, despite her great resolution.

At length the dread announcement was heard!—"Overture on, ladies and gentlemen."

The play commenced, and the first scene of the drama had not been long in action, when a gipsy woman had to enter.

For a moment a sense of sickness overcame the wife-actress, but with an effort of will she shook all fear from her, and walked upon the stage when required to do so, almost as confident in herself as the oldest actor beside her.

The applause which greeted her was loud and general, but it produced no feeling of pleasure, nor of increased confidence, in the young *débutante*. She had taken her position on higher principles than a care of self, and she neither courted praise nor feared censure. She was playing for her husband's life, as she believed, and she would strive to win, whatever she might endure.

In a private box, the furthest from the stage, but yet commanding a good view of the scene, sat Mrs. Gregson and her niece, Marian Mayley. Between them were seated Mr. and Mrs. Warner. Warner clapped his hands to give the young *débutante* courage for the task before her, little thinking whose blood flowed in her veins, or what brave woman's spirit she had inherited.

Her face was stained a deep gipsy brown, and her well-set figure and graceful motion made her seem, indeed, the most honoured daughter of her tribe—a Bohemian queen.

When she spoke, her voice was "soft, gentle, and low," but so perfectly clear that every word she uttered reached the ears of the listeners. It had touched the heart of one of her auditors, filling it with the music which had been hushed for four long years. Yet there were neither the lithe form, nor the auburn tresses, nor the red and white cheeks of the former singer, and the poor mother believed she only heard the echo of a far-off memory. Lucy, with her eyes still fixed upon the stage, took her husband's hand, and pressed it when the gipsy-player spoke, but it was some time before his ear detected the same song that his wife had heard in the first sentence uttered by the Bohemian. When he understood the significance of Lucy's pressure, he trembled as with a gentle ague, and so continued until he could exclaim, "How very like her voice! How very like!"

From that moment the actress upon the stage became endowed with an interest which made both Lucy and Warner forgetful that they were only spectators of a mimic scene, and all the gipsy's sorrows, trials, and temptations became associated with their absent child, until neither could look longer, and, to the surprise of Mrs. Gregson and her niece, Mr. and Mrs. Warner rose, pleading indisposition as an excuse, and left the theatre.

All their way home, and all the night long, the player's voice sang to them of their old homes in the far-off colony, and their beloved Florence; they wondering and wondering whether they were listening in a dream that was to be the harbinger of the return of the old singer.

Vincent Elliott having, most provokingly, missed his friend, came to ask shelter in Mrs. Gregson's box, until the piece was over. The seats of the Warners were unoccupied, and therefore, who could refuse him? Not Mrs. Gregson, as she was glad of his company; and Marian—well, she was too much interested in the play, which was drawing to a conclusion, to care about the presence of Mr. Elliott. The curtain fell, and loud was the applause which followed—Vincent Elliott, at Mrs. Gregson's request, bawling lustily for the gipsy and the manager. The latter soon appeared, and announced the repetition of the piece on Wednesday next. Why Wednesday? Why not on Monday? The *débutante!* The *débutante* was clamoured for. Why did she not appear? When the curtain fell, shutting out the hundreds of faces, the glaring foot-lights, and all but the noise announcing her husband's triumph, Florence, closing her eyes and clasping her hands together, would have sunk down upon the stage insensible, had not Stella caught her as she was falling, and carried her at once to her dressing-room. The faintness was of short duration, and when consciousness returned, the kind actress was kneeling by the side of Florence and smiling an assurance that all was well.

"My brave, brave girl," said Stella, "you have done your part, your woman's part, your wife's part, nobly. Were ours a happier life than I know it to be, I would praise your acting, and urge you to wear this motley for many a night to come. But yours, I am sure, will be a lot more suited to your nature. Home! ah, home without ambition, struggle, success, and failure, will be your future. You must leave to us the tinsel honours of the stage, and the feverish strife which wins them."

Florence was too much exhausted to reply but with the briefest thanks, and then her kind friend assisted her at her toilet, allowing none of the ordinary attendants to interpose their officious services.

"It is a fancy of mine," Stella replied, in answer to a gentle remonstrance from Florence. "It is a fancy of mine that you shall have a pleasant remembrance of this night's work if possible, and that when it comes back to you, you will associate me with it, and think kindly of the poor players: as I have helped you this night, you shall help them, should they ever cross your path in need. I should not like you to forget me."

"That I never shall," said Florence, kissing Stella's forehead. "Never; and I trust that the friendship which has begun so strangely may last our lives." And the wish was realised.

A messenger from Elmsley had conveyed to the doctor the intelligence of the successful progress of the piece, and Florence and the Captain announced the happy termination.

"Thank God that it is over!" said Edward, as he clasped the hands of his faithful clever wife, little thinking then how much he owed to her love.

"I am ashamed of this emotion," he continued, "but the production of that piece had taken such possession of my mind, that to have had to bear longer with doubt would, I fear, have been productive of terrible results; and now to have been so successful! My work and the good kind actors' work also! I will write and thank them to-morrow."

"By-the-by," said Florence, "here is a note for you from Mr. Weaver. Shall I open it?" He answered "Yes;" and therefore she broke the seal, and read as follows:—

"MY DEAR SIR,

"I congratulate you most sincerely on the reception of your drama, and I enclose your cheque for £100, being quite contented to bear any future risk.

"Yours truly,

"B. WEAVER."

Kind, considerate man! Such acts will be remembered where our good deeds are recorded, and when the denunciations of fanatic praters, who judge without inquiry and condemn without charity, have passed into air. His name was not forgotten, when earnest words of thankfulness went up to heaven that night from a sick man's bed.

The first battle of life was over, and the spoils had to be gathered only to make the great victory complete. The money was, no doubt, a welcome part of the gains of conquest; but that would be spent in time. There was other booty which remained with Edward and Florence all their lives, and never grew less, but seemed to increase in value as they grew older and dearer to each other.

Florence sat down by Edward's bedside on the following morning with the newspaper; and spreading it out on the bed, began reading the criticism of her dear husband's play. The plot was ingenious—the language fresh and scholarly, the moral undeniable, and the subject one of domestic life. Then came comments on the acting. Mr. Weaver, one of the best actors of the day, was never more successful; others of inferior merit played most satisfactorily; and Mr. Ranton would have been really excellent but for the exhibition of over energy. "The charming *débutante*," said the critic, "was undoubtedly the attraction of the evening, and gave a value to the piece which cannot be over-estimated;" and then Florence read such praises of herself, that blushes suffused her face and neck, as a consciousness of self-laudation possessed her, although the words she read had been written by another. Edward observed her flushed cheeks and hesitating manner; and when she paused and could read no further, he requested to know the cause of her confusion. To tell him an untruth, to equivocate even to him, were impossible; and so, creeping nearer to him, and laying her head upon his bosom, she confessed to her share in the dreadful conspiracy of the day before, and was pardoned by a hundred kisses from lips no longer feverish with anxiety, and which had received their new health through her bravery and self-sacrifice.

"How noble of you!—how loving of you, dearest Florence," Edward said. "I could not have braved so much, I fear, even to attain the result. How very proud I am of you, my wife! How gratified I am to know that this our first step towards independence has been made together!"

"I am so happy now that you have approved of what I have done," said Florence. "My greatest anxiety was the fear that you might blame me for risking so much. But the end I had in view justified me to myself. And now, dear Edward, there need be no more miserable ponderings on the future. No more fancy pictures of a poor young wife left homeless and penniless, as I have known you paint when you thought your gloomy canvas was seen by you alone. No, my dear proud husband, we are now at liberty to seek those who, having loved me through years of waywardness, will not leave me unforgiven for discovering where the happiness of my life was to be found."

Why press him to your bosom, Florence, that he may not reply, and urge the objections raised by his own proper pride to becoming a dependent?

Do you not hear a knock at the door of your old house at Primrose Hill?

No; it was a visitor to Captain Elmsley, who, not having the least idea that he was being received on the door-step by the Captain's lady, did not hesitate to say—

"Captain Elmsley's at home, I believe; I'll announce myself;" and then brushing past the lady into the house, entered the spacious but dilapidated parlour.

The Captain was engaged as we have before described him, attired in the morning garment of many patches, and darnings, and washings.

His surprise was considerable at the intrusion of the newcomer, for it was Vincent Elliott.

"Aha!" cried Elliott, snapping his fingers. "Is Columbus outdone? Is Captain Ross extinguished? Have I discovered the domicile of Captain Elmsley?"

The person addressed was too much a man of the world to show that he was taken at a disadvantage, and therefore he replied in the most pleasant of tones,

"What, Vincent Elliott! How do you do? Delighted to see you."

"I must shake hands with you," said Elliott, suiting the word to the action, "to satisfy myself that you are substantial! Ha! ha! Then you do live in a house and sleep in a bed like other people?"

"Yes!" replied Elmsley, not quite liking Elliott's manner.

"Very retired out here," continued Elliott. "Are villas dear in this neighbourhood? Rather queer quarters, Captain! What are you out here? An Indian chief, a refugee, or a field-marshal?"

"Fie, sir; fie!" said Elmsley, rather seriously. "You are young. No, my dear boy, I am Captain Elmsley still."

Vincent was rather abashed at this reproof, but he had been induced to be impertinent by the extraordinary contrast presented by the Captain at home and abroad. Elmsley saw that he had countered his man, and wishing to keep friendly with him, pressed his advantage no further, but inquired :—

"By the bye, have you heard anything lately from your innamorata?"

"Yes! I have come to friendly terms with her guardian," replied Vincent.

"That's good news!" said Elmsley. "And is that the reason you have hunted me up?"

"No," replied Elliott, "for, strange to say, he entertains a singular opinion of you—he thinks you—"

"What, sir?" asked Elmsley, sharply.

"Something like a swindler."

"A what, sir?"

The blood rose red in Elmsley's face.

"I hope, sir, you removed such an impression."

"No; I did not," replied Vincent; "but I will, if you give me authority."

"My authority, sir. Do you consider that necessary, being in this room?" asked Elmsley, putting down his pipe, and rising. "I cannot imagine that you are here to insult me, Mr. Elliott."

"I really came with no such intention," replied Vincent. "Come, Captain, we must not quarrel. I think I know you better now than I did from your own account of yourself, which you must confess was not very explicit. You live more for the world than upon it. Now tell me, you have two lodgers of the name of Norwold?"

"I have."

"Are they at home?"

"They are."

"Could I see them?"

"That is for them to determine."

" You're angry ? "

"Rather—swindler is a very nasty word, Mr. Elliott. I am a poor man—an idle man—a vain man, but no swindler."

"I believe you, Captain Elmsley, and apologise for so unceremoniously communicating an impression which I am sure will be very soon removed," said Vincent.

"Say no more ! say no more ! " replied the Captain; "but permit me to introduce Mrs. Elmsley to Mr. Elliott."

He had been constrained to do this, as Mrs. Elmsley, having swept the doorstep to calm her ruffled temper, had no notion of being kept out of her own room by the rude stranger. She had, therefore, entered, and busied herself about until the conversation, taking the animated turn it had done, brought Mrs. Elmsley to the side of her husband, and, by way of conveying the moral support she intended him to receive from her presence she put her arm through his, and leaned upon him, staring Vincent full in the face.

Elliott expressed the pleasure he had in the introduction, and Mrs. Elmsley was equally charmed at knowing Mr. Elliott. The lady's face was perfectly familiar to Vincent, and associated with some pleasurable recollections, but it was not until she had left the room to announce his desire to speak with Mrs. Norwold, that this impression became sufficiently definite to allow him to assign her a place in the Bar of a well-known hostelry, also in Fleet Street, and rivalling "The Cock" in the succulence of its chops and steaks, and the confusion of its arithmetic.

"You have seen Mrs. Elmsley before, I presume?" asked the Captain, with a smile.

"Such is my impression," answered Vincent, smiling also. "I thought you had been a bachelor. I had no idea that you had practised—what you once called the madman's arithmetic —multiplying misery by two. Sly dog!"

"My dear boy," said Elmsley, resuming his old manner and his meerschaum, "I'll not wrong Mrs. E. A house is not a home without a woman—a paradise with one. Mrs.

Elmsley is a pattern to her sex, and makes gin-punch better than any woman in the three kingdoms."

"I see"—said Vincent—"you married her for contrast. She is the useful, and you are the ornamental—"

The Captain's lady returned to say that Mr. Elliott being a stranger to Mrs. Norwold, and Mr. Norwold not able to receive him, would he kindly communicate his business to Captain Elmsley?

"Oh! certainly," said Elliott. "The fact is, your lodger, Mrs. Norwold, is the daughter of Mr. Warner!"

"What, *your* Mr. Warner? Strange, indeed!" said Elmsley; "and that they should have been lodging here, and that I should have been of some service to them!"

"I am heartily glad to hear you say so! I have had a long hunt for them, and might have saved myself and others much anxiety, had I made a confidant of you. But——"

"Oh, you were justified in your silence," said Elmsley. "Mr. Norwold told me something of his history, but not all. I gathered there had been love and elopement in it. He was the author of the new drama you saw on Saturday night!"

"He the author? Indeed! Quite a romance!"

"Quite—for the lady who played the gipsey was his noble, loving wife!"

"Bless and save us!" cried Mrs. Elmsley. "Why, none of you never told me that, Joe!"

The Captain rather regretted that occasion had been given for Mrs. Elmsley to make a remark.

"And Warner and his wife were there," said Vincent, "looking upon the beloved daughter they had travelled thousands of miles to find! No wonder that the young actress had such a powerful effect upon them both. I had promised to waylay you, and find out who the young lady was, as Warner, I believe, is desirous to make her acquaintance."

Elmsley then explained the circumstances under which Florence had become an actress, and Vincent was loud in expressions of admiration, declaring that Elmsley had proved so good a friend, and so clever a general, that he deserved the pleasure of communicating to his young friends the next act of their Life's drama. He therefore left the room to carry the news to the two hearts which had sorrowed long for the one who had been so near to them, and yet they knew it not.

CHAPTER XXXII.

FROM the time Jasper Jellifer brought home Barbara Raymond as his wife, his condition had been made more comfortable, although the most fanciful of observers would never have discovered Cupids perched in the corners of his dwelling, or turtle-doves cooing under his eaves. No, Mrs. Jellifer moved about her house like an intelligent cat, catching such stray mice as came in her way, rarely showing her claws, and never having scratched Jasper more than once or twice during the long course of their connubial connection. She sometimes, it is true, was betrayed into expressions equivalent to a cat's "swearing," although her expletives were moderately feminine. We are pleased with our simile of a cat, for Mrs. Jellifer went now purring about the house, and rubbing round Jasper, as though she had been suddenly endowed with such a stock of affection that its concealment was unendurable.

Jasper was really pleased at these unwonted demonstrations of domestic felicity, and never remembered that the velvet paws were armed with implements of torture, or that cats are of most uncertain natures—loving and treacherous, docile and ferocious, in the same moment.

Mrs. Jellifer was, in reality, quite as good a wife as Jasper desired, and much better, being what she was, than he deserved. There had been small pretence of affection between them; but, as we have said, Jasper loved money, so did his wife, Barbara; Jasper was thrifty, so was she; and Jasper could drive a very hard bargain, and so could Mrs. Jellifer as our prosperous, lucky, cunning friend was about to discover.

To avoid the expense of a respectable clerk, and to keep the knowledge of their own affairs to themselves, Mrs Jellifer assisted Jasper in managing his books, and being naturally a quick woman, she had readily acquired an insight into the commercial mysteries of single and double entry—mysteries by which ragged boys, with but a shilling in their pockets, are converted into lord mayors with thousands upon thousands at their bankers. Mrs. Jellifer, whilst consulting her husband's ledgers and cash-books, had been much puzzled during the last twelve months to account for moneys which Jasper had received, and, passing them through his books in various complicated forms, would possibly have mystified Mrs. Jellifer herself, had she not had her faculties quickened in a remarkable degree by recent circumstances. She had, therefore, during Jasper's daily absence from the office, made a sort of balance-sheet of their possessions, and after setting down the money at the bankers', money invested in loans and mortgages, and other securities, she arrived at the conclusion that Jasper had applied upwards of fifteen hundred pounds to some concealed use. This discovery, instead of annoying her, gave her extraordinary satisfaction, as being another proof of Jasper's perfidious disposition, and a further justification of herself for the revenge she had in contemplation. "He would cheat even me!" she thought; "the wife of his bosom —the woman he has endowed with all his worldly goods! You shall keep your word, Jasper, before we have done with each other."

Jasper's tea was very strong that evening, and he slept soundly for three hours.

Mrs. Jellifer, meantime, gave an audience to Jack-in-the-Box in the lower office. That tatterdemalion had brought himself to his present condition by starting in life as a jolly fellow, and "the best of all good company." He had sung and joked himself out of many respectable offices, where drunkenness and irregularity were considered objectionable habits, until he had been glad to hide his seedy garments, and his blotched face, in the dungeon which Mr. Jellifer called his office. He was a shrewd fellow when sober, and the pittance he received was hardly enough for a single debauch in the course of a week—barely sufficient to place two scant meals a day before him, and keep a bed under him at night. He still managed, when some of his old cronies did him the unkindness to entertain him, to make a night of it now and then; and the effect of recovering from one of those evenings was to render Jack-in-the-Box very impertinent to his employer in the morning. He had had an orgie on the evening preceding, and Mrs. Jellifer found him in a very consequential mood. He was usually addressed by Mr. Jellifer as "Now, then!" and sometimes as "Now, then you sir! look to this, and look to that;" but on the days of his exaltation he would answer to no name but Mr. Jerningham.

Mrs. Jellifer was glad to find him so lively, and fancied she could improve the occasion, by requesting him to fetch a quart of ale, or of stout, if he preferred the heavier liquor.

Mr. Jerningham would in his soberer moods have been surprised at this communication and unwonted liberality of Mrs. Jellifer, but the terms he had established with himself throughout the day had become so very high in his own favour, that he considered this quart of liquor as a sort of recognition of his proper merits, and he offered no opposition. As he bore the foaming tankard from the public-house to the office, the thirsty devil in his throat cried for a draught, but honour prevailed over it, and the foaming pewter was placed untasted before Mrs. Jellifer, who had during his absence procured two glasses.

Mr. Jerningham, at the lady's request, proceeded with rather an unsteady hand to pour out the nut-brown ale as he called it, and then to bow gracefully, and "wish her every blessing that this transitory world could bestow."

The glass again filled, and Mr. Jerningham seated at his ease on an office-stool, Mrs. Jellifer opened the business she had so pleasantly inaugurated. "Mr. Jerningham," she said, "I have observed with more regret perhaps than you have given me credit for, the very unworthy position you occupy in this office."

The words struck a chord in Mr. Jerningham's bosom, and he instantly seized his glass, and drained it of its contents. Having wiped away the foam from his lips with a piece of waste blotting-paper, he merely said "Proceed, ma'am," and resumed an attitude of attention.

"It is not my fault, Mr. Jerningham, that it is so," continued Mrs. Jellifer; "but Mr. Jellifer is, as you may have remarked, a close man."

"———— close!" observed Mr. Jerningham.

"Please don't swear," said the lady. "Now, I am anxious to better your position, if you will allow me."

Mr. Jerningham sat upright on his stool, and rubbed his inky fingers through his exuberant hair, until it looked not unlike a Turk's-head broom, but he said nothing.

"You are, I am sure," continued Mrs. Jellifer, "a gentleman—pray fill your glass again." Mr. Jerningham instantly complied with the request. "I am therefore sure that a woman may trust you."

"With life! with honour!" cried Mr. Jerningham, holding high in air the well-filled glass, some of its contents bedewing the extraordinary hirsute crop on the speaker's head.

"I was sure of that, Mr. Jerningham; but as the service I require of you may interfere with your leisure, I beg you to accept of this half-sovereign as a compensation for the trouble I am about to give you."

Mr. Jerningham knew his own value too well to hesitate a moment in pocketing the unfrequent coin, and to allow the lady to recover from any temporary embarrassment she might be experiencing he again hid his face in the tumbler.

"Now, sir, for my confidence. You know, I presume, that Mr. Jellifer objects to my being more in the office than is absolutely necessary. I must therefore solicit your assistance in making a discovery which is needful to my peace of mind. Mr. Jellifer is in the habit of receiving certain sums of money which he, for some reason, does not choose to account for in the regular way, and I fancy that you might possibly discover in time some clue to this regular misappropriation."

Jerningham's eyes had dilated during this statement, and he looked round towards the door which led from the office to the dwelling-house. Mrs. Jellifer noticed the action, and said—

"You will not mind taking a glass which I have not touched," rising and handing her tumbler to the confused Mr. Jerningham. "You need not be alarmed that our conference can be disturbed. Mr. Jellifer sleeps occasionally after his tea, and soundly sometimes. I fancy he will do so to-night. What do you know?" This inquiry was made so abruptly, that Mr. Jerningham bounded up and down upon his stool—and therefore the lady added in a much milder tone, "You do know something, I am certain, Mr. Jerningham."

"You are sure the governor is all right?" asked Jerningham; and being informed that he was, the now half-tipsy fellow continued, "'Woman and wine,' I never could resist ye, and never shall! Madam, you have unlocked my bosom, not with this golden key, but by your condescension and obliging conversation. Through the panel of yonder distant desk, where I pass so many hours of my miserable existence, you will see, upon close inspection, a hole bored by a gimlet. Why? A pardonable curiosity, I trust, to keep an eye on what interests my honourable employer. Well, Madam, about twelve months ago, Mr. Jellifer did me the honour to ask me into this inner office, and to take a seat—and nothing else. You were away, ma'am, at the time, and the governor

said he was very lonely, and all that sort of thing, which
men are who have no resources, no drink, no smoke. Well,
ma'am, I tried to cheer him up by a recital of my own misfortunes—my own poverty, when he started up and said,
'That's it! That's what I live in fear of! Poverty! a
workhouse end! I don't know why, but I believe that the
few pounds I have saved will some day slip through my
fingers, and I shall be a beggar.'"

"He said that," said Mrs. Jellifer, with open eyes and
nostrils. "He said that was his fear. Well, what followed?"

"He then told me of a man whom he had known, who
had been possessed with the same fear until he took to rob-
bing himself, and secreting his plunder against the evil day;
but his terrors grew too much for him, and he died by his
own hands."

"Well, drink what you have there and then go on. You
shall have more money, if you are honest with me," said
Mrs. Jellifer.

"The next morning I bored that hole in my desk, and
discovered that the governor received small sums, which he
did not put into the cash-box, but into his pocket. On those
days I have seen him busy at the iron chest; and once I
entered, unperceived by him, as he was locking the right-
hand drawer at the bottom. I should have thought nothing
of that, had he not started on seeing me, and, calling me an
idle scamp, sent me a longer journey than any mail-coach
ever accomplished, ma'am."

"Mr. Jerningham," said Mrs. Jellifer, "what you have
told me has removed much of the anxiety I have lately had
on my good husband's account. I am sure I may rely on
your secresy, as you may on my best services at any time."

Mr. Jerningham believed in this protestation, as it was
accompanied by another half-sovereign, and he went home to
his dismal lodging that night as happy as a king, if not quite
as sober as a judge ought to be.

By the light of a single candle, Mrs. Jellifer—her two

elbows resting on the table, and her face between her hands—sat watching the face of her sleeping husband. Her eyes glistened at times, as though her thoughts were so malignant they shone out to warn the doomed man that danger was near him where he sat, beside him in his bed, and afar off in Morden. Yet he had never suspected the chance of evil less than of late, and since there had been moving about his home a gentleness which had been pleasant to him.

When he awoke, he said, with a great yawn, " Dear me, Barbara! I have slept a long time."

" Yes, nearly two hours," replied his wife, with a little hollow laugh. " You would be pleasant company for any one who cared for talking; but I excuse you. I know how much my poor man has to tire him. Here is your biscuit, and glass of table-beer. Take them, and let us go to bed."

Such spare diet, and such thin potations, were not likely to produce heavy slumber; but, throughout the night, Jasper Jellifer was insensible to all that was doing in his house.

Mrs. Jellifer was astir about midnight, as Jasper had not gone to bed until past eleven, little thinking how soundly he was to sleep. Having partly dressed herself, she took a bunch of keys from the pocket of her husband's coat, and went down-stairs to the office. She then opened the iron chest, and the inner drawer to which Jerningham had referred. There was nothing of value there; two or three canvas money-bags, an odd key, and some letters, tied together by a piece of red tape. She had glanced carelessly at the little bundle of papers, but, as she was about to replace them, the writing appeared familiar to her, and she untied the tape, and read the letters. They were from her dead brother, Raymond Ray, reminding Jasper of their sworn compact to stand by each other in the case of difficulty, and calling upon him to remit the money which had been obtained by the bill of sale. There were painful descriptions of misery endured, and of hope deferred; and in the one of

latest date a terrible invocation of retribution on Jasper if he
was betraying the trust reposed in him by his old confederate.
Mrs. Jellifer's eyes glistened with tears at times as she read
these miserable proofs of Jasper's treachery and her brother's
sufferings; and then all traces of womanly feeling passed
away, the lines of her face deepened, and her brow con-
tracted and lowered, whilst her mouth became compressed
until the blood left her lips. She refolded the letters carefully, and placing them in their proper order, secured them
again with the piece of tape. She was startled by a loud
knock at the street-door. Again! it was repeated. She
knew that Jasper "slept well," or she would have been
afraid, perhaps, of detection. Perhaps she had become too
desperate, and he too hateful, for her to fear him in any way.
Before she could open the door, the knock came again, and
she inquired who was there.

"Police," was the reply; "open, if you please."

She complied instantly with this request, and learned that
a light having been seen in the office at that unusual hour,
the officer had considered it his duty to inquire the cause.

"Oh, thank you!" said Mrs. Jellifer, calmly. "I was
looking for some medicine in Mr. Jellifer's desk. He has
been a little unwell. Nothing unusual. Good night, and
thank you for your caution."

To be certain that Jellifer had not been disturbed, she
returned to her chamber and looked upon the sleeping man.
His face was very pallid and woe-begone, and but for the
slight twitching of the mouth might have been that of a dead
man. His wife looked upon him unmoved by any touch of
pity; and perhaps if he had slept on until the great
awakening of all men, she would have rejoiced, had her own
work been accomplished. She returned to the counting-
house, and sat pondering before the open chest, confident that
there was a hidden secret within it. At last she uttered a
sharp Ah! and drew out the drawer which had been so
carefully locked, yet contained such worthless matters. She

had been recalling all the cunning tricks of concealment of which she heard in her early life, and at last it occurred to her that Jasper's hoard was behind the drawer, as it was not in it. She was right. Carefully folded and pressed together she discovered bank-notes of various sums, and amounting to nearly fifteen hundred pounds. That knowledge was enough. She carefully replaced them, locked the drawer and the safe, and then returned to her bed-chamber to lie down calmly by the side of the wretched man she had condemned to a death of torture.

When Jasper rose in the morning, his head was confused and his spirits depressed more than they were usually of a morning, and he complained of his discomfort.

"I am afraid you are over anxious, Jasper," said his wife, "you must not press business so much. You want rest and quiet."

"No, no," replied Jasper, "I could do much more than I am doing. It's not that—I'm out of sorts, as they say; I'll call at a chemist's and buy a penn'orth of something."

"Well, be careful, Jasper, there have been many deaths lately."

"Always are many deaths," interrupted Jasper.

"Sudden deaths," continued his wife, and Jasper nicked his chin with the razor.

"Husbands and fathers, men of business, cut off in a moment, as it were."

"Well, well, not more than the average," said Jasper, who hated death so much that he had retired from the undertaking business before he left Morden.

"I don't know," replied Mrs. Jellifer. "I think the suddens are on the increase. I suppose, my dear, you have made your will?"

"What an odd question to ask a man before breakfast," said Jellifer.

"I once made the same inquiry at night, and you said what an unpleasant question to ask a man at bed-time. As

I am somewhat interested in the inquiry, I will put the question again at dinner-time."

"Of course I intend making my will," replied Jasper; "but it's not the most lively thing a man does. It's not pleasant to be bequeathing away all you've got, being certain that you shall be—I hate to think of it. And then to know the robbery that you—that is, your property, is subject to."

"You mean the legacy duty?" said Mrs. Jellifer. "I confess I never think of that but I could cry! How much per cent. is it on legacies to your own family?"

"O horrible!" replied Jasper. "That is the reason I never can make my will."

"But Mr. Greyford avoided it so cleverly; don't you remember?" said Mrs. Jellifer. "What was it he did?"

"Eh?" Jasper did not reply further.

"What was it he gave his wife—a bond—no, it wasn't a bond—what was it, Jasper?"

"I don't exactly know," said Jellifer; "it was a something—a deed of gift I think they called it."

"Ay, that was it!" cried Mrs. Jellifer. "A deed of gift. As he had neither children nor relations—just like you, Jasper—he made a deed of gift to his wife of all he possessed, and so evaded the iniquitous legacy duty. That is what you must do, Jasper. You have no one to care for but me, nor have I except you, and so I will give our lawyer instructions to prepare such a deed before the world is a day older. Eh! dear?"

What reason on earth had Jasper to urge against such a proposition? Had she not helped to scrape and scrape through the twenty and more years of their wedded life, and was she to be liable at last to pay legacy duty should she unhappily survive Jasper? He was pressed all through his breakfast and his newspaper-reading for any proper objection, and he could find none. The deed of gift was to be prepared.

Jasper walked up and down several times in front of his lawyer's office before he could summon resolution to enter and give away—it was giving away—the gains of his mean, grasping, cheating life. There seemed to be no danger in the act, but still he would be on the safe side, and therefore he limited his donation to Lady Norwold's bond and certain other properties, reserving to himself some three thousand pounds for the purposes of business, he said, and——his secret hoard, of which he said nothing, either to wife or lawyer. The deed was duly prepared, and to Jasper's surprise Mrs. Jellifer only laughed when she heard the reservation her husband had made. Neither did she show the least displeasure when Jasper desired to wait until the next day before he signed the deed that would make Barbara Jellifer richer than himself. He was restless and thoughtful, but his wife only noted his disquietude to utter words of tenderness and considerateness.

"My dear Jasper," she said—it was not often she had called him dear—"if you regret consenting to this act of prudence, tear the papers, and there is an end. I have no wish to consider myself if it gives you pain. I have told you one and only one of the considerations that moved me to make this request. In justice to myself, I will now mention another. I have seen, how year by year as we have grown more prosperous, our plans of business have enlarged also, and hitherto we have been successful. But every day, almost, I read or hear of some thriving man, by an ill-advised speculation, or mis-placed trust, becoming ruined, utterly ruined, when he was thought to be above the danger of such a catastrophe. Are we less liable to error? or to become the victims of some misplaced confidence?"

She paused, as Jasper showed by look and manner how closely she had touched him.

"However," she continued, "let us talk no more at present. Think over what I have said, and then do as you consider wisest, and for the best. I can have no interest apart from yours, dear, any more than you can from mine. Hark! There is the clerk calling you."

Jasper rose without speaking to her, although he appeared wistful to say something in reply, but he could command only a ghastly smile, which did not last until he had left the room. When the door closed upon him, the expression of devilish triumph on his wife's face told plainly enough that her revenge was approaching accomplishment, and that if Jasper signed that deed it would be his death-warrant.

Oh, how she purred about him throughout that long, long, evening, and patted him with her velvet paws, until he forgot there had been treachery ever between friends, or strong, destroying hatred begotten by it!

Mr. Jerningham's summons was not to communicate very cheering intelligence. He had heard that a large commission house in the city had been declared insolvent that day, and he was fearful that his worthy employer might have done business lately with them? No. He was glad to know that all accounts were closed between them. He hoped also that the report might prove untrue, but he had heard it. He did not add, however, that it was from Mrs. Jellifer.

Jasper passed a restless night. The strong fear that had of late possessed him lest he should come to want, increased every hour he laid sleepless on his pillow, and Barbara's proposal might therefore be a premonition from the good destiny which had hitherto made him a prosperous man. He would at least divide the risk of ruin by placing confidence in Barbara.

He knew not what he had parted with when next day he wrote in the presence of proper witnesses, at the bottom of a sheepskin—"JASPER JELLIFER."

CHAPTER XXXIII.

Lucy was the first to meet Florence and her husband. The
poor mother had sorrowed so long for her lost child, that
there was not one reproach remaining in her heart when they
were restored to each other. And when she heard the story
of her daughter's love, and the strange accidents which had
made her marriage seem rash and clandestine, all cause for
censure vanished in Lucy's judgment, and nothing remained
but thankfulness that Florence had chosen so wisely. Warner
loved his child very dearly, also, but his fatherly pride had
been offended, and his fatherly love hurt, if not outraged.
Yet when he heard the story, first from Lucy's lips, with such
extenuations as her mother's love had found, he gave his
anger to the winds, and condoned his past distress in the joy
of once more folding in his arms "the sole daughter of his
house and heart." Edward Norwold had won his own claim
to honour and regard, and he whose life had been one long
exile from home and its affections, now realised them to their
full in the devoted tenderness of mother, wife, and father.

Florence had told her parents what Edward's life had been,
as he had scarcely referred to himself during the short time
they had all been together, partly on account of his present
weakness, and partly because he had no pleasure in recalling
the past. Warner appeared at first to be incredulous of
Florence's statement, not that he doubted her husband's word,
but his own parental love had been so strong that he could not

E E

compass the idea of a father abandoning a son—an unoffend-
ing son, until his marriage with Florence.

When Edward had somewhat reluctantly recapitulated all
that we already know, Warner folded his arms as though to
control his rising anger, and walked up and down the room
before he spoke.

"And this was his treatment of you, poor boy—his son,
and for years his only child!" said Warner. "From his
earliest youth he was always crafty, cold-blooded, mean, and
deceitful; but the most savage treacherous beast that lives has
care for its young, and that instinct secures to it some human
sympathy.   But this man, gently nurtured, sometime loved,
tramples out all the natural affection in his own heart and
yours, without remorse or apparent sorrow, to live his own
selfish life."

All this was true enough, and Edward had thought it over
a hundred, hundred times, from his youth upward, but it
sounded strangely coming from another's lips, and for a moment produced a feeling of resentment against the speaker.

"He is still my father, sir," said Edward.

"Your father, Edward Norwold? By what tie, what
touch of nature does he claim kindred with you?" asked
Warner, passionately. "Your mother, neglected in sickness
as in health, her love for you made into her torture, ultimately
killing her mind first and then her poor weakened body.
You, left among strangers to grow into a good man, or a
wicked devil; the chances were equal.   Thank God! there
are kindly, noble hearts as well as evil ones, and you have
found them—but what cared he? As you lived, he dared not
to desert you—had you died, he would have buried you, and
with your bones all fatherly memories and regrets, as he
would have buried a hound."

Edward felt his blood stirred by this passionate harangue,
and he would have struck one blow for the honour of his
father, but there was something in the tone, look, and manner
of Warner, which awed him as no man had ever done before.

"Edward Norwold," Warner continued, after a short pause. "You have chosen, unsolicited and unsought by me, to make my child your wife. You have taken from me the one being for whom I have lived and laboured, and I ask, in exchange for that of which you have deprived me, a share in your confidence and affection. I have not spoken without a knowledge of the past and present, and even with some prescience of the future. You are not, cannot be, a son to such a man; and must not affect to have an interest which you cannot feel, or I shall mistrust you in all things else. You have to choose between us. Be prepared to answer."

"Have you then any knowledge of Sir Gilbert beyond what I have communicated?" asked Edward, more perplexed by Warner's excitement.

Warner paused in his walk about the room, and sat down in a chair by the table, and covering his face with his hands, said:

"Edward, I dare not pursue this subject further. Never resume it except when I desire you to do so. There must be peace, always peace between us—my son!—my dear son, given to me by my beloved daughter. I will give you half the love of my heart, and will be your father. You must believe that in all I do I am guided by one desire—your happiness—your honour. Florence is the bond which unites us until death comes."

He raised up his head, and there was a strange beauty in his face, a solemn earnest look that begat at once the gazer's love and reverence.

Florence had seen nothing of Uncle Jack at present, as from some cause or the other, he had not been to Warner's lodgings for three days. We have told how he had been employed part of that time, and it is fitting that we should account for the remainder. When he returned to London with his exhumed casket, he soon got at the concealed treasure. He first brought forth some papers, and as they afterwards became documentary evidence, we will transcribe them at once.

NUMBER ONE was slightly discoloured, and the ink browned by time, although the writing was perfectly legible. It bore date twenty-six years past, and was headed Norwold Mill. Then followed:

"This box was deposited in Morden churchyard, at the above date, by me, Raymond Ray, Miller, for my own especial purpose. As it is possible that it may be reclaimed by others, I now state my reasons for its concealment. I have experienced in my intercourse with the world treachery where I least expected to find it, and I have suffered want when there were none to help me, so that I have resolved to secure myself against such chances for the future. None ought to blame me for this precaution should it ever come to the knowledge of others concerned in my proceedings; and it will not do so if I am fairly dealt by. My present business exposes me to great risk; and, therefore, I have given to my brother-in-law a bill of sale over everything I possess, in order that he may take precedence of any other claimant. For my own security I have received from him a similar instrument, which will be found enclosed with this statement."

Jack looked into the box and found the paper referred to by Ray. It was a bond apparently duly drawn and signed by Jasper Jellifer, and acknowledging his indebtedness to Ray for twelve hundred pounds. It was dated six and twenty years ago, and one day earlier than the preceding document. Jack remembered well that Jellifer had produced a similar deed after Ray's conviction, and superseded the claim made by the Crown to the property of the felon. Cunning Jasper Jellifer, thought Jack, there can be no doubt now that he was aware of all Ray's villany, and a sharer also in the gains accruing from it; but, fox that he was, he kept out of the reach of the law. No doubt, either, that when he grew fearful of discovery, he had betrayed his less careful partner, and that all Ray had suspected in later years was true. The long forgotten incidents of the detection, trial, and after consequences came back to Spraggatt's recollection as plainly as though a day only had intervened since their occurrence.

Treacherous—heartless villain !

The wretched man who had crawled to Jack's home in the Bush came vividly before him, and seemed to demand justice at his hands. Was it his duty to become the avenger?

Let him read on.

"What else the box contains was obtained by our joint means, and with our mutual knowledge ; but as it provoked some very unpleasant consequences, I promised to bear all blame, and therefore claimed possession, as the time might come when its value would rescue me from such poverty as I have known more than once in my short and eventful life."

Jack removed a small quantity of tow, and as he did so, was surprised to observe something glitter beneath it. He removed the remaining covering and found a diamond bracelet, containing a faded miniature of the late Sir John Norwold!

Jack's brain swam when he saw this, and he fell back into his chair ! If Sir John himself had looked up at him from the grave, he could hardly have been more overpowered.

That bracelet which had changed the current of more lives than one—that had brought shame and misery, and large happiness also,—buried as it had been from the sight of man for all the years those changes had been coming and departing,—was now brought again into the light of day to work more good or evil by his agency ! How many years he had borne about with him the secret of its existence, and yet knew it not. How it had found him thousands of miles away in the lonely Bush, when he had hardly thought to tread English ground again. How the wretched, dying convict had struggled through the tangled forest, and over the great plain to make him this bequest. All ! all impressed him with the certainty that the hand of Providence was here, and that he had Its work to do.

There was more writing folded up within the circle made by the bracelet.

What would it reveal? He almost feared to open the folds and read. When he had done so he fell upon his knees, and his broad breast heaved like a troubled sea.

The lines which he had read were common-place, and "earthy" enough.

Simply these:

"I have this day received £200 of Raymond Ray, Miller, and placed with him a diamond bracelet as security, until the repayment of the money."

Ray had written those lines, but there were two words more affixed to them, which gave such value to the whole that John Spraggatt, remembering the friend of his youth, had fallen upon his knees and given thanks for them. Those words were "GILBERT NORWOLD."

Warner had gone into the City, and Florence and her mother were standing at the window, each encircled by the other's arm, when Uncle Jack was seen coming up the street. Florence uttered a little cry of delight, and hoped that the dear old uncle would look up, and see her at home again. She was to be disappointed, for Jack kept his eyes bent on the pavement, as though he were in deep thought, but he sailed along at a tremendous rate, and must have run into much craft, on his way from the City, if he had kept such a blind reckoning and carried such a press of sail.

Why those nautical metaphors should have overtaken us, we know not, unless they came consequent upon Jack wearing a pea-jacket, his hands thrust into its pockets, and his elbows very much a-kimbo. When the door had been opened, Jack entered the passage, and was considerably surprised at being violently assailed by some one, who nearly strangled him in the embrace of two soft arms around his neck, then nigh smothering him with kisses,—kissing his great grizzly beard, shaggy eyebrows, rosy nose, sunburnt cheeks—indeed everywhere that a kiss could be implanted. What a shout he gave when he discovered that his assailant was his pet, his darling, his lost Florence! It was a wondrous sight, to see that burly fellow sitting on the stairs, his face hidden by his knuckles, with which he was punching his eyes, to keep back the joy that was trying to find vent, welling up from his great loving heart. And when he had succeeded, and made his eyes very red, he looked at his darling again, and opening his arms hugged her to the bosom of his pea-coat, till the embrace became painful to Florence on account of the buttons. She bore it all, however, as though she had been nestling on the downy breast of a halcyon. Dear old Uncle Jack! who had blamed himself so often for having advised that terrible journey to Paris, and which had ended in making her so very, very happy. And now to be sitting on that broad knee, whereon she had ridden to Banbury Cross in the old location kitchen, and under the old location verandah—that knee, which had been bent in humble prayer for her when her after-fate was unknown—seemed so like a dream, that she was obliged to pull his great bushy whiskers to satisfy herself that all was real again.

And then she led him up-stairs, like Beauty and the Beast, to be introduced to her dear husband—Jack's new nephew. He loved him at first sight, did Jack, and was perfectly of Lucy's opinion, that had Florence made herself miserable for life, by rejecting such a good fellow, Aunt Letty and brother-in-law Monsieur would all have been to blame. As Jack was an old-fashioned Church of England man, and took a very simple view of the Bible, he fancied he could trace a guiding hand in all that was known, and in all that had been revealed by himself, in the box which he had dug out of Morden church-yard.

Jack had come direct to Warner's house, hoping to find him absent, in order that he might take counsel with Lucy upon the course of action to be followed in consequence of his great discovery; and his purpose would have been defeated, as Florence would not let him out of her sight for some time, had not Warner been detained by an unexpected visitor from the City, in the person of Mrs. Jellifer. She had come to see

Mr. Spraggatt, but as he had told her he was only the agent for Mr. Warner, in a certain matter of business with her husband, she asked to see that gentleman, in Mr. Spraggatt's absence. Mr. Warner was averse to the interview, but the lady was so pressing that he consented at last to receive her.

"She had come," she said, "at the request of Lady Norwold, who had a particular favour to ask. In the ensuing week would be the birthday of Sir Gilbert, and it was her custom to wear the family jewels upon family occasions. She was not prepared to repay the money, but she asked the custody of the diamonds for the one night, pledging her honour for their return."

The request was unreasonable. Any other business?

"Yes." Mrs. Jellifer produced the bond her ladyship had given to her husband, Jasper. It secured three thousand pounds, but as money was needed, and Mr. Jellifer could not press for payment, it would be transferred to Mr. Warner for a much less sum.

Mr. Warner would consider that proposal, and answer it on the morrow. "Anything else?"

"Yes. Mr. Spraggatt had given Mr. Jellifer a large sum of money for some very trifling information concerning Mr. Edward Norwold. Might she ask the reason?"

There was no secret now. Mr. Norwold had married Miss Warner, and his residence could not be discovered by Mr. Warner on his coming to England.

"I concluded that was the cause," said Mrs. Jellifer. "I remembered that he had married a governess named Warner, and been turned out of doors by his father. You would like, I suppose, to have them reconciled?"

"No."

"Oh, yes, you would, sir; and I fancy I could make Sir Gilbert listen to you, if you desired it. I don't care for—I mean I don't want money for my assistance," said Mrs. Jellifer; "but you must be resolute if you would be successful!"

"It is useless speaking in riddles to me," said Mr. Warner; "either make your meaning clear, or leave me to my other business."

"What is the punishment for perjury?" asked Mrs. Jellifer—"transportation, is it not? Or, at any rate, long, very long imprisonment?"

"I believe it is," answered Warner.

"Then I can tell you when Sir Gilbert profited by another man's false-swearing, Mr. Warner; and if he knows that you are aware of that fact, will he not listen to any proposal you may make for the acknowledgment of your daughter?"

Warner guessed at her meaning, but he was anxious to hear further.

"Perhaps it would," he replied. "Yes; I should say certainly it would."

"I will do this on one condition, Mr. Warner," said Mrs. Jellifer—"that you pledge me your solemn word that when you have served your turn you will serve mine—that you will prosecute the perjurer—hunt him down, sir, as he once hunted another. I can show you the way, and without compromising Sir Gilbert, should you not wish to do so. Sir Gilbert is an unscrupulous man, and will be glad to be rid of the miserable tool he wants no longer."

Warner was amazed at his own conjectures, so unnatural did they appear, and he asked:

"Who is the perjurer?"

"No," replied Mrs. Jellifer. "I have not done my own business yet. I have this bond to sell—here is my authority to do so—a deed of gift. I want your pledge, also, to follow the other matter to the end."

"I will buy the bond," said Warner, "and I will pledge my word to see justice done. Who is the man?"

Mrs. Jellifer sat silent for a few moments, and then she said in a low voice:

"I will come again to-morrow. I thought I could have been bold enough to have spoken all I wished to say. I cannot."

"To-morrow be it then," replied Warner. "Come to my house in —— Street, by ten o'clock, and if Lady Norwold will call upon me at one on the succeeding day, I will possibly accede to her request."

Mrs. Jellifer thanked him, and then withdrew.

Mr. Warner walked home very thoughtful and perplexed. He had been long convinced that some chicanery must have been practised to have made his brother's possession of the title and estates so easy; and now he was to have forced upon him a knowledge which he had not sought to obtain since his return to England. Who could be the man? He had thought of Jasper Jellifer—yet he was the woman's husband; a generous one, it seemed, by the deed of gift which had been shown that day. Conjecture was at fault, and the morrow must be waited for.

When Lucy had listened to Jack's revelations, she anticipated with sad forebodings their probable effects upon her husband. She believed that he had never entirely overcome his desire to regain his lost position, despite his frequent struggles with himself, and she now foresaw that the resumption of the subject would be likely to produce results which would militate against the future happiness of all who were most dear to her; and she therefore awaited Warner's return with great anxiety. When he came home she called him into the breakfast-room, and, having prepared him gently for a disclosure of some importance, informed him of all which she had learned from her brother. The production of the bracelet affected Warner greatly, and the paper which had accompanied it much more so. For some minutes he could not speak, but held the two evidences of his innocence and the injustice which had been done to him in his hand, gazing at them vacantly.

"At last!—at last the proof has come," he said. "The dead has spoken, and his voice shall be obeyed. The cold heartless villain shall meet the punishment he so richly merits. He shall be humbled in the dust, and the finger of

the scorner shall. point at' him as he lies grovelling in his
shame. Eternal justice would. nott let such iniquity live
prosperously to the end, and. I—the dishonoured—am
destined to declare the hypocrisy. and baseness of: this bad
man's life. Remorselessly as he has pursued his wicked will,
I will pursue him.. I will forget' nothing which I suffered,
but, remembering all, will repay my own wrongs, my father's
miserable end, when knowing that he had dealt unjustly by
his misjudged son. I will reach this man where only he is
vulnerable, and beggar him in name and fortune. Liar, thief,
and perjurer,—without one kindly touch in his whole heart
—I will drive him into exile as he drove me, but without
one solitary hope, one sustaining recollection."

. Exhausted by his passion, he paused, and Lucy regarded
him in painful silence for some minutes. At last he looked
at her, and noting her mute distress, said, "Am I not
right?"

"No," she replied, gently. "Is revenge to be your
acknowledgment for all that God has done for us? For
enabling you to resist the terrible temptations which beset
you in your first sorrow, and you have told me what they
were? For giving you strength of·will and energy to shape
a new course, and make it prosperous? For giving you my
love, which you have proved and tried in many an hour of
sorrow, and said, how often! that in my well-deserved devotion you have found more happiness than you had ever
dreamed of? For our beloved child, whose infant life was
one long blessing, hardly known, hardly acknowledged, until
we thought that she was lost to us! For the inexpressible
joy which her return has given, knowing now that her love
for us was unchanged, and that she has proved herself worthy
to be loved and honoured? Are blessings such as these to be
paid by revenge, when God has commanded us to forgive, and
shown us how much we need forgiveness when striving at
our best?"

She had risen whilst saying this, and had placed her arms

around her husband's neck; but the evil spirit which had been raised was not then to be driven forth; so he unclasped her hands, as though to avoid further reproof or remonstrance, and went out into the street.

Lucy did not despair of her words having reached his heart, and she had prayed earnestly that they might prove of good avail more than once before he returned to her, silent and sorrowful.

CHAPTER XXXIV.

WARNER was reserved and silent the next morning when the family assembled at breakfast, and as this was unusual with him the influence extended to the whole party, until no one spoke a word. Lucy strove hard to conceal her own disquietude, but in vain; and, at last, feeling unable to command herself, she rose and left the room. Warner followed her with his eyes, as did Florence also; and when he perceived that Lucy's uneasiness had become manifest to her daughter, he said:

"Florence, dear, go to your mother; she will be glad of you."

The request had not to be repeated, and Florence left the room instantly.

Warner remained silent for a few moments, and then said, "Edward, we once spoke upon a subject which was painful to both of us, and I requested that it might not be resumed until I desired it. I was unduly excited, perhaps, at that time, and may have misunderstood the exact relations which have existed between you and your father. Did I understand rightly that he had separated you from your mother when she was ill—dying?"

"I am sorry to acknowledge that such was the case," replied Edward.

"You were then taken abroad, and left entirely to the care of strangers?"

"Nearly so. My father visited me at long intervals, and

upon one occasion—only one—took me to England for a very short time."

"But you were always in communication with him, and could have advised with him on the important step you took when marrying Florence?"

"Yes, sir," replied Edward, colouring slightly; "and had I not been certain of his answer, I should have done so. But he had made himself no place in my heart—he had never shown me that I had a place in his—and the new existence I had found in Florence's love, and the sympathy of her friends, was such a blessed change from the isolated life I had lived hitherto, that I resolved to brave the worst that he could add to his previous cruelty, and so I married."

"Have you regretted offending him?" asked Warner, looking at Edward steadfastly as he spoke.

"Regretted it, sir! No—not even when my future appeared to be almost desperate, except for the sake of her whose fate I had made my own. What has he since done to call for regret? Without one word of inquiry, has he not remorselessly abandoned me, nor cared whether I starved or prospered!"

Warner again paused before he spoke.

"And Lady Norwold, was she as indifferent as her husband?"

"I had no claims upon her," replied Edward. "She, a woman of the world, was only anxious to pursue her pleasures undisturbed; and Sir Gilbert was not the most amenable of husbands, even to her who had brought him wealth, which my poor mother had failed to do. Lady Norwold dared not risk the slight hold she had upon her husband's courtesy, for he showed her nothing more—and to have advocated my cause, would have been to have incurred uselessly my father's displeasure. During my stay in their house, she endeavoured to make it a home; nor was she altogether unmindful of Florence either. I have no resentment against her. She acted according to her teaching. She lives only for herself."

" You have no resentment against her ? Have you against your father ? " Warner asked, again regarding Edward most earnestly.

" I dare hardly answer no, for I cannot speak untruly to you," replied Edward, "although I would take no active means to show my feeling towards my father," adding, after a pause—" even to regain my proper position."

"Why not?" asked Warner, sharply. "Why should you hesitate, if, by humbling this proud, bad man, you could compel him to recognise you as his son, and—" he stopped speaking.

" Perhaps you will condemn my reasons and think them foolish," answered Edward, with some hesitation. "You may fail to understand them, perhaps."

"What are they, Edward ? Speak freely, that I may judge correctly."

"I will, sir. You, as I have heard, have made your own name honourable, and the wealth you possess has been acquired by your own skill, probity, and endurance. You have a right, therefore, to consider no other qualities, no other distinctions, valuable or ennobling. I have been accustomed to think differently. I am not the first of my name—I have an ancestry, and any shame or humiliation which touches my father, must sully the bright memories of those who have made our house noble and honourable. Do you understand me, sir ? Do you excuse, even if you cannot approve, the motives which make me tolerant of my wrong, and which, even for her dear sake, I hesitate to cast aside ? "

Warner's face appeared aglow with pleasure, and that strange beauty which had before possessed it came back, and commanded, as it were, the love and reverence of his son. He rose and took Edward's hand.

"Do I understand you ? Yes. Do I approve your motives ? Yes, as though I claimed kindred with the ancestry of which you are so worthy ! I will try to school myself by your example; but I have also a wounded pride to cure, and a sense of wrong to tame into forgiveness, my noble, honourable, much-loved son. I may come to you for counsel."

Mr. Warner then left the room, and Edward remained pondering on what had passed, naturally attributing the concluding words addressed to him as referring to Warner's resentment at the insulting rejection of his daughter, and was not surprised, therefore, when he had narrated what had occurred to Lucy and Florence, that the former uttered earnest words of thankfulness, that the sorrow which had threatened them was about to pass away, and leave them a future unembittered by an irremovable regret.

Warner had scarcely recovered his usual equanimity when Mrs. Jellifer was announced. As the door opened to admit her, Warner felt that indefinable sensation which accompanies the presence of a noxious thing, and it required some effort before he could speak to her, and desire her to be seated. He had a great end to obtain, and therefore he controlled the disgust he felt for this treacherous woman, and whose wicked purpose he had not the intention to accomplish.

"I have considered your proposal, Mrs. Jellifer, and will take your bond; but I decline to make a profit of your necessities. This note to my lawyers authorises them to pay you the money, and to take the proper transfer. Read it, madam; and see that it is satisfactory."

"Really, sir," replied Mrs. Jellifer, with some trepidation, "you are very kind, and I accept your liberality with thankfulness."

She folded the letter again slowly, and was about to return it to Warner, when he motioned her to retain it, as though unwilling to touch anything with which she had been in contact.

"Yesterday," he said, "you proposed to make a certain revelation to me affecting, I presume, your husband, and, as I understood, made it a condition that I should act upon it. Are you still desirous to do so?"

"Yes, sir."

" Well, go on."

Mrs. Jellifer continued silent for some moments.

" Will you permit me first to make some excuse for such apparently unwomanly conduct, sir ? "

Warner bowed.

" You must be surprised that, after obtaining such liberal gifts from my husband, I should seek to do an act of justice by which he may suffer. There was no favour conferred by his gifts, as I had earned, by many years of care and industry, all that I have obtained at his hand. I am not, therefore, ungrateful."

. " Why, then, revengeful ? " asked Warner, coldly.

" For that I can give you sufficient excuse, sir," said Mrs. Jellifer.

She found great difficulty in going on, as it was evident to her that Mr. Warner held her somewhat in contempt. She therefore changed her tactics, and continued.

" Why I have sought to acquaint you with this particular act of villany may seem still stranger to you, sir ; but when I saw you yesterday, for the first time, it came into my head, as it were in a moment, that I might accomplish my own object, and serve you in the business which has perhaps brought you to England."

" Serve me ? " asked Warner, with more interest than he had otherwise shown.

" Yes, sir. It had reference to the Norwold family, for I had not been talking to you five minutes when I felt as though the late Sir John was sitting before me. I then remembered your connection with Mr. Spraggatt—the late Mr. Gerard's going away so strangely, and I believed he had come back again to claim his rights, and that you were he."

Warner had not been prepared for this, although he had thought some recognition of him not impossible, and therefore he had avoided hitherto all places and persons connected with his early life, except Mrs. Jellifer. He, however, kept command of himself and replied calmly :

"People are apt to fancy resemblances which only exist in their own imaginations, and your mind had been set upon this revelation, and so connected me with the object of it. What is it you have to disclose?"

Mrs. Jellifer was beaten back. She had had the impression which she described, and the remembrance of Jasper's perjury had come after it. She then proceeded to describe the part which Jellifer had taken when Sir Gilbert sought to recover the title and estates of Norwold, and detailed the circumstantial and positive evidence of Gerard's death in Italy, as sworn to by her husband.

"And this with Sir Gilbert's knowledge?" asked Warner.

"Yes, sir, although that would be difficult to prove. In that paper you will find Jellifer's evidence arranged by him in order to keep it in his recollection."

She laid the paper upon the table, as Warner did not offer to take it from her.

"Will you write out your knowledge of that transaction, and let me have it to-day?" asked Warner.

"I will, sir; and I have other papers confirming what I have stated to you."

"Mrs. Jellifer," said Warner, after a pause, "I have known some and heard of many bad men and women who have lived by fraud and crime until detection overtook them and brought them to punishment; but even when the husband has been brutal, and the woman lost and depraved, it has never fallen within my knowledge that the wife has betrayed the guilty partner of her life; but has rather sought to suffer, and striven to screen him at her own self-sacrifice. Your life may have been made up of trickery and fraud, but you could not have become so debased as to be guilty of the treachery you design without other cause than you have named to me."

"True, sir," said Mrs. Jellifer, stung to the quick by Warner's observation; "true—I should have deserved all the contempt I can trace in your looks and words. I would not have deserted any man I had loved, or had even professed to have loved, for twenty times Jasper Jellifer's possessions. It is because I did love one man dearly—he was my brother, sir—and know that he was hunted to death by this cold-blooded man whom I must call my husband, that I have resolved to revenge his miserable end. Here are copies of my brother's letters—the originals shall be forthcoming, if needed—showing the misery he suffered, and the treachery Jellifer practised towards him. Read them, sir, and then say if he deserves pity from you, or consideration from me—the sister of Raymond Ray, whom he murdered less mercifully than if he had shot him down on the highway."

Warner hesitated to read the copied letters from Raymond Ray to Jasper, but Mrs. Jellifer was so earnest in her appeal, that at last he consented to do so.

"A wretched story, truly," said Warner, when he had finished, "and more so, if I understand that all those appeals were made in vain."

"They were," she exclaimed, "and be my brother's death mine, if I do not requite his betrayer."

Warner was sickened by the perusal of such wretchedness, and the knowledge of such wickedness, and therefore he rang the bell.

"You will let me have the statement I require, and be sure you communicate its contents to no one."

"I will not, sir," said Mrs. Jellifer, going; she paused at the door to say, "I had forgotten to tell you, sir, that I have seen Lady Norwold, and she will be with you at two to-day. She was very angry, but for that you need care but little. She must at any price have the jewels, sir. Good day."

When Mrs. Jellifer left Mr. Warner, she went direct to a coffee-shop, and there fulfilled her promise of committing to paper her knowledge of her husband's perjuries; having completed her work, she left it at Warner's door, and returned to her home in the City.

Warner had remained alone in his study, deliberating upon

the course he should pursue.   His wife's remonstrance, and
the interview with Edward, had tended greatly to shake his
resolution to resume his ancestral rights, although circumstances had conspired to make the establishment of his claims
easy of accomplishment.   He had only to proclaim himself
the wronged heir of Norwold, like some hero of fable, to
confound his wicked brother and revenge his own great
injuries.   Was this to be his course?   He would seek the
counsellor—the friend whose simple wisdom and truthful love
had been his guide and comforter through years of happy
exile in the distant Bush, when all the feverish dreams which
now made his days restless appeared to have been dispelled
for ever.   Yes, Lucy should be heard again, and by her
decision he would abide, if possible.   When she had joined
him in his room, he placed in her hands the confession of
Mrs. Jellifer.

"These proofs multiply, my love," said Warner: "they
are thrust into my hands as it were by some special influence,
to be used for good or evil.   Even my father's look has not
left my face.   Hard toil and business cares have not
removed the Norwold impress from me, and this base woman
Jellifer recognised in me the resemblance to my father.   The
dead have given up their secret, and placed proofs at my
command.   For whom?"

"Your daughter, whom you love!   For the noble son who
has come to bless our old age, and to wear some day your
ancient honours without tarnish," replied Lucy.   "Shall it
not be so, my dear, dear husband?   Shall we present to
them as their wedding portion the knowledge of Gilbert
Norwold's wickedness, to raise in the young husband's mind,
perhaps, mistrust of his own worthiness, being the son of a
bad father, and create an ever-present fear in that of the
young wife, that Edward may do such injustice to his own
deserts.   Where we would sow only flowers, shall we scatter
the seeds of poisonous weeds, which in time may destroy the
sweetness of their lives?"

"Be it as you decide. From this hour, I crase my name from the roll of chivalry, and inscribe it in good text-hand in the Commercial Ledger, 'George Warner,' provided always, as those cunning lawyers say, when they would find a loophole for escape from a doubtful bargain—provided always, that I can bring this bad baronet—what is his name?—Sir Gilbert Norwold, to such terms as I shall dictate. So kiss me, good wife, and there—I deliver that as my act and deed." The kiss he gave as he pronounced those words of power, was not upon a skin of parchment, but upon a buxom cheek, now glowing with happiness unspeakable.

"You must not be jealous, dear Lucy," he said; "but I am about to receive a lady of fashion at two o'clock; guess her name!"

Of course Lucy could do no such thing.

"Lady Norwold. Oh! quite on a matter of business," said Warner, smiling; "and I promise you, for the honour of my new profession of money-lender, she shall pay good interest. 'The pound of flesh nearest her heart'—if she have one. Until her arrival, I have a letter of importance to write. Let her ladyship be shown into the drawing-room, but do not you receive her, as she comes upon business—mere business."

He had scarcely finished his letter, and despatched it—it was to Sir Gilbert—when a hack fly, containing Lady Norwold and her maid, drove up to the door. Her ladyship only entered the house, and was shown into the drawing-room. The house in which Warner resided had been taken furnished as it was, and Lucy's taste and Warner's liberality had made the apartment very elegant, to the evident surprise of Lady Norwold.

"Well, sir, good morning; you seem to take a pleasure in putting me to as much inconvenience as possible over this business, Mr. Warner."

"I regret that your ladyship should think so," replied Mr.

Warner. "I endeavoured to lessen your trouble by inviting you to call here, rather than at my agent's office."

"Well, this is a more agreeable place than that horrible hole in the City. I declare, some of your things are charming. Well, Jellifer has told you what I require, and you consent to oblige me?"

"I have not done so at present," replied Warner; "though I daresay your ladyship will not object to the terms I shall require."

"Not if you show any conscience at all; and I must say you were not so rapacious as Jellifer, who holds my bond. By-the-by, that's a very dangerous thing, is it not?"

"Very, my lady; unless it receives the greatest attention, it becomes very troublesome. Will not your ladyship be seated?"

"No, thank you; I like to walk about and look at your *bric à brac*, much of it being pretty. But don't let me keep you standing with that armful of papers."

Warner accepted her permission to be seated, and arranged his papers very methodically before him.

"Well, what is this interest to be? Is this Sèvres?—it is, I declare—and I shall pay for it, I suppose. What is this interest to be?" said Lady Norwold.

"I am no stranger to your ladyship's liberality," replied Warner; "but these diamonds are very valuable security—very valuable to me."

"And to me also, I can assure you. They are family diamonds, and there is always a family fuss about them."

"Do you not admire diamonds?" asked Warner.

"Of course I do," said her ladyship with a pretty laugh. "What woman does not? Many hearts have been won by a suite of diamonds."

"Hearts?" asked Warner, archly.

"Well hands," said her ladyship; "they are nearly synonymous now-a-days."

"Too true, I fear," said Warner, displaying the gems upon

the table, "the happiness of a life bartered for a piece of crystal, to which fashion alone gives value."

"Poor fashion!" replied her ladyship, examining through her glass a painted cabinet of great beauty, presented to Warner by his colonial friends. "Poor fashion! Why affect to despise that which you take so much pains to imitate? Who would think that the chrysalis of the City would develop into such a butterfly at the West-end!"

"Surely a pardonable love of good taste——"

"Taste! Pshaw! and yet you pretend to despise fashion! You railers at the follies of the world have the cowardice to follow without the courage to lead. Well—have you done figuring? What am I to pay? I must not be without my diamonds on Sir Gilbert's birthday."

"Nor shall you, my lady," said Warner, calmly.

"Well, that's kind of you, my dear sir. I cannot expect you not to charge for the accommodation, and I have no right to ask you to confide in my word."

"You have not heard me to an end, madam," said Warner. "As your ladyship cannot give me any equivalent security for these diamonds, you shall have them for the night, provided——"

"What? Go on, man."

"Provided I am allowed to be present during the evening."

"In what capacity?" asked Lady Norwold, in surprise.

"As a friend."

"As a friend of mine! In my own house. Does the man think me mad?" cried her ladyship, looking daggers or bodkins at Warner. "Place a money value on your obligation, and I will pay it——"

"I have money obligations sufficient of yours already, Lady Norwold," said Warner, "and am not disposed to increase them. There is your bond to Jasper Jellifer, which I have purchased, beside the advance made upon these gems. Are you prepared to redeem them to-morrow, madam?"

"To-morrow! You know I am not, sir! How can you ask such a ridiculous question?" replied Lady Norwold.

"Then I shall sell these diamonds forthwith by public auction."

"What, sir?"

"I shall describe them as late the property of Lady Norwold," said Warner, calm as ever.

"You cannot be such an unfeeling monster!" cried Lady Norwold. "You would not estrange husband and wife; and for an act of indiscretion consign me to exposure and disgrace!"

"Why not, madam?" said Warner, rising up, and confronting the angry lady's glance unmoved—"Why not? For a more venial fault than deceiving a husband, did you and Sir Gilbert Norwold condemn his son and my daughter to penury, for what you cared."

"Your daughter! Was Miss Warner your daughter?"

"Yes, my lady. Is not the retribution a just one? My child's virtues, helplessness, and true position, were unregarded by you. When, perhaps, a word might have obtained justice for her and her husband, you would not speak it."

"I did not dare to do so, Mr. Warner."

"No—your own selfishness would not let you risk the chance of some discomfort; you knew your husband was a hard man to move to pity or to justice, and your love of ease would not let you make the trial."

"My first impulse was to have done so, but I knew my words would have fallen upon a deaf ear."

Warner was pleased at this admission, though he said:

"You should have listened to your woman's heart, not silenced it by the louder voice of self, Lady Norwold. You knew how good, how worthy of her husband's love, my daughter was; and yet you would not disturb one indolent hour to rescue her from days of sorrow. Why should I spare you?"

" Why should you ? I have nothing to urge in mitigation of your just retaliation. I cannot descend to plead," replied Lady Norwold, with dignity.

"Madam "—said Warner, in a softened voice—"you need not. There are your diamonds. Keep them as your own until I require them of you."

" Sir ! "

" Pray accept them on my conditions. Now you are at liberty to act as seems most worthy your position and your duty."

" Mr. Warner, I will accept these gems in trust from you, and, perhaps, they may have returned to me of greater value than when I parted with them. To prove that may be so, I will now endeavour to extenuate myself, and strive to gain some of your good opinion. Imagine, if you can, what has been my nurture. From my earliest years I have had every wish considered, if not gratified. Those from whom I have exacted service have rendered it so readily—sometimes abjectly—that I have never thought I was receiving favours from creatures like myself, but only accepting as my birthright what I needed at their hands. You were right. I did not care to have my ease disturbed. I saw no claim that your daughter had to make her interest paramount to my own, and it was mine not to offend Sir Gilbert. I think I should not be so minded, were like events again to give me a choice of action."

" You do ! " said Warner, joyfully. " If you knew the pain those words have spared me, madam, you would no longer think yourself my debtor. It may so happen that your intercession will be needed. May I count upon it ? "

" You may, Mr. Warner, to the uttermost."

" I thank you, madam. Possibly you will fail the first time in your advocacy—you shall not the second, take an old man's word."

Warner then conducted her ladyship to her carriage, and bore himself so much like a gentleman, that the invitation he

coveted did not seem to be so impossible, certainly not so
alarming. The selfish crust about Lady Norwold's heart had
cracked in many places, and possibly she might come to have
a freer pulse and a wider sympathy.

The mirthfulness of the guests assembled round Warner's
dinner-table that evening, was in pleasing contrast to the
tristeness of the morning gathering. By one of those remarkable arrangements of the fitness of things, Marian Mayley was
seated between Edward Norwold and Vincent Elliott, and
Uncle Jack had found anchorage between Florence and Mrs.
Gregson. The yellow turban was disposed to be frolicsome
and mischievous, as it was shaken more than once playfully
at Marian, and again oscillated fearfully when its owner remarked, "that she did believe Feberawary had come again,
and that they were pairing as though it had been Valentine's
day"—so much was Mrs. Gregson tickled at her own funni-
ness. Marian had been too long accustomed to her aunt's
little eccentricities to be angry with her, and the others were
too kindly and gentle to create any embarrassment by appearing to notice them.

Dinner over, Florence pretended suddenly to remember
that it was Uncle Jack's birthday, and in a pretty, loving
speech, proposed his health, and holding his great rough head
between her hands, gave him a dozen kisses at least, upon all
the clearings she could find in his forest of beard. Mrs. Gregson seemed disposed to follow Florence's example, but was
deterred by the effort necessary to rise, and the hirsute difficulties to be encountered. Before Jack could say a word in
reply, Mr. Warner, taking advantage of the occasion, declared
what a true, steadfast friend, what a dear, loving brother, and
affectionate uncle, Jack had been, and how much they were
indebted to his unselfish nature for happiness, past, present,
and to come.

Jack returned his thanks in a short blundering speech,
which Mrs. Gregson declared to be quite as good as the Re-
corder's any day of the week; and so their pleasant humour

continued, relieved by an extemporised waltz or two in the drawing-room, until Vincent Elliott conducted Mrs. Gregson and Marian home, giving the younger lady's fingers at parting a very gentle squeeze, of which she said nothing to her aunt, or to any one else, until long afterwards.

CHAPTER XXXV.

JACK SPRAGGATT had not been idle in the interests of his country and of Jasper Jellifer. He had had a long interview with Vincent Elliott, which resulted in "preparing a case," and submitting the same to the proper authorities. Elliott received that immediate attention invariably paid to persons in a position to confer a benefit, and so remarkably in contrast to the reception of those asking a favour.

At Jack Spraggatt's suggestion, old Mr. Higgler, owing to his connection with the former transaction, was again put in commission. The ex-runner was at all times delighted to have the monotony of his retirement relieved by any little job in which an old friend was interested; and as Jasper Jellifer stood in this professional relation to him, Mr. Higgler would have grieved greatly had the execution of this little bit of business devolved upon any other person than himself.

Mrs. Jellifer had gone to keep her appointment with Mr. Warner, and was busy enough giving Jasper a bad character to that gentleman. Jasper had waited dinner for her, until his scanty provisions had grown cold and uninviting, and as unfed men, even when without appetite, are usually despondent or prone to melancholy, Jasper had been making numerous fancy sketches on the ceiling, wherein he represented himself as revelling on pauper allowance, or sitting on the pavement beside the well known legend, "I am starving." Yet he had pinched, and saved, and sinned, to acquire more

money, and it had become a mocking fiend that threatened to
fly away every hour, and leave him a beggar.

> "O cursed lust of gold ; when for thy sake
> The fool throws up his interest in both worlds,
> First starved in this, then damned in that to come."

He was in this pleasant frame of mind when Mr. Higgler
and a friend entered the office, and had a brief audience with
Jack-in-the-Box. Mr. Jerningham was for some time in a
state of uncertainty whether Mr. Jellifer was within or not,
and was only brought to the conviction that he was up-stairs
waiting to take his dinner, by Mr. Higgler intimating his intention of ascertaining the fact for himself. Such a proceeding would have involved unpleasant consequences to Mr.
Jerningham, and he therefore, with more agility than any one
would have suspected him to display, jumped over the
counter, and slipping past Mr. Higgler, ascended the stairs
three at a stride. Mr. Jerningham had scarcely made his
communication to Mr. Jellifer (who was always more or less
disturbed by a vague fear whenever any stranger wished to
see him), when Mr. Higgler entered the room, smiling faintly
and wheezing audibly.

"How *do* ye do? My old friend. How do ye do?" said
Mr. Higgler, blowing off each short sentence, like a jet of
steam from an engine coming to a halt.

"I knew I should be welcome—so I didn't wait for ceremony
—but came up. Well, how do ye do? We haven't met for
some years,—that is, to have a chat. We've passed in the
streets now and then; but somehow or other, you always
seemed too busy to stop and speak to one."

"Well! It is many years since we did meet," replied Jasper, his lip twitching convulsively,—"certainly many years.
What has brought you now, sir?"

"You can go, Mr. Agility," said Higgler, addressing Jerningham, who had shut himself in between the door and the

door-post, and pretended to be going down-stairs again; "my business is private."

Mr. Jerningham took the hint and descended to the office, where he was much surprised to find "the other party," as he described himself, making very impertinent inspection of the fixtures and fittings, in Mr. Jellifer's *sanctum*. Mr. Jerningham felt, at first, disposed to remonstrate, but the man was so cool in his manner, and so sinewy in his proportions, that Mr. J. retired to his box, and observed the other's proceedings through his secret look-out—the gimlet hole.

Mr. Higgler, having wiped his forehead with a large bandanna handkerchief, deposited the same with an airy jerk in the crown of his broad-brimmed hat, which he had placed upon the table, as though the business, upon which he was about to enter, was of the most cheerful character, and peculiarly agreeable to Jasper. In fact, such a communication as would have compelled a friend, of six-and-twenty years' standing, to have sought out Jasper, merely for the pleasure of being the communicator.

"Why, let me see, Mr. Jellifer," said Higgler, closing one eye, and sucking his teeth, to assist him in the calculation; "it must be as near six-and-twenty years ago as may be, since you were kind enough to put me up to that bit of business at Morden, and to 'nose' on your friend, the miller."

"Yes, yes," replied Jasper, as though anxious to dismiss the fact. "It is as long as that, I dare say. But to what am I indebted for this present visit?"

"That turned out a very good job for me," continued Higgler. "That little circumstance that came out of it—you remember—made Sir Gilbert very grateful, and he behaves like a gentleman to me annually. It seemed to have been likely to have turned out to your advantage also."

"It seemed to have turned out!" thought Jasper, repeating the words mentally. "It has done so."

"You remember little Cobby, as played the dulcimer so nicely?" asked Higgler; but not waiting for a reply, continued. "He's dead now, or how he would have laughed to have seen this day! You remember too, I dare say, how when he was put in possession for the Crown, how your good lady came and turned him out, under a Bill of Sale, and in charity let him stay the night over, almost compelling him to sleep in his box of music."

"Yes," said Jasper, getting very uneasy, but not defining the cause in the least. "Well, Mr. Higgler?"

"It is very strange how things do turn up, to be sure. Who'd have thought, that after the cheek you exhibited, and the luck you had to get possession, and the laugh you had of little Dulcimer, and me—oh, yes—I own it!—me also, that I should come here after these years, with a warrant in my pocket, to take you into custody for a fraud upon the Crown, in that very matter! It's really as good as a play. Don't you think so?" and Higgler laughed till his eyes watered.

Jasper evidently considered the play too serious to be laughed at, and he sat with an aghast look until Mr. Higgler had done laughing.

"You can't be in earnest?" he said; "you are joking for some reason?"

"'Pon my word, Mr. Jellifer, it's a fact," replied Higgler, "and it makes the case altogether the most beautiful affair I ever had in hand, in my long professional life. As we are keeping the Lord Mayor waiting, would you mind putting on your hat and coming at once?"

"You really are serious, then?" cried Jasper, starting up. "What does this mean? What has happened?"

"Some document signed by you, and given to The Silver Eel,—I mean Raymond Ray, has turned up; but they'll explain it all to you at the Mansion House."

Jasper's face had assumed the hue of death, and large drops of sweat streamed down it, as he saw in an instant what the churchyard had given up, although he had believed the instrument destroyed long, long ago. Ray had almost told him as much, or perhaps he might not have braved his confederate's revenge, as he had done, by his neglect and silence.

"Come, Jasper, my man," said Higgler, in the kindest tones, "don't give way at such a moment! It's been a long time coming, and you have had a prosperous innings. You've ane consolation—you've the Crown for prosecutor, and I shouldn't wonder if the Attorney-General don't attend to the case himself. I don't want to be pressing, but I must trouble you to be moving along, as we shall come to grief, now that we've made the caption, if we keep the Bench waiting."

"Of course," said Jasper, rising. "Of course! There is nothing for it, I suppose?"

"Nothing, Jasper; never was with me," replied Higgler, with proper dignity. "I would not spoil such a beautiful case as this will be, when quite completed, by the finish you'll give to it, for half the Bank of England."

"Very well. I wish my wife was at home, I'd just change my shirt."

Jasper's mind was evidently confused.

"I wouldn't change, if I was you," said Higgler, going to the door by which he had entered, and which Jasper was approaching mechanically. "They won't mind your appearance. They'll know you are not in your Sunday best. Oh! that's the room you are going to?" continued Higgler, as Jasper turned to another door which led to his bed-chamber. "Sleep there, I suppose? Is it airy?" and with more activity than might have been expected, the old runner reached the door, and, opening it, satisfied himself that it was a bed-chamber.

"Rather close, isn't it?" said Higgler. "You had better leave the door open while you change;" and Jasper, understanding the motives for the officer's consideration, made no objection. Jasper lingered over his toilet, wondering at the adverse turn in his fortunes, and conjecturing to what it would lead. Prison—confiscation—perhaps transportation!

It *must*, if he should be found guilty of fraud on the Crown! Long, long imprisonment at least!   .

As these thoughts rushed through his mind, he became desperate, and, acting on the impulse of the moment, he threw up the window which opened to the back of the house, and with the quickness of youth jumped upon a covered cistern, and then into the yard. His evil genius was about him that day, for, alighting on a loose flag, he dislocated his ankle, and lay powerless, and in great agony.

Higgler heard the opening of the window, and then the noise of the fall. Like an experienced huntsman, he did not look after his game, but instantly made a fresh cast, hastening down-stairs, and calling out to his companion, "Back-yard!"

Jasper was brought into the office, and allowed to seat himself in his own peculiar chair.

"Haven't hurt yourself much, I hope, Mr. Jellifer?" said Higgler, quite tenderly. "Those loose flags are very dangerous to tread on—much more to jump on a matter of ten feet. You'd call it ten feet, Mr. Jellifer, wouldn't you?"

Jasper neither knew nor cared what the height had been; he was in pain both of mind and body.

"Let us get this matter over, Mr. Higgler," he replied; "send for a hackney coach."

"Or, perhaps, one of those new street-cabs will do, Mr. Agility," said Higgler, as Mr. Jerningham, standing on the rail of his stool, peered out of his box; but without showing any disposition to understand Mr. Higgler's suggestion.

"Now then, sir, why don't you go?" cried Jasper. "Don't you see I've met with an accident, and these gentlemen are taking me to the hospital?"

Mr. Jerningham was off like a swallow.

"Very clever of Mr. Jellifer going to the hospital, was it not?" said Higgler, addressing his companion. "Shows such presence of mind; and suffering as he does. You need not be under any anxiety about Mrs. Jellifer and the

premises," added Higgler, when the coach drew up at the
door, "because my brother-officer will stay here, and take
care of everything, and I only wish he was little Dulcimer,
that he might show your good lady how he would return
good for evil. Lean on me, Mr. Jasper; don't be afraid!
That's nicely; why, you'll dance a hornpipe in fetters in less
than a week."

With this consoling remark, Jasper was assisted into a
coach, and under the tender care of Mr. Higgler, conducted
to the Mansion-House, where, as Mr. Higgler had suggested,
he met with every attention on the part of the Lord Mayor
and the law officer of the Crown. The examination was very
soon at an end, and in consideration of the accident which
had overtaken the prisoner, he was committed at once to the
Infirmary in Newgate, Mr. Higgler kindly going out of his
way to see his old friend, Jasper Jellifer, safely rendered to
his new lodgings. Having performed this act of friendship,
he returned to Jasper's house a few minutes before Mrs.
Jellifer got back from her visit to Warner, which had
extended much beyond the time she had contemplated. Her
employment during the morning, and the thoughts consequent
upon it, had given her mind a criminal tendency; so when
Jerningham met her at the door, and told her rapidly the
occurrences of the preceding hour, with a quickness not
unusual to persons whose lives have been passed in scheming
and deceit, something like the truth flashed upon her, and
she unlocked the drawer, behind which Jasper's secret hoard
had been placed, and secured the notes as she had purposed
doing at some later period. She was not one moment too
soon, as the officer left in charge returned from an inspection
of the house, and politely informed Mrs. Jellifer that none of
the property upon the premises could be removed for the
present.

Higgler was rather disconcerted when he recognised in
Mrs. Jellifer the liberal lady at the Station Inn, and instantly
suspected that some "plant" had been put upon him.

"Well, I never!" he said; "if I didn't think you and I had seen each other before, Mrs. Jellifer, the night we had that pleasant party at your expense. But we hadn't met, you see, for five-and-twenty years; and ladies do change so much in that time."

"Ah!" replied Mrs. Jellifer, laughing, "when we first met, I was a buxom woman enough, Mr. Higgler, and not the old——"

"Not a word against yourself in my hearing," interrupted Mr. Higgler. "You're much too good for your husband. He's committed, my dear."

"For what?" asked Mrs. Jellifer, more coolly than affectionately.

"A little matter of fraud against the Crown," replied Higgler, entering into the full particulars of the discovery of Ray's papers.

"I'm glad of that! Very glad of that!" said Mrs. Jellifer, with much earnestness. "I am glad the first blow is not of my striking—though I would have struck it—and will drive this nail home for my poor brother's sake."

"Then you were not in the old plant?" exclaimed Higgler. "Thought you were not. I thought sister couldn't sell brother, as poor Ray was sold. I was sorry for the fellow; but duty was duty, you know."

"I don't blame you!" said Mrs. Jellifer. "It was your trade, and your duty; but to him that did betray him, and left him to die a worse death than a dog, I would do anything cruel. I have him at my mercy, and he shall——" She paused, and gave a fiendish smile at Higgler, adding: "I forgot to whom I was speaking. You now know why I made your acquaintance at the station. I had begun to suspect, from other causes, that my *dear* husband was a bitter villain, and what I overheard you say seemed to confirm it. I was determined to be quite sure before I set about my work. Mr. Higgler, even you must have a contempt for such men as Jasper Jellifer, and will not mind keeping what I have said to yourself. You must get me to see him to-night, if you can manage it. I suppose he will be in the infirmary. I will pay you liberally—more liberally than any broken-hearted wife that ever entered those gloomy walls."

Higgler promised to do his best, and the kind-hearted governor of the prison at that time yielded to Higgler's representations of the poor wife's distress, and allowed Mrs. Jellifer access to her husband, Higgler being present.

There was only one other patient in the ward where Jasper lay, but had there been a thousand it would have signified little to the remorseless woman who now sat by one sufferer's bedside.

"Well, Jasper," she said, "is this all true that I hear?—that your clever scheme to get possession of poor Raymond's property has been blown into the air after twenty-five years?"

"Yes, it seems so," replied Jasper, in a whisper; "but don't speak so loud about it—here, walls have ears."

"So I have heard, and some terrible stories they must have heard in their time, Jasper; but none more cruel, treacherous, and revengeful, than that which they are about to hear now from my lips."

"What do you mean, Barbara?" asked Jasper, alarmed at the words she had hissed into his ear, and still more terrified when he looked at her haggish face in the dim light of the prison ward.

"It is to be all known at last to living men, as it has been known to the devils which have been about our home for more than twenty years, that for fourteen hundred and odd pounds—that was the sum, I think—you sold into the hands of justice your foolish, confiding friend, and my dear and only brother. You told me that he owed you that sum—that it was all that you had scraped together at that time, and that its loss would have ruined you. You lied, and you deceived me. You held that money on trust for the miserable man sent away to do a convict's work—work so terrible, that to any man like poor Raymond it would become intolerable, if there was no hope somewhere for the wretch. My brother's hope was in you—in the friend to whom he had confided all that he possessed, believing that if he lost in the desperate game he was playing for their mutual advantage, his almost brother would stand true to him, and that he should some day overcome his trials. You deceived him, you left him to drag out a miserable life, until his sufferings ate into his heart, and day by day he sank into the grave—every hour marked by renewed or increased pain, and then he died—leaving his blood upon your guilty soul."

"Barbara, what is the meaning of this? Why have you come at this time to aggravate my distress?" asked Jasper.

"I loved my brother. Is that an answer?" replied Mrs. Jellifer. "You sold him for money—money which will slip through your fingers after all your cunning. You will pay dearly for your gains. I now see how Willy Hayes was murdered—cunningly murdered by you, Jasper."

"Are you mad, Barbara?" cried Jasper, starting up in his bed and confronting her.

"No. Had I been a good woman, I should have been long ago, but I have learned to love money as well as you. Yet I would not have betrayed, tortured, killed men for it, as you have done!"

"You lie, Barbara!"

"No, Jasper—I speak the truth as it will be heard, they say, at the Day of Judgment. You killed Raymond by slow tortures. You killed Willy Hayes by slow poison. You knew that brandy was destruction to him, and until he was of age you kept him from it. When he had left you money, you placed the destroyer in his way; and though you neither strangled him, nor shed his blood, yet, at your door lies his death!"

"I will not listen to such madness!" said Jasper. "I will call the warder and have you removed."

"Listen but a little longer, and then I will go of my own accord, never to look upon your miserable face again."

"What do you say? Great Heaven! You will not leave me—now——"

"Now that you are lame, miserable, and about to undergo a disgraceful trial? Did you not abandon Raymond?—Did you not, you treacherous coward? So will I abandon you. You have given me nearly all your means, and I have them safely; even the hoardings behind the drawer in the iron chest—"

Jasper clasped his hands together over his head and uttered a cry which made Higgler come towards his bed.

"It is nothing," said Mrs. Jellifer—"a paroxysm of pain —he moved his foot—he is quieter now."

Higgler retired to a distant part of the ward, and she continued in a low, calm, irritating tone:

"The means you have reserved to yourself will barely satisfy the Crown's demand, principal and interest, even should you escape the consequences of your perjury. You will leave your prison—wherever that may be—an utter beggar, Jasper Jellifer; and the presentiment you have had so long that you would die in a gutter, bids fair to be realised."

"You will not be so cruel, so heartless, Barbara, as to rob me of all, and leave me! How knew you of that hoard? Oh, you cannot be such a devil as to take all—to take all and let me die mad, as I shall do if half you have threatened come to pass."

"Die mad! Die starving! and then you will die as you deserve, according to your evil acts. Had you been the felon that my brother was, yet had been a true man, I would have worked my flesh from my bones—have shared beggary, exile with you; but knowing you to be most treacherous, cruel, and cowardly, I leave you to your fate."

Mrs. Jellifer rose and said, most calmly, "I am ready to go, Mr. Higgler."

"No! she is not," cried Jasper. "She must not go! If

she leaves me now, I shall go raving mad. Mr. Higgler keep her here. Let her be searched before she leaves this place. She has money upon her which is mine! Barbara! Remember I am your husband still! Do not leave me! If you do, may every hour you live be cursed—"

He then raved more fiercely, and uttered fearful imprecations, whilst Barbara, his wife, looked back upon him with a devilish smile on her face, and waved him adieu!

When she had gone, Jasper could not realise the scene which had just taken place. She still seemed to sit by his bedside, whispering those terrible words which were never again to be long out of his mind—no, not when he stood in the felon's dock, and heard the story of his treachery and fraud told over again, and proved piecemeal, and commented upon by counsel and judge: her voice then remained louder than all, pronouncing the hard sentence, that she had possessed herself of all his ill-gotten wealth, and had fled with it.

Throughout the night he could not sleep, the pain of his sprained limb scarcely felt, through the misery of his mind. He could not for some time distinctly remember the threat she had made to see him no more, and when he did so the fierceness of her look and the serpent-like hissing of her voice made him believe that she had spoken too much in earnest, to admit of the slightest hope that she would relent. Then how he raved! upbraiding himself for his confiding folly, which had made her mistress of his fortunes. When he had exhausted that cause of wretchedness, he could not shut out the hideous picture she had drawn of Ray's betrayal, and his subsequent miserable sufferings and death. Why had he not bought, for the small sum which Ray had demanded as a test of his good faith, the damnable knowledge brought from the Bush by Spraggatt? He would have given then ten times the amount—but it was too late. All was too late—his deed of gift could not be recalled. His betrayal of Ray—his indifference to the convict's suffer ing—all too late for remedy in this world, and he had long since ceased to look beyond it. Ten days before the Sessions! and during the intervening time these thoughts came back to him until he longed for his trial to be over, although he could not define any expectancy which was to bring alleviation from his torment.

Oh! false money, so to deceive him! Oh! wicked money, so to have tempted him! All his little cheats had prospered so well, all his meanness had caused him so little shame before it became habit, and so much gratification after, that he had never imagined his greater villanies would bring this double ruin, loss of character and loss of wealth. One ray of hope at last! He would send to Sir Gilbert Norwold, and use his guilty secret to induce him to obtain an easy sentence. Still his gold would be gone! His wife—his wicked, deceitful wife!

He sent to Sir Gilbert, and that gentleman, imagining that the required interview had reference to his own affairs, went to his incarcerated agent.

Jasper told him of the peril in which he stood, and of the cruel desertion of his wife. He reminded Sir Gilbert of his long devotion to his family, and even ventured to refer to certain services rendered to Sir Gilbert's mother. Was that all? If so, Jasper might as well have talked to the stone walls around him, for any touch of human sympathy awakened in the dead heart of Gilbert Norwold.

Jasper grew desperate, witnessing the indifference of the employer for whom he had not hesitated to swear falsely, and in his despair he reminded Sir Gilbert that men had been driven to make revelations sometimes, even when they could receive no benefit from their disclosures, although others had lost station, honour, and wealth, by such confessions. If they hunted him to bay, if he saw every hand armed against him, he would not fall unavenged. Sir Gilbert had bought his wicked services in beforetime, let him now buy silence of the evil done by himself, or beware of the consequences!

"Contemptible creature! Impotent bravo!" said Sir Gilbert. "Beware of you? Fear anything which you can say? I am ashamed to have listened to you so long! If, by holding up this finger, I could save you from the punishment you so justly merit and will receive, I would not raise it."

Sir Gilbert went away, and when Jasper was taken back to his ward, he threw himself upon his prison-bed, and in the agony of mind, produced by a consciousness of utter desertion, he beat his head upon the hard pillow, and howled like one in bodily pain. The warders used gentle words at first to silence him, but finding them of no avail, threatened him with the punishment awarded to the refractory. That quieted him, for even his gaoler's presence was some relief, some little evidence of human sympathy, whereas, to have been shut up alone in a dark cell—to see nothing but the fearful shadows of his past crimes, to hear nothing but the hissing voice always present in his ears when alone—recounting his misdeeds, and reckoning over his lost wealth, appeared to be anticipating the grave and the dread beyond.

The day of trial came at last. Those among the witnesses who had known the smug trader in the little town of Morden, looked at him for some time before they could connect their lucky neighbour with the haggard conscience-stricken wretch who stood shuffling about in the felon's dock. He could readily recall the faces upturned to his, and knew them to be those of honest plodding men, who had had to hunt the wolf from their doors when he had refused them a neighbour's service. Yet some of them had grown grey and wealthy by hard striving, and others had only won respect and honest names, but were richer by those acquisitions than he had ever been. After a while he looked at them one by one, hoping to find some expression of friendly recognition or neighbourly sorrow. He looked in vain! He saw that he was sentenced already in their minds, and that none believed his punishment undeserved.

The trial did not occupy very long. The facts were readily

proved, and had all the wickedness of the man been known his sentence could not have been more severe, as it left him penniless.

The Morden witnesses went from the court to have dinner at one of the neighbouring taverns, and as they drank, and cracked their old jokes, they paused now and then to wonder at the fate of Jasper Jellifer, the lucky, always lucky man— whom they had known so many years.

"It has long been a saying of mine, Mr. Spraggatt"—Jack was in the chair, at the request of many an old acquaintance —"it's long been a saying of mine : before you envy any man his good fortune, or bemoan his bad, 'Wait for the End.' "

The speaker was the Morden sexton, and a very good man in his way. Jasper Jellifer's was a bad end enough, but not worse, perhaps, than he deserved to find at the close of such a life. Detection he would have cared for but little, as he had well known that few—if one—of his acquaintance cared anything for him beyond the bargain of the hour. He had assisted to transport the only one who had ever shown much sympathy with him, and had been repaid for his treachery at last. The other human being with whom he had lived and toiled, and shared what small affection he could separate from self, had hit him a foul blow. She had cheated him by her skill in playing on the only string that vibrated in the muscle which he called his heart, and when she had charmed him into an idiotic confidence, had plundered him of all, and was free to carry it away to the uttermost parts of the earth, if it so pleased her. That was his terrible punishment! That was the end of his cunning.

When the trial was over, Jasper was taken back to his cell, and a letter placed in his hands. He knew the writing. It was from Barbara. She had written :

"I have been in court, and heard your trial and condemnation. My brother's fate will come back to you every day. To-morrow I take with me all *we* scraped together with so much privation, and leave England for ever."

Jasper never saw her more. So let them both depart from our story.

Mr. Jerningham lost his place and his box, but he was by no means depressed at the turn matters had taken. Mrs. Jellifer had evidently been a good pay-mistress for the gimlet-hole information, as Mr. Jerningham was the first of those sanguine gentlemen who believed that an independence was to be obtained by having their names and the words " Coal Merchant " engraved on a brass plate, and placing the same on a door in any locality where building was progressing. His penultimate was the Insolvent Court, and his termination the workhouse. The Jellifer gold had ceased to be lucky.

CHAPTER XXXVI.

GERARD AND GILBERT MEET AT LAST, AND OUR STORY ENDS.

Mr. Warner's letter to Sir Gilbert Norwold received an unsatisfactory and laconic answer: Sir Gilbert never called upon persons with whom he was unacquainted, nor concerning business on which he was uninformed.

Mr. Warner's rejoinder was equally short but effective, as the messenger returned within an hour and brought a note stating that Sir Gilbert would keep Mr. Warner's appointment. He did so punctually, either from habit or a desire to learn the nature of the information possessed by Mr. Warner, and which, he had been assured, affected him seriously.

Warner had darkened the room and put on a broad eye-shade, fearing that Sir Gilbert might too readily recognise him, as Mrs. Jellifer had done; and, therefore, when the brothers met, it was as strangers.

Warner made brief excuse for the darkness of the room, and then requested Sir Gilbert to be seated. A host of recollections connected with their boyhood passed rapidly through his mind at the sight of his brother, and those old memories kept him silent longer than suited the patience of his visitor.

" Are you the writer of this letter, wherein it is stated-that my property and title are in danger?" said Sir Gilbert.

" I am, sir."

" Am I to learn your reasons for such an assertion?" asked Sir Gilbert.

" Yes—but first to my own business," said Warner; " my name, sir, may have suggested it."

"Warner!" exclaimed Sir Gilbert, rising. "I have been dull, indeed, not to have suspected this subterfuge."

"The thought is worthy of you, sir," replied Warner, hastening to the door and locking it.

"Surely you dare not offer me violence, or detain me here against my will?" said Sir Gilbert.

"I will offer no violence; but here you shall remain until I choose to close our conference. You then are free to go," answered Warner, in a tone which proved his earnestness.

"Well, sir," replied the other, "as I am compelled to listen, speak on."

"I am the father of your son's wife," said Warner, "and I claim your recognition of their marriage, unless you can declare some valid reason for refusing it."

"Valid reason! Do you require other than the fact that she is your daughter? My son forgot he had a father," replied Sir Gilbert.

"Who taught him that forgetfulness, but you? Have you throughout his life ever sought his love—his obedience—by one act of fatherly affection? Had you the right to be remembered?" asked Warner.

"My son was brought up according to my will and judgment, sir, and fitted to have maintained his proper station in the world. He has chosen to make his own election of position, and forgot the name he bore. I will never overlook his unworthy marriage."

"I had looked for no other answer," said Warner, "and for the present dismiss the subject. I have told you that your property and title are in danger. You know well how you obtained them, and I am prepared to prove that both are yours unjustly."

"Those are bold words, sir," said Sir Gilbert.

"They would be so, if uttered rashly," was the reply. "Be pleased to read that paper," and Warner placed in Gilbert's hand Mrs. Jellifer's statement.

As Gilbert read what she had written, he laughed scornfully at times, and when he had finished, threw the paper
upon the table. "Is that your proof, sir? The assertions
of a felon and his fitting companion. I have already been
threatened with such a disclosure, and treated it with the
same contempt as I do now. What further, sir?"

Warner unlocked a cabinet, and took from it the earth-
stained box, which he had received from Spraggatt.

"Some years ago," said Warner, "your brother Gerard
was accused of theft, and driven from his father's house, dishonoured and disclaimed. One person only could have
proved his innocence, and was silent. Need I name him to
you?"

"Yes," answered Gilbert, boldly, although a deadly feeling
of fear possessed him.

"Gilbert Norwold, you were the only witness to your
brother's innocence, and were silent. Do not stir until I have
ended. You did not speak because you must have accused
yourself."

"Insolent libeller," said Gilbert; "you would not dare to
utter such a calumny before others. Do so, and I will make
you prove your scandalous assertion, or bitterly account to me
for it."

"Let me prove it to you alone, sir," replied Warner,
calmly, "for the sake of the name you bear. After all these
years, a witness comes to confront you, in your dead father's
image. You know these features?" and Warner held before
him the long-hidden bracelet.

Gilbert recoiled as he looked upon it, and could not speak
for some moments, but sat regarding it as though he feared
the painted face would speak, and denounce him.

"Yes," he said, at length, "that bracelet was my mother's,
and was lost some time before her death. It is now mine,
and I claim it, sir."

"Dare you? Dare you take into your hand again this
evidence of your Cain-like perfidy? Listen to what has lain

buried with it for six-and-twenty years, before you do so."

Warner then read the paper, which had been found with the bracelet, and to which Gilbert's signature was attached, and, as the words came slowly from his lips, Gilbert trembled visibly.

"Dare you take it now?" continued Warner, as Gilbert Norwold sat, his eyes bent upon the ground.

"There was no subterfuge in my request to see you here," said Warner, as he drew up the blind, and removed the shade he had worn; "and if you doubt your danger still, look at me,—others have discerned what you may not fail to see also."

Gilbert obeyed, and when he had looked at Warner stedfastly for a few moments, he hid his face in his hands and exclaimed, "Great heaven! my brother Gerard!"

"Yes, sir, your deeply injured brother, prepared, as you have seen, to claim my own at the cost of all that makes life valuable to you. I have no wish to prolong this painful interview; therefore listen to me. I know your unthankful nature, and look for no return for the concessions I propose to make. Indeed, I deserve none, for it is not for your sake, but for your son, and for those whose future is unhappily bound up with yours. Do you hear me, sir?"

"Yes," replied Gilbert, his head resting on the table.

"I will forego my just claims to title and inheritance on the conditions I am about to make. First, that you acknowledge your son's marriage with my daughter openly, and with the consideration due to their mutual worthiness. Do you consent to this?"

"I do."

"So you yield to fear what you denied to justice. Secondly, I require you to make such provision for Mr. Edward Norwold as I shall think fitting, and secured upon those estates which my father bequeathed to you in ignorance of the wrong he was committing in making you his sole heir. Do you consent to this, also?"

"I do! I do!", cried Gilbert, "and thank your generous nature—"

"Hush! There has been enough of falsehood already, Gilbert Norwold. On the conditions I have mentioned being honestly fulfilled by you, I promise to remain, as men have known me for years past—George Warner; and further, for our children's sake, never to disclose to them that it was your wickedness which made me an exile, and drove me to assume a name which was not my father's. Do you accept these conditions? Will you fulfil them in truth and honesty?"

"I will," answered Gilbert, holding out his hand; but Warner disregarded the action, and proceeded:

"As your future course is shaped, Gilbert, so will I strive to forgive you. At present I should mock at truth, to say I can forgive the impenitent. You can never deceive—never betray me again. You are free to go. Shall I ring the bell?"

Gilbert bowed affirmatively, and Warner having unlocked the door, rung for the servant; and the two brothers parted, never to meet again.

The proposals made by Warner were duly carried out, and society was not much shocked or surprised when, in the course of a year afterwards, it heard that Sir Gilbert and Lady Norwold had separated by mutual consent, and that he had gone abroad, few knew, and none cared whither.

Warner proved the truest friend that Lady Norwold had ever known in her purposeless life, and she came to believe that to discharge her duties properly, and to enjoy the good with which she had been blessed, she must have regard for more than cold, ever-exacting Self.

Our story is nearly ended, and we would part pleasantly with those who may have waited for the end without weariness, if any such there be. So let us blow the prompter's whistle once again, and change the scene for the last time.

The hour was four in the afternoon, and Vincent Elliott, with a slightly flushed cheek, and uneasy manner, was alone in Warner's drawing-room. A carriage, containing Mrs. Gregson and Miss Marian Mayley had driven up some short half-hour before, and the ladies having been received in Warner's room, were there detained to listen to a certain statement from that gentleman, which in no way concerned himself, further than that it enabled him to repay in part the debt of gratitude he owed to Mr. Elliott, for the sympathy he had shown when Warner's heart was aching at his daughter's absence. Marian Mayley blushed very much, and Mrs. Gregson giggled as she had done thirty years ago, when she was Miss Protheroe, and had had a private interview with the late Mr. Gregson, in the days of his retail business, and long before he had been elected alderman, or even common councilman of his ward in the City.

Mr. Warner was a capital diplomatist in some matters, and he had not failed in his present mission, as he entered the drawing-room with a smile upon his face that spoke success to Vincent Elliott.

" Well, my dear sir," said Vincent, somewhat impatiently, " have you seen Miss Mayley ?"

" Yes; and I think you may take up the wooing for yourself," replied Warner. " Here are the ladies."

As Mrs. Gregson and Miss Mayley had entered the room, and exchanged the usual civilities, though with more embarrassment between the younger people than either had exhibited of late, Mr. Warner, in the most malicious manner possible, requested Mrs. Gregson to favour him and Mrs. Warner with a few minutes' private conversation. Mrs. Gregson gave him a knowing look, and slapped his arm with her substantial fingers, shaking her yellow turban so violently at the same time that the bird of paradise seemed spreading its wings for flight.

When the young people where left together, Vincent said, his voice falteringly tremulous :

"Miss Mayley—May I venture to continue the subject which Mr. Warner has commenced ?" No answer.—"I did not dare approach it myself without his intervention, re-membering my former impertinence. Have you forgiven me that act of folly?"

"I am afraid so," replied Marian, very softly, and the con-fession emboldened Vincent to take her hand.

"How very kind of you!" said Vincent; "but I was desperate."

"I also was a mental invalid, Mr. Elliott,"—her voice grew stronger, and she ventured once to raise the long fringes which hid her beautiful eyes,—"Mr. Warner's treatment was anything but agreeable; but I trust it cured me of much vanity and some careless confidence in outward appearance. It was rather cruel to tempt me with such a glittering deceit as 'my lord.'"

"Nay, Mr. Warner has told you that I was indebted to your maid for my barony," said Vincent, pressing the un-resisting hand he held between his own.

"So I have heard, I confess." Her eyes were unveiled again, and looked kindly at Vincent.

"Then I may hope?" said Vincent, reading that look with a lover's quickness.

Marian shook her head rather archly. "My vanity might have received the lord—my heart must now elect the commoner."

"Then be a generous constituent," said Vincent, raising the hand to his lips, "and give a plumper in my favour." He hardly knew what he was saying.

"I believe it is usual to know a candidate's qualifications, is it not?" asked Marian, all smiles and blushes.

"I am a gentleman by birth and education," said Vincent, —proving it, we suppose, by placing his arm around her slender waist.

"Most candidates have those qualifications," replied Marian, making a preposterously slight effort to disengage herself.

"I am six-and-twenty," said Vincent.

"That is a questionable recommendation," replied Marian,

archly, and quite reconciled to the alien arm.—"Recollect, your election would be for life."

"True!" said Vincent, a little confused; and therefore he added, "I'm a barrister-at-law."

Marian was content with her little advantage, so she smiled more beautifully than before, and said, "I think a wig would spoil you."

"If I promise it shall be a Lord Chancellor's?" cried Vincent.

"Oh, bribery! bribery! You are tempting me with a ladyship again!" answered Marian, laughing at her own cleverness, until Vincent made her utter a sweet, feeble scream, by fairly pressing her to his bosom.

What then they said to each other, the young may imagine, and the old remember; but when Mr. and Mrs. Warner, followed by Mr. Gregson, Edward, and Florence, entered the dining-room, they were seated by each other, to all outward appearance, affianced lovers.

"You see, Florence," said Warner, "the force of your example. It is useless to write up 'Dangerous!—Beware of matrimony!'"

"You forget, dear father, that Love is blind, and cannot read the warning," replied Florence.

"That is an error of the old painters," said Warner. "Hymen should have worn the bandage."

"What then, dear sir?" replied Edward. "He would have had Hope for a guide."

"Hope! life's will o' the wisp," said Warner, laughing.— "No: Experience is our only safe guide, young people."

"Not so, sir!" cried Elliott from his seat on the sofa. "Experience has his face to the past. Youth must have a companion that looks to the future."

The servant announced Captain Elmsley.

"I am glad we are interrupted," said Warner, "or I should have been led to think the present generation no wiser than their forefathers. Why do you not ask Captain Elmsley up-stairs?"

"He requested to be announced, sir," said the servant, " whilst he arranged his cravat, and put on his pumps in the parlour."

"What a strange compound of vanity, meanness, and benevolence," said Warner, smiling.

"Nay, meanness is surely an exception in his character!" replied Florence, remembering all his kindness to her husband and herself.

"What says Mr. Elliott?" said Warner.

"Ah, you puzzle me," replied Vincent. "The Captain is a living enigma which I am incapable of solving. If you speak of him, or think of him, he is smiling at your elbow, *par exemple;*" and Captain Elmsley entered the room with all the grace, and somewhat the appearance, of "a friend of George the Fourth."

The gentlemen received him with courtesy, and the ladies with smiles, especially Florence, who could not forget her great obligations to him.

Miss Mayley also felt that she was under some obligation to the bold Captain, and therefore curtseyed to him, saying, "I am afraid Captain Elmsley has forgotten me."

"My dear madam, I wish you hadn't said that," replied the Captain; "but in your presence I feel a little diffidence."

"Diffidence!" exclaimed Vincent.

"Yes—I hope the sensation is not likely to last; if it does, I am ruined," said Elmsley, laughing; "but I cannot forget, though I will endeavour to forgive, an opinion that was once——"

"Expressed by me, sir. I retract and apologise; but one word in private," said Warner, motioning Elmsley to the window.

"I think you will excuse me in some measure, when I ask, Do you remember Lieutenant Hammerton, with whom you served in New South Wales many years ago?"

"Hammerton! Yes!" replied Elmsley, "an ungrateful scamp. He emigrated to Boulogne three years ago with my opera-glass and crush hat, which I had lent him."

"Did you never lend him anything else?"

"Nothing," answered the Captain.

"Never your name?" asked Warner, pointedly.

"I meant, nothing of value," replied Elmsley.

"Is that your autograph?" and Warner showed him a bill of exchange for 100*l.*, faded now, being dated some eighteen years before, as long ago as the time when Hammerton was recalled suddenly to England.

"Why, yes," replied Elmsley, examining one of the signatures to the long-forgotten document, "I believe that is my 'Elmsley.'"

"You see how my mistake arose," said Warner, presenting the paper to the Captain. "Will you accept of this as my written apology?"

"Really," replied Elmsley, rather taken aback. "Really—why—yes, with much pleasure; for it will remind me how easily an injury may be inflicted—how kindly redressed. I'll have it framed, Mr. Warner, as a proof of my respectability."

The two whisperers then joined the others, Elmsley attaching himself for a moment to Elliott, who did not want him, and who could be a little rude at times.

"Well, Captain," he said, "I am glad to see you here, by Jove; how expensively you are decorated!"

"My dear boy," said Elmsley, undisturbed by the remark; "it is the boast of some honest people that they are always prepared for the worst; it is mine, that I am always dressed for the best."

The Captain then glided away to where Florence and her mother were seated, and told them how kindly Mr. Warner had explained away an expression which had given him much pain, and showed them what he was pleased to call "one of his early indiscretions." Warner approaching the moment,

Florence threw her arms around his neck, saying, "Oh, you dear kind papa! You have made every one happy and contented!"

The advent of Uncle Jack completed the little party met to celebrate, unknown to all but Warner, Lucy and her brother, the consummation of the struggle of long years. When they assembled at dinner, Jack again found himself seated by the side of Marian's good-natured, vulgar Aunt, whose attentions to him might have suggested the possibility, that the Gregson relict, and the yellow turban wreathed with orange blossoms, were within his reach, had he desired to possess them. But Jack had planted all his true love years ago, and when it came to an untimely end, he resolved to cultivate bachelor's buttons to the end of his days. As he knew little of the world of London, or indeed of the world generally, he took the Captain into his pay as a Mentor and amanuensis, although Lucy and Florence always asserted that the engagement was only Uncle Jack's clever way of adding to the Captain's annuity.

Our story is told. The wise man of Stratford has said—

> "There's a Divinity that shapes our ends,
> Rough-hew them how we will;"

and we have striven to illustrate this truthful text.

Are the shadows which we have conjured from the Past worthy to be remembered? Or must they pass away again, only to shame him who has evoked them?

THE END.

BRADBURY, EVANS, AND CO., PRINTERS, WHITEFRIARS.

CHEAP EDITIONS OF POPULAR NOVELS.

Each in One Vol., with Illustrated Frontispiece, price 6s.

VERNER'S PRIDE. By Mrs. HENRY WOOD, Author of "East Lynne."

THE SILVER CORD. By SHIRLEY BROOKS.

LORD OAKBURN'S DAUGHTERS. By Mrs. HENRY WOOD.

WAIT FOR THE END. A Story. By MARK LEMON.

LOVED AT LAST. A Story. By MARK LEMON.
[*In the Press.*

EVAN HARRINGTON. A Novel. By GEORGE MEREDITH.
[*In the Press.*

SPORTING WORKS.

Illustrated with Coloured Etchings, &c., by John Leech.

MR. SPONGE'S SPORTING TOUR. By the Author of "Handley Cross," &c. With Thirteen Coloured Engravings and numerous Woodcuts, by JOHN LEECH. 8vo, price 14s.

HANDLEY CROSS; or, Mr. Jorrocks's Hunt. With Seventeen Coloured Engravings and numerous Woodcuts, by JOHN LEECH. 8vo, price 18s.

MR. FACEY ROMFORD'S HOUNDS. A Sequel to "Mr. Sponge's Sporting Tour." With Coloured Illustrations by JOHN LEECH and H. K. BROWNE. 8vo, price 14s,

ASK MAMMA; or, The Richest Commoner in England. By the Author of "Mr. Sponge's Tour," "Handley Cross," &c. With Thirteen Coloured Engravings and numerous Woodcuts, by JOHN LEECH. 8vo, price 14s.

PLAIN, OR RINGLETS? By the Author of "Handley Cross," &c. With Thirteen Coloured Engravings and numerous Woodcuts, by JOHN LEECH. 8vo, price 14s. cloth.

LONDON : BRADBURY, EVANS, & CO., 11, BOUVERIE STREET.

BOTANICAL WORKS.

THE LADIES' COMPANION TO THE FLOWER GARDEN. Being an Alphabetical Arrangement of all the Ornamental Plants grown in Gardens and Shrubberies. With Full Directions for their Culture. By Mrs. LOUDON. A New Edition, considerably Enlarged and Corrected to the Present Time, by CHARLES EDMONDS, F.R.H.S., Gardener to her Grace the Dowager-Duchess of Sutherland, Chiswick House. The Eighth Edition, cloth gilt, price 7s.

HOW TO LAY OUT A GARDEN. Intended as a General Guide in Choosing, Forming, or Improving an Estate, from a quarter of an acre to 100 acres in extent. By EDWARD KEMP. Illustrated by numerous Plans, Sections, and Sketches of Gardens and general objects. A New Edition. In One volume, demy 8vo, price 18s.

NATURE-PRINTED BRITISH FERNS: being Figures and Descriptions of the Species and Varieties of Ferns found in the United Kingdom. By THOMAS MOORE, F.L.S. The figures Nature-Printed by HENRY BRADBURY. In Two volumes, royal 8vo, price 3l.

PAXTON'S BOTANICAL DICTIONARY: comprising the Names, History, and Culture of all Plants known in Britain, together with a Full Explanation of Technical Terms. Crown 8vo, price 16s., cloth extra.

THE HANDBOOK OF GARDENING. By EDWARD KEMP. For the use of Persons who possess a small Garden. Price 2s., in cloth.

Works by Dr. Lindley.

THE VEGETABLE KINGDOM; or, the Structure, Classification, and Uses of Plants. By Dr. LINDLEY. Illustrated upon the Natural System. In One volume, 8vo, cloth, price 36s., with upwards of 500 Illustrations.

THE ELEMENTS OF BOTANY, Structural and Physiological. With a Glossary of Technical Terms. By Dr. LINDLEY. The Glossary may be had separately, price 5s. In One volume, 8vo, cloth, with numerous Illustrations, price 12s.

MEDICAL AND ŒCONOMICAL BOTANY. By Dr. LINDLEY. In One volume, 8vo, cloth, price 7s. 6d.

SCHOOL BOTANY; or, the Rudiments of Botanical Science. By Dr. LINDLEY. In One volume, 8vo, half-bound, with 400 Illustrations, price 5s. 6d.

DESCRIPTIVE BOTANY; or, the Art of Describing Plants Correctly in Scientific Language, for Self-Instruction and the Use of Schools. By Dr. LINDLEY. Price 1s.

LONDON : BRADBURY, EVANS, & CO., 11, BOUVERIE STREET.

www.ingramcontent.com/pod-product-compliance
Lightning Source LLC
Chambersburg PA
CBHW052342110726

47901CB00005B/1321